WE WERE KINGS

We Were
KINGS

THOMAS O'MALLEY

and

DOUGLAS GRAHAM PURDY

MULHOLLAND
BOOKS
HODDER

First published in Great Britain in 2016 by Mulholland Books
An imprint of Hodder & Stoughton
An Hachette UK company

1

A CIP catalogue record for this title is available from the British Library

Trade Paperback ISBN 978 1 444 75432 2
eBook ISBN 978 1 444 75433 9

Printed and bound by Clays Ltd, St Ives plc

Hodder & Stoughton policy is to use papers that are natural, renewable and recyclable
products and made from wood grown in sustainable forests. The logging and manufacturing
processes are expected to conform to the environmental regulations of the country of origin.

Hodder & Stoughton Ltd
Carmelite House
50 Victoria Embankment
London EC4Y 0DZ

www.hodder.co.uk

People say: "Of course, they will be beaten." The statement is almost a query, and they continue, "but they are putting up a decent fight." For being beaten does not greatly matter in Ireland, but not fighting does matter. "They went forth always to the battle; and they always fell," Indeed, the history of the Irish race is in that phrase.

—James Stephens, *The Insurrection in Dublin*

History has to live with what was here,
clutching and close to fumbling all we had—
it is so dull and gruesome how we die.

—Robert Lowell, "History"

And it is those among us
who most make the heavens their business
who go most deeply into this death-weaving.

—Thomas Kinsella, "Death Bed"

WE WERE KINGS

1

THE *MIDIR*, A seventy-eight-foot fishing trawler out of New York carrying five tons of firearms, ammunition, land mines, and explosives, ran low and heavy through the water. It wasn't yet midnight and the air was still and charged with heat, and a mist moved like a separate sea a foot or so above the waves. The boat was an hour from Boston Harbor, had come down the Cape Cod Canal in darkness from the Brooklyn docks, its crew watching the lights of Buzzards Bay and Scituate emerge from the black landscape and the flickering lights of lobster boats moving along the crooked coastline and heat lightning trembling the darkness above.

Two crew members, dressed in oilskins and carrying guns, brought the man out onto the deck. He was similarly dressed but a smear of blood glistened on his face and his legs were bowed as if from a length of time kneeling. His hands were bound behind his back and he was gagged with a kerchief soaked with paraffin oil. His eyes were wide in his bloodied face as he struggled against his holders. Pushing and pulling, they walked him to the stern, turned him so that he was facing south against the railings, the way they'd come, pressing into the morning tide.

Beneath the boat's props the sea churned blackly. He had a moment to consider this and the intermittent, sweeping light cast by the lighthouse on Minot's Ledge and the clanging buoy of the eastern marker as they entered the waters of the bay, and he suddenly, urgently spoke aloud the Act of Contrition: "O my God, I am heartily sorry for having offended Thee and I detest my sins above every other evil because—" and the larger of the two crewmen shot him through the back of the head. The sound of the shot reverberated off the fog shoals and close coastline and as he pitched forward they allowed his momentum to take him. They released their grip and the body upended itself over the railing and into the frothing water. Within a minute the body lay, bobbing, two hundred feet behind them, and, quickly, it was out of sight, lost in the darkness of the heaving sea and carried swiftly by the current southward to deeper waters where above the horizon the sky was lit by brief shimmering flashes as lightning arced violently within the clouds.

2

THE CRYSTAL BALLROOM seemed as if it could barely contain them, hundreds of men and women dancing to "The Siege of Ennis"—stomping back and forth upon the dance floor so that it thundered and shook and the only thing louder than their feet was the sound of the band: accordions and saxophones, trumpets, drums, fiddle, and piano.

Women in lipstick and crinoline petticoats sat on the long benches lining one side of the hall; men with Brylcreem in their hair, wearing pressed jackets, ties, and trousers, stood in small groups on the other side. It's hours since the first waltz began the night, and, fortified by a pint or two from the downstairs bar, men have lost their inhibitions and most everyone has asked a woman to dance. Above, a crystal ball sends spots of reflected light down upon the heads of the dancers, turning slowly as they spin themselves about the room.

On the stage at the front of the hall, a band of intensely sweating musicians moved from the earlier waltzes and set dances to reels and jigs.

A man approached the edge of the dance floor as the song "Biddy Murphy's Cow" came to an end and nodded almost imperceptibly to the accordion player, who gave the pianist quick instructions for the next set—a round of slow vocal ballads—and then rose from his stool and strode to the edge of the low stage, greeting the female singer, Moira Brennan, as she went to the microphone and the pianist began "The Lass of Aughrim." A trumpeter came to him before he stepped down and he said, "Get Finney on the pipes for the finale."

The accordion player's name was Martin Butler and he was a slight man with an unassuming boyish face and a receding hairline, and he smiled to men and women on the dance floor who called out to him. He walked the hallway to a back room and the man who'd nodded at him earlier followed. At the end of the hall they entered Mr. de Burgh's empty office and the man closed the door after them. Inside, the windows were open and they could hear the sounds from the street and the trolleys and buses rumbling from Dudley Station. Amber light spilled from wall sconces and a fan ticked loudly on the desk, rustling papers.

The accordion player dabbed at the sweat on his forehead with a handkerchief. "What is it, Donal?" he asked. "Quick now, I've got to be back on for 'The Boys of Wexford.' Did they get word in time?"

Donal Phelan was tall and lean and built like cable. His face was weathered and his brow constantly furrowed as if something were eating at him but he had no way to express what it was. The accordion player doubted whether he'd ever seen him smile. On his lapel he wore a gold Fáinne and a Pioneer pin with an image of the Sacred Heart and an inscription declaring his abstinence from alcohol.

"We got word to them in time," he said. *"Buíochas le Dia."*

The accordion player nodded. "Thanks be to God. And they know what to do?"

"They do."

"By the time we're through here tonight, make sure it's done. All of it."

"It will be."

"Good. On your way out, send in Cleland."

When Donal left, the accordion player looked out the window onto Dudley Street toward Harrison Ave and Warren Street. The Square was still jumping. There were couples going in and out of the Hibernian, the Rose Croix, and the Winslow. Men spilling from the bars and taverns, and still more coming down the street from the Dudley Station El. Most of them would miss the last train home and they wouldn't mind. Waves and waves of them coming in every week since the end of the war. Everywhere neon and people and music and even with the heat it continued like some great heaving and convulsing beast. You couldn't stop it if you tried. Once it had its legs beneath it, it was too powerful to be stopped. It was a machine, he thought, with himself at the controls, making sure everything happened in the way that it did and it could never be stopped.

Above the rooftops and toward downtown Boston, the sky flickered from one end of the horizon to the other as currents of lightning sparked and raced, but no storm and no relief from the heat. There was a lull from the dance floor before another slow number began and in the cessation he heard in the distance the low peal of thunder and the sky continuing its stuttering, sparking dance. There was a war coming and he was ready for it. He waited and listened to the ballad nearing its end and considered the final set when they'd blow the roof off the place and bring all the walls down on them.

There was a knock at the door and a large man in his late forties entered. He had sad eyes and a heavily lined brow, as if he'd worked hard from a young age and seen his fair share of trouble and pain.

"Ah, Michael," the accordion player said and paused, watching as the older man absently reached for the wedding ring on his heavy-knuckled finger and slowly rotated it back and forth. "Mr. de Burgh's got a job for you."

3

DORCHESTER AVENUE, DORCHESTER

THE SLIGHT BREEZES of the afternoon had been left to die on the banks of the harbor, never reaching inland. And even with the sun long set, the temperature climbed as the minutes ticked away toward midnight. In the thick, swelling heat the sound of cicadas vibrated and thrummed hypnotically down the deserted streets of Dorchester. Houses and apartments along the Avenue remained silent, as if some sudden evacuation had been called for the neighborhood, yet in the shadows behind screen doors and wide-open windows and among continuously whirring fans, people tried to find shelter. From radios, exhausted broadcasters claimed that a Boston city record would most likely be broken by midday tomorrow—102 degrees—and for the rest of the week, no relief in sight. One doctor came on and warned of edema, heat cramps and heat rash, malaise, dehydration, and even death. It sounded like all the proper makings of a plague.

Parked along the Avenue, Dante listened to the radio and took a sip from a can of beer, the aluminum hot in his hand. One moment he felt his gut spin, and the next, he was breathing as if through a pinhole. *It's only going to get worse,* he thought to himself.

Beside the car on the sidewalk, a stray dog lumbered along on branch-thin legs, paused to catch its breath, and glanced across the street, tongue hanging out over its bottom jaw like a piece of spoiled meat. Stepping out from an alleyway, a tramp unzipped and swayed, then leveled off by pressing one hand against the wall. He pissed on the side of a shuttered storefront and then guided whatever fluids he had left into a potted plant. The stray dog watched the tramp for a moment and then, eyes bleary from both hunger and exhaustion, lowered its head and continued ambling down the sidewalk. A police siren wailed off toward Savin Hill, and then suddenly, as if swallowed by the oppressive heat, it stopped midscream.

All the way down the Avenue, traffic lights changed from red to green but barely a car came through. From the passenger side of his '46 Ford Tudor sedan, Dante looked across the street. Two men stood out in front of the Emerald Tavern. The green neon of the shamrock sign above the door reflected off their skin, shining with perspiration, and hollowed out their features, making them look wan and sickly. Both wore sleeveless undershirts and smoked.

Dante stepped out of the car and crossed the street. Trash littered the curbs and the stench of it was heavy. In an alley between the bar and a hardware shop with its metal grate pulled down and padlocked, he caught a glimpse of a woman's pale thigh, the swell of her buttock, the flash of bleached-blond hair in tangles, falling over and hiding her face. She had both hands pressed against the brick wall as a man slammed into her from behind. Her moaning didn't sound like pleasure, and the man's exhausted grunts increased in intensity as he pounded into her with the desperation of a feral animal.

At the entrance to the Emerald Tavern the two men in front eyed Dante. Perhaps they were just waiting their turn with the whore in the alley. Perhaps they were too out of it to even notice.

One had cauliflower ears and the nose of a hopeless boozer, thick and veined with crimson. He wore the gray, navy-blue-lined slacks of a postal worker. The other had the complexion of a man a few steps away

9

from a fatal heart attack. His lower jaw was swollen with tobacco chew, and Dante watched him take another haul off his cigarette, and then proceed to spit out a stream of black juice onto the sidewalk.

"You the electrician?" the man asked.

Dante ran his hand through his sweat-soaked hair. "No."

The other guy asked, "You the iceman?"

"Do I look like an iceman? Or an electrician?"

The man's lips tightened into a filthy grin. "No, I guess you don't."

The man with the boozy nose began to chuckle. "The refrigeration went to shit, so Gerry got the iceman coming. We thought you could be him, even though you got no ice."

"All the ice in the city is probably a puddle by now," Dante said.

The neon sign above them suddenly dimmed and then flickered. Down the Avenue, in a chain-reaction-like effect, the lights faded in storefront windows and above the transoms, the lamps in apartment windows sputtered, and the streetlamps curving over the road pulsed weakly, and then they all came back to full strength.

"Fuck me," the guy in the postal slacks said. "Just what we need. A goddamn blackout."

The other said, "The lowlife blacks and Ricans will have a field day looting."

Dante looked down the length of the Avenue, waiting for it to go dark.

He became worried. Claudia and Maria were back home in the North End. He imagined them in the dark, calling out his name. He nodded to the men, who didn't return the gesture, opened the heavy wooden door, and went inside.

A few ceiling fans spun but did nothing to break the stifling heat. Cigarette smoke webbed the air, and the sour stench of men was thick and unrelenting. By the looks of it, they were mostly from construction, some with paint still on their shirts and their hands, plaster on their knuckles, faces marked with soot and grime, and skin caked with dust.

All of them were drinking from bottles. Empty shot glasses glistened along the bar, and the bartender did his best refilling them. A jar of pickles and another full of pickled eggs sat beside the beer taps. The bartender had a dishtowel wrapped around his head; his white T-shirt was sopping wet and sticking to him like cellophane. He pulled the glass top off one of the jars and reached inside with his bare hand, fingers fluttering wildly until they grasped a dill pickle. He pulled it out and passed it to one of the men at the bar, who quickly went at it, chewing it on the side of his mouth that had more teeth, the green-yellow juice trickling down his chin.

Dante eased into a spot at the bar, raised his hand to the bartender.

"Nothing cold, buddy," the bartender said. "Refrigeration went out this after."

"I just want a bottle of whiskey to take home."

"We charge an extra buck for that."

"That's okay with me."

The bartender charged him even more but Dante was too damn tired to start an argument. He paid up, took the sealed bottle off the bar top, and walked back outside. The two men were still standing there, one of them lighting another cigarette. "That's what the doctor ordered," the postal worker said, nodding toward the bottle in Dante's hand.

Dante ignored the man, crossed the street and got back into his car, turned the engine over, pulled a U-turn on the empty Avenue, and sped toward Savin Hill.

At times, mostly at night, Cal returned to Savin Hill, to where he and Lynne had once lived and the place where Lynne had died. The building was still a burned-out husk, blackened frame and timbers pebbled with flash-scorched grease. No one had attempted to rebuild in the three years since, and city officials seemed uninterested in tearing it down despite the condemned signs plastered on the warped wood. Perhaps they'd forgotten. There were countless other buildings like it through-out the city.

He stood in the wreckage where the porch had been and then pro-ceeded through what had been the front door to the scorched boards that rested upon the stone foundation. Here, he stood directly over the basement furnace, but on the third floor this would have been in the space of their kitchen, and over there the dining room and the hallway leading to their bedroom. He went in that direction, walking through the rooms as if the walls still existed, turning left and then right. In his mind's eye he reached for the doorknob to their bedroom and then turned it and opened the door. He looked at their unmade bed, the tou-sled sheets, her underthings on the floor. Through the window at the front of the room, he could see Malibu Beach, still and gray beneath a blue sky. He heard water running in the bathroom and, through the door, Lynne's voice singing off-key as she bathed.

He approached the bathroom door and again his hand turned the doorknob. White steam and heat spilled from the room. The sound of her voice was louder—no longer muffled, he could hear her clearly now—and he could just make out the shape of her through the steam, lying back in the bath, becoming more visible as he stepped forward on the damp tile. Rising from the water, she smiled at him. Her skin was flushed pink with the heat and he reached for a towel to wrap about her.

The humidity had brought down upon the house a huge, muffled silence; it buzzed in his ears along with the other buzz that was the effect of alcohol and the electric lights farther down the street, the heady thrum of cicadas hidden in the trees. He closed his eyes but the darkness made him feel queasy—things were spinning and within this vertigo, images were emerging: black-ashen faces and flashing red lights, orange flames racing up the side of a building, windows exploding, glass burst-ing in the heat and raining down on the black sidewalk, and flames licking hungrily at the same space where just moments before there had been windows—and he had to open his eyes again. And then suddenly

Lynne was there, as if she had somehow materialized out of the silence and the heat-light and the steam.

It's okay, Cal, it's okay, she said to him. *I'm here. I'm right here.* And she was holding his face up to hers so that he might see her fully and then pulling his head against her so that it lay upon her damp, warm shoulder. He let her, feeling so weak and empty inside, as if something important and necessary—a small flame of sorts—had just been extinguished and all that remained was a whirling, black vacuum and the sense of plummeting, falling without end into that blackness. He was afraid and only now realized that he had always been afraid—years of being afraid and of trying to keep the fear at bay. Lynne's hand stroked the back of his head, his hair plastered to his scalp with sweat. She whispered soothingly into his ear. He wrapped his arms around the warmth of her, pulled her to him, squeezed, and held on, afraid to let her go, and then he allowed her to lead him out into the street and into darkness, away from the flames and the fire and their home, the last place they would ever make love to each other.

They came down the staircase and out into the yard amid the rubble of scorched and blistered clapboard and overgrown grass and weeds smelling of cat piss, and the dream collapsed in on itself. He could taste a sourness in his mouth, feel the sweat beneath his armpits, smell the sweet, charred scent of burned timbers. A patrol car rolled by, sweeping a spotlight at the house, and he blinked in its glare. "That you, Cal?" one of the cops called from the open window and he shouted back, "Yeah, it's me," and they switched off the light and he waved and they rumbled on.

It was high tide and kids hollered as they jumped from the John J. Beades Memorial Bridge, a drawbridge over the inlet from Dorchester Bay. Cal saw flashes of them as they passed through the light cast by the lamps on the bridge and into the water below.

"I thought I'd find you here."

Cal turned at the sound of Dante's voice. He emerged out of the darkness grinning, the street a spear of light at his back. He wore chinos and a T-shirt damp with sweat. In his hand, a bottle wrapped in a brown paper bag. He held it aloft.

"You in the mood?"

Cal laughed. "Sure," he said. He was glad for the sharpness of clarity that sobriety brought, but only in small doses; sometimes reality needed something to soften it a bit and blur its jagged edges.

They sat at the water's edge passing the bottle back and forth and watched the lights reflected in the water shimmering as ripples shuddered the surface. They looked at the kids jumping from the bridge into the water, thrashing toward the rotten spars, climbing out, and returning to the top of the bridge wall, daring one another to risk more and more dangerous spins, somersaults, twists into the water, the cars rumbling past on the narrow spans of metal behind them. It was so hot the kids would probably keep it up till midnight, till their parents called them in or the cops sent them home.

"Seems like a long time since we did that," Dante said.

"Yeah. Seems like a long time since we did a lot of things. And I don't ever remember a summer this hot."

"Does it make it any easier, coming here, going through the house?"

"I don't know." Cal frowned, considering, and his brow creased. He took a swig from the bottle. "I guess it's something I just have to do until I don't have to do it anymore."

A kid dropped from the bridge and started swimming toward the shore, crying. He swore at one of the older kids above him who had, it seemed, pushed him into the water. When he was done with the swearing but not with the crying, he ran across the beachfront to a side street.

"It feels like it only happened yesterday," Cal said. "I see everything over and over again. It's like a bad dream. Every single day, a bad fucking dream."

"Nobody's putting a clock on it, Cal. It doesn't work that way."

"Listen to me—you know better than anyone. I'm sorry."

"Time, man. That's all it takes, time."

Cal grunted and sipped from the bottle. "I used to think that way about the war. After I got back. I'm not so sure anymore."

"No," Dante said, "neither am I. But what else are you going to say to yourself? You hope time changes things—I mean, it's got to, right? Eventually? Otherwise, what's the fucking point?"

Cal handed him the bottle. A haze had come down out in the bay, and although they could hear boats out there moving across the horizon and see the signs of their passing in the swells rolling through the channel, they could not see them; even the lights of Marina Bay were lost in the haze. Distant thunder, out toward Quincy, sounded but they saw no lightning. The rumble seemed to circle the bay, coming to them loud and then diminished and then loud again.

"So," Cal said as they stared toward the sound, "how long do you wait, how long until things change?"

"I don't know. I'm still waiting."

The tide slowly went out and at close to eleven the kids left the bridge. They watched them passing between the streetlights, towels draped over their shoulders, as they crossed the two lanes of traffic and headed south toward Neponset. A brief breeze came up but not even that brought relief. It was the type of heat you sat in without moving, aware of your lungs working, slowly taking air in and forcing it out. The whiskey mellowed the mind—made you forget about the heat—but it also made you aware of the fragile shell you wore, a heap of skin draped over bones containing nothing but ballast and barely functioning pumps and shunts. Cal felt his heart working, a tight ache at the center of his chest, as if he'd taken a savage blow there and days later the pain had ebbed but still persisted.

"It's Owen's birthday tomorrow. They're celebrating in Dudley Square. Anne said you and Claudia should come. It'll be fun."

Dante continued looking toward the bay. Only a few cars moved along Morrissey Boulevard. "Why?"

"What do you mean, why? Why wouldn't you be there, after everything we've all gone through?"

"Owen hates my fucking guts."

"He doesn't hate your fucking guts. All that's in the past. What we did...back then..." Cal shook his head. "Jesus, he stood by you, didn't he? He saw to it that you and your sister could adopt Maria as your own. He did all that paperwork, saw it pushed through, no questions asked. He put his ass on the line, for the both of us."

"I know he did. I don't forget it."

Lights flashed on the giant gas tanks. The sound of the engines of planes bound for Logan came to them long after the planes had gone by, lost somewhere up there in the murk. They passed the bottle and listened to sirens wailing in other parts of the city. The streetlights dimmed and surged and dimmed again. Window fans turned in slow metallic circles, changing speeds with the current. Cal could hear the small, electric clicks in their motors as they stopped and then engaged, whirring like summer bugs.

"Look, it'll be fun," Cal said, "and it'll get you and Claudia out of the house for once."

"Oh, she's been getting out of the house plenty."

"Yeah?"

"Her boyfriend. She's barely around anymore."

"The same guy?"

"Yeah, it's the same prick, going on four months. The way she carries on with him—" Dante shook his head angrily. "You'd think she was eighteen or something."

"For her it probably is like being eighteen again."

"Fucking embarrassment, that's what it is."

"So come then, have a night where it's just the two of you. Tell the boyfriend to go fuck himself."

"Okay, okay. I'll ask Claudia. We'll get a babysitter. We'll fucking come."

"Yeah? Good."

From the Hennesseys' front window a pale incandescent light spilled onto the curb. They had one of the few televisions in the neighborhood.

Dante and Cal could hear *The Jack Benny Program,* which was blaring because old man Hennessey was almost deaf. They listened for a while and then the sponsor's commercials came on. Tonight it was Lucky Strike. Cal murmured the slogan aloud—"Be Happy, Go Lucky"—and Dante looked up. Assuming Cal wanted a cigarette, he pulled one from his pocket. He lit it up and passed it down, and Cal drew long and deep on the cigarette that he hadn't really wanted and the smoke seemed to coil in his lungs and got his gut writhing. It was too much in the heat and he felt sick to his stomach. He handed the cigarette back to Dante and, taking another pull from the bottle, stared out over the water. Together they watched as the city went to sleep—nothing but a lone car passing over the drawbridge every once in a while—and until their bottle was done, they listened to thunder rolling, it seemed without end, through the starless Boston night.

4

Shortly after dawn Owen was on a BPD patrol boat with a federal agent and two of his own men, the vessel churning across the inner harbor toward the Chelsea waterfront, where ships and boats shimmered vaguely. Seagulls swooped low across the water—white on silver—and then Owen lost them as they rose into the silver glare of the sky and the low sun. He had to squint and look away.

Their speed and the spray from the water offered only a mild relief from the heat, and the water became choppy from ships and tankers moving out in the bay, sudden swells lifting the pilot boat and dropping it so that the hull banged loudly and the engine seemed to sputter and groan, and spumes of spray lashed the deck. Owen felt the shuddering in his feet and up through his legs as the small boat took each wave like a depth charge to the keel. He could smell the greasy odor of oily gasoline, the carbon monoxide seeping from the port exhaust and up from the engine room, and when he looked at the water, everything seemed to swirl in the same sickening, myopic haze.

Somehow something had gone wrong and their tip-off had been found out. They'd laid a network of cops and patrol boats around the harbor, waiting for the shipment of contraband that the informant had told them would be arriving from New York at noon, had locked down the docklands on both sides of the harbor since midnight, but still a boat had found its way in through their snare at some point during the night and only now had they discovered it, moored in Charlestown, with no sign of its crew or its cargo. Someone had gotten word to them and if it was one of his own, there would be hell to pay. The thought of all the work they'd done that was now wasted—all for nothing— made him feel sick. He considered telling the cop at the wheel to slow it down, that the motion and the heat and the diesel fumes were bringing on one of his migraines, then thought better of it. A wave of nausea forced him to close his eyes and breathe deeply. When he opened them again, the federal agent was looking at him, and he nodded to assure him that he was okay.

The two-way sputtered from the wheelhouse and Owen called out to the pilot. "Tell them we're coming in," he shouted, "and not to touch a thing until we're there." The pilot looked at him, uncomprehending over the noise of the engine; a wave buffeted the boat, and the nausea forced Owen to clench his jaw. "I said to fucking tell them to maintain their perimeter and not to touch a fucking thing!" he shouted, and this time the pilot got it. He pulled back on the throttle and got on the two-way to the main units waiting on the docks, and Owen glared at the approaching wharves, wishing he could just puke and be done with it.

The trawler was empty. Owen walked from the aft to the wheelhouse and galley in the superstructure toward the bow. He had his men scour the deck and he climbed below into the crew's compartments but this too was empty. In the insulated fish hold he scanned the space with his flashlight. It was as dry as a coffin and despite the smell it was difficult to believe that it had ever transported fish. He sniffed the air for the scent of something that might tell him what had been there only hours before. He smelled diesel, oil, and brine, a foul, brackish smell that seemed to come from another part of the boat, perhaps from water in the bilge that hadn't been properly pumped out. Whoever had sailed aboard the vessel had taken great pains to remove everything from it.

He stood in a square of light provided by the open hatch over his head and looked up above the pinioned trawling arms to where two cormorants beat their black wings at the sky, listening to his men moving across the deck and in the engine room, and he imagined how slow a process it would have been to heft crates of guns and ammunition up onto the deck and then into waiting vehicles in the middle of the night. He considered the number of crew—four to five individuals—and then the driver of the waiting vehicle, and perhaps the muscle he'd have with him. The informant had told him that the boat was carrying five tons' worth. They might have used multiple vehicles to transport the shipment once they'd unloaded it. Say three trucks, with a driver and help per truck. That made a good ten bodies. With that many people, perhaps the job hadn't been that difficult after all.

His men found blood on the sheets in one of the crew's bunks; he told them to take pictures of the sheets and bag them, and he discovered more blood on deck, at the stern. There was a spatter trail across the transom. Either someone had been shot during the trip or there had been some manner of event after they'd docked. He stood at the rail and stared from the aft deck out across the water toward the stunted Boston skyline, which seemed even more stunted beneath the leaden sky. Even at a short distance, heat shimmered on the water and caused the city to blur.

"Detective!" the pilot of the patrol boat called to him from the dock and he made his way hastily off the boat and down the pier to the wooden walk, which, rising and falling on the tide beneath him, caused his nausea to return.

The pilot already had the engine running, the prop churning the water at the boat's rear and the pipe pumping exhaust into the air, and he was undoing the ropes from their moorings. The two-way squawked in the wheelhouse. Owen removed his sunglasses to wipe at his eyes.

"What is it?" he asked.

"They've found a body," the pilot said and gestured for Owen to pull in the last rope before he climbed aboard. "Near the immigration holding center on Armitage, at the other end of the docks." And before he even thought of arguing, Owen had climbed in, tossing the mooring rope to the floor, and the pilot backed the boat into the channel.

The body had been dumped just above the waterline on a stony promontory—a breakwater of sorts—marking the end of the docklands, where the harbor opened up into the outer harbor and the bay. As Owen's boat approached he could make out six cops assembled on the piers, creating a police line. Three stood on the promontory below. He jumped from the patrol boat just as it bumped the stone and strode toward the officers. When they saw him coming they stepped back and out of his way, but they continued watching and he could tell they were waiting to see how he'd react.

The body had been tarred and feathered, but it wasn't like anything Owen had ever read about in history books. It was streaked with black pitch and here and there feathers poked up from the blood and gore. The skin had been burned off the victim because they'd used boiling pitch and not warm pine tar, which, Owen knew, had been used once upon a time mostly to shame and humiliate, not to torture or kill. The man's face, black with flies, looked as if it were moving; caught and struggling in the tar, flies crawled slowly upon his cheeks and open mouth, across the glazed surface of his eyes, and in the shattered front of his skull; a large section of the bone at the glabella—the center of his forehead—was gone. He'd been shot through the back of the head.

Owen held a handkerchief to his mouth and swatted at the flies buzzing around him. Another wave of nausea assailed him, but, breathing deep and slow, he held it off. He knew that this was the worst of it and if he could get through it, he'd be all right. But the heat wasn't helping. The sun had risen higher since they'd come across the harbor and now it beat down on his head like a ball-peen hammer. One of the cops, a veteran named Caputo, walked to the water's edge and puked loudly.

The pitch tar was a bad touch; it had been spread on the man at an extreme temperature, so it was almost a liquid, torching the epidermis and making the skin blister and pull away from the muscle and tendon below—he would have been in agony before they shot him. Although they'd rushed the unloading, they had taken their time with this particularly gruesome act and hadn't feared they'd be caught. The act, its audacity and its brutality, worried at him. He had the sense that with the boat emptied of its cargo and its crew gone underground and into hiding, this was just the beginning of something much larger; his interception of the trawler had set events in motion and this death was only the start. He realized that he'd broken out into a sweat and that it was sour with adrenaline.

"We found the buckets of tar they used up on the dock along with a barrel of industrial pitch," one of the cops said. "There's the charred remains of a fire, but nothing else."

"Never seen anything like it," said the cop standing to his right.

"Nope, me neither," said Owen, "except in history books, and then nothing like this."

He resisted touching the body for it looked as if the clothes and skin had melded in the heat of the pitch; he feared that if he checked the man's pockets, his skin might come away with the tugging. He'd wait for the medical examiner to arrive before having his men attempt to move the body. "Did you check for ID?" he asked one of the cops.

"You told us not to touch anything," said Wolinski.

Owen looked at him; he had a long nose shiny with sweat and had taken off his hat. His eyes were shielded by aviator sunglasses.

"I know I did. Well?"

The cop sighed and nodded. "He's got nothing on him."

Boat horns sounded out in the channel. The water glistened with an oily sheen. Small waves lapped at the stones. Owen looked at his watch. It was now eleven o'clock. They had a good chance of catching all the workers along the docks before they left for the day. He glanced up. A couple dozen were already beyond the police line, trying to get a look at the drama. A white sedan with the Massachusetts Office of the Chief Medical Examiner's seal on it pulled up, and Fierro got out. Owen watched him step through the police line; he was already pulling out a pack of cigarettes.

"Take eight officers," Owen said to the cop, "pair them off and get them talking to everyone they can along the docks. Have half begin at the south entrance and half at the north." He gestured to the fishermen, dockhands, and longshoremen peering down from the wharf. "And you can start with that group up there. I want to know who this guy was. I want to know why he was killed this way."

5

DUDLEY SQUARE

AT DUSK THE streets still carried the heat of the day but there was a welcome relief when the sun went down. Young men and women filled Dudley Square for the Saturday-night dances. The sidewalks were so packed with people that many moved into the road, and cars had to slow to accommodate them. They came off streetcars and trolleys and off the Dudley Square El, heading to the Intercontinental, the Hibernian, the Rose Croix, Winslow Hall, the Silver Ballroom, and the Tuxedo Ballroom, the women flitting like moths in the late night as the streetlights buzzed on, their crinoline skirts bouncing and swirling as they walked in groups, heels clacking along the pavement as incessant as a streetcar's wheels upon the rails.

It had been years since Cal had come into Dudley for the dance clubs, and the area still surprised him. The last time he'd been here had been with Lynne, before the war—God, had that much time passed? They'd been in their mid-twenties. Back then they'd often step out in Dudley Square; it had one of the best club scenes in town. And he was amazed to see how it had grown and thrived since then, stunned as he often was to find that the world had continued to exist without him.

Dudley had even changed in his absence and become something other, something of which he no longer felt a part.

The streets were thronged with hundreds of people. Listening to the accents, he felt as if he'd been transported back to Ireland. He could tell that some of them were fresh off the boat.

He saw Dante and Claudia on the street walking from their car and he called out to them and strode to catch up. Owen and Anne were waiting for them at the entrance to the Intercontinental. Anne kissed Cal and Dante on the cheek and then took Claudia's hands in hers and made her spin so that she could admire her dress. Owen looked pale; a sheen of sweat shone on his forehead. Anne squeezed his waist and teased him about his birthday and his age, and he smiled vainly. Just inside the door an Irish cop, who seemed to recognize Owen, tipped his cap to them and, having heard their talk, shouted merrily, "Happy birthday, Detective!" and this seemed to bring a genuine smile to Owen's face as they paid the doorman and climbed the stairs to the Crystal Ballroom. There was another cop at the door and at different points about the room tuxedoed men observed the crowd, all watching for anyone getting too loud or physical or trying to sneak in a bottle from the bar downstairs. They all knew the rules: No drinking in the dance halls and, above all, show respect to the women.

They took a table before the dance floor and sat for a moment. On the stage a dozen or so musicians played a slow Irish ballad that Cal had some vague memory of—it was an old air, something his mother and father had once danced to in the good days, but done in a contemporary way. With the steady bass and snare accompaniment, the flourishes of trumpet and saxophone, it had an unmistakable drive to it, and it showed in how the dancers sped to grab dancing partners. He watched the hundreds of couples flowing across the floor and the sense of them filling the space with heat and energy. Above them a crystal ball spun slowly, reflecting the four filtered spotlights cast upon it, and showered the dancers with diamondlike prisms of soft light, as if it were raining.

Claudia reached for Dante's hand. "Let's dance!" she said, but Dante shook her hand off. "I can't dance to this," he said. "It's not my thing."

"Oh, you," she said, but not angrily. "You can dance to anything if it's got music in it—dance this waltz with me, please."

Dante shook his head. "Ahh, give it a rest." He nodded to the men about the room. "If I dance with you they'll think we're a couple; you'll lose your chance with one of these lucky stiffs."

Undeterred, Claudia turned to Cal. "What about you?"

"With these legs, Claudia? My dancing days are long over."

"Go on, Cal," Anne urged as she took Owen's hand and he rose from the table. "Nobody sits here."

"Nobody but me. Tonight I'd rather watch."

For a while the three of them sat and looked on as Owen and Anne danced but when it became clear that Claudia was a woman without any attachments—Cal and Dante had been discussing Dante's need for work and his recent job hunt—men began coming to the table. Now the dance floor filled as men walked from their chairs and asked the women sitting on the opposite side of the room to dance.

A young Irishman with black hair greased back with Brylcreem approached their table, and his pale cheeks flushed with blood.

"Would you mind?" he said, and the three of them looked at him as he held out his hand to Claudia. "I mean, might you be up for taking a spin on the floor?"

He glanced at Dante and Cal, who smiled encouragingly, and Claudia said: "Of course!" And, grinning, the young man took her hand, and they joined the crowd as the band began another waltz.

After the waltz, the music picked up, Irish-inflected big band merging with jazz and bop, and a thousand pairs of feet banged the wood so that the room seemed to vibrate as if from distant thunder, and Dante watched Claudia with her dancing partner and saw the carefree way she now had about her and something stiffened inside him. He realized he resented this new Claudia, so capable of throwing off her yoke of martyrdom. How easy she made it look—she was almost flaunting this new person in his face. It was as if he were looking at a stranger; he didn't recognize this woman at all. Gone was her grief, her need to exist in solitude and pain. Gone was her desire to inflict suffering upon herself, to descend into her despair and isolation, her spinsterhood, as if it were somehow a badge of honor.

He stared at her in the dress he hadn't even known she had as she spun beneath the shafts of reflected light. Her petticoat swirled back and forth about her wide hips. He looked at her face, smiling and then laughing at something her dancing partner said to her. The way she placed her hand partially over that smile in mock horror at what he'd said. Dante realized that Claudia's newfound freedom and the release of inhibitions that came with it was a sort of betrayal.

Cal nudged him. "Claudia," he said, "she's a fine dancer. I never knew she could dance like that. You should get her out more often. She looks like she's having the time of her life; I've never seen her so happy."

"She thinks she's Irene Dunne in *Anna and the King of Siam*."

"And what's the matter with that? Can't she be whoever she wants to be? Look at her. She's having a ball, for Christ's sake."

"Jesus, since when did you become so chipper?"

The room was sweltering, the air hot and still with hundreds of bodies pressed together. Cal didn't know how they could all fit in the room. The tuxedoed attendants and the cops were lost in the throng. Up on the stage the band worked furiously; above their jacket lapels, the collars of their dress shirts had darkened with sweat.

Cal looked at the dancers moving across the parquet. He felt the familiar dissonance now, keenly, and tried to contain it, ensure that it did not affect Owen's birthday celebrations, but every time he looked at the dance floor and the dancers there, he was transported to a time ten years before with Lynne—only the clothes and music had changed slightly; it was like looking at two images superimposed over each other until you could no longer clearly make out either. The important parts were gone. Lynne's face was gone.

There was a reverberation of sound, the treble created by two identical records playing on phonographs alongside each other, their music half a second apart and so creating a partial echo. The lights and sounds and movement of people blurred; everything was shuddering. The edges of his world were turning black, as so often happened, the darkness moving slowly inward toward the center of his vision. He took some bennies from his pocket and popped them back quickly with a glass of water before Dante could notice his shaking hand, then with a smile plastered to his face he focused on a straight line toward a single spot— through the crowd to where the band played upon the stage; he focused first on the pianist, then the fiddler, the horn section, the drummer, the bass player, the accordionist, and gradually the room widened, the blackness at its edges retreated, and he saw the world fully again.

At the intermission between sets, while Owen was in the restroom, Anne took Cal aside. She wore a blue sequined dress that sparkled and shone under the light. Her red hair was done up in a bun and she had large, wide, and serious eyes. But there was almost nothing serious or demure about Anne Kelly—she'd grown up in a family of all boys, most of them firemen now, and she had a flippant sense of humor that Cal enjoyed.

"Cal," she said, "would you do me a favor and take Owen down to the bar? It's his birthday but you would think someone had died—buy him a couple of drinks, cheer him up. I want him to have a good time. Us ladies, we'll be just fine."

When Owen came back to the table he looked a hundred times worse. Anne, who was talking with Claudia, pretended as if nothing were wrong, but she glanced at Cal and he got the hint.

"Owen," he said. "You look as if you're gonna puke. C'mon, you need a drink. Let's you and me and Dante go down to McPherson's. I'm dying of the heat in here myself."

Downstairs, the long bar at McPherson's stretched the length of the building and men were lined up at it five deep. Fans turned slowly above their heads. They were putting back their drinks, loosening up their feet and tongues to go talk to women and ask them to dance. It was after ten o'clock and soon most of them would file out in anticipation of the band's playlist, which they knew down to the minute. As the three of them made their way to the back of the bar someone shouted from the hallway, "They're playing 'The Star of the County Down'!" and half the men put back their pints and began moving toward the door.

At the end of the bar Cal ordered them each a beer and a whiskey and when the drinks came he and Dante raised their glasses to Owen and drank them down and then Cal ordered them another round. Above their heads they could feel the vibrations from the ballroom. The strains of the fiddle, blasts from the trumpets, and the steady boom of the bass drum tremored throughout the building. Owen and Dante lit cigarettes and Cal took off his jacket, loosened his tie. Sweat stained his pale blue shirt dark beneath his arms and along his spine.

Cal looked at Owen. "Owen, you're as pale as a ghost."

"Ah, I'm fine. It's just this fucking heat."

"Anne thinks you're not having a good time. It's your birthday, she wants you to have a good time."

"I am having a good time, it's a fucking gas." Owen shook his head in frustration, lifted his glass, and finished his whiskey.

Dante raised his hand to the barkeep for another round.

"Drink isn't going to help," Owen said.

"Have one anyway," Dante said. "It's too hot not to."

Owen took a deep drag of his cigarette and exhaled, tapped the butt end into an ashtray, and left it smoldering on the rim. "We set up a net to catch a boat coming into Charlestown this morning," he said. "We received a tip that it was carrying guns, possibly other contraband, for the IRA. We had the whole harbor locked down."

"Sounds like you didn't find out what they were carrying. Did they figure you?"

"They sure did—they knew we would be waiting and came in sometime last night instead. We found the boat empty, tied up at Ross Wharf. The harbormaster said he had no records of it coming in. We know it's from New York but we're still trying to find out who the owner is."

"And no one saw any of its crew leaving the docks?"

"We think someone might have, but that someone is dead. We've got a body but no ID yet. They tarred and feathered him, shot him in the head, and left his corpse tied to the Charlestown locks."

Owen picked up his cigarette from the ashtray and sucked on it.

"What's the meaning of that?" Dante said.

"It means," said Cal as he finished his whiskey and signaled the barkeep again, "that he was a rat, an informer, or at least they believed he was."

"Yeah, that's exactly what it means." Owen ran a hand through his hair; some color had returned to his face with the whiskey.

Dante frowned. "The IRA in Boston? I've never heard of it."

"Neither have I. Not since my father's day, anyway. And it worries me—if there's a boat that was supposed to be going somewhere and it doesn't get there and the IRA's involved..."

"There's going to be payback—but do you really think they're that organized? Aren't they mostly just shooting at their own or blowing themselves up?"

"Some of the Feds I talked to seemed to think so, say that they've seen more and more arms being smuggled out of the country to Ireland in the last six months, that something is about to happen. Which is the last thing we need here. The town's a powder keg already with every gangster and his brother thinking he's the next Blackie Foley, all trying to get a piece of what he left behind."

Dante and Cal exchanged a look. It had been two years since any of them had mentioned Blackie's name, although whenever they saw one another, the weight of the thing left unsaid was like a tenuous chain that bound them all—that and Sheila's daughter, Maria. After Blackie's death, Sully had taken back some of his dealings and territories that, over the years, his general had gradually adopted as his own, and for the first year, with Shaw at his side, Sully had seemed like the Sully of old, a force to be reckoned with, someone not even the mob or the new gangs emerging in Roxbury and Chinatown would mess with. But in the past eight months, his mind had begun to deteriorate—he was suffering from the early onset of dementia—and with his mind went his ability to manage the town. Now, on the days when he could remember who he was and he wasn't shitting himself, Sully ran everything out of a nursing home in Dorchester, up on the hill, in Mount Bowdoin, above Ronan Park, with Shaw as his errand boy, and the only thing he seemed to care about was clean sheets.

"We've had twelve murders in the month of June," said Owen. "You know the last time we had a number like that? And that's just in Dorchester, Southie, Roxbury, and Charlestown. And now the Italians are pushing in as well, which doesn't help any."

"They must have unloaded the cargo in a hurry," Cal said, "which means they most likely transported it somewhere local. They'll need to find another way to get it to where it was going."

"Probably," said Owen. "Although they might always have had a contingency plan. Our tip-off thought it was a done deal, but someone else already had the get on us."

"And on him," Cal said. "You think this dead guy on the docks is the rat, your informant?"

"We don't know—that's the thing, we don't know much of anything right now. I have to wait for an ID on the body and for the registry on the boat."

"That's some birthday present," said Dante.

"Yeah, a real great present."

"Happy fucking birthday," said Cal, raising his glass, and Owen and Dante banged their glasses against his. "Happy fucking birthday," they echoed and the Irish bartenders glanced down from the other end of the bar, stared at them for a moment, and then looked away.

They climbed the stairs back to the main ballroom, with Cal trying not to show how inebriated he was and testing each step carefully with his feet. He waved Owen and Dante on and they went ahead and rejoined the women. He stepped gingerly on the wood, resting to knead the muscle in his bad leg as men and women passed him.

As he stood before the ballroom, trying to collect himself, its doors opened suddenly. A couple emerged, arm in arm, the man smiling, the woman's head thrown back in laughter, the sound lost in the cavernous space of the ballroom and among the dancing couples on the crystal-lit floor, and he was in that illuminated space, holding Lynne close to him and together they were twirling effortlessly about the room. The sound of the orchestra seemed to swell and in the rectangle of light cast onto the balcony he could see her—for the first time in months, he could see her face clearly—and she was smiling and happy, wearing an olive gown made of some type of silky material that clung to her body. Cal's breath caught and he remained still, lost in and transfixed by the sight before him as if he were in a dream even as men and women bustled about him.

"Lynne," he said quietly. "There are times, baby, when I need you more than ever, when I don't know if I can do it without you." He knew it was a selfish thing, but as bad as it had been after the war, it had never been as bad as this. Lynne had helped him keep it in check, reminding him of the difference between his two experiences, the one in Europe among the dead, and his life back home among the living. She'd reminded him during the darkness, when he'd become incapacitated by fear, shame, and self-loathing, that he was alive and he had only to make the choice, if he wanted, to keep living. And because of her he had made the choice. He'd kept living.

After he'd said good night to Owen and Anne and walked Dante and Claudia to their car, Cal stood on Dudley Street smoking a cigarette, watching the street life and waiting for his buzz to fade before he got on a trolley. The moonlight flickered on the rooftop stacks and water barrels, glowing like embers on the broken glass in the alleyways and glimmering on the chrome of cars parked along the street. Couples, arms entwined or wrapped around each other, passed by him. Cal stubbed his cigarette out on the brick wall and threw it in a trash can. The top floors of the dance halls shone light out onto the Avenue—he could see people there at the windows—and the strains of music filled the steamy night with a charge that prickled the skin, sent the hairs up on his arms.

On the corner opposite the Waldorf, half a dozen men lounged, hair greased and combed back, smoking intently and talking loud. Cal watched them for a bit and he knew they were looking for trouble. By the way they stood he could tell that they'd been drinking. One of them already seemed drink-sick; he had his head pressed to the brick wall as if it were the only thing that might save him. The others stared at the couples as they left the dance halls, eyeballing the men who might challenge them. The usual tension weighed like a lead slat across Cal's shoulders and neck as he considered which one was the ringleader and how he might take him out, and then a large group of Connemara men crossed the street from Winslow House and their faces were flushed and their fists balled and they were talking angrily among themselves in Irish as they walked the street, and the greasers turned away and just as quickly Cal let his anger dissipate and the need to fight left him.

6

JULY 4, SOUTH BOSTON

Bottle rockets tore into the sky, whistling threads of smoke that arched out over the harbor and exploded in sudden blasts of fire. Their reports were no louder than a .22-caliber pistol's, but each reverberated off the still, dark waters as though signaling a war that was making its way to Boston.

Wiping his brow with a handkerchief already soaked through with sweat, Michael Cleland walked along the chain-link fence that bordered the truck lot and separated it from the small, sloping patch of land that led down to the derelict pier. There were about a dozen of them, mostly teenage boys and some smaller, likely their younger brothers who, with their mothers and fathers out at the bars and saloons, the older boys had to keep an eye on. Two of them prepped another round of rockets, placing them in empty cola bottles that were wedged at angles between the pier's wooden slats. One boy lit a match and brought the flame to a long string of firecrackers, and once the wick sparkled white, he tossed it at the two kneeling on the pier. It flared up and blossomed violently; sparks and fire rained down between the rotting planks to the shallow waters below. The two boys hunched down and, with their bare arms shielding their faces, fled through the assault, hollering mad cries and curses. Smoke hung heavily in the air. Cleland couldn't see them, but he could hear them laughing and screaming at one another, like children pretending to be men, their voices loud and courageous with liquor.

Today was the Fourth of July, Independence Day.

Once the smoke had cleared, the acrid odor of it biting at his throat, he could see one of the smaller boys standing at the very edge of the pier. The boy lit a Roman candle with the smoldering end of a cigar and raised the flaming stick high above his head. Blasts of red, blue, and white sparks shot out over the water, and Cleland could see that the boy clutching it was shirtless but unflinching as the bits of fire streamed down on him. The boy appeared possessed in the light, a young savage showing the others that no matter how much pain he suffered, he would hold his ground and never let go.

In a few years, he'd be a menace, Cleland could tell. No longer a troublesome delinquent but a young man cleansed of innocence, a criminal, chin always raised and fists always clenched. All to make his father proud. His father's father proud. The whole line of hard men who were born in the States and saw Ireland as a mirage, a mythical land where their blood belonged but that their hearts had forgotten. They could never be royalty, but here in Boston, they could be kings.

Cleland cursed under his breath. Not even a single breeze to be found along the whole coastline. The city was three days into a heat wave, and he had the feeling it had just started, making Boston a great, miserable furnace, and that it would be this way until well after Labor Day. More sweat gathered along his brow and he wiped at it again with the handkerchief. He tried to breathe deeply and heard himself wheeze. It was as if a massive slate pressed hard against his lungs. *I'm too old for this,* he thought, his heavy-knuckled fingers grasping the chain-link fence as if he were trying to hold himself upright.

He watched one of the boys kneel down to light a whole brick of firecrackers. His friends hollered foulmouthed threats as they rushed by him, hopping off the pier and back to the bare patch of land where empty bottles of beer and broken glass glistened under the half-moon. The wick appeared to dim and then go out. Several of the boys turned inquisitive and cautiously stepped toward the brick, but suddenly the wick sputtered back to life. One of the teenage boys screamed like a young girl. And then blasts of light seemed to multiply and never end, but when the last firecracker exploded, the silence reappeared suddenly, jarringly. The cloud of smoke hung low off the pier and drifted up toward Cleland. The acrid odors of gunpowder burned at his eyes and filled his nostrils. The smell triggered a memory from his childhood, grabbed hold of him and brought him back.

Mum, will it ever end?

Dublin. Easter. The third day of fighting and him ten years old again, standing at the bedroom window and looking at the silhouette of the church two streets away that spired above the rooftops and cut into the great, dark sky. Reflecting off the church came the light from the other side of the square, illuminated with low blasts of artillery and the flashing bursts of rifles. On the street below, a blockade of scrap wood and furniture burned brightly. And from the flames came the shadows of men, elongated and stretched as they flickered against the storefront across the way, skipping through the night like ghouls. He had no idea if they were rebels or looters or Royals. He glanced down at his younger brother Samuel, who was standing beside him, his small hand hot and sweaty in his own, and him clasping at it because if he didn't, Samuel would start up again. He noticed how the boy's large eyes had had the blue sucked out of them; they glistened as black as river stone as he fought against tears. "Be a man, Sam. Crying will do us no good."

And with their mother pacing the upstairs hallway, the floorboards creaking with slow, tired groans, the two of them waited it out and stood at the window well past their usual bedtime, watching as arcs of fire rose and fell beyond the church and listening to the dueling gunfire as it rattled and echoed against the buildings and along the cobblestones, and they waited, waited for Daddy to come home.

Will Daddy come home?

Yes, once this is over, he'll be home.

Forty-eight years old again, Cleland felt his palms sweat and for a moment had the sensation of a small hand clutching his own. He stuffed the handkerchief into his back pocket, reached into his front pocket, and took out a butterscotch candy. He unwrapped the cellophane and popped it into his mouth. He rolled the sweet around, careful not to let it touch his back teeth, which pained him like rusted nails burrowed deep into the bone of his jaw.

Behind him, a truck's engine suddenly came alive. The headlights of Dick Creeley's Chevy flatbed flared brightly, two beams that carried over the gravel lot and illuminated a flurry of mosquitoes battering against one another. The driver, old Creeley, worked odd jobs in the warehouse—cleaning, restocking parts, keeping guard on a shipment awaiting pickup, whatever was necessary. He honked the horn once.

The truck slowly pulled out of its space, the old man pressing the horn again. The brakes cried out, metal on metal, and the beat-up vehicle rolled out of the lot. Cleland turned back to the pier, which remained quiet as the boys moved within the smoke and gathered more ammunition.

Cleland had cursed himself for owing a favor; for "the Cause," they had told him at the club, as if it meant as much in this place as it did in Ireland. And now here he was, on the lookout for a pickup, when he could have been at home with a cold bottle of Pickwick listening to the Sox on the radio, Mel Parnell on the hill against those lowly Pinstripes from the Bronx.

He walked toward the only light on in the back lot, a caged bulb flickering above a steel door to the office. Along the other side of the warehouse came the scrape of a gate against the roadway. Cleland assumed it was Creeley taking his sweet time leaving, and he imagined the old man idling as he nipped at a pint of rotgut whiskey before heading back to his basement apartment outside Quincy Center. But the battered Chevy truck was already a half a mile away on Summer Street,

Creeley singing a song to himself, the heels of his hands drumming against the steering wheel as he pushed the engine as hard as it could go.

Cleland walked under the light. Above him, moths battered against the caged bulb. He checked the door to make sure it was still locked, then moved back into the darkness.

His eyes had trouble focusing. He squinted, sucked hard on the lozenge, and felt sharp tremors vibrate in his jaw. There was movement in the lot. Perhaps just that homeless black Labrador passing through. He spit out the candy, and it cracked against the concrete. His hand clutched at his back pocket and twisted anxiously at the handkerchief. And then he realized he wasn't alone.

Several yards ahead, the ember of a cigar flared and pumped red as if someone was trying to keep it burning evenly. Eyes adjusting, he could see the shadow of a man smoking it. The man was of a large build, and his bald head reflected the moonlight that came through a jagged cluster of low-moving clouds. Cleland raised a hand to get the man's attention.

"Over here." And then he repeated it, softer this time. "Over here."

It should be so simple. Truck comes in, he opens the garage, it pulls in, and they load up the crates. Then he shuts the doors, chains and locks them, and heads home, Mel Parnell probably still on the mound, throwing that sweet curve with a mind of its own, and him drinking a cold beer, knowing that another one awaited him in the icebox.

Down on the pier, whistler rockets popped off in the distance. A bottle crashed and shattered against the rocks. One of the teens hollered with drunken song, words slurred and nearly unintelligible.

Cleland pulled the revolver out of his pocket, kept it at his side.

Without its headlights turned on, a long, black Cadillac pulled into the lot, the slick and polished surface gleaming with the moonlight's reflection. Silent, as though rolling without the engine on, the car moved toward him. Cleland offered a halfhearted wave. He watched the car come to a stop, saw the elongated, ornamental hood, the sweeping curve of its roof, and, behind the backseat, a window, rectangular and covered with white curtains, parted at the center.

"You got to be kidding me," he said, walking toward the hearse. He could see a shadow holding on to the wheel with both hands. The face was without definition, yet he could feel that the eyes were on him, and without seeing it, he knew there was some manner of a grin in that darkness.

Headlights suddenly beamed on and cut across the lot, flashing into his eyes. With his arm, he shielded himself from the light, backpedaled, heels digging through the gravel rocks. He heard a door open and then slam shut.

The headlights dimmed and smoldered with an electric amber, illuminating only a few feet ahead. Spots of light danced wildly in Cleland's vision. Off to his side, he heard the crunch of a boot on gravel. He turned quickly and saw another man walking across the lot toward him, one hand in the pocket of his sports coat, the other clutching a 12-gauge sawed-off shotgun.

"Where's the truck?" Cleland called out. "There's supposed to be a truck. Ryan's Kitchen Supplies."

"That's right, old man."

"Don't you worry," another voice called to him. He turned in a dizzying circle and couldn't see who had said it. The man smoking the cigar was no longer there. The hearse remained still.

Cleland turned and moved toward the lone light above the office door. Maybe he wouldn't have to fumble for the right key. Maybe he could get inside quickly and lock the door behind him and then get on the phone for help. His heart hammered in his chest. Three steps in, he watched the glass bulb explode. Sparks showered down in a bursting pop; the cage protecting the light fell and clattered onto the concrete walkway. He turned around and, without aiming, raised the gun and moved it from side to side.

"They asked me to do a favor," he called out. "I was told to wait for a truck, that's all."

Below the warehouse, more fireworks tore off the pier into the night. But close, on this side of the chain-link fence, only yards away, Cleland saw another man with his arm raised, the glint of black, polished steel, and then the sudden, white flash of fire. He tried to move away, felt his knee give out, the bone and joints buckling. He turned and tucked his chin down, rolled his shoulder inward to protect his head from smacking the hard ground.

But he didn't turn in time and landed full-on, his skull cracking against the gravel. The heat of the wound filled his head, and he rolled to the side and felt blood drip down into his right eye. Frantically, he reached before him and searched for his gun. His fingers grappled with nothing but broken stone until, fingernails cracked, fingertips bloodied, he finally came into contact with the gun's grip.

"Our Father, Hail Mary, Glory be to the Father," he said to himself, waiting for the men to come out of the dark. He raised the gun and fired off a haphazard shot. Another blast came from the darkness and his hand erupted in a spray of blood and bone that spattered across his neck and face. He clutched his wrist and bowed his head over it. He bit down on his tongue and fought back a scream. The hearse's headlights flicked on full, and he was awash in bright light. He managed to get up on his knees and, clutching his arm, saw with painful clarity that three of his fingers had been blown off above the knuckles.

His mouth filled with the taste of copper. He fell to his side and curled into a fetal position. A pool of blood at the back of his head, the throbbing in his legs weakening, Michael Cleland realized he was dying.

Two men had come from the light and, standing before him, one of them said, "I think I know this guy."

"It doesn't matter, does it?" The other spoke with the lilt of somebody from the south of Ireland. "Now search him for keys."

Cleland couldn't talk. Blood filled his throat. He shut his eyes and listened to the fireworks whistling toward the islands in the harbor, and the pain suddenly subsided as he felt the sensation of a child's hand pressing his own. A comfort, no matter how brief, and he took a ragged breath and was back in Dublin again. It was 1916 and his younger brother Samuel was beside him. Through the window, they could see the fires lighting the city of Dublin, gunfire echoing like the distant cracks of newborn thunder ushering in a storm far, far away.

"Once in agony, pity on the dying," said the bald man in a tone mocking a preacher from the old country. He raised the sawed-off 12-gauge and pulled the trigger.

7

ALBANY STREET, SOUTH END

PHILLIP CONNELLY PRESIDED over the room like a man expecting trouble. With hands clasped behind his back, he walked among the poker and craps tables, his face expressionless. About twenty customers played the tables, and four men dressed in black silk vests with red bow ties worked the cards and the dice. The lone woman worker in the den, Gretchen, carried a tray plated with small sandwiches, ham and cheese with mustard on rye bread, and to make them look more appealing, a toothpick bearing a green olive was speared into each one. Phillip raised a finger and motioned her to come over. "Just watch the lad with the hairpiece," he said to her. "Over on Lou's table. He's twitching an awful lot. Not sure if he's sending secret messages or if he's a goddamn epileptic."

"Got it," she said.

"Let Neil know. I'm going to the head, be back in a couple."

She walked to the small oak bar that had been scavenged from an old Prohibition-era speakeasy in Fort Point, its original varnish painted over one too many times. Neil stood behind it and listened as she whispered something in his ear. He looked across the room at Phillip and nodded, then went back to making a drink, squeezing a quartered lime into a gin and tonic.

Phillip left the room, tapped the bouncer on the shoulder, and motioned for him to put out his cigarette. The bouncer took a last pull, dropped it to the ground, and pressed his heel on it. Cross-eyed and with a confused look, the big man shrugged.

"Anybody else comes, tell them we're full up for the night," said Phillip.

"Doesn't look all that full. You expecting something bad, huh?"

Phillip paused and eyed the man from his spit-shined shoes as big as Boris Karloff's in *Frankenstein* to his square, nearly imbecilic face. "Best to be safe rather than sorry, that's all. And no more smoking, you got it? Makes it look like you're hustling our fine establishment, not protecting it."

Old ragtime music drifted down to the lobby from the second floor, where Madame Crane and her whores ran their own games, peddling opium and skin. He could smell burning sage along with reefer and cigar smoke. A man's laughter bellowed, a low operatic tenor, and one of Crane's ladies joined in, her voice shrill and piercing. At least somebody was having a good time tonight, Phillip thought to himself.

The heels of his shoes clacked and echoed as he walked down a marble stairwell to the basement level. The damp hallway smelled of mold and standing water, and it was lit with only one working bulb, leaving much of its length in darkness. Exposed pipes clanged and vibrated above his head. He walked past a janitor's closet that had been left ajar and into a men's room, old black and white tiles faded and cracked, a brackish puddle pooling over a clogged drain. He stood before the urinal he knew still worked, unzipped, and closed his eyes. The door opened behind him, but he paid it no attention. A stall door opened and shut, and then came the loud flushing of a toilet.

At the sink, he rinsed his face in cold water, felt the weight in his front jacket pocket: a fold of cash an inch thick, bound with a heavy-duty rubber band. Perhaps that young lady from New York upstairs would be without a john, he thought, and he could have a nice ride before heading on home. Cindy, Carol, he forgot what her name was but remembered her pinched nose, the full lips, her overall delicate appearance despite her harsh Brooklyn accent.

The toilet flushed again. The stall door slammed open, and pulling a paper towel from the dispenser, he glanced into the mirror before him and saw a dark shape rushing his back. The mirror had dulled over time, exposing the mercury plating below—he couldn't see the face of the attacker, nor his own. He tried to turn but the hands reached up over his head quickly and looped a steel wire across his neck. He watched his reflection in the glass as the wire cut into his skin, and he felt the tremendous strength of his attacker as his body was lifted upward, the tips of his shoes scraping the tiled floor and then kicking at nothing but air. Blood gurgled up into his mouth, and a surge of it sprayed against the mirror as the wire cut through the muscle and the arteries. And then he was dropped to the floor and kicked in the chest with a steel-tipped boot, just to make sure there was nothing left.

At O'Casey's Bar in North Quincy, the taps had closed early. Three men sat in the back room and counted money, what little of it there was. Brendan smelled the smoke first, and one of the other men said he smelled nothing but somebody passing gas. A half a minute later, he sniffed loudly, said he smelled it too, got up from the table and opened the door. Flames danced and twirled along the bar top; blue fire rolled across the ceiling. He reared back and stumbled into the room and saw that Brendan and TJ were already rushing for the back exit.

Brendan got only a few feet outside before a shotgun took off his head. TJ got a few feet farther before a second shot tore through his chest, misting the air with blood and smoke. His body landed hard on its back, twitched uncontrollably, and then went still. The last man almost made it out of the lot and to the street, but a giant of a man, broad-shouldered and balding, cut him off, raised a pistol, and fired. The bullet snapped his head back, and two more bullets brought him to the ground.

Across the street in a five-floor apartment building, bedroom lights flickered on. A woman screamed from an open window. Three men got back in their car, and the driver gunned it down the street. All of them kept quiet until they were a mile away from the burning bar, and in the distance, they could hear a fire engine wailing its sad, desolate song.

"Time for a drink, I say."

"I say we all deserve it."

"We sure as hell do."

"Not a scratch, not one scratch. Pray to the Mother Mary and may she bless us all."

The laughter they shared was loud and quick, and before they knew it, the quiet returned as they made their way back to Boston. The killing was over for tonight. Perhaps one drink, or maybe two, but not much more than that. They had to be on their toes for the morning, bright and sharp and ready. Because they knew damn well that tonight was not the end of something but the beginning.

8

THE BIG COP, Brennan, hulked in the doorway, waiting. He was almost as tall as Phelan. "He was a cop, a detective, Martin," Donal said. "Brennan recognized him."

"We have a lot of police that come in here. Sure most of them are our own. Where else would they go?"

"He was on the docks the other morning. Some of the lads—dockworkers—saw him there."

"Was he? That could just be coincidence."

"And he's here that night? That's a quare coincidence.."

"It's Boston—you can't go four feet one way or the other without banging into someone who knows someone else. Besides, he has no way of knowing the two are connected. Was he talking to anyone?"

"Not that we know."

"Well, then, there you have it—if he was on police business, he'd be asking questions and not dancing."

"Still."

Martin nodded and raised a hand to placate them both. "Right, right, I get your point."

46

He rubbed at his chin with his pen and, for a moment, looked very far away. He tapped absently on the marble patina of the accordion resting with its clasps closed upon his desk. The reeds had swollen with the heat and he'd need to find another instrument to play tonight.

"I'll let Mr. de Burgh know," he finally said and Donal looked at him, and Brennan, seeming satisfied, left them.

"What do you think?" Donal said.

"I think that things we have no control over have already been set in motion, and, God willing, those things will take care of themselves. We shouldn't get involved."

"You're sure?"

"They'll already be on their way so?"

"They will."

"Then I'm sure."

After Donal left, Martin went back to his work—arranging the music for the Fitzgerald wedding, scheduling a session with the young fiddler from Athlone who was trying to make the band, ensuring that the flower bouquets and Mass cards for the recent Irish dead would arrive at the funeral homes, and writing the monthly check to Mr. de Burgh's mother, sent via airmail to Ireland.

Afterward, Martin Butler drove down to Quincy, as he did every other day, to Mr. de Burgh's home, a brick Colonial on an acre of perfectly manicured lawn on the Houghs Neck peninsula, overlooking Quincy Bay. In the two-car garage sat the Lincoln town car, and, because it was always one of Mr. de Burgh's pleasures, Martin took it out for a spin down to Hull and through the winding coastal roads to Cohasset. There was a clam shack on Route 108 called Tully's Bait that sold the best fresh oysters and fish—baked cod or haddock melting in tartar sauce and vinegar, dripping in a thick bun, and the brine from the oysters slick and tight on your gums for hours after. On the return trip he filled the car with gasoline at a station near the Quincy shipyards, at the rotary just over the Quincy Fore River

Bridge past Kings Cove, and then returned it to its spot in the pristine garage.

In the parlor, he often paused before the carved crest of the de Burgh clan, a red cross on a gold shield, a black lion standing on its hind legs in the left quadrant of the cross, and, atop the shield, a seated and chained mountain cat. Mr. de Burgh had once told him that the cross on the coat of arms came from the time of the Crusades and that it had originally been painted with the blood of a slain Saracen.

On the paneled walls on either side of the crest were pictures of Mr. de Burgh himself and his family, the wealthy merchant barons of Galway, an oil painting of traditional Irish sailing boats on the Atlantic with their red sails bowed by the wind, another of white swans gliding atop the Corrib River in the Claddagh. Butler would often stand before these images for some time—it became a ritual, like lighting votive candles and then stepping into a pew to pray.

He checked all of Mr. de Burgh's rooms, made sure the refrigerator was stocked with food—they had delivery service from the local A&P—and shortly after four o'clock, he locked up the house again. He stared briefly out over the Atlantic, inhaling the scent of the sea, and then got into his own car—a dilapidated end-of-the-war Chrysler New Yorker—and headed back through the late-afternoon commute into Boston, the sun still battering the flat coastal expanse and the waters of the bay off to his right like a hammer on steel, and to his house in Chelsea, with its crumbling red-brick steps, asbestos shingles, bowed roof, and patch of scorched and withered grass at the rear for a yard. Here, beneath the hulking shadow of the Mystic River Bridge, his brother waited in his forever state of waiting—a limbo that, when Martin considered it, very nearly broke his heart, but as they said, God prefers prayer to tears—and attended by the Irish day nurse that he'd hired because she only rarely spoke, and then only in Irish.

9

NORTH END

OFF OF SALEM Street, Dante pulled his Ford into the small lot next to North End Auto Body. He parked beside a dumpster, got out of the car, lit a cigarette, and listened to the Ford's engine ping and hiss and what sounded like a steel ball ricocheting inside a hollow metal tin. Most likely it was the oil pump going to shit. He wondered how much juice the car had left, if any.

There were a few other cars in the lot but they were in far worse shape than Dante's. A junked-out Chevy with its windshield cracked and spiderwebbed, the bumpers hanging off, and four flat tires. A Chrysler DeSoto that had been in a car wreck, the passenger side smashed in as if the metal were no more solid than a foil gum wrapper. And the husk of an old Hudson passenger car from the Depression era, its sides pockmarked with blistering rust, the front hood no longer covering an engine but a family of raccoons.

Dante walked across the lot toward the building. One of the circular lamps above the gas pumps remained on, occasionally flickering as if in some secret code. The garage in back was covered in darkness, the metal dock door rolled down and chain-locked. Tufts of weeds and crabgrass came up through cracks in the concrete. Broken glass shimmered along the walkway leading to the front door. The two large windows were cluttered with advertisements yellowed and wrinkled from the sun: *Golden Shell. Veedol. RPM. Johnson Motor Oil. Phillips 66.* Dante peered between the gaps to see if the owner was still in the back office, but the place had been shut down for the night.

Dante tried the door anyway. It was locked.

He'd done a bit of work over the past six months for the owner, a lean and weathered Sicilian who called himself John even though his real name was Gianni. Changing oil, filling tanks, doing some spot-welding, soldering, touch-ups, and all-out paint jobs. Just last week, he'd spray-painted a pristine red Plymouth all white. He'd known it was hot, probably stolen the night before from one of the suburbs bordering the city, but he was getting twenty-five dollars for it so he kept his mouth shut and made sure he covered the thing twice over. He even got into the dashboard and knocked a thousand miles off the odometer. But in the end, John didn't show much gratitude. He'd stiffed Dante the last few jobs, suddenly losing his grasp of the English language when Dante asked him where his money was.

The bulk of his income was from Uphams Corner Auto in Dorchester, but even there, the work had become too sporadic to produce a steady paycheck. Twenty hours one week, forty the next, and sometimes a Sunday phone call from the owner, Gus, telling him there wouldn't be much work that week and to check back the following Monday. Cal couldn't give him anything reliable either—the occasional trail job or a weekend gig working security at some downtown office building. Dante wasn't even on the Pilgrim Security payroll; it was all under the table.

At home, the bills were piling up. Pay one off, and another three come in the mail. Save up a little money for the holidays, and watch it blow away well before Christmas. He felt he'd been busting his ass for the past two years, and ever since Maria came into his life, he couldn't keep up, even with Claudia working part-time as a waitress. And there wasn't much to show for their efforts besides the bigger apartment in the North End, just as dingy and decrepit as the old place in Scollay Square, but felt much more like a home, although just last week, a letter had been slipped under the door telling them that the rent was going up twenty dollars a month.

Hoping to make ends meet, Dante had auditioned for some night-clubs needing a piano player. All of his tryouts had come up empty, and he wondered if it was how he played or how he looked. With all that time at the garage—sweating in the pit and hunched over engines—and the sleepless nights trying to comfort Maria after bad dreams, he looked grizzled, the stress and the insomnia adding on the years, the hard lines of his face growing deeper, and all the life in his eyes dulled to a dispir-ited glare, as if he were one step away from giving it all up.

Another strike against him: the music was changing. Fewer and fewer people wanted to hear the classics, whether it was jazz or swing or soulful standards. Instead it was pop songs by Perry Como, Doris Day, Bill Haley and His Comets, and a handful of pretty white boys singing love ballads suited for a soda-parlor serenade. Fuck, maybe he'd play those songs if he had to, if he got paid well enough. But in the end, he couldn't see himself in a record store fingering through the Top 40 songbook sheets alongside acne-riddled boys smacked in the face by puberty, and teenage girls showing off their growing curves under tight wool sweaters. Piano men, there wasn't much need for them anymore. A jukebox would do just fine as long as people had spare change in their pockets.

Dante checked his pack of smokes. Only one remained. He reached in his pocket and took out a paper clip twisted around his key chain. He straightened it out, hooked the edge, maneuvered it inside the office door's lock, twisted one way and then the other. A small click, and he was inside by the front desk. The cash box was locked, screwed down into the desktop marked with coffee stains and cigarette burns. Below a shelf lined with cans and jugs of windshield wiper fluid, WD-40, and antifreeze was a metal rack squared up with packs of cigarettes and candy bars. He reached in and grabbed four cartons of Camels and a box of Mars bars for Maria, found a paper bag behind the desk, and placed them all inside. He figured that wouldn't settle the amount owed to him, but at least it was something.

Outside, the air smelled of asphalt and gasoline. His stomach growled and he felt acid crawl up into his throat. With only a few dollars in his pocket, he needed something to fill the hole; he hadn't eaten much since the morning. He walked toward the lights of the North End, passed onto Prince Street, and glanced inside the windows of restaurants where tables remained empty and where waiters idled about with nothing to do. Not even DiGiacamos' Bakery showed a line. Or the ice cream shop serving gelato and shaved iced.

Dante went into a corner store right as they were closing up and picked up the cheapest bottle of wine they had, a film of dust coating the glass, and a day-old loaf of bread costing only a nickel.

On Prince Street, the colorful lights dimmed. Young workers swept the doorways and walkways of cigarette ends. An old cook sat on a stool pressing a wet towel against his face, cursing the heat in Italian. Across the street, a few teenagers with greased-back hair sat on a curb talking with a navy sailor who was asking for directions back to Scollay Square, his words slurred and slow from too much drink. One of the young hoods stood up and paced around the sailor, sizing him up. Dante knew they were about to roll him over, but he looked away, knowing it wasn't any of his business. The sailor should have known better—if you can't handle your booze and don't know your way around, never go off and get drunk all by yourself in a city like Boston.

He passed by more restaurants that had closed early. Left over from the first festival of the year, the Feast of Santa Maria di Anzano, streamers and decorations hung off wires and around poles. Hanging in some storefronts and twined around the railings of apartment balconies were ribbons striped with the colors of the Italian flag.

He crossed the street and came to the storefront window at the De Rossi Social Club. Inside, the life-size effigy of Santa Maria stood illuminated garishly by red and green Christmas lights. Her crown was a wreath of silver stars that enveloped her head like a constellation. The robe draped around her shoulders was heavy with miscellaneous costume jewelry, and dollar bills were pinned together and wrapped around her neck. The crowned infant nestled in the cradle of her right arm, the porcelain of his cheek chipped and the once-vibrant red of his lips dulled to a pale rose. The glass window was smeared with the prints of the many desperate hands that had reached out to touch the saint, and suddenly, Dante felt a great somber weight fill his chest.

He lowered his head before the window and said a prayer—not for himself, not for Margo or Sheila or Cal, but for his niece, the namesake of the saint, three-year-old Maria. He had to pray for her. Who else would? He prayed for her health, her happiness, that he might provide for her, clothe and feed her. He prayed that her mother was in a better place and would look out for her. And he hoped with all his heart that Sheila would want it this way—with him and Claudia as her daughter's caretakers.

Years ago, when it seemed the snow would never end, he had come so close to falling off and never coming back. He prayed that he'd never get so close to that edge again.

The Christmas lights suddenly flickered off, and the silhouette of the porcelain saint stood shrouded in darkness. With a chill gathering at his neck and slowly moving down his spine, he imagined her closing her eyes and lowering her head in her own lost prayer.

It was time to go home. If he stayed out much longer, trouble would come find him as it had for the young, drunk sailor. He took the two bags from the ground and walked down Prince Street, wary as he passed by barrels of trash awaiting the morning pickup, hearing the rats scavenge and gnaw their way through the waste. He saw their dark, glistening bodies hugging the curbs, some of them disappearing through a sewer grate and others darting across the street into the alleys.

The rat problem was only going to get worse. With neighboring Scollay Square being demolished—building by building and block by block—even the rodents needed someplace to go.

❧

The two lamps in the living room had been left on, and Dante walked to each one, reached up under the shade, and switched it off. In his bedroom, he unbuttoned and took off his shirt, pulled off his shoes, removed his sweat-drenched socks, and tossed everything into a corner. The yellow glare from the streetlight outside came in through the windows and cut across his unmade bed with razor-edged lines. The way the sheets were strewn about the mattress gave him the sensation that there was someone frail and thin hiding under them. He pulled the sheets off the bed and fought against remembering how Margo had looked at him: the death-locked eyes glaring, the lips parted and still, even though he heard her calling his name.

He whistled the refrain from "These Foolish Things," forced himself to think of Margo vibrant and alive, but he couldn't go back quite that far in time. He spread the sheets over the mattress, tucked them in, and smoothed out the edges.

Footsteps padded into the hallway and toward his room. A voice came to him. "Uncle." He watched her enter the room and he walked over to her, slowly, as though trying not to startle her.

He turned on the ceiling light and bent to one knee. "What's wrong, darling?"

Barefoot, the soles of her feet black with dirt and the cotton nightgown threadbare at the shoulders, the three-year-old started to cry. He picked her up and she burrowed her face in the crook of his neck.

"Where's Auntie?" he asked, but she didn't answer.

Maria's breath was hot and sour on his skin, and he felt a feverish heat coming through the thin cotton. She smelled ripe too, and Dante could tell that Claudia hadn't bathed her as she'd promised she would that morning.

"It's okay, love. I'm here now. Everything's okay."

He brought Maria back to her bedroom, no bigger than a kitchen pantry, and gently laid her on the small mattress beside her doe-eyed

Boopsie doll. He checked to see if the lone window was open all the way, pressed at the screen to make sure it was firmly in place, and moved the fan to a bedside stool so it blew directly on her. He sat on the edge of the cot's mattress, careful not to put all his weight on it. With his fingertips, he stroked her forehead and her hair until he heard her breath thicken with sleep. "I'll be right back," he whispered.

He knocked on Claudia's door and then opened it and saw that her bed was empty.

On the kitchen table were two glasses and a nearly finished bottle of white wine. In the ashtray, a few cigarette filters stained with red lipstick and two half-smoked Toscani cigars, the ends pinched and still dark and moist from saliva.

An hour later, he heard the front door open, the clatter of shoes on the wooden floor. When Claudia came into the kitchen, Dante looked out the window toward the Brink's Building and, farther off, the hazy lights of Boston Garden and North Station.

"Out late?"

"I was just gone for a bit. I wasn't going to leave her long."

He turned slowly in his chair, looked her over. "I've been home for over an hour now."

"It's nothing. I was just down the street, with Janice and the other girls."

Dante pointed to the ashtray. "Are these Janice's shit-smelling cigars? Don't bullshit me, Claudia. You were out with Vincent again."

"So what if I was?"

"You look drunk."

"I just had one drink. One drink and that's it."

"Did he pay this time, or was it out of your pocket again? Or should I say my pocket?"

Claudia's hair was done up in a roll, her lids thick with powder-blue eye shadow, and she was wearing a sleeveless polka-dot dress that hugged her hips and, above, showed a small thread of cleavage. She went to the fridge, opened it, and looked inside. "Nothing to eat," she said, matter-of-fact.

"Don't complain to me. You were home all day."

She reached in and grabbed a block of cheese, held it in her hand, then put it back. "I don't see what the big deal is. I'll make sure I go tomorrow."

"You can't leave her alone. Not ever."

Her back was turned to him as she went through the cabinets. "She was sleeping like a rock when I checked on her. I already told you I was just down the street. Vincent had good news on a business deal. He just needed to talk it through before making a decision. So don't get all worked up."

Dante forced out a laugh. "Big decision, right. A forty-three-year-old man who still lives with his mother and works the short con because he can't work much else. Yeah, I'm sure he needed your opinion."

"I'm not in the mood, Dante."

"Well, I'm in a fucking mood. I'm in a mood, all right."

She ran the faucet until the water was cold, took a glass from the counter, rinsed and then filled it. "I have to be at work early tomorrow. Maybe we can talk later."

"I have to be up early too. I have an audition at the Commonwealth this week, and I need to practice. Then off to Uphams until eight. We'll talk now."

"Tomorrow, let's just talk tomorrow." She headed to the hallway.

"What is it, Claudia? You're not the same. Before, you acted like her mother, like you wanted to care for her. Now it's Vincent this, Vinny that."

"It's not that. It isn't…" She trailed off, closing her eyes and pressing the palm of her hand against her forehead.

"Then what is it?" he asked.

"She's not mine, Dante. I never asked for her."

Stunned for a moment, Dante drank straight from the bottle of wine and then shook his head. "For Christ's sake, you're her aunt."

"That's what the papers say. They're faked, forged. Owen did you a favor, but not me. If anybody is the parent, it's probably you."

"We said it's our responsibility."

"No, it's *your* responsibility," she said as she walked away.

"So you get your wish. That scum will knock you up, and then what will you do? Go off and leave us behind? Pretend none of this ever happened?"

"If that's what Vincent wants, then probably yes."

He heard her voice from the dark hallway. "I'm tired, Dante. I'm really tired. We can talk tomorrow. Now's not the time."

From the kitchen window, Dante watched as heat lightning flashed against low clouds. An uncomfortable silence pressed down on the room, making the heat and humidity even thicker.

In a couple of days he had an audition for a restaurant on Park Street, the Commonwealth. It was for three evenings a week, four to five hours on the grand piano, taking requests and playing for the tip jar. He should lie down and try to get some sleep, but with all the thoughts twisting around in his head, he knew it wouldn't come easy.

Dante smoked one cigarette after another, finished the bottle of wine and wished he had another. The loaf of bread remained on the counter untouched, and his stomach cried out in hunger. His eyes were getting heavy, and the smoke left his throat bitter and raw. As though he were back before the statue of Saint Maria, he lowered his head and tried to conjure up another prayer that would be able to hold him in place, but nothing came to him, nothing but a memory from long ago.

The day it all changed for him, the day he turned his back and walked away from that edge.

It was only the third week that Maria was with them. The winter still raged on into March, and he was holed up in the Scollay Square apartment with Claudia and the baby, day and night, waiting for something to go wrong. He caught some sleep when he could, ate when the hunger became too much. It was a Thursday, and for once the sun had broken through the heavy slate clouds, but it disappeared almost as quickly. Early night pressed at the windows, making the apartment so cold he swore he could see his breath fog the air before him. Claudia had had to leave for a few hours, said that she had to get out and move around, see a friend for dinner and run a few errands. She'd promised that when she got back, he could call Cal and meet him for a drink. It would be good for them to get out before they both went stir-crazy. She knew he was worried about being alone with Maria for the first time. She'd tried to soothe him, telling him, "You're a natural."

To keep busy as the baby slept, he cleaned up the kitchen, towel-dried the dishes and cups and put them in their proper places. Then he sat on the couch flipping through one of Claudia's magazines and see-ing nothing but women smiling, teeth flashing white, and men looking too dapper for their own good. He heard Maria cry out, and he tried to ignore it, but when she began to shriek, he got up quickly and ran into Claudia's bedroom.

Maria's face was pink and pinched as though in pain. Even before he could smell it, he realized she had shit her diaper again. Dante wanted to reach down and console her, but something had a hold of him, some invisible grip that clamped down on his muscles and even deeper, into his nerves, so that he felt paralyzed. Barely able to get any air into his lungs, he watched as the baby twisted and tried to turn over. From the edge of her cloth diaper, shit trickled out and spread across the thin mattress; the patchwork blanket and once-white sheet were soon soaked through with brown. His nostrils filled with the stench coming off her, and there was a moment where her eyes opened and focused on his, and in that look, beneath the desperation, he saw the eyes of Michael Foley, of Bobby Renza, even of Sheila and himself.

Nauseated, he felt his stomach spin. He broke free from the invisible grasp and stumbled down the hallway and into the bathroom, where he filled the sink with bile and the half-digested remnants of his lunch. The hoarse cries of Maria sounded throughout the apartment, and no matter how hard he pressed the heels of his hands against his ears, he couldn't block them out.

Claudia came home and found Dante sitting in the bedroom, head between his knees, crying softly. The baby still wept, but with her throat so raw and sore, she mewled like a small, wounded animal. Claudia shook him by the shoulders and told him she couldn't trust him anymore, cursed him out and said that he was still a junkie mess and that he wasn't, and would never be, suited to take care of the child. He tried to convince her that he was clean, that this was something he couldn't control, but she ignored him and took the baby to the bathroom to clean her up.

He left, and for a full day and night, Dante walked the frozen and desolate streets of the South End, moving from one flophouse to the next. Eventually he met up with his old friend Lawrence and tasted the junk for the last time. In the hazy half-slumber between dream and nightmare, he had neither revelation nor remorse for the awful thoughts that had come to him as he watched Maria turn in her own feces, but once the sun climbed into the sky, warming the flophouse room with its amber glow, he woke up, walked back to Scollay Square, and strangely calm and clearheaded opened the door to his apartment.

Claudia was sleeping, and carefully, he took the child from her crib and carried her to the living room. He reclined back on the couch with her laid upon on his chest, her soft breaths warming his neck. With his heart beating wildly, he held the child to him, feeling the spittle from her mouth wet his shirt through to his skin. He stroked her back and whispered in her ear, telling her that he was sorry and that he would never let it happen again.

10

CAL WAS TIRED of killing and tired of fighting; listening to Owen had sparked his interest at first, that need to know and discover—there used to be a pleasure in that and in the need for revenge, to make things right. He understood those things; they made sense to him. Payback for a wrong was as old as the Bible but it was the question of the wrong that interested him most of all—what deserved what manner of retribution, what manner of death, and by whom. But the cycle itself was unending, and he'd seen enough in his short lifetime already. He was sick of it and even more sickened that not only could he not prevent it but that he was, most often, its cause.

He lived in a boardinghouse in the Fort Point Channel—the site of the Boston Tea Party—that a century before had been a hotel for bargemen and skippers, a first stop for nearly penniless immigrants just off the boat, and a meat rack for the rough trade from the dockland wharves just over the bridges. The place had a regal-sounding name— the Excelsior—but knowing the area, Cal doubted it had ever been re- gal. Cal mused on the name, thought of the poem by Whitman and almost laughed. He spoke aloud: "'Who has gone farthest? for I would go farther. And who has been just? for I would be the most just person of the earth.'"

He had a closet with a dozen shirts, five ties, and three suits, and his dresser was filled with clean clothes. He had lived in four hotels in the three years since Lynne had died and he knew better than to try to convince himself that this would be the last. It would do for now and he was in no rush to leave when there was no place he wanted to be. He'd been here for so many months that he'd earned the status of a long-timer, someone with no particular date by which he might leave and, most likely, no plans of anything better. His dreams of something better had died with Lynne.

He saw the other long-timers in the hall on his way to the bathroom. Unlike the weekly or monthly stays—junkies and drunks and johns with their male and female whores, grifters and sinners and those fleeing the law or a con gone bad, people who still seemed to have some manner of urgency about them, a need to be elsewhere, a desire to get on living—the long-timers looked as if the living had been knocked out of them. They shuffled in the hallways and remained mostly still and quiet behind their doors, perhaps listening to a baseball game on the radio, some old band tunes, or the Friday-night fights; they barely looked up when you passed them and some seemed surprised when you greeted them with a good morning or a hello.

He'd been here long enough to make the place comfortable even if he could never call it home. He had an icebox and a hot plate, and his heavy bag hung in the corner of the room near the window. By his radio, gleaming dully on a small end table, he had a reading chair, and should he have guests, although he never did—except for Dante bringing Maria over once—there was a small Formica table with a fold-down sleeve and two metal chairs with vinyl seats.

With his towel and toiletries he walked down the hall to the bathroom and had to wait for another tenant, who sounded as if he were wringing his guts out, to finish up. When the door finally opened, he let the tenant pass and then stepped in and the smell assaulted him.

Cursing, he placed his towel on the rack and his shaving kit by the grime-encrusted sink, glanced in the toilet, and stopped. He stepped out again. The tenant was halfway down the hall.

"Hey," Cal called. "You. Come here."

The man turned; he looked to be a year or two older than Cal and had about twenty pounds on him and a couple of inches. His curly brown hair was tight on the sides and high on top. He had a low, wide forehead and a constant squint. There were red-and-black-plaid slippers on his feet with the stuffing poking out of them.

"You didn't flush. Finish your business."

"What?"

"I ain't your mother. I'm not here to flush after you."

"What's your problem, man?"

"Everyone cleans up after themselves. That's how it works."

"Fuck you."

"Come flush your shit or I'll take it and smear your face in it."

"You've got a real big mouth for a little man."

"I'm not asking you again."

The man stared at him, frowning, undecided, and then he wavered, sighed deeply, and came back toward the bathroom. Cal noticed the drawn look to his face, the tightness in the skin about his eyes.

Cal waited in the hall as the man flushed. When he was done, he walked past Cal.

"You're an asshole," the man muttered. "And I know what room you're in."

"That's okay, sunshine. I know what room you're in too."

Freshly bathed and back in his room, Cal stood in his pants and undershirt before the ironing board and moved the steaming iron slowly and methodically across his shirt. His skin was tight from his morning shave, stinging slightly from aftershave. Coffee steamed from the decanter on the double-burner hot plate. This was part of his daily ritual: he rose just after first light and performed the rosary, kneeling at the side of his bed, then he put the coffee on and let it brew, tuned the radio to the morning news, and showered and shaved and dressed.

At the center of his thoughts, like a prayer itself, was the memory, the word: Lynne. Sometimes he spoke to her, imagined her with him, and other times, it was more difficult to draw her essence—the sense of her—and though she felt farther away from him than he liked to imagine, he knew she was there regardless, listening, and so he talked to her as he went about his day. He made sure he rose from the bed and dressed like a man should to start his day of work, to be one of the living, as only she would have expected of him. He knew it was the memory of her, the need to respect that memory, to not allow it to become something cheap, tarnished, or diminished, that kept him rising, climbing from his bed, one day after the other, until days joined days and became weeks and months and then years. And in this illusory way, he created the structures and rhythms of a life.

This morning as he stared through his open window and sipped his coffee, there was no sense of her, only the still water of the channel glimmering silver with sunlight and oil-belching fish trucks passing over the Northern Ave and Congress Street Bridges and the haze already lifting from the tar rooftops of the derelict textile buildings across the channel and the sweat trickling down his spine. His undershirt stuck to his back. "It's gonna be a hot one, Lynne," he said to the emptiness. "Too damn hot."

11

IN THE KITCHEN of a stone cottage overlooking the slate-blue waters of the bay, Sean Mullen stood before a large butcher-block table, an apron spotted with blood tied tightly around his waist. In one hand he held a large carving knife and in the other a whetstone. He moved the blade across the stone as if tuning some long-lost instrument, and only once did he look across the kitchen to the man sitting in a chair beside the window.

The man watched Sean, sometimes called the General, pull a large salmon from a wicker basket, the silver of its scales shimmering and speckled with black.

Sean Mullen was a short, stocky man with the build of an iron-worker or a boxer; he'd been both in his life, among many other things. What hair he had left was raked over his scalp. His skin was dark and weathered but not deeply wrinkled, and his face was clean-shaven but already filling in with a coarse stubble. His hands were thick, roped with veins, and while his fingers appeared stubby and callused, they could maneuver with the dexterity of a well-trained embroiderer's. Nearing sixty, he had a boyish twinkle in his eyes that betrayed others into believing he was a pleasant man. He could be, from time to time, especially around his sons and daughters and a few select friends whom he trusted.

Low clouds passed above the cottage, and the midday light staggered from shadow back to the sun again. Wind pressed against the window, making the screen clatter in its frame.

The man in the chair coughed into his hand and watched as Mullen sliced into the fish, running the blade smoothly along its belly, cutting up to the backbone, turning the fish over, and removing its head with ease. He scraped out the guts and cut off the fins.

"Pat, mind fetching two ales out of the icebox?" he asked.

The man grabbed two brown bottles, gently placed each one down on the table, found the iron church key nearby, and fumbled with the caps until they opened. He returned to his seat and didn't say a word.

After he deboned the fillets, Mullen wrapped them in brown paper, took some string, and diligently tied them into a package. He placed it at the edge of the table. "For your wife to cook for supper."

"Thank you."

"Now." He paused, took a big draw off the bottle. "Now, how much of a mess is it?" He took the flat end of the knife and scraped the guts across the cutting board and into a pile of innards from the other fish he'd cleaned moments ago.

"It's a mess, yes. But one that can be fixed."

"Is that so, Patrick?" He wiped both sides of the knife against his apron.

"I believe so. I wouldn't worry."

From the basket, Mullen grabbed a net full of oysters still glistening wetly from the Atlantic. He laid down the fillet knife, picked up a small shucking knife, and, holding it as if he were a surgeon, went into a large oyster, splitting it open quickly and placing the half shell on a chipped porcelain plate.

"Let's be honest."

Patrick cleared his throat. "Five men gone. No word from a couple of others. They may turn up yet."

"Gone, eh? Just like that?" He opened two more oysters with ease. "You've been there before, haven't you?"

"I've been to Boston, New York…quite a few times."

"So tell me, in Boston, on a scale from one to ten, how likely is it that things will be back in order by the end of the week?"

"Can't really say yet."

"Can't really *say* yet," Mullen said, mimicking him. "Well, when *can* you say it, then?"

"I know it's not what you want to hear. I wouldn't be sitting here otherwise. Nearly half the shipments are gone. The men, we can replace. But I think we wait it out. Let the heat from the police die down. We stay patient and we watch."

"You've known me a long time, right? Have you ever took me for a fool who sits and watches the paint dry?" Mullen shoved the knife into a large, knobby oyster twice the size of the others. His forearm tightened and his upper body bent low over the table. He sucked through his teeth and then hissed. The oyster shell cracked in his hand.

He looked down at his finger, watched as the blood began to bead out of the wound and drip down onto the table. "God Almighty, will you look at that?"

Patrick hesitated and then stood up from the chair. "Is it deep?"

"I've had much worse." He raised the knife and pointed it across the table. "I got to say, I'm having a bit of a problem with your casual attitude toward all this. You make it sound like we just lost a crate or two. That tomorrow will be a new day, a glorious new fucking day."

"I told you not to worry. We have men there that can take care of it. Believe me on this."

"Who do we have in Boston with de Burgh?"

"That would be Donal Phelan."

The General nodded and paused for a moment, looking down at the blood flowing from his finger, considering.

"It's important to remember," he said, "that de Burgh is a sympathizer, not a martyr—that when it comes down to it, he has nothing to lose, it's merely an investment, just like much of his philanthropy work. Still, as long as Donal is working with him, I suppose we can live with that.

"We've seen a drop in American funds. We need their money more than ever, but more important, we need the shipments. Our stockpiles are still depleted and Ruairí's border campaign can't proceed without them being filled. I'm not about to go to him and the rest of the leadership and tell them we've bollixed this up."

He clenched his hand tightly around the handle of the knife, and the blood flowed freely from the slice in his finger.

"To be honest, I don't trust many over there in Boston. And even here, I'm losing more faith each day in our own."

"Sean, it's going to be fixed. I trust Donal implicitly and de Burgh's a businessman—he won't do anything that would jeopardize business."

The General took a deep breath, sighed, and then spoke. "I'm not sending an army. Just the four of them."

"What do you mean?"

"I mean I'm taking care of it on my own. They're already on their way. Myles and the others."

"Myles and the others? Now you're talking mad."

"Myles will be on a plane from Dublin to London. Fitzgerald, Kinsella, and Egan will meet him there and they'll all take a ship to New York. And then from there they'll go to Boston."

"I say we just wait it out. Fitzgerald's the only one who knows that city well enough. Myles and Kinsella will be lost there."

Mullen went into another oyster, cracked it cleanly open. Blood dripped into the gelatinous gray and white meat. He put the shell to his mouth and sucked down the oyster, chewing it and then swallowing.

"All will be settled with the Yanks the right way. My way, Patrick."

Patrick took an oyster off the porcelain plate, chewed at it, left the half-full bottle of ale on the table, and picked up the salmon neatly wrapped in brown paper.

Mullen watched him. "It's funny to think about all the times somebody goes to America and they can't help but get greedy. That country does that, doesn't it? No matter how hard you try."

With his face flushed, Patrick offered a mere nod. He realized he was at a point in the conversation where he could say no more to the General.

Mullen smiled, flashed his bright white teeth. "Now, you take the fish to your wife. Tell her I caught the fish, I gutted the fish, and I dressed the fish. Tell her that I told you not to worry. So you go home. Go home and give my best to your family."

12

DUBLIN, IRELAND

With the Irish Sea below him, Bobby Myles said farewell to Dublin. He wouldn't be back again. Not even for his mother's funeral, which he knew deep in his gut would happen sooner rather than later.

The doctor had said a year, if she was lucky. Bobby thought a month, maybe two at best. Yesterday afternoon, he had sat with his mother at a restaurant on Essex Street. The lights were dimmed and wisps of a dissipating fog smoked against the windows, and even with it so dark, he could see how sick she had gotten. The shadows seemed to seek her out and gather in the shallows of her face, the bags under her eyes, and the concave cheeks, the skin so brittle it might have been old parchment paper. In the blueness of her veins that wormed their way along her hands, he could see that even inside her, there was a darkness taking over.

The food had arrived silently, and she pretended to enjoy a meal of lamb, roasted potatoes, and spring vegetables—cutting something, moving it across the plate, but rarely ever putting anything in her mouth. She kept clearing her throat before she talked, as though she needed to startle and force out the words she wanted to say. Clearly, she had spotted his lie about spending a week in London on business. She knew he wasn't coming back. Yet she asked questions about the trip, and he did his best, giving her brief answers to make it seem authentic yet insubstantial, nothing to worry about. "That's nice," she'd said. "It's good to keep busy. Onwards and upwards."

He paid the bill and told her he had to go home and pack. He didn't tell her that in London he would meet three other soldiers, Kinsella, Egan, and the Ox—Fitzgerald. And he didn't tell her there would be a journey across the Atlantic to New York, followed by an airplane to Boston. And then from Boston, whenever the job was finished, as far out west as he could get. "I trust you'll be okay," he said to her. "The nurses at the home, they'll take good care of you." He had stood and kissed his mother on the top of her head. His nostrils filled with the strong scent of her lilac shampoo and something deeper, the sourness of death that came with living too long. He gently pressed down on her hand, felt the coldness of her skin and the fragile bones beneath, and told her that he loved her and would be back to spend Christmas with her.

"Don't forget that you'll always be from here, Robert. This was my country, not your father's," she said, trying to come across with humor. She was referring to her side, the Galway side, and not his father's Liverpool and Merseyside roots.

"How could I ever forget that, Mum?" He laughed, giving her a pained, crooked smile.

With her fork, she speared a stem of asparagus and moved it from one end of the plate to the other, and then her lips turned up in a sickly grin, yellowed teeth bared and exposing her discolored and receding gums. Even though she was smiling, her eyes remained lowered, as though heavy with the weight of oncoming tears. Where had her beauty gone? Where was that woman he had once feared? In the lobby of the restaurant, he grabbed his sports coat and hat and made his way to the exit. Outside on Essex, he walked along the sidewalk and stole a final glimpse through the restaurant window. His mother sat there, no more significant than a mannequin propped behind the dusty window of a tailor's storefront. Fighting the urge to go back and tell her the truth, he kept on walking and didn't look back to watch the tears roll along his mother's cheeks, cutting pale, gummy lines through the rouge she wore so thickly.

Now, in the fixed-wing, dual-engine airplane, Bobby Myles lowered the brim of his hat so it rested at his brow. Sunlight broke through the clouds and reflected off the wing of the Douglas DC-3. The light up this high was different, less tainted. It flared up under his hat and warmed his face—a pleasant sensation, but in his chest there was a leaden weight, and from that came an anxiety that made him feel as though he were a mere bag of bones in a floating vessel constructed of aluminum, gears, gasoline, all of it bound together by a lonesome prayer that the heavens wouldn't let it buckle and come crashing down.

The aircraft could seat twenty-five comfortably. On this trip, it was half full. One man in the front was saying prayers in Irish, occasionally clearing his throat with a poorly veiled curse. Behind him, a mother and son sat quietly, as if they were still inside a crowded pew at Sunday Mass. A woman across the aisle softly chewed on sweets that she plucked from a cellophane bag between her legs. Her attention was focused on a paperback novel she held up with one hand, her thumb pressing hard in the center. Bobby could tell it was an American book by the lurid cover showing a bosomy brunette in the arms of a square-jawed cowboy; the cowboy was apparently about to either smack the woman in the face or tear off her blouse and ravage her breasts. *The irony of it all,* he thought. America: the lustful frontier mapped by greed, avarice, skin, and sin. He amused himself with images of how the Americans saw their own country (America the Beautiful, the Land of Opportunity, the Great Melting Pot), and then he imagined it as he'd always wished and hoped it would be—a great wide expanse of sky and land, a sanctuary of deserts, mountains, forests, and lakes where one answered to nature only, lived with what one had, and didn't rely on handouts from others.

A sanctuary—he liked the way that sounded.

Sanctuary.

A safe, sacred place.

71

The plane hit turbulence and it felt as if the aircraft were moving against a tempestuous sea. He had a flask in his chest pocket, and he took it out, unscrewed its thimble-like cap, and filled his mouth with brandy. Instantly it softened the panic.

He forced himself to listen to the buzzing of the engines, hoping they'd lull him into a peaceful state. The attendant moved through the aisle as silently as a ghost, and when she spoke, it startled him so much that he quickly pushed the hat up from his brow. Her fingers gently touched his shoulder, and she smiled apologetically. "I didn't mean to give you a start. We'll be landing in an hour. Would you like a pillow for your neck?" He said no, thank you, and watched her move down the aisle, stiff-hipped and without much grace, an Irish country girl who seemed to have just started out on the job; perhaps this was her first time leaving the island and she was already missing home.

The Douglas DC-3 hit more turbulence. Another taste of brandy, but instead of calming his busy mind, it filled it with the reality of the situation ahead, his real reason for going to the States.

Was he really going to abandon the outfit and call America his own? Informer, traitor, fugitive—what would they say of him once they found out he wasn't coming back? What guilt would they shame him with?

He couldn't count the number of hours he had spent going through scenarios, times when he'd lain idle but with his mind working frantically as he imagined all manner of miscues, hiccups, and errors and tried to find a way out of each mishap without one wrinkle, one wasted second. In the end, no matter how hard he tried to cement the plan, he realized that only being there in the moment would show him the way out, that right moment to flee.

And maybe, just maybe, the farther away from Ireland he got, the less he'd see her. No more nightmares, no more moments where her porcelain face and coal-black eyes exploded into his consciousness, obliterating every other thought, almost everything else in the world.

That terrible day in Belfast—God bless her poor young soul.

❧

He always saw the road first.

Through the windshield speckled with rain, he saw mist rise up off the wet tarmac like steam, and above, the clouds rolling dark and heavy as if hidden behind them some great behemoth powered a dangerous, unspeakable machine. Pedestrians scattered along the walkways, and as Bobby drove by them, they appeared to him like faceless mourners trudging through the misery of another day. Even though it was only two in the afternoon, it felt as if night were already pressing down on Belfast.

Bobby was wired tightly, his knuckles pale as he gripped the steering wheel with both hands. He watched out for the potholes that threatened the threadbare, mismatched tires of the Hillman Minx he carefully drove north toward Old Falls Road.

In the Austin Saloon in front of him, Gedrick was driving in a messy way. He was drawing unnecessary attention, making sloppy turns on narrow cobblestoned roads and, earlier, an abrupt, skidding stop at an intersection that had been clear of traffic; the RUC officer standing on the corner had eyed the vehicle warily but in the end didn't raise a hand to pull him over.

In the passenger seat next to Gedrick was Marcus Coyne, no more than twenty years old, all high-and-mighty Dubliner—the type who thought he could change the times with his fists, a pugilist who lacked all restraint and nuance and who in public stood out like a leper at a high-collared English tea party. Bobby didn't like him, but he thought at this moment that he should be the one driving the lead car.

"Geddy, you ripe bastard, slow and easy," Bobby said. "Don't make a fool now. Steady, steady."

The car ahead of Bobby swerved over the center, then quickly straightened out and slowed down. Black smoke twisted out from the tailpipe. A stretch of terraced houses leaned into the street, dark wood and gray paint. In that moment, Bobby sensed that something was amiss.

Earlier this morning, he had sat with Gedrick at an empty lot south of the city in Dunmurry and watched him drink straight from a green-hued bottle that bore no label. It wasn't to calm his nerves but to keep a monthlong drunk from falling apart. Gedrick had been in a bad way since his wife had left him and gone south back to her childhood home in Waterford. Ever since then, he'd scuttered and drunk without end, a right mess pushing his luck to the brink. But it was in that moment this morning before they squared up and set the bomb in the trunk of the car that Bobby noticed a look of determination and clarity in his friend's eyes, a look that held true to the past when he was a soldier through and through—once the best bomb maker in all of Europe, a magician in the way he mixed the nitrobenzene and fertilizer or nitrosamine and ethylene glycol to duplicate the British PE-4.

Bobby wished he hadn't noticed that look. If he hadn't seen it, he would have forced Coyne to drive the lead car instead of Gedrick.

Even last week, Bobby had put in a call to the General and said that Gedrick was in a bad way, not right in the head. He'd suggested that he be taken off the Belfast factory job and that if they couldn't get somebody else, two men could do it instead of three. The General gave him a whole line of staying true, that Gedrick could handle it, that he was the best they had.

Manpower's thin, the General had said, *and Gedrick is a right fucking master at making the goods. He could wire one in his sleep, for Christ's sake. About the drinking, now, c'mon, who hasn't had their fair share of misery? Every so often, it comes when you're not looking and you grin and bear it and you take it as your own. That's life; that's what happens to us all.*

The General had ended the call with *Just keep an eye out. Use your magic. You see things before they happen, and that's why we trust you, Bobby.*

Ahead, the Austin Saloon was pushing forty miles per hour.

Bobby checked the rearview to make sure they weren't being tailed. They weren't.

And in that second where his eyes flashed from the rearview back to the road ahead, the Austin swerved around a large pothole and caught the edge; the hubcap popped off, the tire burst, and the car began to skid out, spinning into the opposite lane. Instead of letting up on the gas, Gedrick hit the brakes.

Bobby would always remember that the world had gone mute and time slowed down so that he could see the car careening and flipping over, sparks flaring out as the metal scraped against the asphalt. The vehicle turned over, once, twice, and then a white blast of fire tore through its frame.

Bobby pulled the car over and left the keys in the ignition, the engine idling. He had been holding his breath, and he forced himself to take in air, shouldered the door open, and ran out. The flames consumed the wreck, and a mushroom of smoke billowed up into the sky. He felt his lungs constrict and he fought to breathe evenly, the burning petrol stinging his eyes and making everything around him indistinct and blurred.

Other sounds filtered back into reality. Car doors slammed behind him. Brakes squealed and tires screeched along the road as more cars stopped to see what had happened. And then he heard it: the sounds of a man miraculously still alive, his body pinched and punctured by metal, the flames eating through his skin and flesh and cooking the marrow and the bone. There was nothing Bobby could do except listen to Gedrick scream and ask God for forgiveness and to stop the pain.

Step away from the fire. You don't know these men. You don't know anything about them. You just saw it all happen and you did your good deed by checking to see if anybody could be helped. That's all.

He closed his eyes and tried to calm himself. When he opened them, he noticed movement at the curbside. Underneath a tree that had caught fire, most of its branches sheared off from the shrapnel and the impact of the explosion, there were shapes strewn about on the walkway. Human shapes. The smoke was burning his eyes, the heat of the flames blistering, but he moved in closer, noticed that one of these shapes was still moving.

A woman wormed her way off the curb and into the street like some half-crushed insect. He couldn't tell which were the tattered threads of her red sweater and which were the tattered and torn shreds of her own flesh. In shock, she tried to turn over but with one of her arms completely torn off at the biceps, she floundered and then went still.

Beside a storefront window shattered from the blast, a man sat against a wall. The shrapnel had shaved off his face, leaving nothing but pulp and bone. And lying next to the man was another shape; Bobby couldn't tell if it was a dog or a small child.

And then he saw her, standing there on the walkway. She had stepped out from behind the tree and now she stumbled toward him, her eyes locked on to his. She was just a schoolgirl. He could tell by the checkered dress, the thick stockings up past the knees, and the black, clumsy shoes. Her hand gripped her stomach. Blood seeped through her fingers, and something pale and glistening slipped from her grasp. He squinted his eyes and saw that it was part of her lower intestine. Her eyes never left his, and she tried to speak, lips forming words, apparently saying the same thing over and over again, but no sound came to him. Her eyes were black against her skin, which shone white and vibrant like porcelain. She took one uneven step, and another, and then she stumbled to her knees. She stayed that way, upright, as if in some manner of penance. Bobby looked from side to side to see if anybody would help her. There was an older man dressed in a sopping tweed hat and a slicker standing there, but, like Bobby, he was immobile, nearly paralyzed.

The girl's body shuddered and she fell forward, her hands hitting the ground. She was trying her hardest not to fall down all the way, and for a moment, she held steady. Her stomach opened up and her innards uncoiled beneath her. Almost tenderly, she lowered herself to the ground, as if she were merely going to sleep, turned to her side, and rolled over onto her back. Her eyes remained open.

As the fiery wreck lost its strength, more people congregated in the middle of the road. The flames dimmed, exposing the blackened metal husk, the broken glass, the remains of two men smoking, hissing, as the rain came down harder. A high-pitched wail of an ambulance came from the south.

Bobby walked over to the girl's body. He took off his jacket, fanned it out, and placed it over her torso but not her face. He reached into his pants pocket, brought out his rosary beads, and knelt down beside her. He held her left hand, placed the rosary in her bloodied palm, and closed her fingers over them. The lifelessness of her body carried through him, momentarily possessed him.

He didn't care what side of the line her family stood on, whether they were nationalist or unionist, Catholic or Protestant. She needed something to accompany her, something that wouldn't leave her abandoned and alone. He reached down and parted the black hair above her dark eyes and he tried to say a prayer but the words caught in his throat. He held on tight to her hand. Only when an ambulance medic touched his shoulder and said, "Son, we'll take her now," did he let go, noticing that the string holding the rosary had snapped, and some of the beads stuck to her while others fell to the road and were washed away by the rain toward the gaping hole of the sewer grate, back into the earth, forever.

13

CAL SAT AT the desk in his office and stared at the two young men sitting opposite him. The ceiling fan above them turned its wooden slats slowly in the heat. The windows were open and the din of wrecking balls and pile drivers came to them, a steady *thump-thump-thump,* like a clanging iron heart sounding out the final days of the Square. Toward the harbor, a milky haze covered the low skyline, still and unmoving. The men were in their Pilgrim Security attire but he'd taken them off their regular shifts after they'd been caught gambling with the employees in the place they'd been hired to provide security for, the Chinese Merchants' Association Building on Hudson Street in Chinatown. After the pissed-off owner called and berated him in Mandarin and broken English, Cal had replaced them with new guards; these two had shown up to find their jobs taken, and now Cal was having to explain why he'd done what he'd done and he wasn't happy about it.

Albert was Polish and Jimmy was Greek, and each was bad medicine for the other; they had grown up in the Triangle, had been incarcerated together for transporting stolen goods across state lines, and in the past two years he'd moved them to and from more jobs than he could remember. Why he'd ever put the two of them together in the first place was beyond him. Their Pilgrim Security shirts were wrinkled, the armpits dark with sweat, and he wondered how long it had been since they'd washed them. He could smell the both of them from where he sat.

"I know you two think this is a joke," he said, "but I'm not laughing. This company has been in the red for the better part of a decade and now that we're starting to get work again I'm not going to jeopardize everyone else's job for a couple of jokers. I got an earful from the owner and now you're going to get an earful from me."

Albert, who'd been masticating a stick of gum, stopped chewing. "Yeah, but Cal, we won that money fair and square."

"You took their paychecks from them!"

"It's not our fault those fucks bet their paychecks and they got nothing to bet on."

Jimmy shook his head. "I knew they were bluffin' all along." He glanced at Albert for support. "They learned a valuable life lesson. Now they won't go and do something stupid like that again. You could say that we helped them out."

"Watch it, Jimmy. Do you want this job or not?" Cal looked from one to the other. "Well, do you or don't you?"

"Of course we do," said Jimmy.

"Then this is the first thing you're going to do. You're going to go around there directly after we're done talking and you're giving those people back their money." He held up a hand when they began to protest. "After you've done that, you're going to go and apologize to the owner, Mr. Lin. I'll be calling him later today and if that apology isn't sincere, if he feels that it wasn't sincere, then we'll be having this talk again, but this time I'll be handing you your pink slips. Are we on the same page?"

"Yeah, yeah, sure thing, Cal," Jimmy said, and the two nodded in unison. "We'll fix it."

"Good. Now get out of here, you're ruining my appetite for lunch."

They stood, scraping their chairs against the floor, took their plain, black-billed eight-point service hats off the table, put them aslant their heads, and left. "And," Cal called after them, "make sure you wash and press those shirts. You two look like slobs!"

In the outer office, the door opened and Owen stepped in. He sat in one of the wooden chairs as the two men filed out into the hallway—he eyed them and they eyed him back—and then he came in, pulled a chair out from the desk, and sat heavily. His hair was slicked back and he was freshly shaved. Perspiration beaded on his upper lip.

"You must be getting desperate if you've resorted to hiring those two."

"Ahh, they're all right."

"Their rap sheets say different."

"Their rap sheets don't see the whole picture."

Owen smiled, amused. "Saint Cal, savior of the down and out and the misunderstood. You never change."

"We all change but sometimes it just looks the same."

"Yeah, I guess."

"You look better than you did the other night, so that's something."

"Well, that's good, because I don't feel better." Owen held a fist to his chest. "Acid, it's keeping me awake at nights. I haven't been able to sleep since this boat business started."

"That bad?"

"There's been five more murders."

Cal whistled though his teeth and poured them coffee even though it was too hot for it and it tasted bitter and left a bad taste in his mouth.

"We managed to ID the first body, the one found tarred and feathered. His name was Mickey Flynn, a part-time night watchman for the docks. Played music around town. Some of the dockworkers knew him from the Irish Starlight Express. You know the band?"

"I've heard the name. You see their posters about. They're big in the Dudley scene, right?"

"Yeah, that's what everyone tells me. Anyway, it looks like someone killed him once the boat was unloaded."

"Was he your tip-off?"

Owen sipped his coffee and grimaced. "No, he wasn't." He took a deep breath and held it, rubbed at a spot over his heart. "I had to meet his wife—Mrs. Flynn—and tell her. She insisted on seeing the body, wouldn't believe he was dead until she saw for herself. I wish I hadn't let her see him like that. I doubt she'll ever forget it."

"Jesus."

"Yeah."

"And the others, what about them?"

"All in the one night." Owen extended his arm and mimed holding a gun, then moved his arm left to right, his mouth sounding minor explosions: "*Boom! Boom! Boom!* One after the other," he said. "Fierro says that the times of death were so close together—perhaps thirty to forty-five minutes apart—that it's difficult to tell who got it first and who got it last."

"Someone's cleaning house, that's what it looks like."

"Sure."

"So what's the connection between all of them?"

"Besides the fact that they're all Irish?" Owen shook his head. "I assume it's the boat and like I said, that this is only the beginning."

"Haven't the Feds taken over?"

"If the boat had been found with guns aboard and transporting them from New York to Boston, yeah, they would have, but no guns, no crime, and nothing to connect them to this, four murders in our jurisdiction. Even Giordano doesn't want to admit a connection."

"Giordano couldn't see a connection if it hit him in the face."

"He thinks this was a random night of violence in a city that has been turned upside down by it lately—he's blaming everything on the breakup of the Irish mobs, the Italians, the Chinese, the blacks, the heat."

"He's like a Boston weather forecaster. What a gig! I don't know how he's managed to stay in his position for as long as he has."

"He'll be superintendent in chief next."

"Yeah, I believe it."

After a brief pause, the jackhammers, sounding like machine-gun fire, and the pile drivers started up again, and Owen squinted.

"Sorry about the racket. It's too hot to close the windows."

"It's always that loud?"

"Yeah, I suppose it'll be that way until they've torn down every last brick of the Square. Look at what they did to the West End and the North End."

From the window Owen could see the Central Artery that now cut the North End and the waterfront off from the rest of the city. The government had seized properties and demolished them to make way for the monstrosity. McAllister had had a part in that and he'd gotten even richer because of it, sucking on the ruin of Boston and growing fat and bloated like a leech feeding on blood. In the end, Senator-Elect Foley had served his purpose—people rarely spoke of his brutal death or his years in political office; they spoke only of the corrupt and twisted connection between him and his murderer brother and how they'd both gotten theirs in the end.

It had been a year since construction began, workers driving the concrete piles to support the steel columns that would hold up the elevated roadway. The destruction of homes had displaced over twenty thousand people, and the excavation of land—what had been billed as redevelopment—had deeply traumatized the city. Seeing what had once been sprawling immigrant neighborhoods reduced to six square miles of blight and ruin had been too much for many, especially those who'd already experienced similar destruction in the war in Europe. Not a building left, the area flattened and leveled, as if those places had never existed. A black smog from the cranes and derricks and dump trucks had turned the sky toward the harbor gray and soot-colored. Every day he smelled the fumes; they seemed to come through the open windows and coat the furniture, his clothes, his skin. When Cal left Scollay at the end of the day, the Square looked grayer, dirtier, and more beaten down because of it.

Cal poured Owen some water in a paper cup, reached into a drawer, took out the vial of bennies, and pushed it across the desktop. "Take two," he said. "It'll help."

Cal rubbed his brow, where the sound of the machines continued to pound. "So, the body count has gone up, and you're slumming in Scollay."

"Giordano says I have a short leash to find something that I can string together to make sense of all this, if it can be made sense of—he doesn't want to call it a case, not yet, and he's not supplying any men. We're stretched too thin as it is. I need some legs on the street, legs of guys who have a clue about what we're dealing with and who know people who they can get to talk."

"You want to see what Dante and I can dig up?"

"If you can, I'd be grateful. Any little thing will help."

Owen pushed a manila envelope across the table. "That's the basic info we've scrounged together, including pictures of the crime scenes, the name and address of one victim, possibles for the other five, definitely Irish, non-Nationals. There's pictures of the boat in there as well as my info from the informant on what they were carrying and, from the Feds, the names of New York and Boston gunrunners. Their info was old, so who knows if it still holds up."

Cal looked at the envelope and then widened his eyes quizzically. "You came prepared. What if I'd said no?"

Owen shook his head, smiling, and stood, yanking his tie lower on his neck. At the door he turned. More perspiration beaded on his upper lip. "I knew you wouldn't say no."

"You're pretty sure of yourself." Cal leaned back in the wooden chair, the springs underneath the seat creaking.

"I'm not promising anything, but you do some good on this, word will get around."

"What word is that?"

"With people..." Owen paused and cleared his throat. "With people who could get you your job back."

Without amusement, Cal laughed. "That's real funny, Owen."

"I'm being serious. You get us some solid info to work on, it can help you get your old job back. I mean it."

"Stop fucking with me."

"I ain't fucking with you. You've always been good police."

"You forget about me and Giordano?"

"Don't worry about him. There are other people I know who can pull the right strings. And me, I'm not just a lowly patrolman anymore. I have my own connections. Trust me, Cal. That envelope there can help you leave this shit show behind."

"Maybe I like this shit show."

"Yeah, dealing with dirtbags like those Greek and Polack fools day in and day out."

Owen gestured to the stenciling on the frosted-glass window of the door: *Pilgrim Security*. "Shit, with all the ex-cons on your payroll you might as well change the sign to *Bondsman*. It's a pain-in-the-ass life you live, and you know it."

Cal leaned over the desk, grabbed a silver pen, and pressed his thumb against it hard. "I'll let you know if I find anything out."

Owen opened the door. "I need all the help I can get."

14

UPHAMS CORNER, DORCHESTER

In the dim, hot gloom of Uphams Corner Auto on Columbia Road, Cal found Dante in one of the three pits welding the undercarriage of a car, and when Cal stepped closer he saw that he was working on his wreck of a Ford. The heat hovered in the small space, intensified by the metal, stacked rubber tires, and rusted oil drums. It felt twenty degrees hotter in the place and difficult to breathe. Water dripping from a tape-wrapped pipe above his head had created a riffle in the oil-stained concrete. Sparks from the acetylene torch lit up the helmet's visor as Dante leaned into a violent blue and white halo, intensified and concentrated like a flare burning in the dark. The sparks arced in a shower, clanging and bouncing off the lip of the pit and spiraling; flickering hot filings skittered across the concrete and glowed there like embers. Cal watched from a distance until Dante finished and lifted his visor.

Dante considered his work on the undercarriage of the car, tracing the weld line slowly with his eyes until he caught sight of Cal standing beyond the pit. He dipped his head, angled it below the rocker panel to see him full-on. "Hey, Cal, what's the word? Want to help me weld a joint? My eyes are for shit."

"Isn't that your car?"

"Yeah, we're slow right now."

"That's good, then, because I could use your help."

Dante took off his helmet and climbed from the pit. He put his gloves and heavy welding apron on a hook by a workbench and began scrubbing his hands in the sink. When they were clean he lowered his head and put it under the faucet and let the water rush onto his neck.

"Is it work?" Dante said.

"You mean, does it pay?"

"That's what I mean."

Cal reached into his pants pocket and pulled out an envelope with the Pilgrim Security logo on the front. "Here," he said and laid the envelope on the bench.

"What's this?"

"It's for a job you did three months ago, back pay. Seventy dollars in cash. The way you like it."

Dante harrumphed and turned off the water, roughly toweled his face. Every job he did was under the table and on the side and Cal knew it. When Dante looked at him, his dark eyes shone with moisture; water dripped from his hair and slid down his cheeks.

"I was thinking of trying out for a piano job at the Commonwealth. I heard it doesn't pay half bad and it's steady."

"You'd be a sure thing there."

Dante nodded and opened the envelope. "I don't have the luxury of doing anything for free, Cal."

"I know, I know. I can give you daily expenses, a small per diem, just until this other gig of yours pans out."

Dante leaned back against the workbench and lit a cigarette. Hanging over the bench top, a yellow fly strip with half a dozen still-struggling flies twisted back and forth with a sudden gust of air. Cal took Dante's silence for reluctant assent.

"That boat that Owen told us about," he said, "there's been more killings."

"Jesus. And you want to get involved in that type of shit."

"No, I don't, but I told Owen I'd ask around just to help him out. And we both know enough people from the old neighborhood who might have a hand in this or are keeping quiet about those who did."

"And they won't talk to cops."

"Sure as shit they won't, but they might talk to us."

15

DANTE WOKE IN the morning after little sleep. He stood before his dresser, where a steel fan purred steadily, and rubbed at the stubble along his cheek. The vague impression of a bad dream teased at his memory. He lit a cigarette and tried to remember. But besides the anxious feeling of what the day would bring, nothing came to him.

First, he checked on Maria. She was still asleep, the sheets twisted around her legs and her face pressed into the pillow. Claudia was in the bathroom getting ready for her morning shift over at the diner, the pipes moaning as the water rushed through them, and he heard her singing to herself, a melody tuneless and without pitch. He knocked on the door. "Don't be too long. I have to be out of here by quarter of."

In the kitchen, he put the kettle on, filled a pot halfway with water, and gently placed in four eggs to hard-boil. Standing before the window overlooking Commercial Street, he lit another cigarette and watched the early-morning sun reflect off the windows of the neighboring buildings. On the street below, a barrel-chested vendor and his teenage son un-loaded crates of fruits and vegetables and carried them down through the open cellar doors of a small grocery. Another truck was parked up on the sidewalk in front of Hagman's Bar and Grill. The truck's side was painted with the Falstaff Brewing emblem, and in the open back, two black men sat reading the *Globe,* waiting for somebody to arrive and sign off on the delivery.

Claudia called out from the hallway, "It's all yours."

In the shower he ran the water as hot as it could get. At the mirror, he pressed at the can of shaving cream. Very little came out. He shook the can and pressed the nozzle again. Only a hiss of air, and he knew it was empty. He used soap instead, lathered it up and rubbed the white foam into the sharp contours of his face. The stubble came off smoothly, and he rinsed the razor clean. He always did his upper lip last, and when the blade staggered across his skin there, he flinched and cursed, felt the sting first and then watched as the blood beaded out from the nick, cutting a crimson stream through the white lather. The taste of copper came into his mouth, and he wondered how many times he had tasted his own blood. *Too fucking many,* he thought.

From a jar of Brylcreem, he fingered out a generous dollop, ran it through his hair and then combed it to the side. He brushed his teeth and gargled with Lavoris until his gums stung raw and slapped some cologne along his neck. He was already sweating, and as he left the bathroom, he patted at his face with a damp towel.

Back in his bedroom, he pulled out a white shirt that was wrinkled but clean; it was a little tight in the shoulders but he muscled into it anyway, secured the top button around his neck without much room to spare. He knotted a black silk tie and slipped on a pair of pressed pants, black socks, and shoes in need of a shine.

Claudia was in the kitchen. She was wearing a waitress outfit, garish pink and white, the hemline high up on her thighs. Her hair was still wet from the shower and she sat before a steaming cup of coffee. Her lips were painted a vibrant red and her cheeks lightly dusted with rouge. She had a cup of coffee waiting for him. He contemplated pouring a shot of whiskey into it. It might help with the nerves, he thought, but he decided against it and drank the coffee black.

He looked her over. "New outfit?"

"Yeah. What do you think?"

"Just looks a little cheap to me."

"Cheap?"

"Showing all that leg."

"The new owner likes his girls showing more, not less. It was his idea. He knows his food ain't that good so he needs to make the men come back somehow." She forced a smile. The lines of her brow deepened. "What time do you get back?"

"Not until late. The audition this morning, then I'm off to the garage."

"You nervous?"

"About what?"

"The audition."

"Not really. I'll be fine."

"What song are you going to play?"

"I'll figure it out," Dante answered. "Probably an old standard or two."

She stood up from the kitchen chair, walked over to where he stood, and straightened his tie. Her perfume smelled medicinal and overpowering. The rouge on her left cheek seemed heavier than it was on the right, as though she were covering up an old, lingering bruise. "You should play something pretty," she said. "The Commonwealth seems like a place that wants pretty songs. Not sad ones."

"I'll try and remember that, Claudia."

He paused, looked down at his sister, and fought the urge to remind her of the other night and about how she could never leave Maria alone again. Perhaps she was able to see the anger rising in his eyes because she turned and walked back to the kitchen table, took a last sip of coffee, and, without looking at him, said, "Sorry, Dante. I won't let it happen again."

He checked his watch. "You hurry up then. I'll wake her up and get her over to Mrs. Berardi."

In Maria's bedroom, he sat down on the edge of the small mattress and laid his hand on the child's shoulder. She turned into him, kept her eyes closed. Her small hand moved on top of his. "I want to stay home."

"Sorry, my sweet, it's time to get up. Auntie will be back later."

"Will I be alone again today?" she asked.

"No. Not ever. That was just a onetime thing, Maria, just one time, that's all."

In the kitchen, he put cereal in a bowl, sliced in thin cuts of a banana, and poured in milk. She ate only a few spoonfuls and he dumped the rest into the garbage. In the bathroom, he helped her change and then watched her brush her teeth. After she was done, he wiped at the white foam clinging to the sides of her mouth with his knuckle.

Five minutes later, he put on the charcoal-gray hat with a broad black band. It had been a birthday gift from Claudia, and he'd never had an occasion to wear it. Something about wearing a new hat made him feel stiff and clumsy, made him feel as if he were trying too hard to impress somebody. It was too large and came down low on his ears, so he tipped the brim higher up on his forehead, took hold of Maria's hand, and brought her into the hallway. He locked up and then knocked on his neighbor's door.

Mrs. Berardi wore a beige housedress and no bra; her breasts hung low by her waist. Coming from the kitchen, the smell of bread baking in the oven momentarily comforted him. Maria, still groggy from her own sleepless night, looked up at Dante as if she didn't want him to go. He got down on one knee and kissed her on the cheek.

"Thanks again for this," he said to Mrs. Berardi. "You've been such a help. I hope you know how grateful Claudia and I are. We don't know what we'd do without you."

The woman looked him over. "No worries. No worries at all. Maria is such a good little girl. Sometimes I forget she's even here with me. So quiet, she is. In her own little world." She reached down and took Maria's hand. "You look nice, Dante. Not going to the garage in that, no?"

"Not today."

The woman raised a finger caked white with dough and pointed to his face. "You cut yourself shaving."

He reached up and touched the cut above his lip. Blood stained his finger. He looked down at Maria and noticed that there was a smear of it on her cheek from where he had kissed her. He wiped it off and then said good-bye.

Pressing his upper lip with a handkerchief, he moved quickly down the three sets of stairs, his shoes clacking and reverberating in the concrete stairwell, past closed doors where radios sounded with the early-morning news and where the smells of bacon and coffee wafted about the hallway.

Dante jogged out the front door and then launched into a run. A large truck honked at him as he crossed the street without looking. From its open window came a baritone voice heavy with a Charlestown accent: "Look both ways, you stupid fucking idiot!" Dante got to the curb, turned around, and watched as the guy in the boxlike vehicle painted red with *Brink's Security* in bold white lettering revved the engine and took a hard right onto Hull toward the company garage.

Dante turned a corner onto Causeway Street and ran to the North Station depot, through the revolving door, and down the escalator, the mechanical steps groaning and shuddering as if the big belt driving them were about to snap in two. There was a large group of children on a day trip, most likely waiting to catch a train that would bring them up north to Salem or even farther, the beaches of Manchester and Gloucester. They were boisterous and loud and their voices filled the air. The two supervisors of the group were at the booth settling the proper amount of fares with an MTA worker who kept shaking his head as if in disagreement. Dante dodged through the rowdy crowd of children and, at the turnstiles, jammed a token into the slot. He pushed through and hustled toward an idling trolley car tightly packed with passengers. He slid between the doors just before they closed, knocking shoulders with a man reading the *Herald*, the headline "Heat Wave," and moved to an open spot midway into the car. Accidentally brushing up against a young woman wearing a thin summer dress, Dante offered a smile, but she didn't return it.

"Pardon me," Dante said.

She lifted the thin strap of her dress higher up on her shoulder, the swell of her breast trembling. He nodded apologetically before moving his eyes to the window, seeing nothing but the pitch-darkness of the underground. The car was full with body heat and the stink of the unwashed, and Dante, already breaking out in a sweat of his own, closed his eyes and tried to breathe, in and out deeply, as the trolley screeched over the bending tracks toward downtown.

16

BOSTON POLICE DISTRICT D-4, SOUTH END

IN THE POLICE station, Owen took note of the businesses he planned to canvass in Dudley. He'd begin there, the center of the Irish cultural scene, and then work his way back to Southie and Dorchester. Mickey and the Irish Starlight Express had a large following and a reputation among the Irish club goers; he would get information, he just needed the right information, the kind that might keep the investigation going. He had to shed some light on Mickey's involvement with the gunrunning boat, find a connection to the other victims, if there was one, and figure out if he'd been targeted or if it had just been a case of his being in the wrong place at the wrong time.

He looked about the room; most of the beat cops were out on patrol, although a few roamed here and there—because of the heat, the streets were fairly quiet. But it might only be a matter of days before violence erupted and spread through the town like wildfire.

Window fans stirred the briefs, police reports, and arrest records on the desks. The desk sergeant was listening to a young black woman. Another woman stood behind her, white and young and obese, glaring at the posters on the wall, staring balefully at the cops as they passed—

Owen could tell straight off that she'd probably had two or more siblings who'd done long stretches, but she also looked afraid. He could almost guarantee that she knew some of the people whose faces were on that wall, and she probably knew where they were hiding; the real reason she was here was to do reconnaissance, to see if the cops were still beating the bushes or if they'd lost interest, and then she'd relay the info to her father, brother, cousin, or boyfriend. He'd seen this before, and he considered going over to shake her up a little and then decided against it. Instead, he flicked a pencil onto Caputo's desk and when he caught the cop's eye he nodded toward the hall. It took Caputo a moment but then Owen could see that he'd gotten it, and he rose from his desk and stepped toward the girl.

Two other detectives were sitting opposite each other and tying up reports; one was poring through an old record of mug shots. A large beat cop named Peter Molloy stood looking over his shoulder. Every once in a while the detective would ask him something and Molloy would shake his head and then the detective would turn the page of the enormous missal.

"Peter," Owen called, and waved him over. "Can I ask a question?"

Peter shambled over, put his weight on his left hip, leaned against the desk, and folded his arms across his chest. He said, "Detective," in a formal but friendly way and in a deep baritone that might have come from an actor upon the stage.

"Do you ever get over to Dudley Square?"

"Oh, for sure. It's great *craic* over there of a Friday and Saturday. I met my wife there."

"You did?"

"I did. At the Hibernian. Ten years ago this October."

"So you know the scene well."

"Haven't been to the halls in a while but you hear people talking and the same bands are still around."

"Did you happen to know Mickey Flynn from the Irish Starlight Express?"

Peter frowned and all humor left him.

"Everyone knew Mickey. Hearing about his death came as a great shock. My wife's brother often played with him at the social clubs in Dorchester and West Roxbury. Mickey would play any session there was and often for no pay. He was a hell of a man."

"Do you think he would have had anything to do with the IRA?"

"You mean the guns and all that?"

"Yeah."

Peter looked as if he were thinking about it, and he pursed his lips, but his eyes said something else entirely—he was considering Owen and deciding what he should tell him. He was a much smarter man than Owen had taken him for; his easy smile and manner made you think you were instant comrades, friends even.

"There's lot who support the IRA," he said. "You've got function halls all over Boston where they're raising funds every weekend, but you won't often find family men there. I didn't know Mickey well enough to know his politics, but I never took him for a supporter."

"Okay, but there would be plenty in Dudley who are, yeah?"

"Sure, of course. You're talking about every Irishman and woman in Boston. Everyone wants a united Ireland."

"Including yourself?"

Peter smiled. "If you don't, you shouldn't call yourself Irish."

"So all these clubs—they have owners, people I can talk to about these recent murders. Do you know any offhand?"

"De Burgh is the fella everyone knows—he lives down the South Shore now but owns most of the property in Dudley, not to mention the social clubs around town. They lease their properties from him. He has a hand with the unions around Boston too, even the policeman's union. He sets up relief funds for struggling Irish who have just come over, for Irish families with sick children, for people who need help with immigration. He arranges the travel for people who need to get back home."

"I've never heard of him."

"Did you come off the boat recently?" Peter teased, all humor now.

"No. My mother and father came off one, though, in 1912."

Peter nodded. "God bless them—are they well?"

"They died some time ago."

"My condolences. May they be at peace in heaven."

He paused and rubbed a big hand across his thick chin.

"Well," he said, "I can't name all the people who run the small venues and bands, and there's tons of them on the wedding circuit, but you should start with de Burgh. If it's about Ireland, a fund-raiser, a benefit, a *céilí*, then he's involved. Everyone recognizes him by his car, a big flashy Lincoln with whitewalls. If you see that, you know de Burgh is in the house."

"Thanks, Peter."

"You're welcome. Keep me in the loop. If you need anything, just ask."

"I will."

17

DURING THE DAY, in the absence of club goers thronging the streets and music spilling from the dance halls, the Square was a bustling place of retail and business: trucks idling as they unloaded their shipments and cars honking as they moved north along Washington Street into downtown Boston. Almost immediately, Owen marked the long, wide Lincoln town car parked before the Hibernian—it stood out among the other cars, like a yacht surrounded by rowboats—and pulled in behind it.

Owen was dressed simply because of the heat, pants and shirt with his badge clipped at the belt and his snub-nose hanging in its holster at his side. Without a blazer to cover it, he felt strangely exposed; everyone could see that he was a detective, but that might not be a bad thing this morning. He rolled up his sleeves; he was like any other workingman out for the day.

He'd called beforehand and was told that de Burgh's office was on the top floor of the Hibernian. He'd asked the operator to connect him, and he'd waited and listened to the line ring until the operator came on again and told him what he already knew, that nobody was answering.

In the Dudley Square Tavern, a half a dozen men sat at the bar.

Many were laborers who had stopped in for lunch; they wore T-shirts stained with plaster and paint. On the television behind the bar, the Red Sox were playing the Athletics and Spook Jacobs of the A's had just slapped a run-scoring single through the infield. One of the men, meat loaf and potatoes spilling from his mouth, swore and then took a pull from his bottle so as not to choke.

The bartender came over. He looked the part: tall and thin, his posture so bad that he was hunched over. Owen imagined a life of leaning against things—bar tops, doorways, ledges, the bar back where the bottles gleamed dully—and then always leaning in farther, conspiratorially, to catch the whispers and rants and confessions of his clientele.

"Officer," the bartender said, eyebrows raised questioningly.

"Detective Mackey."

"Detective Mackey, what can I do you for?"

"I'm looking for Vincent de Burgh. His office said I might find him here."

"Mr. de Burgh? Haven't seen him in here in some time. But you might look over at the Biltmore or the Intercontinental, that's where he is when he comes in town."

Owen nodded, asked for a lemonade, and looked about the room. Two men in Sears overalls were talking, one of them agitated and gesturing wildly and then shaking his head. Another man sat at a corner booth reading the *Globe* and sipping on coffee or tea. Owen wondered how many men in the room might have known Mickey Flynn, how many might have had some part in his death.

The bartender came back with his lemonade, the glass beaded with condensation, and said, "If you don't mind me asking, why are you looking for Mr. de Burgh?"

Owen put back half the lemonade in one gulp, his mouth puckering at the sweetness, and then set the glass on the bar.

"I was hoping he might donate to the Boston Police Gaelic Column, the pipes and drums band."

"Oh, he'd do that, all right, he's certainly one for the music. It's him that keeps the music alive. Wouldn't be a thing happening here or else-where in town without him."

"I was also hoping he might tell me a little bit about Mickey Flynn."

"Mickey Flynn?"

"Did you know him?"

"Ah, God, sure I did. Poor Mickey. Everyone knew Mickey. I was just talking with the lads"—here he half turned and waved an arm at the rest of the bar—"and we were saying what a shame it was, how hard it's been on his poor wife and their children."

"I know," Owen said.

"Mr. de Burgh's arranged a charity drive for the family," the man said, wiping down the bar. "There's going to be a raffle this weekend to help them out, and all the local musicians are donating their time."

"That's generous of him."

"He's a generous man."

"And Mickey, he was a musician too, wasn't he?"

"A brilliant tin-whistle player."

"Where did he play?"

"All over town, but his regular gig was at the Intercontinental with the Irish Starlight Express."

"Would you know the names of people he played with?"

"Well, sure, there's lots of guys. Mickey played the kitchen sets around town and the weddings and baptisms. Mickey played with any-one that could hold a tune."

"Anyone who's here right now?"

The bartender glanced along the bar and then shook his head. "No, not at this time of day, but if you really want to know the steady ones, the ones who played with Mickey for a living, you should ask Mr. de Burgh. He's in charge of headlining the acts. You don't play anywhere without his say-so."

"You heard about the boat that came in, where Mickey was killed."

The bartender stared at him; he seemed to straighten slightly from his slouch, as if a metal rod had been driven into his spine. He stopped wiping with the rag. "I don't know anything about a boat," he said and turned abruptly to watch the Sox game as if Owen were no longer there.

"Hey," Owen said, but the bartender ignored him. "Hey," he said again and banged his glass sharply against the bar. The room quieted. The men at the bar looked down its length to the two of them. The bartender turned back to Owen, and Owen stood. Color had risen to his cheeks and he seemed about to grasp the man by his collar and pull him over the bar. He lowered his head. "A man was brutally murdered," he said. "So when I ask you a question, you fucking well answer me and you don't turn away. Have you got it or do I need to make myself clearer?"

"No, Detective, I've got it."

"Good. Now, about the boat?"

"We all heard about it, but I don't know anything. This isn't that type of bar."

Owen was aware of the other men watching them. Three of them, longshoremen by the look of their getups, rose from their stools and stood, feet planted wide on the floorboards. Owen watched them, turning his body halfway so that they could see the gun, but they held their ground.

"So where is that type of bar?"

"Jesus, I don't know, in Southie or Dorchester, but not here."

Owen nodded toward the men. "What are you three doing?"

The smallest of the three spoke. "Nothing. We was just finishing our lunch and need to get back for our shift." He wore a light flannel shirt with the sleeves rolled up to his biceps. Hooked to his belt was a utility knife.

"Where do you work?"

"At the South Bay rail yards, unloading freight."

"Well, it won't hurt you to sit your asses down for one minute longer, will it?"

Owen stared at them until they sat and then looked back at the bartender. "Give me the name of a bar," he said, "and then I'll be out of your hair."

"Jesus, man," the bartender said weakly. All rigidity was gone now and he seemed to have curled further into himself. "That's not my scene. You'd know as well as me."

"A name. Any name."

He shrugged. "Feeney's, Cullen's, the Twelve Pins, I don't know…"

"That's good enough."

Owen raised his glass and finished his lemonade. He walked the bar, making sure that the men kept their backs to him. The bartender watched him the entire way.

So much for truth and simple answers. Owen hadn't expected this level of resistance so quickly and he regretted having had to bully information out of an average Joe; they'd all clam up with the police now and word would spread like wildfire.

Outside, he walked quickly to his car parked on the opposite side of the street, waited beneath the shade of an awning, and watched as the three dockworkers came out. He expected that they might come looking for him but they got into an old Harvester pickup with rusted blue panels and drove away. They hadn't been looking for a fight after all.

At the Intercontinental, Owen took the steps up to the main floor and the ballroom where they'd celebrated his birthday. Music came to him faintly, the sound of a chanter or bellows and a metallic rhythmic tapping. From down below, in McPherson's, the soft tinkling of glasses, the legs of bar stools scraped on wood. Deep in the building's belly, the flushing of toilets. Otherwise the building was still, his footsteps loud on the tile. He stopped beneath the gilt chandelier, its beveled-glass diamond-shaped jewels catching the sunlight from the surrounding windows and sending it in glancing arrays about the broad hallway and staircase. He stepped across the light-dappled entranceway and into the ballroom. A cleaning woman pushed a damp mop back and forth over the gleaming parquet floor. She looked up to acknowledge him before going back to her work.

In the corner of the room near the bandstand two men sat, one playing the uilleann pipes and the other a tin whistle, the unaccompanied sound swelling out into the high open spaces of the room. They leaned into each other, huddled, as if listening to the other's notes, and as they played, the one with the tin whistle, a smaller man with a receding hairline, nodded and hummed to himself. The uilleann player had his eyes closed. A tall, lean man watched them; he was writing something in a notepad. As Owen walked across the dance floor, the man looked up and then came forward and met him halfway. Owen watched him, saw him glance at the gun and the badge and then back to his face. He smiled but it was without warmth; there was something of the clergy about him, Owen felt. A certain severity that showed in his gaunt features, his pinched look. Two brass or gold pins on the lapel of his jacket caught the light, sparked briefly. Owen recognized one as a pin of abstinence. When the man smiled, it didn't touch his eyes. He held out a hand. "My name is Donal Phelan, I'm the manager here. How can we help you this fine morning?"

Owen noted that the bagpiper watched them for a moment, and then looked away again. The melody was a familiar one, he thought, but he couldn't put a name to it; it was much older than the usual standards, perhaps something from his parents' time. He handed Donal his business card.

"I'm Detective Owen Mackey of the Boston Police. I understand that Mickey Flynn worked here regularly, as a musician?"

Donal nodded his head. "Yes, poor Mickey. May he rest in peace."

"Your employer, Mr. de Burgh, would he be about? I'd like to talk to him if I could."

Donal looked at him and then turned to the bagpiper. He seemed to hesitate before turning back to Owen.

"Mr. de Burgh's not in his office at the moment."

"Where is he?"

Donal turned again and called out to the two men and the music stopped. "Do you know where Mr. de Burgh is?" he asked. "The detective here would like to talk with him."

The bagpiper was the one to speak. "He went to the bank, said he had business there. He should be back after lunch."

Donal nodded and looked at Owen. "If there's something you need, perhaps I can help?"

Behind them a metal pail banged loudly on wood, and, grunting, the charwoman offered up a prayer to no one in particular.

"I need a list of the musicians who play here as regulars, members of the Irish Starlight Express and others, if you can provide that."

"Of course. It's the Irish you want, not the Irish Americans."

"Is there a difference?"

Donal smiled, and again Owen was aware of how little warmth showed in the man's eyes—it was telling. There were only a few men he knew who could manage that trick.

"I'd be happy to get the names of all the musicians we have working for us and their information."

"I assume you pay them under the table, so many coming in just off the boat?"

"Not at all, Mr. de Burgh wouldn't hear of such a thing. We're running a business, not a rooming house. Everyone who works here has valid papers, and they're also established musicians. Mr. de Burgh keeps everything on file."

The music started up again.

"Very good."

The tall man strode to a back room and Owen walked to the two men playing. The older one, who seemed to be leading the session, continued to play with his eyes closed. The man squeezed the bellows beneath his elbow, and his fingers moved across the chanter as he rocked back and forth, and a sweet but sad air sounded from the instrument. He finished on a spiraling downward sequence and the dirgelike drone that had been a fixed note throughout the song moaned one final, despairing appeal that Owen could feel the vibrations of it through the wood beneath his feet. The man glanced up, and, seeing Owen listening, he smiled.

"You liked that?"

"I did. Very nice. What's the name of it?"

"'Cu Chulainn's Lament.' An old sad song but a good one." The man looked at him quizzically. "I remember you," he said. "You were here the other night."

"There was quite a crowd, I'm surprised you'd remember a face like mine."

"The music has kept me sharp. It's rare that I don't recall a face once I've seen it."

"Then you know all the musicians you've played with around Boston."

"Yes, certainly."

Somewhere along the hall a clock chimed. Its toll reverberated off the wood and tile. Owen was thankful for a breeze that had suddenly come in from the open windows across the room. He took a moment to wipe his brow.

"Did you know Mickey well?" he said.

Nodding, the man took the pipes off his lap and laid them gently on the floor. "Well enough," he said. "He was a fair musician who was always open to learning new things. A good man to play with. If you decided to change it up, all you had to do was look at him and he'd be right along with you."

"Did you know his politics at all?"

"You're asking was he involved with the Cause?"

"Yes."

"There's some that talk loudly about stuff like that, especially on the American side, but that wasn't Mickey. He liked playing the old rebel tunes at the end of the night or during practice, but that doesn't mean a thing."

"Do you know if he was in debt to anyone? Was he getting by financially?"

The tin-whistle player and the bagpiper laughed, and the older man shook his head. The soft skin of his cheeks trembled. He had all the warmth that the tall man lacked. "Ah, that's a good one, a musician who's not in debt to somebody. Mickey, like everyone else that plays the circuit, made very little from what he loved to do, and any man you ask around here, despite the *craic,* is just making ends meet. He worked double shifts at the docks and even with that, I know it was difficult on him and his family."

"So he wouldn't have had time to be gambling?"

"No, not that I ever heard of."

"Has your boss, de Burgh, has he ever been strong-armed by any of the local Irish gangs?"

"You mean the Americans?"

"Again with the Americans. I mean any gangs—has anyone demanded kickbacks from the money you guys bring in off a weekend? Do you have people pressing you for security or to be the sole suppliers for your booze?"

"No, none of that here. They wouldn't dare."

"Why not?"

"Because it wouldn't be wise, Detective. We can look after our own."

"The way you looked after Mickey."

"God rest his soul, now that's not fair. It wasn't anyone here who did that to Mickey."

Owen nodded. The thin man's polished shoes stamped the tiles of the hallway as he returned; he carried a sheet of ruled paper in his hand, his face as expressionless as ever. He held it out to Owen, who took it and glanced briefly at the names written there in a fine penmanship.

"That's the name of Mickey's bandmates and the musicians from bands they regularly played with here and at Mr. de Burgh's other venues around the city. Perhaps they'll be able to shed some light on the unfortunate circumstances of Mickey's death."

"Unfortunate circumstances? That's an odd way of putting it."

"How else would you put it, Detective?"

"*Unfortunate* is when I spill coffee on my best white shirt or when my horse comes in last or when the Sox lose to the Yanks. *Unfortunate* is that washerwoman with the broken back scrubbing the floor. *Murder* is what I call it when a man is beaten to a pulp, tarred and feathered, then shot through the head. Nothing fucking unfortunate about it at all."

"I stand corrected, then. That is a more precise way of putting it, surely."

Owen was suddenly sweating. The room seemed much too warm, and though it was a vast space he felt the air close and stifling. He coughed into his hand, felt the sweat trickling down his back. He pulled a notepad from his shirt pocket and the pen from its binder clip. "Do you mind," he said, "if I get your names again?"

"Donal Phelan," the thin man said.

"Peadar McGann," said the whistle player.

"Martin Butler," the bagpiper said and looked up at him. Owen glanced at his face, wrote the name slowly, pursed his lips, and then put the notebook back in his pocket. He looked at the pins on the thin man's lapel and then at his eyes. "Would you tell Mr. de Burgh that I stopped by, and if anything comes to mind, even something you don't think is important, would you mind giving me a shout?"

"We'll do that, Detective," said the thin man curtly, tapping the pocket of his jacket blazer where he'd deposited Owen's business card. "Most certainly we will."

On the street, Owen considered the placards stapled to telephone poles and the posters in storefront windows announcing the upcoming shows in the Square: Tommy Keenan and the Big Brass Céilí Band was in for a string of weekends at the Crystal Ballroom, and Patrick Costello and the Boys of the Glen were being flown in direct from Ireland for a special concert at Dorchester's Florian Hall and two nights at the Hibernian. He reached for his notebook and opened it again, considered the names there. He thought of Martin Butler, the bagpiper, and the thin man, Donal, with the cold eyes. The world was becoming a dangerous place and you had to know where to tread and then you had to tread lightly. Eisenhower was exploding nuclear warheads by the hundreds in the Pacific as a show to the Soviets, and in the less than a decade since the war ended, the world seemed to have changed so much.

He crossed at the intersection of Dudley and Washington and a woman stepped out of DeWitt's Travel Agency before him, causing him to stop. She was still adjusting the clasp on the brown handbag slung over her shoulder when she looked up. It was Mickey Flynn's widow.

"Mrs. Flynn," Owen said.

"Hello, Detective." Despite the heat, she was wearing a black mourning dress and a black shawl, her red hair pulled back beneath a dark kerchief. Her eyes were wide and red-rimmed, her cheeks flushed from the heat. To him, she looked the same as she had on the evening he'd met her down at the coroner's office after he'd agreed to show her the body and Fierro had lifted back the sheet covering her husband. The light had been different then, certainly, brighter, harsher, diminishing the lines and creases on her face so she seemed very young and vulnerable, and the morgue was a cold room, but little else seemed to have changed. It was difficult to imagine that only two days had passed since then.

"Are you—are you okay? The children—"

"Yes, yes, I think we are," she said, slightly breathless, as if the question were of such a serious complexity she was trying to understand what it meant. Her eyes looked about as if she thought someone might tell her what to say. "Mrs. Ryan is looking after Mairéad and Finn today," she said, almost as if it were a question to herself, and she frowned, as if she were in doubt of the fact, and then continued, "while I run some errands."

Owen didn't know what to say and felt helpless. He went to speak—some commonplace-yet-safe nonsense about how he was glad to see her out and about so soon—but Mrs. Flynn spoke first.

"It still feels so queer," she began. "I don't think I have my head wrapped about it. I expect to go home and see Michael, but I know

108

that isn't going to happen." She looked at him briefly, red-rimmed eyes blazing, and then looked away to where people moved about the street. There was the thrum of traffic, the clang and squeal of distant trolley cars, the sky high and bright above, and she squinted into it. Owen didn't think she was squinting because of the light but rather because she was trying to find a way to explain something.

"I don't know," she said, "I don't know at all."

"What's that, Mrs. Flynn?"

"I don't know what we'll do now. I'm just after getting our tickets back home, and meself and the children are taking the boat next Wednesday."

"You're going back to Ireland?"

She bit her lip and nodded. "Sure there's nothing for us here now anyway. It was always Michael's idea to come to America, to Boston. It's a hard, cruel place and I never did get used to it. Thank God, Mr. de Burgh has arranged everything. It will make it less of a hardship. It will be good to be settled back home, good for the children to be around family, around their own."

"Mr. de Burgh took care of the trip for you?"

"He did and he's going to get Michael's body shipped home and Mr. Phelan says they're arranging a dance and all the proceeds will go to help us get started again and—"

She still stared at a point above the passersby and the traffic, looking as if she were lost, as if she had woken to find herself in a place she didn't recognize.

"I see him in my dreams, Detective," she said, and her voice had a hushed, awed quality to it. "He's come to me every night since I saw what they'd done to him, and in the dream he's always whole and himself again and I wake up happy but then I realize I haven't woken up at all."

She tottered slightly and for a moment he thought she might fall. He reached out an arm to steady her. "Mrs. Flynn, if there's any way that I can help—"

"I don't need your help," she said quickly, her cheeks reddening, as if she were embarrassed that she'd momentarily lost herself and had said too much. "But thank you," she said, her voice trembling now. "I hope you find the men responsible for this. I hope the men who killed my Michael get justice for what they did to him."

"I promise you that they will. If you leave a forwarding address, I can contact you with any news of the case, I'll let you know—"

"No!" Mrs. Flynn shook her head fiercely. "When I leave here I don't want to hear another thing, I don't ever want to remember this place." She turned and strode away with her hand held to her face, her steps quickening as she began to cry, and the words came to Owen, muffled with grief: "Thank you."

Owen watched her go. Sunlight and heat trembled on the chrome and glass of cars, on the traffic moving east and west along the Avenue. The light glanced and ricocheted off metal stanchions before buildings and on mailboxes and newspaper stands and the trolley banging and clanging up Dudley Ave. The migraine grasped his head in its claws and squeezed and shook it so that it seemed horses were galloping thunderously in his skull. A wave of nausea came upon him and he thought he might be sick. He dabbed at his forehead with a handkerchief and cursed the heat and walked weakly back to his car.

18

THE GOLDEN DOME of the State House blazed as the sun rose higher over the city. Dante, hustling up Park Street from the train station, glanced at his watch: 10:26. He was nearly an hour late.

The Commonwealth faced the northeast end of the Boston Common. It was a fine-dining establishment where politicians fine-tuned legislation and where businessmen impressed potential clients or greased up old contacts; a place where the dying blue bloods on Beacon Hill came to dine and bask in a privilege that no longer held any influence in the city. Occasionally the nouveau riche arrived here to show off their newly minted wealth with pompous, unrefined flourish and to prove to others, as well as themselves, that they could afford any entrée in the leather-bound menu.

It took a moment for Dante's eyes to adjust to the darkness of the lobby. Spots brought on by the harsh sunlight skittered in his vision, and he pressed at his eyes until they passed. A worker pushed a large vacuum cleaner across the plush maroon rug. The electrical cord snaked and coiled along the ground. Dante carefully stepped over it and into the restaurant.

Several chandeliers hung from the gilded ceilings, dimmed to the lowest setting. Even in such muted light, he could see that the cherry-wood walls, dividers, and railings were polished to a mirror-sharp shine. Looking as if they'd been taken from the Isabella Stewart Gardner museum, oil paintings hung in ornate, gold-tinted frames. To his right, a smoking area was cordoned off and squared up with black leather chairs, the backs sectioned with shallow button tufts and detailed along the borders with silver nails. Stepping farther into the main dining room, he saw tables draped in fine white cloth, and he watched as several drab women in their fifties carefully placed fine china beside the polished silverware, crystal glasses, and napkins folded into sharp-lined pyramids.

Dante stood there and felt a familiar panic wind its way up his stomach, sucking the air from his chest. He reminded himself that it was for the money and nothing else: thirty dollars plus tips, four nights a week. With that and the work at the garage, he could get out of the red and find a bigger apartment or even rent a small house outside of Boston, perhaps in Medford, where many of the North End Italians had moved over the past few years.

Across the dining room, a very thin man walked out of the connecting hallway, saw Dante standing there, and raised his hand, beckoning him over as if he were demanding a servant to quickly step to it. Dante took off his hat and walked between the tables and nearly stumbled as he hurried up a set of three stairs to meet the man.

"I'm assuming you're here for the audition?"

"Yes. Are you Mr. Jennings?"

"I am."

The man was wearing the pin-striped suit of a banker, the collar of his shirt open at the neck where coils of blondish-white hair glimmered metallically. The suit probably cost well over two hundred but most likely that didn't matter to the man; he looked as if he had slept in it three nights in a row. His skin appeared flushed, and his gray eyes were rimmed with red. Dante could smell cologne and, underneath it, a fair share of whiskey coming through his pores. He could tell the man was suffering the worst part of a hangover and was in desperate need of a drink.

"I'm Dante Cooper. I called you a couple of days ago." He reached out to shake the man's hand. The man's face showed little emotion, and he seemed reluctant to reach out but did so anyway. His grip was limp and clammy. Dante squeezed it tight and then let go. When the man turned around, Dante instinctively wiped his palm against the side of his pants.

"Follow me, David. There's a couple ahead of you. You can just wait at the bar if you like."

"It's Dante."

"What's that?"

"My name... it's Dante."

"Oh yes, Dante it is."

They passed by the steel double doors that opened into the kitchen. The light coming from the circular windows was intense and sterile, the brightness of an operating room in a hospital. From inside, someone called out in Russian, and the sounds of pots and pans banged in response as the cooks scrabbled to get the lunch preparations in full motion.

"This is where the piano is," the thin man said. "We call this the Red Room."

Other than the polished dark oak of the bar and the circular tables arranged on the floor, the lounge seemed to possess every shade of red imaginable. Sangria. Scarlet. Burgundy. Cardinal. Several ornate lamps with tasseled crimson shades sat atop the U-shaped bar, bleeding a subdued and secretive light. Facing north and with velvet curtains pulled back, several large windows looked out onto the street.

"Just take a look at her," Jennings said. "Not bad."

It took Dante a moment, but then he registered whom the man was referring to. On the sidewalk, a peroxide-blond woman passed one of the windows, stopped in midstride, turned, and looked at her reflection in the glass, making sure the lines of her lipstick were clean and that not a hair was out of place. With it so dark inside, she had no idea she was being watched.

"Such a pretty little thing. A mouth like that wasn't meant for singing Sunday hymns to the parish, I'll tell you that," Mr. Jennings said.

When the woman seemed satisfied with her appearance and moved on, Jennings turned to Dante. "Make yourself at home." He gestured to the bar where three other men were sitting.

Jennings walked to the man at the grand piano in the corner of the room, a gleaming and stately Steinway Model M, Louis XV–style. Mr. Jennings sat down on a leather chair, folded his arms across his chest, and told the pianist to start.

Dante listened as the player went into a breezy number, soft and light and pleasant. But the notes seemed to reverberate monotone, no life making them carry across the room. Dante turned back to the three men at the bar. He sat down on a high stool, flicked a match and lit a cigarette.

The man closest to him was wearing a sharp-collared short-sleeved shirt and a watch that hung heavily off his thin wrist, boldly shining in the way that real gold didn't. He looked to be in his early twenties, probably a student over at the new Berklee School of Music, still thinking that the songs he wrote would actually make a difference in the world.

A few stools over, a man in his forties wore a thin olive sports coat patched at the elbows and a porkpie hat that had seen better days. He had hard times all over his face, remnants of failures and bad decisions etched deeply into the crow's-feet that lined his eyes. He was probably the type always trying to stretch it clean but falling for the junk just when he thought he had a handle on sobriety. Dante knew that look well.

The old-timer leaned on the cushioned rim of the bar top and smoked a cigarette that he didn't seem to be enjoying. He turned and eyed Dante, weakly nodded, and then resumed his empty stare to the window and the lines of people passing to and from work like tin figures in a carnival shooting gallery.

The third player was a black man not much older than himself. A pair of black sunglasses casually rested atop his head, and the beginnings of a mustache peppered his upper lip. Boyishly handsome, the man seemed sure of himself as his eyes danced over a sheet of music before him, studying it, tapping his fingers on the edge of the bar to how it all played out in his head.

Dante asked the man with the porkpie hat, "How many have played already?"

"About six or seven others, I forget."

"Any good?"

The man shrugged his shoulders, turned his attention back to the window.

Time seemed to slow. Dante waited and smoked one cigarette after another.

The Berklee kid played Chopin, and he played it well, note for note. But the grandiose ballad sounded through the place too regal and too formal, even for a highbrow establishment like the Commonwealth.

Next up was the older gent with the porkpie hat. Dante could tell he liked Art Tatum, injecting some touches of early bop in the first phrases of "The Breeze and I," but he knuckled through the last part, and right before he reached the end of the song, he had to start the chorus over from scratch. He wasn't getting a callback. That was obvious. He stood up from the piano, shoulders stooped, mumbled "Good day" to Mr. Jennings, and, with his hands shoved in his pockets, padded across the rug to the hallway leading back into the restaurant. Probably the only thing on his mind was where to score next. Addicts like that fucked up on purpose, Dante knew, just so they had an excuse to fall face-first off the wagon.

The hip black guy played something modern—off the Top 40 charts, most likely. Could have been a Perry Como song or the one Claudia had been humming to herself in the shower that morning. He read off the song sheet with ease and played with a natural grace and exuberant charm, at points looking up at the empty tables as though guests were sitting there enjoying his performance. As the song came to an end, he sang out the last line with a high contralto that carried through the empty room. He was mimicking the singer Jimmy Scott, and although he lacked the right pitch, Dante had to commend the guy. He had showmanship, something Dante knew he lacked.

"Nice job, kid," Mr. Jennings said. "Your name again?"

"Evan Williams."

"Thank you, Evan."

"You're more than welcome," the player said, gathering his sheet music from the piano rack. "Thank you for your time, sir."

As the kid walked past him, Dante nodded. "Nice job." Williams didn't say anything back, only smiled. Dante couldn't tell if it was a grateful smile or a cocky one.

"Mr. Cooper. You're next."

Dante sat down on the cushioned bench, lightly tapped out a few notes to see how tightly tuned the keys were. Mr. Jennings reclined back in the leather chair, crossed his legs before him. The bar was now empty, and the only movement came from the bartender rearranging bottles along the shelves.

"Where'd you play out?" Mr. Jennings asked.

"To be honest, it's been a while. The Pacific Club, a short run at the Hi-Hat—afternoons, not evenings. Played at the Roseland with Pomeroy for a bit. Filled in with Sonny Stitt's band a couple of times. Here and there."

"What're you going to play?"

"A medley. Some Porter and Carmichael."

For the first time since Dante had entered the place, the man smiled at him. "Are you going to play it like the coloreds would?"

"I'm just going to play it, I guess."

"Then do what you got to do."

Dante clenched and unclenched his left hand, hoping to get the blood flowing under the scar that curled along his knuckles. He took a deep breath, let it go, and then started to play. His fingers flowed over the keys and he tried to keep nothing in his head but the song itself. Halfway through the number, he felt he was hitting his stride, but from the hallway came the sounds of the vacuum cleaner, and he stumbled over a note like a drunken man misjudging his next step. Quickly getting back into the music, he continued with the medley, changing the tune to "The Nearness of You."

At the bar, a bottle crashed against another bottle. The bartender appeared frustrated, slammed another bottle on the bar top, coughed, and then cleared his throat. Maybe the prick was sending secret signals to Jennings, Dante thought. Perhaps he was the one making the final decision on who would get the gig.

The keys seemed to swell under Dante's fingers. He hit a sour note, followed it up with a refrain that was lost in the sucking white noise of the vacuum moving closer to the lounge. And then his left hand locked, his scarred fingers suddenly filled with concrete, and the last note was struck a half a second behind, ruining his groove altogether. He stopped and looked up at Jennings.

"Sorry, all this noise got to me."

The man grinned, sat forward on the leather chair. "To be honest, sounds a bit too colored for my taste. Try cleaning it up a bit. Make it sound nicer, you know, more gentle." And then he nodded for Dante to continue.

Dante moved into a different piece, "These Foolish Things," Margo's favorite song. He allowed himself to think of her, seeing her at her most healthy and vibrant, right after the war, September 1945. Revere Beach. The sky-blue dress with the snug bodice, a matching sun hat that shaded her mascara-thick eyes, the white heels that staggered her steps and slightly bowed her thin legs inward. And the white gloves nearly up to her elbows, one wrist boldly displaying an aquamarine bracelet that he'd bought her, telling her it cost him a pretty penny, something she'd gracefully accepted even though she could tell it was nothing more than costume jewelry and not worth very much.

He slowed the song down so each note reverberated and resonated just the way she'd liked it.

Halfway through the song, his heart rapidly beating against his rib cage, he thought he was nailing it. But Jennings must have thought otherwise. The man casually stood up from his chair and walked over to the bar. Dante slowed down the number, and when he saw the bartender fix the man a drink, he stopped playing altogether. The last note resonated dissonant and miserable in the belly of the grand piano and died as it sounded across the room. The memory of Margo in her blue dress blurred, dissolved, and then faded to black.

Dante sat there wondering if he should wait for the man to come back or just get the fuck out and call it a day. When Jennings sat down at the bar and lit a cigarette, Dante knew he wasn't coming back. The audition was over. He stood up from the bench, went to the bar, and grabbed his hat from the stool.

"That's it, right?"

"Yeah, that's it."

"When will you let us know?"

Jennings took a pull off his vodka tonic in a large glass tumbler. "To be honest, I wasn't that impressed with any of you today. If I had to choose one, though, it'd probably be the nigger. Maybe if he were a few shades lighter, he'd get the job."

The bartender started laughing, and Jennings joined in. "If I change my mind, I'll let you know, David."

"It's Dante."

"Yeah, okay, Dante," he said.

Dante lit a cigarette, walked back to the entrance, and dropped the cigarette to the floor, where it smoldered and singed the lush crimson carpet. He angled his hat over his eyes and left.

Back outside, he found himself pacing the sidewalk, feeling the heat and humidity weigh down on him. He walked across Park Street to a circle of shade under the branches of a large maple tree that fanned out over the black iron fence bordering this side of the Common. He took off his tie, folded it and shoved it into his jacket pocket, unbuttoned the top two buttons at his collar, and right away felt he could breathe easier.

A tired breeze stirred the leaves above him and cooled the sweat on his brow. He left the shade and walked along the fence. A group of bums, burnouts, and wet-brains gathered on the park benches. Some were asleep, laid out like bags of trash left on the curb. Barefoot and blistered, one man in a tattered business suit sat with his head in his hands, stunned from the heat and from dehydration.

Walking across Tremont before the traffic lights turned green, Dante realized what his next step would be and where he had to go.

Cal had offered him a job. And even though it sounded downright foolish, nothing but trouble, he began to think it was something he had to do. The Irish in this city worked among themselves, made big decisions from the stools of little bars and pubs, and inside the union halls and backroom dens of dance halls, they worked out the new avenues of commerce, verbally laid down their own laws, and argued about how the power would be shared and divided. But there was a big problem. There was no boss in charge anymore, no emblematic figurehead to keep people in line and put the fear of God in those who betrayed them. The empire no longer had a king, and that vacancy would only stoke the fire until the flames couldn't be controlled. Dante knew well enough that Boston was a powder keg. Add in a long, ruthless summer, and it would no doubt be a ripe fucking mess by the time September came calling.

He reached into his pocket for some spare change, pulled out two dimes and a nickel. He needed to find a pay phone, first to call his boss at the garage and tell him that he wasn't coming in today, and second to call Pilgrim Security and let Cal know that he was in.

19

"FUCK JOE DIMAGGIO! Fuck Joe DiMaggio!"

Standing five rows back from Cal and Dante, the man cupped his hands around his mouth and screamed at the empty field. He wore a pair of mail-order sunglasses, the kind with a white plastic nose shield attached to the bridge, a tight oxford shirt, and a checkered clip-on tie that looked as if it belonged to a Catholic schoolboy rather than a middle-aged man. He hacked and spit on the ground, and then, slightly swaying, grabbed his 'Gansett and sucked half of it down before he continued on with his chant. "Fuck Joe DiMaggio! Fuck the Yankees and fuck New York! Fuck you, DiMaggio!"

With the worn nub of a pencil, Dante was hard at work setting up what he thought would be today's starting lineups. Drops of sweat fell off his brow and blotted the paper on his lap. A cigarette was angled behind one ear and a half-smoked one hung unlit from his mouth. In a casual manner, he said, "Somebody has got to tell this drunk shithead that DiMaggio retired in '51."

Cal said, "He knows damn well that Joe doesn't play anymore. He thinks he's a real comedian."

If anything was restraining Cal from going at the man, it was the four women sitting in the row ahead of him. Four nuns, side by side and leveled off like a neat row of bowling pins, each wearing identical, round wire-rimmed sunglasses. One fanned at herself with a folded newspaper; the one next to her sipped from a bottle of Moxie. The two closest to the aisle shared a bag of peanuts, the laps of their habits dusted with salt and bits of shells.

Across the field, the Yankees' batboy came out of the visitors' dugout, his pin-striped shirt hanging loosely off his shoulders, his trousers billowing about like pantaloons, and crossed the green behind home plate. Taking aim at the child, who couldn't be any older than twelve, the man screamed even louder. "Hey! Hey! Kid! Do me a favor and go tell DiMaggio to go fuck himself!"

All four of the nuns turned around. Cal did the same. But the man didn't notice.

Cal took a deep breath and stood up from his seat. Before he could make a move, a lithe young man with a severe crew cut rushed down the steps. Without saying a word, the man brought a hard left fist across the loudmouth's jaw. Like a puppet with half of its strings cut, the loudmouth staggered sideways but didn't go down; his sunglasses hung crookedly off his face, and his eyes crossed as though his vision were on the precipice of going black. The man followed with a right hook dead center and then a quick left to the temple. The loudmouth's head twisted and snapped back, his eyes rolled up into his skull, and he hung in the air for a brief moment before tilting over and crashing shoulder-first into several empty chairs. Some of the surrounding fans cheered and clapped. And then there were those who didn't even notice, or perhaps just didn't care—a drunk with a big mouth getting his comeuppance was a common sight to many of the Fenway faithful, nothing all that special.

Two ushers came down the stairs and grabbed the unconscious man by the shoulders. A nasty wound split the skin above his left eye, and when he opened his mouth, Cal could see that his teeth were stained with blood. Once the ushers had squared him up in an empty seat, they slapped at his cheeks until he fully came to and then helped him to his feet and escorted him to the nearest exit.

"That's what you get, you loudmouth piece of shit!" one spectator yelled out.

A drunk woman in the next section hollered, "What you gonna say now, you no-good jackass!"

Cal sat back down, softly punched Dante's shoulder. "You missed it. Some jarhead kid just went savage on that prick."

Dante sighed. "I've seen plenty of loudmouths go down before. It's all the same to me."

"Well, I think somebody should buy that guy a beer." Cal watched the young man walk up the opposite aisle and over into another section, where he sat down next to a woman holding a baby wrapped in a bright pink blanket. The infant squirmed in her arms and she rocked it violently until the baby began to squeal. Squinting against the sunlight, Cal couldn't tell for sure but it looked as if the woman sported her own bruised eye and swollen upper lip. Suddenly his gratitude to the fighter waned. He turned back around and he saw that one of the nuns was looking right at him. She offered a gentle, knowing smile, as if she were telling him to mind his own business. He nodded and gave her a tired smile in return.

The uncomfortable quiet returned and the temperature climbed even higher into the red. Cal found it hard to breathe.

"Only idiots like us have a death wish to sit out in this heat."

"Dedication, I guess," Dante said, finally relighting the cigarette in his mouth.

"Stupidity is more like it."

The attendance was well below eight thousand, and most of the crowd was scattered about the ballpark, where empty seats far outnumbered those that were occupied. Those lucky enough to have tickets for seats in the shade were a few degrees less miserable. Fifteen minutes past what should have been the first pitch, the game was delayed and Cal had no clue why. People walked up the ramps and went through the gates into the ballpark, saw that the field was empty, checked their watches, and then made their way back down to the humid but cooler concourse, where the concession stands served up soda, beer, peanuts, popcorn, and hot dogs, but not much else.

Cal slipped a capsule of Benzedrine from his shirt pocket and washed it down with his beer, which was already piss-warm and had his stomach turning sourly in the heat. He downed the rest, crushed the empty cup, and let it drop to his feet. The ground was covered in peanut and red pistachio shells and several ends of cheap, foul-smelling cigars. He wondered which was a bigger dump, Fenway or the Boston Garden.

"This is just something special, a grand old time. I should have told Shaw to meet us somewhere else."

With eyes not moving off the score sheet, Dante said, "C'mon, Cal. Get in the spirit."

"Then what's the holdup?"

Dante turned to Cal. "Maybe Mantle is still sleeping off a hangover. Or maybe Yogi Berra is taking a big shit. How do I know?"

Cal lit a cigarette even though he didn't want one. It was something to do, something to help kill time.

Across the infield and the lustrous emerald that defined the outfield, the Green Monster undulated with heat-soaked ripples. Cal stared at the thirty-seven-foot green wall and thought of the two poor saps stuck inside at ground level, the scorekeepers working in the narrow passageway behind the scoreboard. *Must be a fucking oven in there,* he thought, *at least one hundred and twenty–plus.*

He'd been behind the scoreboard once, back in 1946 when he was still a cop. Working the game was a gig coveted by all on the force, and even though he was more of a Boston Braves fan, he didn't mind the shift. An easy way to slack off, take in a game, and get paid for it. The narrow space lacked a proper toilet so the scorekeepers pissed in a bucket they kept in a corner, and he remembered hearing rats scurry in the darkness in search of food. On the way out, before he reported to his post by the bleachers, he spotted a section of the wall with check-marks and lines crossed out in pencil. It was like something out of a prison cell, somebody checking off the days before he went free. When he saw a dead rat with its spine snapped, most likely by the head score-keeper's thick-soled boot, he realized that the markings weren't days but this season's dead rats; almost too many to count.

"I think it's starting," Dante said beside him. "Finally."

The stadium speakers rattled with static and feedback. Once the line cleared, the announcer welcomed the crowd and then proceeded to read off the starting lineups.

"McDougald, Collins, Mantle, Berra, Bauer, Woodling, Carey, Riz-zuto, and, pitching for the New York Yankees, Allie Reynolds.

"Bolling, Goodman, Williams, Jensen, Olson, White, Lepcio, Hat-ton, and, pitching for our own Boston Red Sox, Frank Sullivan."

And then it was time for "The Star Spangled Banner," sung by a local woman who worked for the Red Cross. She began off-key and without much range. Somebody behind Cal and Dante called her a commie. Another said he had heard crows sing better. Cal stood, placed his hand over his heart, and sang the words to the remainder of the anthem while Dante stood beside him, hat in one hand and score sheet in the other.

By the time the game started, both Cal and Dante had unbuttoned their shirts and rolled up their sleeves. They'd grabbed some beers and were sharing a bag of popcorn. A few rows to their right, an old woman sat with a transistor radio on her lap tuned to the WHDH-AM 850 broadcast of the game. The voices of Hussey and Delaney discussed the day's lineup, and with the first pitch approaching, Curt Gowdy came in to call the play-by-play. The four nuns blessed themselves and then stood up in unison to applaud their home team as they took to the field.

Just as Cal started to relax, he heard a familiar voice come from be-hind him, loud and shrill. "Hey, Cal! Dante! I was looking for you two bastards. I got a row in the shade, first-row grandstands. Come get out of this fucking sunshine and join me and my boys."

❧

Dante hadn't seen Shaw in years. He had gained weight, especially in the face. His orange-ginger hair was thinning, and a bald spot grew wide on the top of his scalp, leaving the skin there speckled and blotched. He had the look of a man who knew he was sick but feared going to the doctor to find out what ailed him.

A burgundy Cuban shirt pressed tight against his stomach, and a pair of baggy khaki shorts showed his disproportionately thin legs. Despite all the times he and Sully's boys had knocked Dante around, Dante couldn't help but feel some sympathy for him.

"So it's been a damn good year for me," Shaw said. "My hands are in so many places, I forget how many deals we got going."

Off to the side, two of his men sat and watched the game with apparent indifference. They too looked miserable. Years ago, when Sully had full power over the city, he'd given Shaw some of his toughest men to help get things done. Now, by the looks of it, the men he got were solely the bottom of the barrel.

One of the men had a neck so fat that he couldn't fully turn his head to watch the ball come off Ted Williams's bat and twist foul into the box seats to their right. His face was crossed up with scars, and showed it had taken some serious punishment. The other was about sixty years old. Irish-looking. His skin was weathered like a farmer's, and he had a sad, faraway look in his eyes as though every shitty moment in his life was playing over and over in his head. Occasionally he tried to spit but his dentures were so ill-fitting that when he did, spittle clung to his lips and flecked against his chin. He'd leave it there until he thought nobody was looking, and without much nuance, he'd wipe at it with his knobby wrist and try to clear it off.

Cal went for beers and came back with only three. He handed one over to Shaw, who nodded appreciatively. "Next round on me," he said for the second time during the game. He raised the cup toward Dante. "No hard feelings," he said.

Dante raised his cup. "None taken."

On the field, Olson chipped an outside pitch that rolled to second for the final out of the inning.

"Things are looking messy," Cal said.

Shaw sucked at his teeth. "Yeah, this game is shit."

"I wasn't talking about the game. I was talking about the killings."

"I knew there had to be a reason you wanted to see me." Shaw smirked. "Don't tell me you're trying to play Dick Fucking Tracy all over again? Remember, you're not a cop anymore."

"I'm doing somebody a favor by asking around. So let's just say it's part of the job."

"That's what they all fucking say. Whatever you're asking, we got things under control. Nothing's changed there."

"From where I'm watching, you and Sully are in as piss-poor shape as this year's Red Sox." He gestured toward the field and grinned.

"What the hell's that supposed to mean?"

"It's common knowledge how far you boys have fallen. You've given up and let a new generation of scum come in and walk all over you, right? The old Boston is wondering who the fuck is in charge these days."

Shaw finished his beer and sucked at his teeth again. "C'mon, Cal. If we knew who was behind all those killings, we'd have them hung up by their balls and skinned them alive."

"Just saying, nobody who's from here would do something so stupid as wipe out a bunch of their own in one night. If somebody in Boston is behind this, I bet they're paying others to do it."

"Cal, I'll say it again: We don't need your help."

Dante leaned in. "Out with the old, in with the new. I think it's time to admit defeat, no? So you can get back to robbing stagecoaches, or better yet, get a safe job being a clock watcher on the Schrafft's assembly line. I hear they're hiring. You can eat all the candy you want, isn't that nice?"

"Fuck you, Dante. If you're so bright, who do you think is behind it?"

"I don't know. I'm not a criminal. But maybe it could be the Italians. It's not the first time they fucked things up for you."

"No way. That's too easy. Sully got a promise from them. It can't be the Italians. No way. There's too much that'd come bite their ass in the end."

Dante leaned in farther. "Or could it be somebody from New York? Boston's a small city, but our shipping ports are big. Just think of all the junk coming in and out of Gloucester, New Bedford, even our own waterfront. Not as much heat as it would be down on the Hudson."

"Look at you. Think you're a smart man now that you're off the junk, is that it?"

Cal lit Shaw's cigarette and then one for himself. "Or it's the Irish, fresh-off-the-boat types, wide-eyed and hungry. Men who don't give two shits, it's all a joke to them. They'd wipe their asses clean with the Stars and Stripes if they had to."

Shaw shook his head, looked as if he were ready to say something but kept his mouth shut.

"We heard about the murder at that South End gambling den," Dante said. "Old bastard was strangled with a wire, nearly had his head cut off. And that shitty bar in Quincy, up in flames and three men torn up with buckshot. Either you're lying or like Cal said, the old gang don't have much muscle anymore. Which is it?"

At the crack of a bat the men stopped talking and turned back to the game. Mickey Mantle had just launched one of Sullivan's fastballs out into the empty seats at right field, and Rizzuto and Collins crossed home plate.

Seven to one.

People around them left their seats and made for the exit ramps. As though the home run were a flame to a wick, a section of the bleachers erupted into another fight. Two groups of men were throwing wild, drunken fists at one another. Several ushers quickly rushed over the aisles and broke into the fray, only to get knocked down. Shielding their heads, they cowered by the stairs until a group of police bearing clubs moved in, got some good whacks in, and brought the brawl to an end. From afar, the violence of it seemed faked, and not very exciting at that.

Cal finished off his beer. "I hear Sully's in a bad way."

"Rumors are rumors." Shaw stamped out his cigarette.

"Dementia. That's what I'm hearing from people who know."

"Good days, bad days. He'll be okay."

"You don't sound too convincing," Dante said.

With his eyes glistening somberly, Shaw looked at Dante and then at Cal. He rolled his shoulders and gestured to one of his men for another cigarette. The skinny old man pulled out an empty pack, crumpled it in his hands, and let it drop to the ground.

Shaw sighed and ran his fingers through his sweat-damp hair. "Between you and me, sometimes he's with it, sometimes he ain't. We're getting things in order, you know. We just don't have the army we used to have. Tough to tell who is who anymore. Everybody whispering this or that, talking shit behind our backs. Everybody thinking they can still be a king without putting any time in."

"Can we see him?" Cal asked.

Shaw appeared to think about it for a moment, and his eyes glinted with remembrance as if he were pushing back through the years and visualizing an exact moment when they were young men from Fields Corner trying to make a name for themselves.

"I think he'd like that, Cal. He always said you'd have been a good soldier. Always said that you were like your father. Persistent, not knowing when to quit." Shaw smirked, took his hat off his knee, and put it on, pushing the front brim far up on his forehead. His two men got the gesture and stood up from their seats. Dante looked at the two of them. *Fucking Laurel and Hardy,* he thought, the saddest two musclemen he'd seen in quite some time.

"Where is he?" Cal asked.

"At the rest home near Fields Corner. You know the one. It's been there forever."

"When is a good time?"

"Tomorrow would be okay. Give me a call in the morning."

Dante watched as Shaw stood up and in that moment saw him not as a soldier but as a stepchild of the former boss of Boston. He would inherit nothing of the empire, not that there was anything left to give or to take. He was as good as a servant at this point, a nurse, an errand boy. Dante wouldn't be surprised if he saw Shaw a year from now tending bar at some shithole on the Avenue, wearing the same ugly burgundy shirt he wore at this very moment, slinging weak drinks and singing the sad songs that only bums knew the words to.

"You boys take care," Shaw said, and followed his two men out of the aisle and up the stairs.

20

NORTH END

FEELING AS THOUGH he needed the exercise and also to escape the furnace-like heat of the subway, Dante got off at Boylston and walked north toward Scollay Square.

The sun was setting its dying embers over the city, filling its streets with a somber, otherworldly light. He fingered the change in his pocket and thought he'd get a cold beer or two at Kelly's Rose. But he'd had his share with Cal earlier, and only a block away from the bar, he decided against it. Instead he walked into a corner store, went to the magazine rack, grabbed a *Weird Tales,* a *Special Detective,* and a comic for Maria, paid for them, and then left.

One block up, an empty lot opened before him. There was a building halfway demolished; jagged spires of brick reached up into the fiery sky. Some windows and walls remained intact but without any rooms behind them, it looked to Dante like the photos he'd seen of London after the Blitz. Piles of rubble, slabs of serrated concrete, and chunks of ballast were scattered around the lot. Crickets buzzed in the random patches of green weeds that miraculously sprouted from the dust and dirt.

Deeper down on Prince Street, he spotted flashing reds and blues twirling on the hood of a parked squad car. Closer, he noticed yellow police tape hanging slack from a tree and looped around a telephone pole. A police sawhorse blocked off one end of the sidewalk. A young cop who was dwarfed inside his heavy wool uniform stood guard, his cherubic face pink from the heat. He didn't look much older than a senior in high school.

The storefront window, once stenciled white with the words *North End Pharmaceuticals,* was shattered. Fangs of glass clung to the corners, and on the sidewalk, small fragments glimmered like jewels. A dark stain had pooled on the gray pavement. In the fading sunlight, it looked like something that would leak from a machine and not a human body. Drippings of it ran the length of the sidewalk. Whoever else was injured had made a run for it.

Near Dante, two middle-aged women stood on the sidewalk chatting. One was especially attractive and the other the exact opposite, a raised and bumpy mole right under her nose and protuberant eyes under wiry, bushy brows. They were speaking to each other in Italian. His grasp of the language was still a bit rusty, but since he had moved into the neighborhood, it had gradually been getting better. He could tell they were talking of the crime scene being another one of those youth-gang incidents—the Irish kids from Charlestown starting up with the juvenile North Enders here. He'd already heard of the two rivals going at it once school got out in early June, but he knew it ran much deeper than that. One version he'd heard was that an Italian kid knocked up an Irish girl from Charlestown. He'd tried to solve the problem himself and beat her with a Louisville Slugger until she miscarried. He'd told her to say it was two blacks but once she recovered, she'd told her brother who it really was, and he went up higher, to the local mobsters, mostly Irish American thugs who were bodyguards to the unions and who on the side grafted immigrant-owned shops and manned the betting halls. A whole gang of them used baseball bats on the kid, and to shame him further, sodomized him with one of the bats and left him bleeding to death by the bocce courts along the pier overlooking the inner harbor. And then back and forth it went—no surprise there. Higher up the chain, the older regimes got wind of what was happening and had no choice but to protect their own. Baseball bats became knives, and the knives became guns. It was all part of that cycle that Cal knew so well, and it didn't matter if it was the IRA or the Italian mob, it would never stop. That's the way it worked; that's the way it would always work.

Dante put a cigarette in his mouth. As he lit a match a hand slapped hard against his back. The match fell from his fingers. He turned quickly. It was Vincent Antonelli, the boyfriend of his sister, Claudia.

"I thought it was you. Hell, man. How's it going, Dante?"

Dante stepped aside, still in shock from the slap to his back. Men who did that got under his skin. Hitting a man on the back when he wasn't looking, wasn't expecting it—something was wrong about it. It was almost no different than a sucker punch.

"Okay, Vinny. I'm doing fine."

"I was just across the way, hanging out with the old-timers. Saw you standing here like you were police or something."

Dante looked across the street to the stoop of a building where three hard guys in white T-shirts smoked cigars, talking loudly and gesturing with their hands as they argued. They were no good. Loudmouths, layabouts. The kind that fucked their teenage mistresses every Friday, beat their wives every Saturday, and then cursed out somebody who didn't go to church every Sunday.

"C'mon, let me buy you a drink."

"Sorry, Vincent. I don't have the time."

"Jesus. What are you, my fucking mother? Call me Vinny."

"Okay, Vinny."

"A quick one. Right over there. C'mon, Dante." He pointed to a small restaurant in the building next to the stoop. Its façade was in dire need of a paint job. A wooden sign above the door read *Italian Social.*

A heavy velvet shade covered the one storefront window. It was a place Dante had never seen anybody exit or enter.

Vinny wore a loud green shirt, the top two buttons undone, and a thick, gold chain glimmered against his sun-darkened skin. His short-brimmed hat was damp with sweat. He took it off and, with his arm, wiped at the moisture beading on his forehead. He stepped in closer to Dante. Beneath the vapors of a pungent musk, Dante could smell Vinny's breath, which was like dog shit from the cheap cigarillos he smoked, one after the other. Briefly, Dante wondered how Claudia could stand such a smell.

"C'mon, we've never really had a chance to catch up. We should talk and get to know each other a bit more. Man to man, without anybody else in the way."

There was a youthful gleam in his eyes, but beyond that he looked unhealthy, and at one point he winced, apparently fighting off a lingering pain that had flared up somewhere in his body. He was a tall man, heavy-boned and slow. Dante followed him across the street, noticed how he walked with a limp, which Claudia told him came from his time fighting in the Guadalcanal campaign in 1942. There was nothing that showed Dante that Vinny had been a Marine, though.

The wooden bench in front of the restaurant was caked with pigeon shit, and the gravel of the walkway was cracked. Somebody had done a terrible job of filling in the cracks with black tar; swipes of it marked the concrete.

Vinny maneuvered a key into the door lock. Dante noticed that he had a hell of a lot of keys on a metal ring and wondered what they were for. Either Vinny was a janitor to the whole North End or he had a dupe ring, a set of random keys commonly found among low-level burglars and thieves.

"The place ain't a five-star joint but it does what it does right."

When the door opened, a bell above chimed loudly. Dante walked in and immediately a rancid odor assaulted his senses—something was rotting. Vinny forced the door shut and then turned the lock.

The restaurant was empty. Six round tables were covered in red table-cloths, each sectioned off on a tiled floor. Some of the linoleum squares were missing and left behind were the remains of dry-set mortar. Several shaded lamps hung from the ceiling, and a tawny light came from them. One of the shades was torn, as if by a knife.

"Don't judge a book by its cover," Dante said. "That's what they say, right?"

"Yeah, and they also say don't bite the hand that feeds you."

On the floor were mousetraps. One was occupied and Dante could tell it was a fresh kill. The smell in the room was probably from several other rodents that hadn't been removed from their traps yet.

"My father, God rest his soul, always used to say that. 'Vinny,' he'd say, 'don't bite the hand that feeds you.' But I didn't agree with it. It sounded dumb to me even when I was a kid. I got sick of hearing it so one day I told him that sometimes the hand that feeds you can't cook worth shit. And that I'd rather go hungry than shit my pants and throw up a lung, you know."

"What'd your father say to that?"

"He said that I got a mouth on me, and that if I keep it up, what comes around will come around."

"Sounds like your father had a way with words," Dante said.

"He sure did. A fucking skipping record, my old man. God rest his soul."

They took a seat at the round table closest to the back. Dante could tell the tables were set up for card games and not for eating—the cloth tablecloths had more cigarette burns than food stains, and there was a mildewed smell coming from them, as if they hadn't been washed in months. It was obvious this place was a cover-up, a place for drop-offs and pickups, small-time negotiations and gambling. There was nothing legal about it. It was as blatantly criminal as Vinny's key ring.

Vinny called out in Italian, and a young teenager came through the curtained doorway, hair slicked back from his forehead and a duck's ass cutting a V at the back of his neck. His denim pants were rolled up above his pristinely white sneakers.

"Get me and my friend a bottle of the house. And some ice on the side, like I like it, okay? And two cappuccinos. And some of those pistachios too."

The wine bottle came out, its bottom encased in wicker. In the spaces that were frayed, there was dust, and lots of it. Vinny put a cube of ice in his glass. Dante drank his room temperature, the way you were supposed to. It tasted rich and heavy and very strong. It had been made in the neighborhood, he could tell.

"You okay, Dante?"

"I'm fine. And you?"

"I'm doing great. Really good."

They both took another mouthful from their glasses.

"Looks like business is doing good here."

"You're a comedian, Dante. I didn't think you were capable of making a joke. I'm glad you can. It's important to make jokes."

"I've never eaten here. Is it good?"

Vinny gestured with his hand that it was okay. "*Mezza-mezza.* Some things better than others."

There was awkward silence again as the kid brought out the cappuccinos. Dante blew on his and then took a sip. It was thick and muddy, extremely bitter on the tongue.

"So what's up?"

"Just thought it would be good to chat, that's all. Get acquainted."

"Okay then."

"Claudia tells me you're working for the police?"

Dante leaned back in his chair. "She told you that?"

"She did, yeah. She tells me all about you."

Dante fingered his pack of smokes, lit one, and dropped the match in the cup of cappuccino, where it hissed in the pale foam.

"The stuff with the cops. What's that all about?"

"Nothing big. Nothing that concerns you."

"What? I've met you like twice and you still treat me nose-up. C'mon, enough with the snooty bullshit. I could be your brother-in-law if things with Claudia keep going the way they're going. Let's not start off like this."

"It's not what you think. I work on cars, Vinny. Sometimes Claudia doesn't know what she's talking about."

"She tells me you're looking for steady work. I can help. Good, solid work. And you won't break your back doing it. The kid, too, you'll be able to give her more. Take care of her better."

"The kid has a name."

"Yeah—Maria. Like my mother. I ain't here to bust your balls, Dante. I'm just wanting to be gracious, to be good and offer you some help."

"Just so you know, I'm not a criminal." He tapped the ash in the cup.

"I wasn't saying you were. Relax, for Christ's sake. You're fucking wound tight. Real tight." He grinned. "Tight like some young pussy crying to be fucked."

"You got a nice way of saying things. Maybe you got it from your father."

"I like jokes. They're okay. But I don't like sarcasm." Vinny cracked some pistachio nuts, chewed at them voraciously, and left the shells scattered on the tablecloth.

"I don't mean to be rude, Vinny. You want to talk about Claudia, that's okay. But I didn't come in here to talk about me, or Maria."

"That's actually what I wanted to talk about. Claudia. You know, she has come out of her shell. And I helped bring her out of it. I'm good for her. Some may say that I'm too good for her. But I love her, and because I do, I can say anything I want. You, you kept her in her head too much. I know you had your bad deal and all, you went through some serious shit, I know that. But she deserves a life of her own."

"Claudia can make her own decisions. She's a grown woman."

"Then treat her like one."

"Are you serious? She has her responsibilities, and ever since she's been with you, she seems to be off in some other fucking universe. I don't like it."

"Nobody said you had to like it."

"She's a mother," Dante said, his voice rising.

"Well, that ain't her kid. I know that. She told me everything."

"Everything? What are you talking about?"

"You know. Don't play dumb Polack."

Dante stood up from the chair and tucked it under the table where it hit the edge. The glass of wine shook precariously, drops of it spattering the tablecloth.

"She's going to be with me soon. I know you've been through a lot. She's told me about your wife, the shit you went through with the junk. And how Maria came into your life."

"What did she tell you?"

"She was a bit drunk. You know her. She can't really handle her wine. Anyway, I'm a pretty good listener and I can put two and two together. She told me what you and your mick friend were up to a few years ago. All that business with those cocksucking Foley brothers. And suddenly you pretending the kids were your own. Uncle Dante, Auntie Claudia. What a joke."

Dante moved toward the door.

"I just want you to know that she wants to have her own child with me. As a matter of fact, she wants her own life with me. So make it easy for yourself and let's not sling mud at each other anymore. We could be brothers real soon. Keep it in the family, as they say. I won't say a thing. Won't say one fucking thing, you remember that and we'll be okay."

"Listen, scumbag," Dante said before turning the lock and opening the door. "You keep Claudia away at night when she's supposed to be watching Maria, I'll come find you. Don't think I won't."

"You call that a threat? A real tough guy..."

Dante slammed the door. A panel of glass rattled in the pane and then slid from its hold, shattering on the sidewalk. On the stoop of the neighboring building, the three men stood up and stared him down as he passed, waiting for him to turn around so that they could start something. He kept on walking. They cursed him in Italian. Dante heard the words *vigliacco* and *figa*, but calling him a coward and a cunt wouldn't make him pissed enough to get into a fight. All that bad energy, all that anger—it was brewing up inside him, but he knew it was best to take a deep breath and save it for later. The violent world that Cal knew so well had finally found him, was pulling him in whether he liked it or not, and he decided that starting now, no matter where he went, no matter what time of day, he would carry a gun.

21

GRIFFIN'S, DORCHESTER AVENUE, DORCHESTER

THE CEILING FANS had stopped and the beer was more froth than liquid. Dante and Cal were back on the Avenue to help Owen, sitting at a bar during a noonday blackout in one of the workingman Irish pubs along the Avenue, listening to the men about them cursing the electrical outage and the heat and trying to get a sense of this part of the city again, one that they knew but to a large extent one that was also completely unfamiliar. The bar was almost all Irish FOBs, even though it was run by a Ukrainian whom everyone called Dommo.

There were a few Irish Americans at this time of day, an old-timer who Cal often saw at the bathhouses pushing a mop across the floor or handling the towels, and a young fellow Cal recognized as the last of the Kinneallys, Pauli Kinneally, the twins' youngest brother, sitting by himself on the stool closest to the door. He'd always been a decent kid, the one who'd managed to stay untouched by his brothers' criminal activities; everyone knew he wasn't made from the same stuff, which, to Cal's thinking, was a good thing. He'd gone into the trades, working as a plasterer's apprentice, and now, after getting married and having a child, he had bought a van and had his own small business going. He was listening to the horse races on the portable tube radio above that end of the bar and scribbling in the race section of the *Herald*.

Cal wondered briefly how hard the death of his brothers had been on him, and on his mother, Bridie Kinneally, who was still alive, but he didn't know the kid well enough to say hello or *I'm sorry for your loss, I'm sorry I had to kill your scumbag brothers three years ago.*

It was an odd feeling to share the same space with the family member of someone you'd killed or had a part in killing, but he never allowed himself to consider it too deeply. It was akin to the way he'd felt when, as a cop, he'd arrested someone for hard crimes, helped put him away for a long time—in a way, a sort of death—and then seen a wife or sister on the streets or a brother or uncle in a bar. Dorchester was such a large part of the small city that it was difficult to return home and not be surrounded by it. Lynne knew that, and it was for that reason she had wanted them to leave.

He'd felt the same way when they'd shipped him stateside after his hospital stay in Verdun and he'd been reunited with some of the men from his old platoon. They shared a common grief for lost friends and comrades, men they had witnessed die in horrible ways, but each of them also experienced a particular and singular shame at being alive and that shame, instead of creating a bond between them, produced a distinct estrangement. He looked at Pauli circling the horses as the next race began on the radio. He was a good kid, Cal thought, and had deserved better, but at least he'd been fortunate enough to escape the violence that had been the ruin of his brothers.

"How you doing, kid?" Dommo called to him. "Any luck?"

The kid smiled at him and raised his hands in defeat. "I never have any luck with the ponies, Dommo, and besides, my wife hates it."

"Ahh, every man have a vice, otherwise is not a man. I no trust a man who say he have no vice—either he afraid of living or he bullshitting you. He has vice but he just no tell you, he hide it away."

❧

The radio had just announced the fourth race from Saratoga when the bar's door opened. Cal glanced up, aware of the shifting heat in the room and the sound of honking horns on the Avenue. He registered that it was Pat Nash, John Jo Nash's son, a no-good who was mostly seen with one of the Fitzpatricks, small-timers trying to claim some ground in the city and who were at odds with the Walshes and the McDonaghs, old pals of Blackie's. The boy, no more than seventeen, approached the bar and raised his hand as if to order a drink, and Cal saw much too late that in it was a gun. Pauli was looking at the newspaper when the boy shot him in the head point-blank and then sprinted out the door. Pauli fell hard from the stool and struck the floor. "Jesus Christ," Dante said and they both raced to the front of the bar.

"Call for an ambulance," someone shouted, "call for the cops!" but Dommo was wailing and wringing the dishrag over his head. Blood spatter spotted his right cheek.

"I can't!" he cried. "The phones aren't working."

"Shit!" one of the men said and ran out onto the Avenue for help.

Cal knelt by the body, checked for a pulse. It was there, but weak. He took off his shirt, and Dante helped him position the kid's head so that they could hold the shirt against the wound on the left side of the skull, where the bullet had exited. The other men crowded around. They looked at the kid's pale face; his eyes were closed and it seemed as if he were sleeping. Blood trickled from the hole at his right temple, and Cal tried to stanch that as well.

They stayed at Pauli's side and watched as he bled; the shirt became sodden and dark. Sweat shone on their foreheads. It trickled into Cal's eyes and stung. He blinked but refused to let go of the kid. Someone propped open the door, and a slight breeze turned the pages of the newspaper on the bar. Cal felt the kid's pulse grow slower, and then, almost imperceptibly, it was gone and he let go of him and stood. His undershirt clung to him, soaked with sweat and blood.

By the time two beat cops and the ambulance arrived, the kid was already cold, cold in the way that only the dead can be, even in the heat of summer. None of the men looked at one another. Dommo sat with his head in his hands at the bar, his shoulders shaking softly. The bar rag lay on the countertop beside him, bloodied from where he'd tried to wipe up the spray from the gun blast.

Dante sat heavily on a stool and Cal sat beside him.

"Shit," Dante said. "This is too much."

Cal nodded and watched as the ambulance attendants put the body on a stretcher, covered it with a sheet, and carried it out the door. The cops took all the info they needed from some of the patrons and stood in the corner waiting for the homicide detective to arrive. Cal stared at the spot on the floor where the kid had fallen, at his bloody shirt, which the attendants had left there. The announcer on the radio called the results from the last race of the day at Saratoga and one of the men somehow thought looking at Pauli's newspaper was a good idea. After a moment scanning it, he said: "The kid's got the winning horse circled. Wild Colonial Boy. The fucking kid won in the fourth, sixty-four-to-one odds. A real fucking payout."

Dommo thumped the bar in anger and then wailed some more. Tears streaked his face. "No, the kid never make money bets, he just listen to the races, see if he could guess the winners. He never have no luck at it."

That's right, Cal thought, the iron-rich smell of blood on his undershirt and still strong in his nostrils. The kid hadn't been lucky, he hadn't been fortunate, and he hadn't escaped after all.

22

SULLIVAN, THE OLD gangster, was sitting up in his bed and staring out the window when Cal and Dante came in. An oscillating metal fan ratcheted back and forth, pushing feebly at the air, stirring the tops of newspapers laid out on a reading table. Shaw was in a chair at the other side of the room, sucking on a lozenge and reading a dog-eared pulp novel. He glanced up, gestured with his head toward Sullivan, and held a finger to his lips, and Cal and Dante took it as a cue to wait.

The old man looked like an old man; the flesh about his once-strong jaw sagged, and there was a gray pallor to his skin, the color Cal had seen on dead men or men in shock during the war. Sully's hair, once a fiery bush of red, was a sickly, yellow-tinged white—discolored from the nicotine of cigarettes. One smoldered in a tin ashtray on his bedside table. On the peeling plaster wall above Sully's head, a small wooden crucifix hung. It was the type with the mother-of-pearl inlay that had been treated with luminescent resin so that the figure glowed in the dark, keeping watch over him as he slept. It was sold by the foreign mission headquarters of the Society of the Divine Savior and in the early 1940s you could buy a carton of them on the Avenue for two dollars— Cal's parents had had a similar one over their bed.

A large blond-wood Raytheon console television had been dragged into the room, presumably at Sully's request, and on its wavy screen was the hydrogen-bomb explosion at Bikini Atoll from back in March, a thousand times more powerful than the bombs that ended the war. Cal watched the detonation beneath the waves and the huge funnel of water, dwarfing the surrounding fleet of destroyers and frigates, and its massive, mushrooming head expanding outward, rising to the heavens. But Sully wasn't watching the screen.

Cal tried to see what Sully was seeing and followed his gaze. He saw a stretch of thin grass, a row of juniper bushes burned brown by the sun, the roofs of parked cars upon which the sun glinted harshly, and then, down the hill of Mount Bowdoin and past Ronan Park, the shopping district, the Supreme Foodmart, the library, the post office, and the Fields Corner trolley, which rattled along the overpass rails, bisecting the horizon.

"I remember when I was young," Sullivan said, as if to himself, "playing ball at Ronan Park. We beat every other team in Boston. I played right field because of my arm. It was a cannon, my arm. Could take out a runner stealing home straight from deep right, no hop. They said I could have made it in the majors."

He turned, and his eyes were surprisingly blue and bright, the lower lids damp from weeping. He blinked—his eyes adjusting from light to shadow—reached across to the bedside table, pulled a tissue from a box, and wiped at them self-consciously.

"The mick and the wop," he said, shaking his head. "Haven't ever known it any other way, and now it's just the same, even after all these years. You boys make me laugh."

"Hello, Sully," Cal said, and smiled. "Thanks for meeting with us."

"Ahh," the old man said and he waved the comment away, pulled himself farther up in bed, and straightened the yellowed sheets about him. "Your request for an invite was a show of respect. You didn't have to do it. Hardly anyone does these days. For most of the people out there, I've been dead for years."

"That's not true," Dante said. "They might want it that way, but everyone still knows you're the one in charge."

Sully looked at him, squinting in the dim light of the room. He picked up the smoldering cigarette and drew on it thoughtfully, pensively. When he was done, he lay it back in the tray. "They say I'm mad."

Shaw chuckled from the corner, the lozenge rattling against his teeth as he moved it around in his mouth.

"What the hell are you laughing about?" Sully said.

"You *are* mad, boss, fucking loony most of the time. You've been mad your entire life."

Sully shook his head. "See the shit I have to put up with? The only thing I get to look forward to these days is clean sheets and a regular bowel movement. The rest of the time I'm stuck listening to this fool."

Cal took a chair from the reading table and pulled it close to the bed, and Dante did the same. Cal noted the scent of disinfectant bristling sharply in his nostrils, but underneath that another odor: soiled linens and unwashed bedpans, urine and vomit and feces. The smell was embedded in the blankets, the wallpaper, the sheets, the carpeting. He'd noticed it as they'd walked through the hallway and it had stayed with him and magnified his sense of unease, his dislike of such places where sickness had become palpable, as much a part of the building as the bricks and mortar, and the patients and nurses and doctors and nuns who wearily trudged the halls had resigned themselves to it. It reminded him of the institution where his father had spent the last two years of his life.

"When was the last time you got out?" Dante said.

"Before this fucking heat began, the beginning of the summer."

"We can take you out, if you'd like." Dante glanced at the wheelchair folded by the door.

"No, if I can't walk on my own, I don't need those fuckers seeing me in a wheelchair. I won't give them the satisfaction."

There were many things that could have been said—a shared history of death and murder and blood spilled during one of the worst winters in Boston's history. Until this moment, Cal could almost have convinced himself those things had never happened, but they had, and look at where they were now. It was hard to believe that only three years had passed. Sully was looking at the both of them, and Cal knew that the same thoughts were running through his mind. A narrow vessel at Sully's right temple pulsed dully; his eyes seemed to be the only color in his face.

"Terrible business that," Sully said, acknowledging what hadn't been spoken, and he picked up his pack of cigarettes, took his time lighting one. Shaw turned the page of his book and tsk-tsked at something happening in the world of his crime drama.

Cal considered saying something that might explain or justify their actions and the way Blackie had died, but no words would come to him. Shaw had stopped sucking on his candy and was looking at the three of them. Cal felt suddenly like a child waiting to be reprimanded by his father—his jaws tensed instinctively, as if he were about to be struck hard across the face. Here, now, Sully merely had to consider the punishment and then mete it out. As old and weak as Sully looked, Cal had no doubts about what he was capable of. For a moment he wondered if they'd made a mistake in coming to him, had perhaps put themselves in a dangerous position, but then he dismissed the notion. If Sully had wanted some manner of payback, he would have done it years ago. He had agreed to meet with them, and Shaw, sitting there by himself and watching, wasn't the type to project intimidation; in fact, his presence spoke to a trust that Cal doubted they deserved.

"I was disappointed that everything had to go down the way it did," Sully said, "but you two weren't responsible for that, not entirely, anyway. That's the past, and I don't have time to think about the past anymore. Besides, you're here for something else."

"You've heard about the boat that came into the harbor last week and the string of murders since?" Cal asked.

"I've heard they think the boat was carrying guns."

"That's what they think. Guns bound for Ireland that are now gone. We think they're still somewhere in the city."

"And the murders are because they're trying to remove all evidence of it."

"Something like that—all the murdered have been Irish."

"So far," Sully said, exhaling smoke and squinting through the haze. Cal nodded. "So far."

"I agreed to see the two of you," Sully said, "because I've known you both a long time, because you know how things work and you're from the neighborhood and you have some manner of respect, because of what happened with Blackie, and Cal, because I knew your father. In one way or another, we're all connected in this town, and I don't even mean this neighborhood, I mean all of it. We may not like the others, but everything we do has repercussions and it affects us all.

"You need to keep your heads low. From what you've said, they've already begun to clean house. They won't leave any loose ends and they won't want people going around drawing attention to their activities. There's a reason I haven't heard anything on the streets—they're keeping it tight in the Irish communities. I was always against having anything to do with them—it's not good business and we're not here to further causes—but for a while there, Blackie, unaware that I knew, was trying his hand at getting them guns. I think he liked the idea of it more than anything, liked to say he was supporting the Irish cause like a good son of Erin, a Boston-Irish kid who hadn't forgot his heritage, but even he knew he was treading on dangerous ground. In the end he put up some of his own money to get them guns and get them to Ireland."

"What happened?"

"I don't know. I don't think the guns ever made it and there was some type of falling-out. What I do know is that Blackie never tried to get involved again. The thing is, and what you two have to understand, is that fanatics will do just about anything."

Cal watched him; he could feel his face go rigid. His heartbeat quickened and the smells and the light in the room became more sharply defined.

"I know, I know," Sully said and held up a placating palm. Again, it was as if he were reading Cal's mind. "You're thinking of Blackie, you're thinking of all the crazy bastards out there right now killing to get a piece of the city, but"—and he frowned and shook his head—"that's not fanaticism. A lot of those killers are psychos—Blackie was psycho. Mary, Mother of God! They're the ones hired to kill people because no one else will do it! But a fanatic needs nothing to make him kill other than his belief in a particular ideology. It gives him a higher moral ground, a place where he can rationalize what he does, and it makes him expendable—he knows this. It's the belief in this other thing that motivates him. To work with those types of people is not just bad for business, it's dangerous. There's no profit in it and you can't trust that they won't turn against you."

Shaw brought a plastic cup of orange juice to Sully's bedside and Sully sipped it slowly through a straw. As he leaned forward his white tufts of hair caught in the rectangle of sunlight before the window and it softened his features, made him look, momentarily, less decrepit. From down the hall came the sound of clattering trays and cutlery, the bland, watery smell of boiled food and diluted sauces.

Sully finished the juice, put the cup on the table, and wiped at his chin. "I'll keep my ear to the ground," he said, "and I'll have Shaw and his boys listening, but I wouldn't put much hope in that. There is one person who might be able to help you, though."

"Who's that?"

"Your friend there, the priest."

"Father Nolan?"

"Of course, he's the original Irish gunrunner. I'm surprised they let him into the country at all."

"But that was years before he came to Boston, before he joined the seminary," Dante said. "What could he know about that now?"

"Ahh, you two. You're like the Keystone Cops." Sully shook his head and then began coughing. When his hacking had subsided he pulled up phlegm in his throat, thick and wet-sounding, and spit into the empty cup at his side; Shaw put down his book and retrieved the cup, threw it into the wastebasket.

When Sully spoke again, he wheezed slightly and he seemed tired by the effort. "You two make me laugh. You think that once you're in with that lot, you ever truly get out? Nolan's your guy. There's a reason he became a priest—why many men become priests—a reason that has nothing to do with God's calling. It's to hide from their pasts. He'll know a thing or two about what's going on. I'd lay money on it."

Sully closed his eyes and put his head back against the pillow. In the soft light cast from the window, he looked at peace, content, a fatherly and benevolent figure, almost. You'd never know the type of man he was, had been. The crucifix's mother-of-pearl sparkled. On the far wall, the fan clicked and whirred through its revolutions. Shaw unwrapped a lozenge with a rustling, popped it in his mouth, and began sucking loudly. Cal and Dante watched as Sully sighed deeply and then smiled, and for a moment they thought he might be asleep, his cigarette smoke twining lazily toward the open window.

"Now, you two," Sully said, his eyes still closed, "get the fuck out and let an old man rest."

Shaw joined Cal and Dante outside, and the three of them left the shade of the front porch and walked down to the street. On the lawns, metal sprinklers clicked and grinded as they spun, and staggered streams of water hissed out over the dry grass, wetting the pavement before them.

"He didn't seem too bad to me," Cal said to Shaw.

"There's a word I'm looking for." Shaw stepped to the side to avoid the spray of water. "The doctor said he'd have clear moments. Like he's normal. But then, *wham,* he's all confused and doesn't want to talk to anybody. You caught him at a good time."

A young nurse wearing a crisp white uniform, hat pinned into hair that was stiff with some aerosol product, hurried past them to the building. It looked to Cal like she had encountered Shaw before and was doing her best to avoid him. Shaw eyed her legs, the shimmering nylons covering them, and then her hips as they pulsed from side to side beneath the bleached fabric. He sniffed the air like an animal and then grinned to himself.

"Lucid," Cal said.

Shaw turned. "What's that?"

"Lucid," Cal said slowly. "I think that's the word you're looking for."

"Yeah, that's it. Lucid." Shaw spit out his lozenge. It shattered into pieces on the pavement as if it were glass. He took a cigar from his pocket, unwrapped it, and bit off the end. He had to smoke his cigars outside—Sully couldn't stand the smell of them.

Cal looked back at Dante, who was several yards behind them, his hands in his pockets and his ill-fitting gray hat angled down over his eyes. Water from the sprinkler wet his pants legs, but he appeared numb to it. He seemed preoccupied with something.

"Sully's sick," Cal said. "I can see that, and it's clear he doesn't know much of anything going on. You, though, you're out and about. You must have heard something. Rumors, drunk talk, anything. Nobody sits on a load of stolen guns and keeps it airtight."

Shaw looked away and moaned with frustration. "Sully told you to see Father Nolan. I don't know shit, so stop thinking I do."

When all three of them came to the sidewalk, Dante tapped Shaw on the shoulder and gestured with a raised chin across the street. "That car over there. Your boys?"

Shaw sucked on the cigar as if it were lit, squinted against the sunlight. "Not ours. Why you asking?"

"I saw them in the same spot over an hour ago," Dante said.

"So?"

"When we got here, there were three guys in that car. Now there's only two."

"So fucking what?"

Dante looked at Cal. "Seem suspicious to you?"

Cal eyed the black Chrysler Windsor parked a half a block away. "Yeah, it looks a bit off to me. Somebody should do his job and go check on them."

"Just to be safe," Dante said.

Shaw shook his head. "Could just be two people waiting for somebody. Go find a meter maid and let her know. I don't give a shit if they park there all day."

"Do you have any other men watching this place?" Dante asked.

The cigar end crumbled in Shaw's mouth. He took it out and, spitting, threw the cigar to the ground. Black flecks of tobacco clung to his bottom lip. "Don't worry about it. We got this place covered. Plus, there's no visitors allowed in after six."

Shaw paused, wiped at his mouth with the back of his hand. "You two want me to do something about that car, don't you?"

He waited for them to say something, and when neither did, he stepped off the curb. Once there was a gap in the traffic, Shaw walked across the street to the parked Chrysler.

"It's probably nothing," Cal said.

"Probably not, but it's good to keep the lazy bastard on his toes."

Cal and Dante watched Shaw go to the driver's side and knock on the half-open window. From where they stood, Cal and Dante couldn't see the driver's face.

Something was off.

Cal felt his insides tense and tremor, a feeling he remembered from back in the war, before the first shot rang out or the first bomb tore through the earth around him. It was an odd sensation—the way nature seemed to slow, the sky pressing down and the sunlight flaring brighter, as if his pupils had suddenly dilated. Sounds both sharp and piercing cut through the humid air.

The shrill calls from crows atop the telephone lines.

The opening and shutting of a postal box as a pedestrian dropped off mail.

An old man whistling tunelessly as a nurse guided him along the sidewalk.

He looked to Dante, and Dante cocked his head slightly to one side, as if he too could sense something was off-kilter.

Across the street, Shaw leaned on the car, talking to the driver in a casual manner. The shadow of the driver sat erect and still, and they could see the silhouette of the passenger, who was broad-shouldered. The men in the car didn't seem too concerned with Shaw, nor did Shaw seem too worried about them.

Shaw shrugged his shoulders and let out a bark of laughter. Some more words were exchanged, and Shaw patted the hood of the car, turned around, and started walking back across the street. He was shaking his head as if embarrassed and pissed at the same time, and he was opening his mouth to say something.

An explosive crack rang out from inside the nursing home, followed by a second and a third. A quiet followed, disrupted by a woman's piercing scream. Dante and Cal looked up to the building and saw a nurse on the front steps, the same one that Shaw had given the X-ray treatment to. A black groundskeeper ran up to console her, and she pointed across the porch to the other side of the building.

Cal reached into his jacket and gripped the handle of his gun but didn't pull it all the way out from its holster. He walked down the sidewalk in the direction the nurse was pointing.

Cal caught a glimpse of a man running at full sprint. He was short yet lean, and he wore the powder-blue pants and short-sleeved shirt of an orderly. He was running toward the parked Chrysler that Shaw had just come from. Its engine revved. Smoke pumped out black from its tailpipe as the car edged out into traffic. The man hit the back door, opened it, and leaped inside. The tires tore at the pavement, and with the clutch grinding loudly, the Chrysler pulled off and burned down the street.

Dante was already on his way back to the building. Shaw was right behind him, hobbling as he tried to keep up.

In the dank, carpeted hallways of the nursing home, an old man wearing a food-stained robe comforted a confused-looking woman in a wheelchair who was crying like a child. A nurse sat at the front desk with her face in her hands. Another worker barked into a phone, asking for help.

There was classical music playing from the radio in the recreation room. The canned orchestra and its strings added a surreal, haunted quality to the scene as Cal ran up the stairwell to the second floor.

He met Shaw and Dante at the door to Sully's room.

He was still alive. The nurse who had been in the room with Sully hadn't been so lucky. One bullet had gone through her temple, sprayed the wall with dark blood from her skull. After the first shot, she must have fallen forward, for the second shot had torn through her shoulder.

Now she lay on the carpeted floor, body twisted at the waist, eyes still open; her skin already appeared waxen. There was a doctor in the room, and he briefly looked up at Shaw in a strangely accusatory way before he went back to Sully. On the bed, the old man cursed, his thin arthritic hands clutching and twisting the bedsheets. His eyes were tightly clamped shut as the doctor ripped open his pants leg and pressed at the wound above the knee.

Dante took off his hat and wiped the sweat from his brow. He looked at Cal, and then at Shaw. "Who was it?"

Shaw shrugged. "I didn't recognize the two in the car. They could have been anybody."

Above the bed, the crucifix stood out boldly against the wall. The arc of the nurse's blood had misted the lacquered wood and the figure of Christ. Cal grabbed Dante by the sleeve and they walked back into the hall. At this point they were just getting in the way, and without saying a word to each other, they went down the stairs to the lobby and waited for the police to arrive.

23

CAL DESCENDED THE narrow stairway from the Northampton El to the street. Beneath the shadow of the turn-of-the-century elevated station—the first elevated line in the country, once the architectural pride of the city—electric sparks and flakes of metal as fine as ash cascaded down through the massive steel uprights and arched trusses. The sidewalk tremored beneath his feet as trains passed overhead. In the shadows of the El sat Mitch's Bar, an anonymous brick façade with one small square window covered by a metal grille and a sign above it advertising Budweiser beer. You might pass by without noticing it unless the door was open, as it was on hot nights like tonight.

It was a mixed crowd of black and white at this convergence of two neighborhoods, a halfway house of sorts that had been there as long as Cal could remember. Father Nolan sat at the bar reading the paper and nursing a bottle of Extra Stout and a Jameson. Cal sat at the stool next to him and the priest looked up. The man never aged; he still had sharp, clear blue eyes and smartly swept-back silver hair kept close to his head with pomade.

"Cahal," he said. *"Dia dhuit."*

"Dia is Muire dhuit, Athair."

"What brings you down here? It can't be the beer." He gestured to the taps behind the bar. "Warm as piss."

The bartender came up, and Cal asked for the same as the priest. The bartender was from Lagos—he had come to the United States by way of London—and when he wasn't denouncing the British in a deep pidgin English, he sat at the far end of the bar reading the international papers.

"Hundreds of bars in the city and not a cold beer anywhere," said Father Nolan.

"I haven't seen you down here in years."

"Who told you I was here now?"

"The sexton at the Holy Cross. That your main gig?"

"No, no, not at all. The parish has been run ragged, not enough young men joining the priesthood, so the senior priests often have to do double duty at two or more other churches. I'm just blessed that I've been granted such a high order as the mother church of the Archdiocese. We'll get some new blood in soon, please God, and that will change."

When the Jameson and Extra Stout came, Cal sipped the whiskey slow, like the priest, and then drank from the bottle. They were both silent, the priest waiting and Cal letting the heat of the whiskey shimmer in his throat and head. *Like a song,* he thought, *like a song.* He cautioned himself to have no more than one and, smiling, turned to Father Nolan, who was watching him with interest.

"Tasted that good, did it?"

"It did, yeah. Was it that obvious?"

"I take it you've been dry for a while—that's a good thing, Cal. One day at a time is the best most of us can manage, and sometimes that's enough, that's all it needs to be."

"You mean for drunks."

"I mean for people like us."

Cal nodded, threw back the whiskey so that it swelled his cheeks. He put the glass on the bar and motioned for another. "I need to know something," he said, and he glanced at the priest. "Something about my father."

"Your father?" The priest looked down at the rim of his glass, tilted it so that the amber liquid moved back and forth.

"A boat came into the harbor last week. It was smuggling guns intended for Ireland. The guns are gone now and a lot of men are dead. I spoke with Sully and he said I should talk to you."

"He did, did he?"

"He said you and my father were both involved, deeply involved."

Two whiskeys came, but the priest continued to swirl what he had left. Cal watched him, and after a moment he put the whiskey back, smacked his lips, and set the almost-empty glass down softly on the bar.

"As a longshoreman, your father played a big part in getting weapons over to Ireland during the late twenties and early thirties. Everyone on the docks knew how it worked and that if there was a way to move freight, your father could get it done."

"I'm surprised he didn't work for Sully."

"Oh, I think Sully wanted him to. Your father could make contraband disappear"—Father Nolan looked at Cal and snapped his fingers—"like that.

"Your father was one of our top men before he came over, so he was, and for a while, it continued here."

Cal noted the way the priest had said *our* instead of *their*, and he considered the priest more intently, thinking, as he often did, how little he knew about people he'd spent a large part of his life around. "Even after he got into the politics?" he asked.

"Oh, that was a great boon when your father got on the city council and became a councilman for Ward Eight. A great boon."

"What happened?"

The priest shrugged and folded his paper slowly, as if he were putting the past together in his memory.

"What ever happens with things like this? You see a world of death and pain and you wake up out of the darkness. You decide you want no more part in it. You realize that by what you've done, you've put your soul at risk. You try to make amends. America changes you—America is always working at changing you—and you let it."

"Are you speaking about yourself?"

"I suppose I am."

"And my father?"

The priest harrumphed and shook his head disdainfully, sadly. "Your father was in it till the end."

Cal nodded. "That would be my old man, all right." He sipped slowly from the remaining whiskey and then the Extra Stout. Through the open doorway came the sounds of the subway rattling and squealing. He watched its movement by the shadows that trembled and shook beneath the elevated tracks. The cars passing through that dark latticework flared briefly with embers and sparks. A black woman with lacquered hair and long legs walked by the doorway, and one of the old-timers sitting by the entrance playfully called out to her. From other corners of the bar, the sound of laughter, belly-deep and jovial.

"Over the years, I've heard lots of things about my father," Cal said. "Everyone says he was a good man, but I know better. I know when they say *good*, they mean something else entirely."

Father Nolan remained silent.

"Would you call him good, Father?"

"Ah, Cal, are any of us good?"

"No, I don't suppose we are." Cal smiled bitterly and finished his whiskey. "I need to talk to one of them. Can you arrange that?"

Father Nolan clasped his hands together, rubbed them as if they were cold. His lips tightened. His fingers laced around the whiskey glass, and he held it so that the skin shone white at the knuckles.

"I know a man," he said, "and he might talk to you because I know him and he knew your father. They were both proficient at what they did. And this man still is. I'll see if I can set up a meeting. But in the meantime, you shouldn't be talking to anyone. As far as they're concerned, an informer's an informer. Their allegiance is to country—a united Ireland—and then to God."

"When could you set it up?"

"Two days should be enough time."

Cal nodded and rose, pushing back the bar stool.

"And Cal," the priest said, and he gently grasped Cal's arm. "Don't forget that to them, they're not in America. They're three thousand miles away but they're still home. This isn't about America. Don't forget that."

"Maybe it's time we reminded them," Cal said, and he rapped the bar with his knuckles. The sound of it was startling and bright, like nails being pounded into hard wood.

24

THE PACIFIC CLUB, COLUMBUS AVENUE, ROXBURY

SOME AFTERNOONS, THE stage of the Pacific Club was packed with musicians eager to burn off the slow hours of a lazy summer day. The players who had arrived too late sat at the tables and booths, waiting their turn. They sat impatiently and drank dime beers or bottles of tonic, and, lighting one cigarette after the other, they filled up the glass ashtrays before them. The ceiling fans were turned to their highest settings; they broke apart the smoke but didn't do much to the heat.

A soprano-sax player, Jimmy Rollins, called out to the owner of the club: "Hey, Moody, I feel a chill in the air. How about firing up that furnace." Moody responded with a dismissive shake of the head and went back to scrubbing down the bar top with wood soap, the pine scent both medicinal and heady.

Other than the musky stink of himself and the rest of the musicians onstage, Dante didn't smell much of anything. He sat behind the old, beaten-up piano and played with an intensity that he hadn't felt in quite some time. Some of the young players eyed him up and down, skeptical of a white guy leading the rhythm section. However, the old-timers knew him well, even treated him with a little extra care, knowing some of the tragic shit he'd gone through.

Maxwell Curtis was back from New York, brandishing that old trumpet that could sound like a broken heart or its complete opposite; somebody had once said it "screamed like a fat Harlem whore in heat." Louis Valentine showed up with his trombone. Dante hadn't seen him in well over a year. Louis had done some time up in Walpole for forging checks, and despite not playing for a while, he brought in some challenging edges, and the way he slid in and out of the rhythm kept Dante on his toes. Old Toad was there on drums, all five foot one of him, and occasionally, when he got tired, the old man allowed a teenager who everybody called Blue Hill Slim to take a seat behind the kit and try to keep up.

As the afternoon turned into early evening, a dozen other players switched in and out. Since Dante was the older of the two piano players, he sat through many renditions of Tin Pan Alley standards and some daring takes on popular songs from the war. On the few songs he didn't know, he pulled back and didn't try to showboat. But most of them, he played with vigor and soul. He hadn't had this much fun in years.

By the time six o'clock rolled around, he was dizzy from the heat, and his stomach growled with a raw, biting intensity that flared up even worse when he took a shot of rotgut whiskey from Old Toad's copper flask. After they went to town on a rendition of "Flying Home," they all decided it was time to take a break. Out in the back between a dumpster and stacks of wooden crates filled with empty Pepsi bottles, Dante shared a joint with Maxwell. The reefer sizzled in the humidity, and the bitter taste of it made Dante's throat sore, but going back inside, he was recharged for another set, his head light and his senses sharp.

Jimmy Rollins and Valentine helped Toad bring out the vibraphone that had been gathering dust in the storage room. Rumor had it that it once belonged to Lionel Hampton himself, but by the looks of it now, it was good for nothing but the trash heap. Toad wiped down the aluminum bars with a rag and then brandished a pair of soft wide mallets, the rounded ends a bright cardinal red. He went at it with an odd tenderness, striking the notes and letting them hum and resonate. The sound emitted by the instrument was almost saintly, reverent. Those talking in the booths and at the tables shut their mouths and watched the old man play. Slowly, those onstage joined in, and they toyed with the rhythm until it became a real song with its own melody. They stretched it for as long as it could go, and when it ended, a churchlike silence filled the room.

It was during this quiet moment that Dante sat back on the bench and finished the last of his drink. The bitterness of the quinine made his tongue feel puckered and dry.

A shaft of bright light came across the front of the club. Two women walked in and went to the bar. One was squat, thick-hipped, wearing a purple hat with a halo of peacock feathers. The other was slender and tall.

The owner, Moody, leaned on the bar reading the *Globe* and tugging away at his large half-bent pipe. The short woman offered her hand to Moody. Moody looked up and laughed, removed the pipe from his mouth, took her hand as though she were royalty, and kissed it. Then Moody said something to the slender woman, and she responded as if she were upset with him, but Dante could tell she was just playing around. She leaned over the bar and kissed the big man on the left cheek and then the right; she did it with the affected air of a European socialite. Dante squinted through the smoke, and he watched her come toward the stage. She stopped at one of the round tables, grabbed a book of matches and an ashtray.

Her shoulders were almost bare in a thin-strapped cotton dress, and she wore a pair of leather sandals. She was tall and lean with the muscles of a dancer. Her hair shone with a metallic gleam and was pulled back tightly and tied into a neat bun. She walked without seeming to be aware of her figure or the amount of bare skin she showed from her shoulders down to her long, finely sculpted legs. Besides the dress and the sandals, she wore nothing else. No makeup. No jewelry. Not even, from what Dante could tell, a bra.

Behind him, Maxwell teased his trumpet, blowing at it and clearing it of spit.

She looked up at the sound, saw Dante watching her, and smiled. His lips felt leaden but he managed a smile in return. He went to light a cigarette and pretended he was getting ready to play. His hands were shaking. He felt exposed, examined. She let her eyes linger, as if she were trying to locate his face somewhere in her memory; perhaps she had met him before.

Dante looked down, softly plinked the piano keys.

There was something about her that reminded him of his late wife, Margo, that natural beauty that was averse to gussying up like some forbidden, lustful idol. That was what Margo's sister, Sheila, did, and briefly he saw Sheila too—a woman who carried trouble with her, a woman who found comfort not in the company of a few women but in the company of many men.

Standing behind Dante, Maxwell leaned in and whispered, "I hear she likes them white, Cooper, but there's one thing you ought to know."

He turned, a bit dazed still. "What's that?"

"Guess who her cousin is."

"Who?"

She was standing at the bar, smoking a cigarette. The bartender, Bowie, was making her a drink.

"Big Moody himself."

"I never seen her before," Dante said.

"She moved up here from Baltimore."

"That's nice," he said, trying his best to sound like he didn't give a shit.

He and the band went into the song "My Melancholy Baby." Several chords in, Dante stumbled. As a result, the bass player floundered too. The drummer tried to fill in the hole but couldn't quite make it. Jimmy Rollins ran a finger across his throat. "Cut it," somebody hollered.

He could feel the woman's eyes on the stage watching him intensely, as if she were playing a game to see who could stare the longest without flinching. But when he looked over, he saw that her back was to the stage. Suddenly, the room seemed to be closing in on him. Maybe it was the reefer, he thought. It felt as if his senses were misfiring and dulled around the edges. He knew it was time to call it quits. He glanced at his watch and stood up from the bench.

The other piano player took his seat, and Dante patted him on the shoulder. He grabbed his hat and his smokes and stepped off the stage, walked through the club toward the bathrooms in front, nodding at Moody as he passed.

"Sounded like you were digging for clams there," Moody said, grinning.

His cousin stood at the bar and she turned to Dante. He felt helpless standing under her gaze. She too grinned. He tried to think of something witty to say but nothing came out.

As he stood at a urinal in the bathroom, the door opened. Maxwell walked up to the empty urinal next to him. He unzipped and grunted as he began to piss. Dante flushed and went to the sink.

"What's her name? Moody's cousin."

"Isabelle. I heard him call her Izzy. All I know is she's from Maryland, got no curves for a black woman, and she's living up on Mission Hill."

Dante turned on the faucet, cupped cold water in his hands, and splashed his face again and again.

Behind him, Maxwell kept on talking. "Just remember, Moody will eat you for breakfast you look at her the wrong way. He ain't got no daughter, so I'm sure he's going to treat her like one while she's here. That means you behave like she's a preacher's wife. Off-limits."

"I just asked who she was, that's all. I'm not going to jump her or anything. I know better."

"Do you?" Maxwell touched Dante on the shoulder with one hand while he zipped up his trousers with the other. "I'd say she's trouble, even though she don't want to be. What I gather is she needed to get away from Baltimore. You take that and you fill in the blanks."

Dante jangled the keys in his pocket to make sure they were still there. "Need a ride home?"

"I was just going to get on my knees and beg for that. Seriously, I'd appreciate it."

While Maxwell went to get his trumpet, Dante stood at the empty end of the bar near the exit. Moody and the short woman with the peacock hat had gone off somewhere. Bowie was still behind the bar, and another man had joined in Bowie and Isabelle's conversation. He was large and broad-shouldered, looking as if he'd just stepped off a plane from Miami with his tailored khaki slacks looped with a white leather belt and a bright turquoise shirt neatly tucked in at his wide waist. He leaned toward Isabelle, trying to make her laugh with some foolish story about visiting Baltimore. Dante expected her to turn around and offer him one last glance so that he'd know she still sensed his presence in the room, but when Maxwell came back and said he was ready, Dante reluctantly turned and walked toward the exit.

He held the door open for the old trumpeter and then followed him outside, where it felt considerably cooler despite the temperature holding steady in the nineties. A 1949 bright red Cadillac was parked in front of Dante's junk box. It looked as if it had just been spit-polished and waxed to a virginal shine. He knew that the car belonged to the well-dressed man now talking to Isabelle. He looked at his own car with its dents and rust and four mismatched tires. A weight pulled at his chest.

"Jesus H.!" Maxwell called out. "I ain't even got a license, Cooper, so don't take offense, but by the looks of it, this here old horse needs to be put out of its misery."

"Are you talking about the car or your own sorry ass?"

Maxwell laughed. "Fuck you, Cooper."

As Dante muscled the key into the lock of his apartment door, he could tell that something was wrong. He walked in and closed the door behind him. Afraid that he'd encounter something thrown on the floor, he stepped forward with staggered, uneven steps. He dragged a hand through the darkness and called out for Claudia and Maria.

There was no response.

From his left came a sudden movement. His eyes adjusted.

It was just the curtain shuddering from a dull breeze. From outside came little light and little sound too. It was as though the city held its breath.

He decided not to turn on any lights—if someone was there, he could use the darkness as a cover—but he feared he'd knock over a lamp or bruise his knee against some of the bulky furniture they'd acquired secondhand. He still didn't feel comfortable with the layout of the apartment, even though it was the place they'd called home for well over a year now.

He could hear the pipes in the apartment above; the tenant must have been taking a shower. The three bedroom doors were open. From Maria's room came a pale glow from the streetlight. He could see that her bed was empty. The bedsheets were rumpled and twisted, and one of her dolls peered out from the messy folds, its hair knotted and twisted like a madwoman's. Claudia's room was even darker, no light at all. He could smell a familiar odor lingering inside: the rotten cigarillos that Vinny smoked.

Footsteps from above sounded against loose floorboards. Standing in the hallway, Dante wondered if the tenants upstairs would hear if something bad happened. And if they did, would they do anything about it? Come downstairs and knock on the door, or call the police?

When the footsteps ceased and the quiet settled back in, Dante was able to hear something else. It was the sound of water dripping and it was coming from the kitchen.

The fridge door had been left open, and a rectangle of fluorescent light lay on the black-and-white-tiled floor. There was a puddle of milk, and something red was swirled into it, making it look pink. He knelt down on one knee, looked closer, and saw there was also broken glass.

He stood and reached to the wall, switched on the light. Beside the shattered glass of the milk bottle, small footprints in blood went across the kitchen and into the pantry. From inside came a child's whimpering.

He cautiously stepped into the pantry, reached up to the string and pulled it down. The light from the bare bulb blazed, leaving no shadows, and there, in its unflinching brightness, Maria sat and looked up at him like some savage child, her feet bare and the right one bleeding, the gash nearly two inches long.

"It's okay, love. I'm here now."

He knew what had happened. She had been alone and gotten thirsty. She went to the fridge for some milk and her hands couldn't fully grasp the bottle and it came crashing down. She'd probably panicked and tried to clean it up but she stepped in the puddle and a fang of glass sliced deep into her foot. Claudia hadn't been around to help her. Neither had he.

"It's okay, Maria. I'm here now," he repeated, softer this time.

Her eyes appeared swollen and bloodshot, and some dried snot flecked inside her nostrils. He knelt down and checked her foot, pressed at the wound. Maria screamed but she didn't cry. It would require stitches, and they might have to use a pair of tweezers to pull out fragments of glass.

"Don't worry, we'll get it all fixed up and as good as new."

She whimpered, wiped at her nose and mouth with her thin forearm.

He lifted her up, kissed her on the forehead, cradled her in his arms, and then brought her to the bath. Under cold water, he carefully rinsed her foot and asked her if it hurt, and she said no. "It hurt much more," she added.

"When was that, honey?" he asked. "Was it still light outside, or was it dark?"

"It just got dark."

"When I was a kid, if I got a little cut I'd cry for days. You're much braver than I was." He tried his best to be calming, but inside, a rage grew. It was the same story as before. Claudia had thought she could leave Maria alone again. Just one drink out, maybe two. Just a little alone time with Vinny.

With the wound dressed in gauze, he placed a sock over Maria's foot for good measure, changed her into a clean nightdress, and carried her outside. He would have to walk ten minutes to get to his car, and he started toward it. A cab was crossing over the road to make a three-point turn, and he stepped off the curb and called out, "Hey! Hold up!"

The yellow taxi pulled around on the empty street and came to a stop beside them.

"What's the trouble?" the cabbie asked.

"My daughter," he said, "she cut herself and I need to take her to the hospital."

"Mass General?"

"Yeah, that's the closest."

The cabbie eyed them suspiciously but then reached behind his seat and pulled up the door lock. "Is she going to be okay?"

"Yes. Yes, she is," Dante said.

In the backseat, with Maria on his lap, he fully registered what he'd said just a moment ago: *She's my daughter.*

He looked down at her face, at the nose that would develop a Romanesque sharpness, perhaps too big for her other features as a teenager but fitting just right once she became an adult; the lips that were Sheila's, the V of the upper lip pronounced and sharp, what some people called a cupid's bow; and the dark, troubled eyes—not Renza's, not Michael Foley's, but his own.

Maria smiled up at him, but the smile was pained and worried. "I'll be okay."

He felt his throat constrict and his heart hammer at his rib cage. He put a cigarette in his mouth but didn't light it. He felt utterly and completely helpless.

She's my daughter. The words went around and around and didn't stop until the cab pulled up at the entrance of the hospital.

"How much?" Dante asked.

The cabbie shook his head. "Don't worry about it. I have two daughters myself. I know how it is."

25

BECAUSE THERE WAS little food in the fridge, Dante decided that he'd take Maria out for breakfast. He couldn't remember the last time he'd gone to the grocery and filled the shelves, icebox, and pantry.

Both he and Maria had slept poorly—they hadn't left Mass General until midnight. The emergency room had been full of people waiting to see the two doctors on shift. There was a college-age kid who had been hit with a bottle, and his inebriated buddy sat beside him and pressed what had once been a white towel against his friend's bleeding face. There was a frail Chinese woman who had fallen down and apparently broken her arm. Melodious groans came from her toothless, gummy mouth while, slumped beside her, her husband napped with his chin down, oblivious to all the noise. In the same row of wooden chairs, an obese man complained that he was having a heart attack, and when he wasn't cursing the nurses who passed by him without a glance, he had his face buried in his hands and sobbed like a child.

Eventually a nurse came and told Dante and Maria to follow her. She took them to a room where the doctor was waiting. The doctor had bright, young eyes but the rest of him appeared cadaverous, as though the death and illness surrounding him on a daily basis had taken its toll. With long, thin fingers that reminded Dante of a tarantula, the man treated Maria with such indifference, he might as well have been pruning a plant. But the doctor did his job—he cleaned the wound of chipped glass and, with a steady hand, wove a thick black thread in and out of her iodine-stained skin, closing the gash with seven stitches. Through it all, Dante held Maria's hand, telling her to squeeze tight and look at him, not at her foot. Not one tear had rolled out of her eyes, and Dante couldn't quite put into words why, but her bravery broke his heart, so much so that he had to look away from her penetrating gaze.

Back at the apartment, Maria couldn't fall asleep, and Dante read to her for an hour, first a story from *Weird Tales* about a mummy's curse wreaking havoc on a group of archaeologists, and then part of a comic. When she was finally out, he went into the living room, expecting Claudia to come in at any minute. But she never did, and he woke up curled on the couch with the morning sun coming through the open window, the slightest breeze touching the curtain and giving him hope that today might be cooler than yesterday.

Now, in the front foyer of the apartment building, Dante wrestled with the old secondhand stroller that was supposed to fold out. There was rust covering the joints, and he hunched over it and pulled at the handles so hard that one of the plastic wheels jostled out of its hold and clattered onto the tiled floor. He slammed it back in with the heel of his hand and finally extended the cheap stroller so all four wheels touched the ground.

"C'mon, get in."

Maria was leaning on the wall under the mailboxes, and, with her arms crossed over her chest, she shook her head no.

"I know you're a big girl, but because of your foot you can't be walking."

"Horsey ride," she said.

"No horsey ride. My back can't take it, and you're too big for it anyway." He reached out his hand. "C'mon, don't be a brat now."

Stinking of aftershave and pomade, a man leaving for work opened the inner door, said, "Excuse me," and eyed Dante standing beside the wreck of a stroller. Dante's patience was stretched thin already, and he stared back until the man left, letting the front door slam shut behind him.

"We don't have all day," Dante said, and she finally relented. He helped her into the seat. When she leaned back, her shoulders were pinched by the two metal bars that led up to the curved handles. The canvas material bowed under her weight.

"Where we going?" she asked, even though he'd told her twice already.

"To see Auntie at work and get you some pancakes."

They crossed out of the North End toward Causeway Street. It was still early in the morning, yet the sunlight was as harsh and bright as if it were high noon. The lack of food in his stomach and the lack of sleep made all the edges of the city bleach and blur in the glare. Everything looked like it did on a television set with the tint turned all the way up.

Pedestrians drifted by them on the sidewalk, turning toward them with apparent amusement. Perhaps it was the loud clacking from the carriage wheels. Or how Maria was too large for the seat. Or maybe it was Dante's downtrodden appearance as he pushed her along, a cigarette hanging loosely from his lips and his wardrobe not much finer than a bum's down at the Pine Street Inn.

"Don't let your feet hit the ground," he said to Maria, who kicked her legs up and then lowered them dangerously close to the concrete. Again, she was testing him.

They passed under the elevated tracks that led from North Station to the Lechmere stop. Shafts of dirty sunlight came through the tracks and girders and lit the street in strips, giving Dante the sensation that they were descending underground and witnessing the last of the outside world before darkness completely took them. The windows of the stores and shops were opaque, and trying to see inside as he passed, Dante witnessed his own greasy silhouette in reflection. A man with a horribly thin face and yellow, syphilitic eyes stood inside a doorway. He whistled through his teeth, raised a hand, and waved for Dante to stop. "Hey, buddy, come here. I need to ask you a question."

Above, a train pulled into the station with a thunderous roar, and the conductor announced the stop but the speaker on the platform was so damaged that the words were lost in feedback. As the train moved out, metal tearing against metal, Maria put her hands over her ears and pressed to quell the noise. Cars honked at one another, the sounds of their horns echoing in the air heavy with exhaust.

There was a hump of a homeless man curled up on the sidewalk on a piece of cardboard, his face black with beard and a foul smell coming off of him. Maria turned her head and stared at the bum as Dante maneuvered the carriage closer to the curb. A small flock of pigeons shot up from the gutter, their plumage the same color of the soiled concrete, and flew up to the shit-caked rafters under the rail. Maria watched their ascent, and then she started to clap, her applause muted by all the noise around them.

Back out in the sunlight, Dante winced. A block down, he spotted the sign of the diner Claudia worked at, the Hopscotch.

An older woman held the door open for them, and as he moved forward, the wheels locked up. He lifted the stroller with Maria inside it and settled it down in the alcove next to a gumball machine filmed over with dust. The air was thick with cigarette smoke, and the smell of burned bacon dimmed his appetite.

There were two waitresses weaving among the booths along the wall and the ten tables that were squared up on the linoleum floor. They were seated right away, but they waited for five minutes before someone came to take their order.

"So what'll it be for the young lady? Apple or orange?"

"Orange, please. And coffee for me."

The waitress's hair was blue-black and it was tightly knotted in the back. She listed the specials and Dante couldn't help but notice a cold sore, the size of a raspberry, on the side of her mouth, poorly veiled by the lipstick she wore heavily. He lost his appetite completely but he ordered scrambled eggs and rye toast for himself and blueberry pancakes for Maria. He watched her walk away, the blue skirt wrinkled and her panty hose loose behind the knee, as if they were two sizes too large. Glancing up, he expected to see Claudia coming out of the kitchen.

And maybe this is her now, he thought as a waitress came through the doors, but when she raised her head, he saw a pale-skinned girl barely eighteen tying a checkered apron around her waist.

Where the fuck is Claudia?

In the wooden kid's chair, Maria was restless, taking her fork and stabbing at the place mat. He told her to simmer down but she paid no attention. Funny how the stroller was too small for her but the chair she was sitting in was too big. No wonder she was in such an awful mood; nothing seemed to fit her right.

"What do you want to do today?" he asked.

"Nothing." She shook her head and he could tell that boredom was going to lead to one of her tantrums. He reached into his pocket and found the worn nub of a pencil. He handed it to her, and, still frowning, she started doodling on the paper place mat. He lit a cigarette, tugged at it with deep breaths. Ash flaked down to the table and he wiped at it with the side of his hand.

"I'll be right back," he said. "You stay put, hear me? Don't get out of the chair."

He followed the waitress with the blue-black hair and tapped her on the shoulder before she went through the swinging door into the kitchen. "Excuse me, miss."

"Yeah?"

"Claudia Cooper works here, right?"

"Yeah, she does. Or *did*, I should say."

"Did?"

"Claudia hasn't been in all week. Didn't even give notice or nothing. Just walked out and didn't come back."

"Really?"

"Yeah, really. Why you looking for her? She in trouble?"

"No, she's not in any trouble. But you see her, let her know her brother was looking for her."

When he returned to the table, he saw that Maria had knocked over her glass. The orange juice pooled on the tablecloth and dripped onto the floor. He pulled out napkins from the dispenser and tried mopping up the juice, but it only seemed to make the mess worse.

Dante looked toward the kitchen, and through the ticket window he saw one of the cooks staring at him. When the cook noticed him looking back, he quickly returned his attention to putting the finishing touches on a plate for pickup. In that moment, Dante knew that the waitress had told everybody that he was looking for Claudia.

Five minutes later, the food arrived. Dante got out of his seat and cut up Maria's pancakes, took the syrup and poured it on until she cried, "Too much!" He kissed her on the top of her head, returned to his seat, lit another cigarette, and ignored the rubbery-looking eggs and the burned toast on his plate. The coffee was weak, as if they had used yesterday's grounds, but he drank it anyway. The waitress came and put down the bill. He did his best not to look at the cold sore on her lip.

"Not hungry?" she asked. "Our food ain't *that* bad."

Dante shook his head and smiled. "I lost my appetite."

Back on the sidewalk, Dante tried to fold out the carriage but it wouldn't budge. He got down on his knees, laid it on its side, and pulled at the handle.

"Piece of shit!"

As soon as he said it, the handle snapped off at the point where the rust was thickest. Standing straight, he picked the carriage up and tried to right it, but it leaned at an angle. It was useless now, junk.

Standing a few feet away, Maria was laughing, but he found nothing funny about it. There was a line of trash cans against the building. He grabbed the stroller, swung it high, and tossed it. It spun in the air and crashed against the barrels, knocking over one of them, its lid popping off and clattering like the cymbal from a drum kit. A flurry of flies shot up from the stinking trash. A rat scurried out toward the shadows under the elevated tracks.

"Time to get on the horse," he said. He knelt down so Maria could crawl onto his back, and when he stood up, he felt a knuckle of pain knock at the base of his spine. Her little hands, sticky from the syrup, pulled at his neck.

And they were off, back under the elevated tracks, dodging the bum laid out on the sidewalk, going past the pigeons flapping their filthy wings, past the junkie swaying in the doorway like some destitute marionette, and then out into the sunlight on the other side, that much closer to home.

He jostled her up higher and told her to hold on to his shoulders and not let go.

"The Apache are right on our tail and they're shooting arrows by the hundreds. They want their scalps back and they'll string us up for the vultures if they catch us." He neighed like a horse and she kicked at his hip to propel him forward. Both of them were laughing, and it lasted all the way back to their neighborhood.

When they got back to the apartment, he was drenched in sweat, lungs gasping for air. She needed a bath, so he ran the water in the tub, sat Maria down on the toilet seat and checked the wrappings on her foot. Dried blood appeared on the gauze like a blot of red ink. He'd have to clean it up again. "I'll be right back," he said.

Claudia's bedroom door was partially open and he tried to remember if it had been opened or closed before they'd left for breakfast. Her dresser had two of its drawers halfway pulled out. Some clothes were scattered about her unmade bed. It was obvious she had been in a hurry.

In the kitchen, he fired up the burner, filled the kettle, and poured coffee grounds into the press. A pack of smokes was on the kitchen table and he recognized they weren't his. Reaching for them, he saw the note that had been left there.

Dante, I'm sorry about this but I had to get away for a while. Vinny and I are heading to the Cape for a few days, maybe a week. There are lots of things to talk about when I get back. I spoke to Mrs. Berardi just now. She says she'll help watch Maria when you're gone at work. Sorry again. Love you. —Claudia

On the side of the note, somebody had sloppily drawn a sad face, two

*X*s for eyes and a downturned frown. And next to that was a crooked heart with an arrow stabbed through it and the words *Love you too.*

Dante knew that it wasn't Claudia who had drawn the face and the heart and written *Love you too.* It had to be Vinny who had doodled on the note while Claudia was in her bedroom packing up her suitcase. Dante crumpled up the piece of paper and dropped it back on the table. In his head, he could see the two of them in a car right now traveling down Route 6 over the Sagamore Bridge to the Cape, not a care in the world. As he lit a cigarette, he heard Maria cry out for him, suddenly and with an urgency that could only mean she was in pain.

In the bathroom, she stood beside the claw-foot tub and pointed to the water and all the steam coming off it. He turned the brass knob the other way, and the tap stopped running, and he reached inside to pull out the plug but reared back quickly and shook his hand. The water was scalding. He hurried over to the sink and held his hand under the faucet, letting the cold numb the pain.

"I'll fix it," Maria said. And on her dirty face, dried syrup glistening along her cheeks, a look of worry took hold. "Let me fix it."

"It's okay, love. It's fine."

His heart was breaking again, just like it had when he was with her in the emergency room, but as he kept on talking, he felt a desperation tear into him and open the hole so wide that he was afraid something would get inside that he wouldn't be able to get rid of.

"I got an idea. Just me and you, just the two of us, we'll get dressed nice and go see the matinee. There's one movie that just came out about giant monster ants, called *Them.* How about that? Then, later, a sundae at Brigham's. We'll get jimmies, caramel, hot fudge, the works—"

"Vinny says ice cream is bad for me. Vinny says my teeth will fall out."

"What does Vinny know about anything?" Dante took a deep breath and sighed, grabbed a towel and dried his hands, then picked Maria up, embraced her, and brought her out to the kitchen, where the kettle whistled with a horrible, foreboding pitch.

26

CAL HADN'T TENDED his father's grave in over a dozen years, but someone—perhaps a family member of someone in a nearby grave who'd been embarrassed or ashamed by the state of the plot—had taken it upon himself to cut the grass, pull the weeds, occasionally place a potted flower before the stone, and, on St. Patrick's Day, lay a wreath of shamrock there. Cal knew these things because, though he'd convinced himself that he didn't care, he often stopped by to look at the stone, consider his father's life, and wonder about the man. He didn't talk and he didn't pray the way he often saw others do at the graves; he merely looked and thought and wondered, as if somehow, one day, he might be granted the answers to his questions, as if his father might rear up out of the grave and say, *All right, now it's time, a mhac, come with me and I'll tell you what you want to know, what it is you're looking for.*

He didn't talk and he didn't pray, not as he did at Lynne's grave, and he was thankful that they were in separate parts of the cemetery—his father on the bank beyond the cedars that sloped to the broad, almost regal width of the Neponset before it became a trickle and leaked defeated into the harbor and the sea; Lynne on the other side of the train tracks that bisected the grounds and along one of the paths that wound through small undulating knolls filled with flowers and copses of hardwoods, closer to the chapel.

He stood at his father's grave—his funeral, the plot, and the stone of Connemara marble had been paid for by his mother with most of the funds from his father's pension and donations from various unions about the city. The grass had been cut and was brown, scorched from the sun. Blackened and withered flowers stood in front of the headstone; Cal couldn't even tell what they were. Hornets buzzed the air, savagely going after the apples that had fallen from the trees and were rotting sweetly on the ground. Crickets and cicadas and other flying things thrummed and pulsed electrically in the denser foliage.

"What secrets did you keep? You bastard," Cal said aloud. He sighed and stared about him.

The Old Colony Railroad trolley from Ashmont rumbled through the cemetery, just out of sight beyond the rolling knolls of the grounds. Cal watched an old man in a decrepit rowboat pulling up traps on the far bank of the river. Tree branches, granting Cal welcome shade from the sun, stirred above, making a sloughing sound as they rubbed together gently.

Father Nolan strode up the path between the greenhouse and the stables coming from the riverside, having, Cal guessed, walked along the Neponset from St. Gregory's and Lower Mills Falls. He looked as strong and lean as ever, his stride that of an ex-soldier, quick and purposeful, and his white hair slicked back, but to Cal, he seemed older somehow, a barely perceptible weariness to his face and as if he were pulling his shoulders in against some deep, internal cold. Sweat trickled down Cal's spine. He wiped at his brow and waved and then stepped back into the shade beneath the cedars, and Father Nolan met him there.

"I spoke to your man and he's agreed to a meeting at St. Anthony's shrine on Tuesday evening at seven, after confession and vespers."

"Why the church?"

"He didn't tell me why and I didn't ask—neutral ground, I suppose.

He's a churchgoing man, a God-fearing man. He'll respect the sanctity of the church."

"How will I recognize him?"

"He'll be downstairs by the votives. He's a tall, thin fellow. He'll be wearing a Pioneer pin on his lapel. You'll know his look from your own history, from the war. You can't mistake it."

The priest lit a cigarette and Cal was surprised to see the shakiness in his hands as he brought it to his lips and deeply inhaled.

"It's like a black stain upon all of us, Cal," Father Nolan said, smoke streaming from his nostrils. "It's as if something dark touched your soul and not even the light of God can bring it back. Do you believe that? Sadly, God forgive my soul, at times I do. It's my own weakness, my own lack of faith, perhaps. My own soul is tarnished the same way. There's a place there that even God has no access to, no ability to mend. I have to live with that—we all have our own secret burdens—just as you have to live with those things from your past."

He glanced at the grave and then toward the river where the sun struck the water in dappled lances, making it seem as if it had more movement than it did. "Hopefully you'll get the information you need and then you can put it to rest."

"You make it sound simple, Father. I only wish it were that way."

"God help us, Cal, go easy. This is all I could do, and dear God, I wish I hadn't done it at all. I don't know what is the right thing any-more. You don't have to meet with him, you know. It can end right here"—and he glanced to the headstones that stretched down to the river—"before your father's grave."

"You know I can't do that, Father."

"Then God be with you, Cal." The priest put out his hand and Cal shook it.

"And you, Father. Thank you." For a moment they regarded each other and Cal thought Father Nolan might say something more, but then the man nodded serenely, an acceptance, perhaps of things no longer in his control. He turned away and then paused. The light through the swaying branches dappled his black shirt, blazed in his white hair. He looked at Cal and forced a smile. "I'd better see you in Mass after this," he said, and he strode off.

Cal watched him make his way to the arboretum and the cemetery greenhouse and then take the lane to the towpath and the river. He wondered at what risk to himself the priest had arranged the meeting and if that assignation had brought back dark memories from his past that he'd worked so hard to keep hidden and tamped down. Cal had perhaps asked for too much from him, but he needed to talk to this man who'd known his father and who might allow him and Dante a particular access to de Burgh's world and to the IRA in Boston.

Nothing had changed, and neither had he, Lynne would have said. But she would have been wrong—he almost said it aloud: *You're wrong, Lynne.* He knew that he had only to convince her and, in so doing, he might convince himself. He walked the winding path to her grave, away from the river, and at the watering station he filled a plastic pitcher and watered the perennials he'd planted before the stone. The ground took the water quickly, and he refilled the pitcher and did it again. He said nothing for fear that the guilt he felt for his past actions and the actions yet to come were a betrayal of the promise he'd made to her and for fear that if he talked, he'd hear her voice coming to him in response. So he remained quiet—the first time since her death that he'd failed to speak to her—until, with lowered head, he said, "I love you," and walked back to the entrance and Cedar Grove Station.

27

CHELSEA

Evening and the sun just fading over the city rooftops, beyond the drawbridges and shipping cranes, slipping down into the west. In Martin Butler's kitchen there was a general air of jubilation, the type that comes after a hard workday in the summer. He had been playing the accordion for his brother and Donal when some of the neighbors stopped in, as had Father Langton from the East Boston Parish of the Holy Name. There was Michael Michalczyk and his wife and two day laborers who'd just come with their father from a meeting at the Polish American Political Club on Broadway.

The woman wore a babushka around her head even though she was only in her thirties, but once the music started playing and her husband pulled her to her feet, she loosed the knot under her chin and let the headscarf fly off as he spun her around, laughing, and the other men in the room clapped their hands and stomped their feet. Martin looked at his brother, who sat with his eyes closed, the hair plastered to his damp forehead and the veins rigid in his forearms as he clenched and unclenched his fists—Martin knew this was a sign of his enjoyment and smiled as he played.

The sound of his playing drifted from the windows on the heavy night air and down the street, pressing back the sounds of the cars thrumming over the Mystic River Bridge—a ceaseless vibration like the electricity pulsing through the overhead wires and the insects buzzing in the trees on Admirals Hill, always rising in pitch at the onset of thunder and lightning and only quieting when the air cooled.

The priest had imbibed a small glass of brandy, and his cheeks sparked red. Tea was laid out on the counter as well as some bottles of porter and beer. The older Pole brought out his spoons and played them on the knees of his paint-spattered work pants and everyone laughed when he completed a rill of percussion, slapping the spoons off his thighs, that sent Martin playing faster on the accordion.

"Oh, you ol' devil, you!" he hollered, and his fingers danced across the mother-of-pearl keys and he worked the bellows so that sweat shone on his forehead.

A knock came at the back door, reverberating softly in the hallway, and through his exertions, Martin looked at the clock above the sink, then glanced at Donal and nodded.

Donal closed the kitchen door behind him, stepped into the hallway, and went to the back door, where the streetlights shone through the window and illuminated the silhouettes of four men outside. He opened the door and stepped out onto the porch and into the backyard, where the men stood in the shadows.

"Donal," their leader said.

Donal took a look at each of the men. He hadn't been told who was coming, but he knew Kieran Fitzgerald and the slim, light-haired fellow at the back, Bobby Myles. The other two were strangers to him.

"Kieran," he said. "How was the ride across?"

"A right bitch, that's what it was," said Fitzgerald. "The boat tossed us about so much I didn't know what was up and what was down, and Egan on the rail throwing up the entire time. His stomach still isn't right."

"Ah, go mind your own stomach, you," the one called Egan said. "My stomach's made of cast iron, so."

"And you, Bobby," Donal said, "you still have it in you? I didn't think they'd send you, not after what happened."

"I'm here, aren't I? They wouldn't send me if I didn't have it in me."

Donal nodded. "Are the lodgings suitable?"

The men grunted their assent.

"I'm assuming O'Flaherty gave you the locale to find the second car and the guns. Any difficulties?"

"No difficulties. The driving on these roads is another thing." Fitzgerald gestured toward Bobby with his head. "Our driver is still getting the hang of it."

"I'll be able to drive these roads with my eyes closed in no time. That's not a problem."

"Good. If there's anything else you need, per Mr. de Burgh, you're just to ask."

"The cargo," Fitzgerald said, "is it safe?"

"It is. And it'll be on its way soon. Mr. de Burgh just wants to make sure everything is in order before it's sent."

Fitzgerald stared up at Donal and scratched absently at the stubble on his cheeks. Farther down the side of the house, a slant of light from the kitchen sliced out into the night. It arced over two trash barrels and showed the withered grass and weeds heaving up from the dirt. The sound of an accordion came to them along with a fine voice singing the plaintive "Glen of Aherlow" and then another voice joined in, rougher, gravelly, but filled with passion.

"Donal," Fitzgerald said. "We're here with orders. We're not concerned with what de Burgh wants or doesn't want, we're concerned only with what he does. Do I make myself clear?"

Donal looked at him and let the stillness hold for a moment before speaking. In that tension, the sound of the music and the cars upon the bridge above them seemed to ebb, like a radio being turned down, as if the space before them had suddenly become larger and more expansive than the world beyond. "You've only just arrived," he said. "Don't presume to think you know a thing about what's going on here. Your orders are your orders, but the last time I checked that didn't include a charge to get the cargo home. If you want to take that on as well, even though you know no one here, we can contact the man back home. I'll be glad to wash my hands of it." He turned and stepped onto the porch.

"All I'm saying is that they don't like this situation being left in the hands of Americans."

"Americans?" Donal smiled coldly. The Fáinne and the Pioneer medal on his lapel glinted for a moment as he squared his body. He bent his head slightly, listening to the melody from the kitchen, and then said, "You must all be tired. You'll need to get your bearings and your feet under you, and then we can talk some more." He put his hand on the door and then looked back at them standing there. They could see only the pale gleam of his face with all of its narrow, hardened angles. "Go on now and get some rest," he said. "You're going to need it."

The four of them started to make their way out, but then Bobby stopped and said he was going back to the yard to relieve himself. Driving these Boston streets with a full bladder would be an unwise decision, and as they were bound to get lost again, he thought it would be best to relieve himself right away instead of holding it in and suffering through one wrong turn after another.

He moved through the weedy backyard, unclasped his trousers, and did his business, hearing the din of the music as it rose and swelled from the kitchen. At the window, the warm light framed the scene as if it were a living painting, and it was a strange sensation to Bobby once he realized that they were completely unaware of his gaze. He felt that feathery twinge of homesickness tickle his throat, and he swallowed with regret that he couldn't join these people, share a pint, and play just one song.

Myles noticed they were all celebrating except for one. He sat just outside the circle, settled on a chair lower than the others. There was an odd stillness to his limbs, and he was canted slightly to the side, perhaps from too much drink. It took Bobby a moment to see that the man sat in a wheelchair.

Bobby fastened his pants and stepped closer to the window, and he could see that below the man's combed-flat hair, a bright scar knotted along his temple and down to his jaw. His eyes were closed and dark with shadow, and his mouth was partly agape, one side weighed down as though by the gravity of a stroke. His clutching the armrests of his wheelchair was the only appearance of life. It was clear that he was the victim of some manner of trauma, and most likely that scar told the story of a horrible accident.

The song ended. One of the men left the kitchen. Another grabbed a bottle from the icebox. The accordion player, broad-shouldered and with his sleeves neatly rolled up on wide forearms, stood. He placed the instrument on the seat and went to the wheelchair, put his hand on the man's head and stroked his hair. The wheelchair-bound man didn't show any reaction whatsoever but there was something brotherly about the gesture, and in another time, another place, Bobby would have seen it as a special moment. But then the accordion player squinted and leaned forward to look out the window into the darkness, his mouth set in a grim line, and Bobby could tell his eyes were focused right on him—somehow the man could see him out here; he knew he was being watched. And then Bobby recognized the man's face. A car horn blared from the front of the house—most likely Fitzgerald, always impatient. Bobby hurried to the car, but even though he was away from the window, he still had the sense that Martin Butler's eyes were following him every step of the way.

28

L STREET, SOUTH BOSTON

THE WEATHERMAN ON the radio, Don Kent, had promised rain, at least enough to bring the temps down to the low nineties, but by midafternoon Dante knew there would be no showers, not even a sprinkle. The WBZ meteorologist had been predicting relief for days now, but it never came. He'd be better off setting the odds on the dog races at Wonderland than soothsaying the weather. And with Kent's batting average no better than Eddie Joost's—who had hit a paltry .185 for the 1943 Boston Braves—every New Englander was probably crying for the weatherman's head on a platter.

Kent's voice came from the transistor radio, low and muddied by the static. The bartender limped out from the shadows by the kitchen and turned the radio off. The silence in the place was heavy with a dreadful boredom, and Dante shifted restlessly in his seat because of it. With empty stools beside him, he looked at the window and saw the swath of radiant light cutting across the dark oak bar. The only other patron was a disheveled old man, the sunlight at his back inflaming the wild coils of his white hair. The man's face was blustered and ruddy, and every time Dante made eye contact, the man smiled at him as if he were in possession of the answer to some great riddle.

The pub was called the Castlebar Inn, and it belonged to a turn-of-the-century building that had apartments on the second and third floors that were usually rented out to Irishmen just off the boat and looking for work. It was a place, according to Owen, where not every Irishman would be welcome. Here the Galway caretakers would scope each new arrival's accent right away—if a man was from Dublin or Cork, he didn't stand much of a chance—and if it matched with the last name given, then he would be taken in with some semblance of warmth and brotherhood. The Irishman could get a loan to get him on his feet, a loan to be paid back with significant interest once work came in. Plus there'd be chipped beef and beans and gritty black tea from the closet-size kitchen every morning, just enough to fill the hole and get the blood pumping.

Owen had told Cal that the Castlebar Inn, one of the many bars scattered across the grid of South Boston, would be a good place to check out, and this morning, Dante had taken the train to Broadway and walked the half a mile to meet Cal here. Cal's plan was they'd keep an ear open for any conversations that stirred their curiosity, asking questions when the opportunity arose. Earlier today, there had been nothing but small talk about the weather and chatter about this bloke or that no-good troublemaker or how that piece of shit owed a fin and had given every excuse in the book not to pay it back.

An hour and a half ago, Cal had left the bar and said he had something to do. Dante imagined him in his car traveling the roads, looking at closed doors and quiet storefronts along Dudley Square, cutting through the Polish Triangle, across downtown, to the waterfront and the fish piers, where he'd watch the workers gut and clean their catches for the day. Then he'd head to Savin Hill, where he had once lived with Lynne, and walk along the shore of Malibu Beach where stranded jellyfish lay rotting and stinking in the sand at low tide. After that, he'd get back into his Fleetline and roll through the Avenue all the way to South Boston. That was Cal. Never an idle thinker, and rarely able to sit still.

Dante yawned, and his whole body twitched as the air escaped him. The cigarette slipped from his fingers and scarred the wood black. He picked it up and pressed it down into an ashtray crowded with spent filters and crushed ends.

He had read through the paper twice already. And now he eyed the comics page for the third time—with extra attention to Brenda Starr and how she was wearing one of those fashionable bullet bras that he'd seen models in magazine ads wear under tight wool sweaters, the kind that pushed out their breasts as if they were antiaircraft guns aboard the USS *Iowa.*

Again, he read over Li'l Abner, that little prick Dennis the Menace, and a new strip about a giant dog called Marmaduke. And then he was back at the box scores for yesterday's games, the numbers and names indistinct.

There was nothing left to look at in the papers but the obituaries. The beer was making the small print blur. Dante pressed a stiff finger against the paper and ran it down over the names that sounded Irish.

Cleland. Connelly. Flynn. Hines. Lonergan. Morrison. O'Casey. O'Rourke. Sullivan.

Funny how some of the death notices sounded identical, as if the obituary editor at the *Herald* had used the same copy and simply changed the names of the dearly departed. Six men were to be buried back in Ireland, but the obits didn't say where. Usually the newspapers printed that information—the Irish paid particular attention to what town or region one was from and even more to the location of one's final resting place.

He pressed his finger harder into the page and read some of the obits again. Six of the bodies were being held at two different O'Flaherty's Funeral Homes and would remain there until they were shipped out. That was odd enough, but there was something else wrong, although he couldn't quite pin it down. He closed the paper and folded it. *Flynn.* The name sounded familiar. Why?

"Fucking Irish," Dante said under his breath, and he raised his pint glass and drank down half his beer.

The old man had heard him, and he raised his own beer glass in salute and grinned in that deranged way, the halo of dirty light around his head appearing to scintillate even more.

With his pint now polished off, the man moved painfully from his stool and out through the front door he went.

The door closed and then rattled as it opened again.

A construction worker came in and sat two stools down from Dante. The man's skin was sunburned, and he wore the look of the overworked and underpaid. The stink of oil was heavy on his clothes, and the dirt-encrusted knuckles on his left hand were bleeding. He didn't seem to care. He lit a cigarette and sucked on it loudly, the gray smoke funneling out of his nostrils like the exhaust from an old coal-powered train.

The worker had a whiskey and two beers in the time it took Dante to reread the front page of the *Herald*. When he left, it was just Dante at the bar again. He contemplated leaving as well—Cal could wander around the city all he fucking wanted. He drank down his beer and waited for the bartender, a cockeyed man who hunched over as if years of hard labor had contorted his spine and permanently twisted his gait.

"Another one?" he asked.

"No," Dante said. "I'll pay out."

"Buck fifty then."

Dante reached for his wallet.

The stool next to him scraped the floorboards.

"So what's happening in the world?" Cal asked, and pointed to the newspaper.

"Not much. That anti-Commie board is trying to take away little kids' horror comics. They say they're too violent and will turn them into juvenile thugs. Then there's the Red hunt in Hollywood, the heat wave, the Sox taking another loss by six, and an article about the Cuban narcotics trade."

"That's it?"

"And Brenda Starr's tits just keep getting bigger."

"Jesus, you must be bored out of your fucking mind."

"You could say that. Anything on your end?"

"No, it's quiet out there. Too quiet."

When the clock by the cash register flipped to four o'clock, a new bartender came on shift. Dante got his attention and asked for two Jamesons. They came in glasses still warm from the sink, and a faint soapy taste lingered after he sucked the shot down.

"You ain't going to drink it?" Dante nodded to Cal's untouched whiskey.

"Maybe in a bit," Cal said. "You hungry?"

"Not really. Soon, though." Dante got up from the stool and went to the men's room in the back.

"A lot of Irish wakes next week," Dante said matter-of-factly when he returned.

"Yeah?"

"Six of them."

"What are you talking about?"

Dante pointed his thumb at the newspaper. "In the obituaries, there are half a dozen funerals, one after the other. And all of them are getting shipped back home to Ireland."

Cal lit a cigarette and paused. "Doesn't sound that odd to me."

"But these are all at O'Flaherty's, in Dorchester and Southie. There must be more Irish-owned funeral homes in this city, no? Here, take a look."

Dante slid the newspaper across the bar. Ash from his cigarette crumbled off and dusted the pages. He leaned in and lowered his voice. "Maybe this is something we should look into."

"I'd say it's just coincidence."

"It can't be coincidence." Dante slurred the last word. The beers he'd drunk earlier in the afternoon were getting to him. He had fed Maria this morning but forgotten to feed himself. He warned himself to slow it down. "Flynn? Connelly? Those names sound familiar?"

"Wait a minute." Cal's eyes flitted over the page. "People would notice something like this."

"Perhaps people just check out the names in the obituaries. Maybe they don't waste their time reading each one."

"You're wrong. Most Irish do. My father would get the paper and read them before anything else, even the headlines. And I know my fair share of people who do the same thing."

Cal's hand crept along the bar toward the shot glass of whiskey, which glistened in the afternoon sunlight like some kind of caramel-colored gemstone. Cal lifted it and held it still, perhaps questioning if it was worth it, especially at this time of day, but he swallowed the shot and winced, and Dante knew that Cal had instantly felt its effect winding through his system. He wiped at his mouth with his knuckles and then smiled.

"When I was young, my father dragged me to every funeral from Mission Hill to West Roxbury. Wherever it was, all those funeral homes looked the same to me. The same white paint on the outside, and inside the same crimson carpets lining each and every room. And the same smell too. All those flowers surrounding the dead but not doing shit to cover up the fact that they were rotting away. Jesus, even when I was a kid, the dead all looked the same to me."

The new bartender was at the taps filling a glass. The Pickwick tap sputtered with foam and made a strangled, hissing noise.

"But one place that stood out was O'Flaherty's. I remember my dad would sometimes take me to these even when there wasn't a funeral going on."

Cal paused. "Flynn. Cleland. Those are names of the victims. Jesus. They're all getting shipped back together, aren't they?"

29

NOT EVEN IN America for a full twenty-four hours, Bobby Myles sat in a small, square boardinghouse room with the weary desperation of a prisoner stuck inside his cell. Across from him there was a sink, discolored with rust, and its tap constantly dripped no matter how hard he tightened the ivory handle. Yellowed by decades of cigarette smoke, a length of wallpaper was curling away from the corner of the wall, the glue once binding it now pasty and smelling of mildew. On the bedside table there was a lamp that didn't work and a vase that held dead flowers, the water at the bottom tea-colored and speckled white with mold. And worst of all, the cot mattress was festering with fleas, so much so that last night he'd slept on the floor with his jacket folded into a pillow. That he'd managed to get even a couple of hours of sleep amazed him.

Scratching at the bites on his arm, Bobby decided he couldn't stand the place much longer—the rotten smell from the wallpaper, the stink of his own bitter sweat, and the savage heat that came through the window as though it were the grate of a blazing furnace. He decided to check the car that they were to use for the job. It should be ready by now. And then perhaps a stroll through the neighborhood, if one could call it that, and then, later, try to find something to eat and drink.

Perhaps he should have gone with Fitzgerald and the others into town. After five days of travel—four on the ocean and one in the air—he deserved at least some reprieve, some solid ground to stand on. But while they were enthusiastic about their first couple of days in Boston, he felt on edge. He had felt this way ever since he got on the plane and left the Dublin terminal, and then for the four days in the closet-size rooms three levels below deck on the *Queen Elizabeth*, the sea constantly lapping at the great hull as they dragged closer to America. The edgy feeling only got worse when the plane departed from New York and made its way north to Boston.

When they had stepped out onto the sweltering tarmac at Logan Airport, he had felt as if he couldn't breathe. And later, when the four of them stood under the harsh fluorescent lights awaiting their luggage, the anxious feeling increased. Somebody should have been there to meet them, or at least to point them in the right direction.

Once they got their suitcases from the cart, Egan, Kinsella, and Fitzgerald had gone off to exchange some of their shillings and pounds for American dollars. Bobby already had two nickels in his pocket and he went off to find a pay phone and make a call. On his third try, a man picked up and told him to get the others and go to the drop-off area; somebody was on the way. Egan had purchased several packs of American cigarettes, and the four of them waited outside, watched the big Yank cars pulling in and out of the great asphalt parking lot, smoked, and said little to one another besides how big of a bitch the heat was here.

Two hours later, a man named O'Flaherty, a morose fellow who said he was born and raised in Tullamore, met them and drove them around the city—the Common, the waterfront and the piers, a place called Beacon Hill, down a long strip of desperate-looking road called Dorchester Avenue, and, last, to where they'd be staying, a boarding-house in South Boston.

The mood during the car ride had been pensive, as though they were all strangers sharing a cab. The sites they'd passed were less grandiose than they had imagined, and O'Flaherty as a tour guide was far from captivating. He seemed unable, perhaps unwilling, to put a proper sentence together.

"We'll be in touch with you before anything happens," he had said to Myles as he stood by the car, and then he'd handed him a ring with two keys on it and a piece of paper with two addresses. The first was where he'd find the car they'd use, just a few blocks down from L Street, parked in a driveway of a triple-decker home, and the second was the home of Owen Mackey, 180 William Day Boulevard. There was a laminated photo of the man clipped to the note. It appeared to be cut from a group photo; a ghostly, disembodied arm was wrapped around Mackey's shoulder. There was a boyish roundness to his face, and his bright eager eyes shone as if he was gripped in the swell of a celebration. Perhaps it was taken at a wedding, or some ball or banquet. Despite his innocent face, the man could have done terrible, awful things. And even though Bobby tried to convince himself that that was the truth, he knew that something was off. Why had they sent them all the way here to do this job?

To get out of his head, Myles sat up from the wooden chair, dropped to the floor, and did push-ups until his vision began to blur and his shoulders burned at the joints. He stretched and went to the beaten-up dresser, put on a shirt and his watch—four o'clock—grabbed the two keys, his wallet, the note and the photo, and slipped them all into his pocket. He combed through his hair with his fingers and left the room.

He walked down the hollow-sounding stairs and passed through a hallway that led to a bar called the Castlebar Inn. It was filling up with men arriving after a day of work, most of them with that wild look in their eyes as they started in on their evening drunk. A group of them cawed at one another with the brash accents of Bostonians. His stomach growled but he fought against the feeling. He'd seen what the food looked like here—it would probably look the same going out as it had coming in.

Outside, he surveyed the street and watched as the sun flared a septic light against the multifamily houses across the road. There was much disrepair to these homes, and the shoddy attempts by lax landlords to fix the damage on the cheap made the places look even worse. Patchwork molding, mismatched paints, bubbling tarpaper on porch roofs, shingles hanging at crooked angles, and gutters held in place by rope and twine.

On the second-floor porch of one home, a horribly stained carpet hung over a railing, and Bobby watched as a pink, rotund woman whacked at it with an iron rod and clouds of dust billowed in the thick, still air. A small girl wearing no shirt and a drooping cloth diaper held the screen door open and cried out hungrily.

He didn't trust the area. Perhaps it was the narrow, nameless streets and the sharp, blind corners. And how the alleyways ran deep between the clapboard houses like secret passageways. And how the sidewalks and street corners were too thin, and how they appeared to be manned by hoodlums and juveniles looking for trouble.

Bobby asked a teenage boy where the ocean was, and without looking at him, the kid pointed ahead.

Two blocks down, Bobby was amazed to find how close the Atlantic actually was. In the apartment, it had felt like it was miles and miles away. He made it to a walkway lined with giant blocks of granite spackled white with bird droppings, and on the other side, a narrow curve of beach was nearly swallowed up by the incoming tide. Farther off, through the haze, were the humps of several islands that hugged close to the Boston coastline. For a moment, he wondered if anybody lived out there or if the islands were desolate, abandoned.

A seagull swooped down from its perch on a telephone pole and cried out with both aggression and hunger. Its target was a much smaller gull pecking at bits of trash down by the gutter. Facing off against each other, the birds flared their wings and shrieked. Bobby closed his eyes and saw the gulls of Wicklow, wide-breasted with a seafaring pureness to them, not polluted and squalid like the ones before him.

He fought against the homesick feeling percolating in his gut. He lit an American cigarette and dragged in the smoke, sighed it out, and walked away from the sea.

When he got to the car, he was perspiring heavily. O'Flaherty had told him the house where it was parked was close by the inn, but it took him almost a half an hour to find it. It was a brown triple-decker with a crooked front porch littered with broken furniture and crates of miscellaneous junk. The driveway was barely wide enough to fit one car. The Packard sedan sat far back beside the yard, which, in the heat, smelled of dog shit. Laundry hung from a clothesline, still looking unwashed and filthy. A dog leash coiled along the dirt next to the back steps, the collar split in two.

"Lovely," he said to himself.

He walked around to the trunk. The key scraped inside the lock, and he pushed in hard and maneuvered it until he felt it click open. Inside was a stained canvas tarpaulin smelling of oil. The sensation of somebody watching made him turn back to the yard. Startled by the hanging laundry—the white undershirt of a large man, a pair of gabardine slacks—he inched back, turned around, and looked down the driveway. Nobody was there. He looked up to the windows of the houses pressing over him and saw only closed curtains and torn and patched screens.

At the trunk, he lifted the canvas and saw the guns. They were all there. Four pistols, a sawed-off shotgun, and several boxes of cartridges. There were also two maps, one for the city and the other for the state of Massachusetts. He took the maps, closed the trunk, and made sure the doors were locked.

It was time for a drink and then back to the room to go over the maps.

After walking for some time, he ended up where he'd started—in front of his boardinghouse and the Castlebar Inn. The loud talk of men came through the windows with the intensity of a crowd awaiting a prize fight, yet somewhere within its din, he found comfort.

Through the smoke and banter of the workingmen, he walked the hallway, but once at the stairwell, he had an immense urge to go back—Egan, Fitzgerald, and Kinsella, they were out having fun, why shouldn't he? But he grabbed hold of the railing, feeling the immensity of this new, strange city press down on him, and took out the maps from his back pocket and pulled himself up the hollow stairs to his room on the second floor.

30

CHELSEA

WHEN THE KNOCK came at the door, Martin Butler had just finished singing his brother to sleep in his wheelchair by the bedroom window. Dymphna went to answer the door as Butler laid a light shawl over his brother's chest. It was the latter part of the day and the room was mostly in the shadow of the bridge, a small breeze bothering the curtains, and he worried that even with the heat, Coleman might get a chill. He went to the kitchen, raised the flame beneath the teapot that was always simmering, and listened to the talk at the front door. After a moment Dymphna's heels clicked on the linoleum followed by the sound of a man's boots as she brought the guest the length of the hall and into the kitchen.

Bobby Myles stood in the doorway. "God bless all here," he said and Butler smiled.

"I was wondering when you'd stop by."

"Aye. We've been busy."

Butler put two mugs of tea on the table, and Bobby pulled out a chair and sat. Spread across the kitchen table were a dozen pamphlets and brochures in bright colors advertising the desert: red sand and red buttes and blue pools in which rich, suntanned bathers were frolicking.

Hope Springs in Arizona and New Well Ranch in Nevada—vacation spots and tourist getaways in the American West. Dymphna was still standing in the doorway, and Butler looked at the old woman and then nodded for her to go.

"You found your way back all right, then?" he said.

"I've been studying the maps. I had no problems."

Butler nodded. "That'll be a good thing for the job, it'll help you ac-climate quickly. Still, you were the last person I expected they'd send."

"I think it came as a surprise to a whole lot of them."

"Why then?"

"Because I was told to. I didn't have much choice in it."

"We like to think we have no choices in what we do in life."

Bobby eyed him but remained quiet. He had a keen dislike for such philosophizing. Sure, a man knew he had choices: to be killed or to kill and suffer the penance and the guilt for doing the killing. He noted that philosophers rarely got their hands dirty; they let others do the work for them. He thought of all the commandants he'd taken orders from. So many of them soft, weak men who loved violence and reveled in the carnage it left behind. But then, he knew Butler and the struggles the man had experienced, how hard he'd worked at protecting his brother, whom Bobby had recognized in the wheelchair through the window on the night he'd arrived in Boston. The man he'd once seen as a boy being treated at the Temple Street children's hospital next to the Mater Miseri-cordiae in Dublin, where his own sister had succumbed to tuberculosis at the age of twelve. Martin Butler had been all the rage then, the mys-terious man from County Kerry playing the big ballrooms around the city, and he and Bobby would see each other, sometimes two and three times a week, as they attended to their siblings in the hospital. Even then he'd been talking about America.

From the other room came the sound of Butler's brother coughing, wheezing like an asthmatic, and then moaning softly. Butler was watch-ing Myles; carefully he collected the tourist pamphlets and brochures and placed them in a single stack.

"The doctors say the best place for Colie would be the desert," he said. "They have these spas, natural springs and the like. Dry, clean desert air is what he needs, but here we're underneath a bridge with all manner of traffic belching its fumes and the ships steaming up the Mystic and the empty metalworks and paint companies down the waterfront still polluting the city."

"I've always wanted to go out west meself," Bobby said.

"With the cowboys."

Bobby grinned. "Oh, aye, the fecking cowboys."

He sipped his tea. It was strong and bitter and left an oily taste on his tongue. He could hear the old woman's footsteps on the floorboards above them, moving back and forth. "Do you think you'll ever go?" he said.

"Go?"

"West, I mean, with your brother?"

"I don't know. Perhaps. Ah sure, it might just be wishful thinking. There's a lot of work to be done here but in the end the family should come first, don't you think?"

"Family," Bobby repeated and nodded absently. The word meant very little to him these days. Briefly, he considered his sister buried in Glasnevin Cemetery, and his mother, and those who would tend their graves without him.

"Your sister—" Butler began.

Bobby shook his head. "No, the consumption took her. She didn't live to see her thirteenth birthday."

"I'm sorry for your loss."

He looked at Butler and they held each other's gaze and then Bobby dipped his head to his mug of tea and Butler rose, pushed back his chair, picked up the stack of brochures, and placed them in a drawer by the sink. He glanced through the window.

"Why don't we go for a walk?" he said. "Some of the heat is gone out of the day and it would be good for Colie to get some fresh air. He's been cooped up in the house for too long. Besides, he's sick of looking at my sorry face. He likes new company."

❧

They walked with Butler pushing Coleman in his wheelchair down to the Chelsea waterfront and along Marginal, where the traffic passed over the recently built McArdle Bridge into East Boston, and then they threaded through the narrow cobbled backstreets off Broadway by old brownstones and along the Mystic River, where the remnants of Chelsea's once-thriving industry remained: decrepit and crumbling warehouses and pitched smokestacks.

As they walked, Butler pointed to places out in the channel where this or that had happened during the Revolutionary War; where the battle of the Chelsea Estuary occurred, where the British ship *Diana* was taken by colonists, where George Washington was stationed during the siege of Boston. Bobby didn't know if it was for his benefit or for Coleman's—perhaps this was something they did together every day, and perhaps for Butler it was a penance of sorts. The sound of Butler's voice did seem to soothe Coleman and it wasn't until they went below the supports of the bridge, darkness and heat melding with the sound of cars passing invisibly above them, that Coleman became agitated and tossed his head so violently that it banged against the back of his wheelchair.

They emerged into light and onto the grounds of the naval hospital rising up on Admirals Hill, the green grass being tended to by gardeners with white hoses. Before them, the Mystic widened and sparkled in the sun, and they paused for a moment to take it in. Butler stroked Coleman's hair, and he became calm again. Bobby could see fish flashing briefly on the surface of the dirty water, pecking at flies floating on its scummed top, and for a moment he could forget why he was here, three thousand miles from home.

As if reading his mind, or perhaps because he had been waiting to say it all along, Butler spoke. "Terrible business that, in Belfast."

Bobby looked up.

Butler was looking at him. "Gedrick was a fool," he said. "And may he rest in peace. It wasn't your fault what happened."

Bobby flicked his head, as if to dismiss the matter. He appreciated Butler's words but had already heard it a million times. "So," he said, "what is it you do for Donal, for this fellow de Burgh?"

"I do what I did back home. I play music and run Mr. de Burgh's dance halls. I look after his estate. There's a grand power in that, a great freedom, and a wonderful opportunity for a businessman. There's as many Irish coming now as there were in the days of the Famine."

"You're lucky, then. To be out of all this rubbish."

"I am, I suppose."

"But de Burgh told you we were coming."

"He did, but I know only part of what's going on. I think it works better for everyone that way."

"Then he trusts you, and you trust him?"

"He does, and I do."

"What happened with the boat?"

"The police knew it was coming in and the lads had to rush to hide the guns."

"Sure I know all that, but what else is there? What is de Burgh up to?"

"Didn't Donal tell you?"

"Ah, he's not telling us a thing."

"Well, he must have his reasons."

Bobby sighed. "I just want to be done with it. I don't want Belfast all over again."

"That would be up to your men, wouldn't it?"

"I wish I trusted them as much as you do this de Burgh."

"It will all work out, God willing. Mr. de Burgh will see to it. He doesn't do anything lightly and he takes nothing for granted. I'm sure Donal has already told you that."

"How did you ever end up working for him? Why did you come to America?"

The breeze lifted the thin hair on Butler's brow. His face was perspiring in the heat. Small beads of sweat dotted his upper lip. His pale blue eyes, impassive as ever, didn't change as he spoke. "Sure, what was there in Ireland for me and Colie anymore? The two of us needed a fresh start and Mr. de Burgh gave it to us."

They reached a gazebo with picnic tables that faced a wharf at the center of the hospital grounds; it had a small rotunda at its end where patients might sit and view the river. Butler stopped the wheelchair and looked at him.

"I think Colie and I will rest here awhile, if that's okay? You can find your way back?"

"I can."

"Good-bye then, Bobby. And good luck."

"Good-bye, Martin. I hope the next time we meet it's under better circumstances."

Butler smiled. "God willing," he said. He turned, spoke briefly into his brother's ear, adjusted the shawl on his chest, and pushed the wheelchair down to the wharf. Bobby watched them for a moment and then, with the wide, towering expanse of the bridge looming before him, walked back the way they'd come.

31

BOSTON POLICE DISTRICT D-4, SOUTH END

OWEN SAT AT his precinct desk looking at the *Herald*'s obituaries spread out in front of him; a metal fan, clacking loudly, oscillated back and forth, stirring the edges of the paper. Other cops moved about the room or sat at desks typing up reports. Someone was whistling, and it grated at his senses. He was supposed to be doing his own follow-up on a recent knifing at the Stuart Street homeless shelter that had become a homicide only after the victim—a sixty-seven-year-old black man, Donald Mathies—had bled out while staying overnight at Boston City Hospital. He and another detective were searching flophouses through-out the South End and Roxbury for a young man named Cesar Vasquez, the assailant, but there was something about the case that nagged at Owen. The hospital staff had been covering up something when they'd spoken to them. In fact, he knew they were lying. The other detective was still out on the streets, and when he got back he would expect Owen to have something to offer, but he had nothing. He'd been staring at the obituaries and thinking about the Irish shootings since he'd first seen the paper. Cal and Dante were right.

He glanced up as two youths, their eyes bruised and swollen shut, were pushed across the room toward the holding cells, the cops holding them shouting obscenities at them as they went. He knew the two cops and knew them for the fuckers they were. They were from Cal's days at the academy but had gone no further up the ranks—they were sadists and vicious and they liked what they could get away with on the streets. He shook his head, thought, *One of these days, you bastards will get yours.*

He looked down at the paper again, where he'd circled the wakes of the murder victims that were taking place at funeral homes in Dorchester and Boston. All of them were staggered, one day after the other, over the next week. He wondered at the time frame—why were they waiting so long to wake the dead? The bodies had been released to the families directly after the autopsies, four days ago. The obits spoke of *In the Memory of* and *Loving Husband, Father, Son, Brother,* but there seemed to be no urgency in getting the bodies home to grieving loved ones on the other side of the ocean. The bodies would have Mass services here but there would be no burials as they were all returning to Ireland.

De Burgh had paid for Mickey Flynn's funeral, and, looking at the paper, Owen wondered if Flynn's was the only one—maybe de Burgh had paid for the others' as well. How far did de Burgh's philanthropy go? Perhaps de Burgh had covered the costs purely out of a desire to help the Irish community, or perhaps he had had a more direct connection to the deceased. Owen tore the obit page out of the paper, folded it, and placed it in the inside pocket of his light jacket. He took the jacket from the back of his chair. Giordano would have a fit if he knew Owen was putting time that should be directed to other police work into this, but he needed to go back to Dudley.

Downstairs, he let the desk sergeant know where he was heading and he left a message for the other detective. When he got back, they'd take a ride to Boston City Hospital and question the staff again, but this time he'd get some straight answers from them.

◈

He left his car parked near the precinct and walked across Stuart to Columbus, where he caught a streetcar to Dudley. The car was packed with people in the middle of the day because subway service had been temporarily suspended on the Orange Line El due to the rail ties expanding in the heat.

As the tram rattled along, he watched the city passing—people standing on street corners looking bleached and dazed, others sitting beneath awnings and in the shadows of porches and stoops. Sunlight dazzled off the glass. The heat of the sun's glare filled the interior of the car. He could smell the sweat of the other passengers. Crossing invisible borders between neighborhoods, he looked over the rooftops of the brownstones and tenements at the blue-white, cloudless sky. Boston was not a town of tall buildings and arcing skylines but of neighborhoods, tightly packed and closely linked—if not by tenderness then by history, and each neighborhood emerged as distinctly, proudly its own. They passed a park, empty of children, and an avenue of trees, a shock of bright green when everything else seemed so washed out and defeated.

He stepped off the tram at Dudley Station and walked the Avenue slowly, looking into storefronts. The bars were of little help; the community was closed off to the police, and de Burgh had yet to return his messages, and now Owen was irritated. Situated in the Ferdinand Building, a three-story, high-ceilinged baroque- and Renaissance revival–style structure dating from the 1880s, the Dudley Square Bank occupied a central place in the square.

At the customer-service desk, Owen showed his badge and asked to speak with the manager. The brunette clerk called the office, spoke briefly, and then rose from her chair. He followed her across the wide lobby, her heels sounding loudly on the tile, and he could see that, despite the fans in the room, her blouse was stuck to her lower back with sweat. She knocked on an office door with the sign STEWART NICKERSON, BANK MANAGER, then opened the door for Owen and left.

The manager stood and shook Owen's hand, then sat again, nodding as Owen introduced himself and explained that he was a detective looking into a murder case, all the while saying impatiently, "Yes, yes, yes."

Owen stopped short and smiled, letting time drag out. The manager was slim, pale, with glasses and a receding hairline, and his quick, irritated air made Owen bristle. He waited until he sensed the man growing uncomfortable. The manager leaned forward in his chair and began to fidget with his pen; he widened his eyes questioningly and then cleared his throat. From the lobby came the sound of adding machines, a call over the intercom for a Mr. Roberts, and music playing through the office speakers, up-tempo A-sides of songs Owen knew but couldn't quite place.

"I understand," Owen finally said, "that this bank is used by most of the local businesses?"

"That's correct."

"Including Mr. de Burgh's businesses—you deal directly with him regarding those accounts?"

"Why, yes, yes, we do. Mr. de Burgh's accounts are all handled out of this office. Is there a problem?"

"No, no problem. It's merely part of our investigation. Would it be possible to get a record of his holdings throughout Boston?"

"Why do you need that information?"

"Like I said, it's part of the investigation. We think some individuals might be using his funds inappropriately, funneling the money for their own use. I know that Mr. de Burgh has been generous to many people in the city of Boston, most especially recent immigrants. We think that the distribution of such monies might have been a factor in the recent killings. I can't say more than that."

"Well, why don't you simply ask Mr. de Burgh? I'm sure he'd be happy to assist you."

"Because I'm here, and I'm asking you."

"Well, that's not information I feel comfortable giving out to you, Detective, not without Mr. de Burgh's say-so."

Owen's face softened and he nodded, sharing that he understood the manager's reluctance and the potentially difficult position Owen was putting him in. When he spoke, he tried a reassuring tone. "I don't want any more information than would be publicly available in the records at city hall."

"Like I said—" The man spread his hands as if to say it was all beyond his control, and Owen took the opportunity to abruptly change tactics.

"You do understand that I'm on police business, investigating multiple murders. If you're saying that you're not willing to accommodate the police in a murder investigation, I can make sure that information finds its way into the press."

"No, no, I'm not saying that at all, you misunderstand me—"

"If I have to leave and come back with a warrant, I'm not going to be happy, and neither will my boss, and neither will the DA or the judge he'll have to harass for it. No one, beginning with me, likes having his time wasted. I'll make sure to come back not only with a warrant for Mr. de Burgh's records but also with warrants to open up all of this bank's most prestigious accounts for scrutiny. It'll be mayhem. And when your superiors ask what's happening, you can tell them that it began the day you decided not to cooperate with the Boston Police."

"That won't be necessary, Detective—"

"Detective Mackey."

"I'm sure I can get you the reports you need, but, as I hope you'll understand, I will have to inform Mr. de Burgh."

"Of course."

The manager pushed back his chair and went to the door. His pale cheeks were pinpricked with two dots of startling red, and when he passed by, Owen noticed the dark hair beneath his left jaw that he'd missed while shaving that morning.

Owen glanced about the room. There was a glass tank filled with brightly colored tropical fish swimming in a continually revolving pattern. A portrait of an ancient banking tycoon, white and grizzled with a thick handlebar mustache and small, glaring eyes meant to scrutinize and intimidate—an assurance to a particular class of white people that their funds and their future assets, their legacies, were safe with him. On either side of the wide, levered-blind window stood a large purple vase with a bouquet of lavender roses and daisies offset by fuchsia carnations and white lilies, all surrounded by baby's breath. It was arranged in a distinct fashion—he'd seen similar flowers in other professional buildings in the square and in the window of DeWitt's Travel Agency. Their scent gave the room an atmosphere of calm. He wondered if he could ever be comfortable working in such a space.

The manager came back and placed a manila folder on the desk before Owen. He remained standing, perhaps hoping that this would be the end of their interaction.

He coughed into his hand and cleared his throat. "That's a record of all Mr. de Burgh's properties that this bank holds mortgages and liens for. It also includes those businesses whose finances we manage."

"All of them?"

"Yes, all the ones that our bank manages."

"Good, because I don't want to come back, and I assume you don't want me to come back."

"That is entirely at your discretion, Detective."

Owen smiled. "Nice flowers," he said.

The manager turned, glanced at the flowers, and then looked back again, surprised. "Oh, yes, they are very nice. We have fresh flowers delivered twice a week. It maintains a certain air, a kind of professionalism, don't you think?"

"It's amazing you can keep them from wilting in the heat."

The manager looked at him, a puzzled expression on his face.

"The flowers," Owen said.

"Oh, yes, the flowers." He shrugged and smiled thinly. "Well, we do the best we can."

The manager watched from his doorway as Owen walked through the lobby to the front doors. When Owen stepped out into the square, the manager returned to his desk, picked up the phone, and dialed Mr. de Burgh's office at the Intercontinental.

Staying to the west side of the street, where the sun was blocked by the buildings and allowed some shade, Owen walked to Dylan's coffee shop on Columbus and sat down heavily at the counter. There were only two other people in the place, a man and woman sitting at a booth; the woman was crying softly. Behind the counter, hot dogs marketed as *Fresh and Delicious!* sat in a steamer of greasy-looking water. Stale pie crumbled on a plate beneath the glass of a grimy display. From the kitchen came the smell of frying liver and onions. Owen's stomach churned unpleasantly. He ordered a coffee and a glass of water and opened the bank records of de Burgh's properties and investment holdings in and around Boston. It was a long list, and he glanced over them and then took the *Herald* obit from his pocket and compared the information. When the old man behind the counter brought his water, Owen gulped it down and asked for another.

The wakes for the victims were to take place in various O'Flaherty's Funeral Homes—there were two funeral homes on Dot Avenue and another two in Southie, all of them owned by de Burgh. So the question of whether or not he'd paid for all of the funerals seemed to be answered. Every one of the murdered men was going through his funeral homes and returning to Ireland. And that Atlantic passage might be on de Burgh's dime too. Six bodies, six coffins, all being waked in the same week and then shipped home together, but no dates were given in the obits on when the bodies were to be received or interred in Ireland. Owen sipped his coffee and grimaced at its taste, pulled some coins from his pocket, and left them on the counter.

Outside, he began walking. The entirety of Washington Street along the El route from Dover Street to Egleston was almost impassable due to the road's buckling. Burst water pipes had flooded the street, with geysers shooting up through the ruptured tar and macadam. Road detours and work crews pressed the pedestrians and the traffic down one congested street after another until Owen felt like he was trapped and would never get out of Dudley. At the corner of Shawmut and Lenox, he paused at a phone booth. He had his jacket slung over his shoulder and his shirt was dark with sweat, and one of his headaches pressed behind his eyes. He stepped into the booth and the fan kicked on, and it was a welcome relief. He called the precinct and told them to send a black-and-white to pick him up because it was too damn hot to walk. Then he lowered his head and waited—the fan blowing on the back of his neck, the receiver at his ear to dissuade any passersby from banging at the door—until the cruiser pulled up at the curb.

32

SHRINE OF ST. ANTHONY, ARCH STREET

CAL WALKED FROM the Pilgrim Security offices to J. J. Foley's on Otis and had a warm beer in a room packed with loud suits from the business district, which soured his mood and made his head ache, then walked up Summer Street to Arch. The shrine and home to the Franciscan friars of Holy Name Province had been in Boston for a hundred years but the church was only a couple of months old; its foundation stone had been laid in '52. It was done in an art deco style with dozens of narrow panels of stained glass in the flat façade and a large stone effigy of Christ on the cross over the entrance.

In the chapel, Cal stood at the font and blessed himself with holy water. He looked casually about the room: candles and dimmed lights; penitents emerging from the confessional booths in the east chancel and others moving toward the front of the church with heads bowed in prayer after confession. He smelled the familiar scent of beeswax and incense from the censer during novenas and heard the muted thrum of whispered prayers bleeding one into the other, over and over again, until the room, despite the small number of parishioners, hummed with it.

The man sat by the votive candles at the statue of Saint Francis of Assisi, and Father Nolan had been right. Cal knew the look of him almost immediately. There wasn't another in the place like him. Even sitting, he looked tall, and almost emaciated, with a gaunt, ascetic stoniness to his face, something that Cal had seen in soldiers and in the faces of killers.

At the top of the aisle, facing the Eucharist, Cal genuflected, blessed himself again, and walked toward the pews where the man sat. He took a pew behind him and to his right so that he could see his profile. Lost to the world around him, the man muttered softly the Breastplate of Saint Patrick, candle flame flickering softly on his closed eyes:

> *May the hand of God protect me,*
> *the way of God lie before me,*
> *the shield of God defend me,*
> *the host of God save me.*
> *May Christ shield me today.*
> *Christ with me, Christ before me,*
> *Christ behind me,*
> *Christ in me, Christ beneath me,*
> *Christ above me,*
> *Christ on my right, Christ on my left,*
> *Christ when I lie down, Christ when I sit,*
> *Christ when I stand,*
> *Christ in the heart of everyone who thinks of me,*
> *Christ in the mouth of everyone who speaks of me,*
> *Christ in every eye that sees me,*
> *Christ in every ear that hears me.*
> *Amen*

"That's nice, that is," Cal said from behind him, and the Pioneer slowly opened his eyes.

"We're in a church," he said. "Will you fuck off till I'm done?"

"It's a beautiful church too," Cal said, and as the Pioneer turned slightly to look at him, Cal craned his neck and regarded the marble columns rising to the arched ceiling, and then looked to the front of the chapel, at the exquisitely wrought depiction of Christ with His arms outstretched toward His Father in Heaven and, behind the altar, the elaborate marble and gilt reredos.

The Pioneer sighed. "What do you want?"

"Father Nolan said you were willing to speak to me. Or am I wasting my time?"

"Sure let's see if you can talk sense first, and then I'll speak to you." The Pioneer reached into his pocket.

"Nice and easy now," said Cal. "Take it slow."

"What kind of man thinks I'm going to shoot him in a church?"

"If you were in my shoes, you wouldn't be saying that."

"Why so?"

"I was shot at in a church before. Ended up being a bloodbath. I don't want that happening again. I'm sure you can appreciate my tone, yes?"

"Jaysus, in a church?"

"Yeah."

"Sure what's wrong with this country altogether?"

"We're still figuring it out."

The Pioneer nodded to himself and then sat still, not asking any more. If Cal hadn't known better, he might have thought the man was praying again or in a deep state of meditation. When it became clear that the Pioneer would volunteer nothing, he began again.

"Your boss, de Burgh, he has you set to cause a whole bunch of trouble."

Still the man didn't respond; his head moved almost imperceptibly, as if he were indeed talking to himself or praying. Cal was about to say something when he spoke.

"My father raised pigs outside Cavan," he said. "Pigs will eat anything. They're a great benefit to a farm. They don't cost much to keep, you just need the space for them. A proper run and a trough and another of their kind and they're happy. You keep them till they get fat and it's always pleasant in the spring when they birth a few bonhams. Other

213

than that, you wait till they get fat and you keep them happy and when you put them down for slaughter, all the parts of the pig will see you through the winter. It's a grand, happy animal, a pig. As a boy, I always liked our pigs."

This time, Cal remained silent. A woman began to cough, a long, wet hacking, and when the attack persisted, she stood with her hand to her mouth and made her way to the exit. There was the clatter of coins in the poor box, the hiss of a match being lit, the smell of a candle being extinguished, and the sound of kneelers being raised.

Finally the man spoke. "The priest said you wanted to talk about your father."

"I wanted to talk about the IRA and those involved in Boston."

"Then you want to talk about your father."

"What about him?"

"He was top man for us here. Directly after the war."

"I assume you don't mean World War One?"

"Your father was fighting another war."

Confessions were over and the priest exited the confessional and walked toward the sacristy, nodding and smiling at those in the pews who looked up or addressed him as he passed, his footfalls reverberating on the marble tile. The Pioneer seemed content in the stillness, and he acted as if Cal were a familiar, as if it was the most natural thing in the world to be talking in a church about the past in this way, reminiscing about death and murder. Cal let the stillness stretch. He was surprised to find that he too took a strange comfort in it.

After a while, the Pioneer spoke. "You didn't know your father, then," he said, and Cal's mood soured.

"I knew my father plenty well. What the fuck are you talking about?"

The Pioneer shook his head, seeming amused but also pitying; Cal took it as mocking. "Ahh, you didn't know that man half as well as you think you did," the man said.

"And you did?"

"We knew each other—a lot of people in this town knew each other, before, in the old times, back home."

The Pioneer half turned to regard him, took in his face for a moment, and then looked forward again. He frowned as if he were considering something.

"You would have been very young then," he said, rubbing absently at the medallion on his lapel, "during the time your father made a name for himself.

"I told you he was a top man, but what I meant to say was that he was a top killer. Did you know that about your father?"

Cal watched the bowed backs and bent heads of the penitents kneeling in the pews alongside the confessional. The cloying, thick smell of incense fogged his thoughts, and he closed his eyes briefly, trying to will himself alert.

"Father Nolan hinted at it."

"That was good of him," he said, musing. "It would have saved you some of the shock of hearing it directly, I suppose.

"So, what do you want to know? How many men he killed? The way he killed them? He was known as a vicious man, your father was. A lot of people turned away from the Cause because of men like him."

As if remembering Cal's father's acts, the Pioneer shivered, shook his head, and blessed himself; Cal couldn't tell if it was real or a performance.

"So much anger and violence. I assume he probably brought a lot of that home to you and your mother. It's tragic what parents put on their children. I remember one time—"

"I want to know who's running the show in Boston," Cal said, more loudly than he had intended. The smell of incense burned in his nostrils like formaldehyde, and the lights from the chancel seemed to be growing brighter even as the flickering lights in the aisle seemed to dim. He was aware of his own breathing, of the knot tightening in his chest. He forced himself to exhale long and slow, and gradually the pressure eased.

"I want to know who killed those men last week," he said, more calmly, "and I want to know where the guns are."

The Pioneer's head rocked back as if he were laughing. "Guns? I have no information about that."

"So it wasn't the IRA?"

"Haven't I already said that I have nothing for you?"

"I suppose you and my father made a great team."

"Aye, we did. For a while there."

"And you still work for them."

"No one *works* for them."

Cal gritted his teeth. The man was infuriating with his penchant for talking around things. "Right, but you're with them, you're in the organization."

"I'm in no such thing. Father Nolan said you wanted to know about the past, about your father. That's why I'm here, that's why I'm sparing my time for you. If you have something to ask, ask it and be quick."

Cal persisted. "You're a contact man for the IRA in Boston."

"I'm an employee of Mr. Vincent de Burgh and I work hard for a living. I've worked hard ever since I came to this country twenty years ago. I've come here tonight at the request of Father Nolan and owing to the past I had with your father, a past that most of us, including the priest, have done a good job leaving behind. If you're done, I have nothing else to talk to you about."

"What about de Burgh?"

"What about him?"

"He's a hard man to track down. What's his role in all this?"

"Mr. de Burgh's a successful man, a busy man. He doesn't have time for this nonsense."

"Do you know of a Detective Owen Mackey?"

The Pioneer stiffened, but only slightly and so fleetingly that if Cal hadn't been searching for some manner of response, he might not have seen it.

"Detective Owen Mackey," the Pioneer repeated.

"He went to see Mr. de Burgh last week sometime. You wouldn't forget him. Anyway, I was talking to him and he has all these interesting ideas about de Burgh and, I suppose, about you.

"See, whether you talk to me or not doesn't really matter. Detective Mackey has already got a really good picture of what happened on the night of the Fourth, and pretty soon he'll be able to prove it, because we all know that those guns haven't left Boston yet, and the longer they remain here, the more antsy your real bosses are going to get. If I were you, I'd start praying a whole lot harder."

Shoes dragged on the marble—someone with a limp much like Cal's. At the head of the nave someone sat heavily in a pew, and Cal felt the vibration through the wood. The thrum of muted prayer still held the space, but something, Cal felt, had shifted—something within himself. At his rear, a match was struck and a votive lit, and he smelled the sulfur of the extinguished match. He watched the Pioneer's chest rise and fall slowly. Again, Cal had the sense that he was meditating, so when the man spoke, low and deep, it surprised him.

"You should stay out of our business. We will do what we have to do. And son of Luke O'Brien or not, you'll have plenty of trouble coming down on you if you get in our way."

Cal smiled at the Pioneer's use of *we*. As calm as the man seemed, Cal had gotten under his skin. It didn't mean much, but it meant something, and that was enough for now.

"I'm used to it," he said, and he rose from the pew, leaving the man to his prayers.

Cal stepped out of the church and paused for a moment on the street, staring up into the Savior's anguished face near the hour of His death. It was hard not to stare at His face—at the severity and extent of His pain—for Cal could never tell or decide if His was a look of acceptance, a powerful embrace of what was to come and the knowledge that He would soon be with His Father, or simply a giving-up, a weary and resigned, pain-washed succumbing to events over which He had no control. At times there seemed to be an incredible power in that sacrifice—the thought of it, when Cal conceived of it fully, as he had as a child performing the Stations of the Cross, contemplating each moment of Christ's suffering before the end, was overwhelming. And yet, at other times, it seemed as if there was no power at all in it, that it was the antithesis of power—that it was powerlessness.

He tried to conjure up an image of his father's face but it would not come to him—the man remained amorphous, perhaps even more so now that Cal had parts of the man's life and nowhere to put them. If anything, he was more fragmented and Cal further estranged from him. The only times he could see his father's face clearly lately were in the nightmares of the beatings he'd given him, the shattered cheekbone and the ruptured spleen at eleven that had required emergency surgery at Boston City Hospital, the broken nose and arm that had kept him from boxing for six months. He wanted to be done with those terrors and have something else to associate with the man, something that might begin the forgiveness that Father Nolan always talked so much about, but it seemed as if that would never happen. Leaving aside his own abuse, he now had the knowledge that his father had been a murderer and good at what he did. No matter how much penance Cal did, no matter how much love he tried to seek within himself, there would never be enough for him to forgive that.

33

O'FLAHERTY'S FUNERAL HOME, DORCHESTER

OWEN AND CAL sat in the last row of hard-back chairs put before the coffin, watching the mourners filing into and out of the room. After an hour Cal grew restless; he'd had his fill of grievers, the interested, the excited, the death flies of funeral homes. He'd seen enough of them and of the insides of dozens of funeral homes as a child, when his father had hauled him to a different wake every weekend during his years as a ward boss and union rep and then, later, when he campaigned for city councilman. This was the death flies' drinking hole, the bar that delivered their drug and fed their obsessions. An old woman in a black shawl entered, and he recognized her from when he was young. A stranger to the bereaved, she'd been coming to these things all her life.

"I can't believe this is your fourth this week," Cal said to Owen.

"It's been a busy week. I wanted to see just who might show up to these things."

"You're waiting for the killers?"

"Killers do strange things—some of them are like pyromaniacs. They like to return to the scene of the fire, to see the carnage they've wrought, to relive it."

Cal lit a cigarette and shook out the match. "I know. But I don't think that's this lot."

"Perhaps not, but I've still got to see."

Owen craned his neck around to look at the crowd, grunted, then turned back. "I would have thought de Burgh would make an appearance," he said.

"He doesn't need to when he has him." Cal gestured to a man who had just stepped through a doorway bearing a wreath of white carnations and roses in each arm, his hair shorn tight to his skull and his mouth hard-set in a gaunt face—the severe mask of dignity required for such occasions.

"That the guy who warned you off at St. Anthony's?"

"Yeah, that's him." O'Flaherty met Donal Phelan at the casket and together they arranged the bouquets on pedestals, one on either side of the coffin. They spoke briefly and then Donal turned to leave, pausing as he caught sight of Cal and Owen. He held their gaze for a moment, then nodded and left the way he'd come.

"I met him in Dudley Square," Owen said, "when I was inquiring about Mickey Flynn. He's got an edge to him, for sure."

"My father used to quote Martin Michael Lomasney to me all the time: 'Never write if you can speak. Never speak if you can nod. Never nod if you can wink.' You know that one?"

Owen nodded but continued to stare after the man. Cal flicked his ash into the standing black and brass ashtray next to his chair. "Well, to my father, it was a code. If you could follow those simple rules, one day you'd be a congressman, a senator, mayor of Boston. He always said that politics was a game and if you played it well and always kept the other fella thinking that you had a better hand than you did, you'd win."

"The Lomasney quote doesn't sound much like your father."

"No, my father liked to speak, and if he could use his fists rather than nod, he would."

Two old women in heavy black dresses and with black kerchiefs about their heads genuflected and then slowly lowered themselves onto the kneeler before the coffin and began to pray. They were there for a long time and much of the queue behind them simply blessed themselves before the coffin and then went to offer their condolences to the family standing by the table that held the Mass cards. Cal watched as O'Flaherty moved about the room, shaking a hand here and there as people left, speaking with another funeral director, receiving flowers arriving at the front door. Cal had been in this room when he was younger, and it looked and smelled the same. He stared at the floral-patterned wallpaper. There was a sickness in his stomach that he could not describe or put a name to, as if the place—the memories from childhood—were making him ill. He ground his cigarette into the ashtray and popped a mint in his mouth, waited for the acid in his stomach to settle.

"His connections to the IRA," Cal said, referring to the Pioneer, "do you think de Burgh knows?"

"I'd like to talk to de Burgh and find out."

They waited until the room had mostly cleared and then rose and went before the coffin. Family and friends had placed photographs of the dead man and his children and grandchildren against its base. Someone had been thoughtful enough to leave a fifth of Powers. "Nice flowers," Owen said, lifting the card on the bouquet and looking at it.

"What is it?"

"They're from de Burgh, from a florist he owns. Quite distinct. I've been seeing arrangements from them all over the place."

"He *is* the Irish philanthropist. You said he paid the first victim's funeral expenses?"

"Yeah, and I'm pretty sure he paid for the others' as well," Owen said.

"But some of these guys—I looked at the obituaries, they'd lived here their entire lives. Every single one of them is going back to the home country?"

"I talked to the funeral director, O'Flaherty, and he confirmed it. He doesn't seem to like me much." Owen laughed, and the old woman in the black shawl looked in their direction and glared balefully at them.

"All of the funeral homes belong to de Burgh," Cal said. "That doesn't seem strange to you?"

"It does, yes."

"What do you think the connection is?"

"Right now," Owen said, tapping the casket, "only the dead know."

He saw the woman still looking at them and lowered his voice. "I've had enough. Let's leave him to his family."

Cal genuflected before the coffin and blessed himself, then placed his hat on his head. "I've known her since I was little and my father dragged me around to every wake in town. She's no family to this man. This is like a hobby for her. It's how she gets her kicks."

"Well, let's leave her to it, then."

At the entrance to the vestibule Cal looked back. The old woman had her head lowered and was praying loudly, fervently, hands clasped together so hard that her knuckles showed white, a rosary entwined in her fingers. She'd be here until they kicked her out, helping the dead along in their passage to God.

Christ, how he hated funeral homes.

34

ACROSS THE STREET from Dante, a person walked with uneven, staggered steps. Nearly at the apartment building, keys already in hand,
Dante assumed it was just another bum winding along the sidewalks in
search of a drink. Drunks unfamiliar with the city came from Scollay
into this neighborhood all the time.

The person stepped off the curb, momentarily leaned in between two
parked cars, and then stumbled into the street.

Something was off, and Dante couldn't quite pin it down.

A car was coming, and seeing someone in the middle of the street,
the driver pressed down on the horn. Headlights flashed, and the face
was lost in shadow.

"Watch where you're fucking going!" the driver screamed from the
open window.

When the person got to the curb, Dante realized it was a woman.
He heard a strange mewling coming from her mouth, the sound of a
dog that has been brutally beaten. A word took form, a horrid moan.
"Dante," she said.

The streetlamp's flickering light touched the face and showed him who it was. He stepped in closer and caught Claudia before she fell to the pavement.

Lifting her head into the light, he saw that her right eye was completely sealed, knotted with bruises, and the skin above the left eyebrow was scraped raw, crusted with dirt and bits of gravel. Her mouth was almost swollen shut by the egg-shaped contusion that doubled the size of her left cheek. Blood and spit came dribbling from the thin space that was her mouth, a pinkish string of it hanging off her chin.

He reached around and held the back of her head and pressed her to his chest. Her voice was clogged with tears, and that horrid sound continued to bleat from her throat.

"Who did this?" he asked.

He could feel the feverish heat coming off her body. Blood seeped into his shirt.

"Who fucking did this?" he asked again.

"It was him... Vinny."

Dante took her into the foyer of the apartment building. The bright fluorescent lights showed how awfully she'd been beaten, and he tried to look away but couldn't. This was his sister. This was Claudia. Blood was bright on her face, neck, and shirt, which was torn at the shoulder and showed bruises along her arm. He made sure she could stand on her own and fiddled with the front lock until the key slid in and he opened the door.

There was no elevator in the building and he took his time bringing her up the three flights of stairs. With his help, she climbed the steps slowly. Inside the apartment, he turned on a small amber-glassed lamp to keep the light low and made her sit on the couch. After getting some towels sopping wet with cold water, he did his best to clean her up.

"I'm going to find him. Where is he, Claudia?"

She was breathing steady again. With the blood mopped off her face, the swollen cheek appeared even more obscene—it looked unreal, like the makeup in a Lon Chaney film, grotesque but not actually flesh and blood. She put a cigarette in the side of her mouth and, with a shaking hand, managed to flick a match and light it.

"Earlier he said he was going to watch the bocce games. By the water."

Dante reached under his khaki jacket, grabbed his revolver. He flipped it open and saw the silver ends of five bullets. With a whip of his wrist, the cylinder snapped back into place. The sound startled Claudia and she looked up at him. She shook her head. "There's nothing you can do now, Dante. Nothing."

"Maria is next door. She can't see you like this, so you stay and rest. When I get back, I'm going to take you to a doctor."

"I'll talk to Vinny later. Stay out of it."

Dante walked to the door, then turned, expecting her to say something else. Clumsily, she tried to put out the cigarette. Half crumpled in the ashtray, it smoked wisps of a charcoal blue. She lowered her head into her hands, and he left the apartment, closing the door quietly behind him.

He knocked on Mrs. Berardi's door. After a moment, it opened a few inches, the chain lock dipping and then leveling taut as she peered out. The old woman saw it was Dante, closed the door, unhitched the chain lock, opened the door again.

"I thought I heard you come home," she said.

He spoke so low it was almost a whisper. "I'm sorry but I have to go do something. Can she stay just a little bit longer? I'm really sorry and I won't let this happen again."

The old woman sighed, and, unwilling to make eye contact, she looked down at the floor. "When will you be back?"

"Soon. It's okay, right?" He asked the question but was already sidling toward the stairs, raising his hands in an apologetic manner.

Just as Dante turned in the stairwell, he saw the old woman bless herself three times over, probably hoping to ward off the aura of trouble he'd left behind. Hurriedly, she closed the door and turned the lock, the bolt slamming into its groove so loudly that Dante was sure it had startled even her.

❧

Across the inner harbor, the Bunker Hill Monument speared the night sky above Charlestown. Like clusters of cotton being pulled apart, clouds stretched in slow-fading wisps across the yellowed moon. At the opposite shore, the skeletal shape of the USS *Constitution* appeared in the night like a shipwreck, and down a half a mile, Dante could see tiny clusters of fireworks sparkle and reflect against the still, dark waters, their explosions muffled and sounding minuscule from so far away.

Off the sidewalk and down a grassy incline was the section of park where the bocce games were played. Two courts ran parallel to each other, and ropes twined with white lights, their bulbs blazing, hovered above them, illuminating the two games being played simultaneously. Clusters of mosquitoes danced around the lights, and below, groups of men congregated on the borders of the two courts packed down with dirt, granite, and oyster-shell flour. Smoke from their cigars and cigarettes clotted the humid air. Some of the men rubbed halved lemons against their skin to ward off bugs. There wasn't a woman in sight.

Most of the men watching were middle-aged with potbellies, white T-shirts and suspenders. A few younger men stood out. They wore loud-colored shirts and smoked fancy cigarettes and drank liqueur from plastic cups. There were elders too, stoop-shouldered, white haired, and they were sitting in foldout chairs with a clear view of the players.

It was a festive scene—the loud chatter, the playful bad-mouthing in Italian, the clattering of the balls, and the cheers that followed when somebody rolled a shot in to kiss the *pallino,* all of it augmented by the wine flowing from homemade jugs.

And then Dante saw him.

Vinny stood near the scoreboard on the first court looking like he didn't have a fucking care in the world. He was smoking one of his cigarillos, the smoke escaping his mouth a toxic yellow, and he held a cup of wine that he drank from casually.

Dante moved down the grassy incline, making sure to stay within the darkness. From his limbs came a great weight that bore down on every inch of him. It felt as if everything had been sucked right out of him, and the only emotion left was a sharp, intensified bloodlust that drummed maliciously at his temples and allowed his eyes to catch every detail, every shift of light, and every slight movement.

The two games ended, and a young boy cleared the scoreboard. Another group of players manned the ends of the courts, eager to get in a last game before it was time to call it a night. Vinny crumpled up his cup, dropped his cigarillo, and ground it out in the grass with his heel. He shook hands with a couple of men and then walked toward the water, where a path wound its way back to North Station.

Dante waited until Vinny was out of the other men's sight, and then he followed him.

The gravel path curved around a small island of shrubbery and thornbushes and then straightened as it ran beside a wrought-iron railing that protected pedestrians from a fifteen-foot drop into the harbor.

Dante took this turn slowly. Close to the bushes, he felt a thorn branch clinging to his leg, and he pulled it away. If Vinny knew he was being trailed and was waiting for him to get closer, Dante wanted to have enough room to get at him first. He knew if Vinny got him down, he was probably done for.

A breeze came off the water, and the metal No Trespassing sign clattered on a gate that led down to a small boat dock. An orb-like light on a lamppost hung over the path, and the big man stood under its diffuse glare, lit a match, and puffed at another cigarillo until its tip burned red. Dante could hear him hack, and then spit, and then whistle with a razor-sharp intensity, as if he were calling out some secret warning.

Suddenly, the heaviness in his limbs left him, and Dante felt light and weak, as if he might float away and never touch ground again. He quickened his step, and Vinny stopped and slowly turned around.

Dante raised his gun, and he heard a click of a blade snapping out of its handle.

"You son of a bitch!"

227

The world turned slow again, the gravity pulling him down. A glint of steel flashed and cut the air.

Dante sucked in his gut and arched back. The knife sliced through his shirt, and a burning pain flared on his skin. He swung the gun toward Vinny's head, but the fat man threw up an arm. The gun clattered to the ground, and before Dante could reach down for it, Vinny put all of his momentum into a second swipe of the blade.

It missed Dante's face by inches.

Lumbering as though weighed down by broken stone, Vinny tried to straighten up, but he stumbled. Dante squared up and brought a left fist against the jaw. Pain rattled the bones in Dante's hand, and he reached in with his other hand and raked his thumbnail across the man's left eye.

The big man grunted and cursed, crouched down, and, like a bull, rammed his shoulder into Dante's midsection. Dante left his feet and landed on his back. The breath was knocked out of his lungs, and he clutched his chest and gasped for air. His vision quivered but he was still able to see Vinny pressing a hand to his damaged eye.

"You fight dirty, you no-good prick."

Dante's fingers grappled at the gravel. One fingernail cracked and bled. Where had his gun gone?

"Figured a piece of shit like yourself would sneak up on a man like that. I know all about you, I know what you've done. I know that you and that mick buddy of yours fucked with the Brink's job, stuck your noses where they shouldn't have been. I'm surprised you lasted this long."

Dante waited until the man stepped closer, then he reared back his right foot and kicked out. The thick of his heel shattered the bone right below the man's knee. Vinny cried out as he fell forward, his chin bouncing hard off the gravel, head snapping back.

Dante got to his feet as fast as he could.

Vinny rolled onto his back. "You don't know how connected I am. You have no fucking idea."

Dante reached down and grabbed the switchblade off the ground.

His stomach was still burning, and he lifted his shirt to see the undershirt soaked through with blood. He was lucky he wasn't cut too deep.

Vinny tried to sit up. Dante wound up and kicked him in the face with the sharp tip of his shoe.

"Why'd you do it?" Dante asked. "What did she do to you?"

Vinny's nose was broken and his mouth was black with blood. When he grinned, it appeared that he had no teeth left. "The crazy bitch got what she deserved."

Quicker than Dante thought possible, Vinny reached down to his belt, where a snub-nosed revolver was hidden. Dante fell on top of him before he got it all the way out. With one hand, he pushed him down, and with the other, he shoved the blade under the man's ear and pushed it in until its tip ground against bone. A horrible hissing came deep from Vinny's throat. His eyes locked onto Dante's. His pupils dilated, wide with shock as the reality set in that he was going to die. There was a ferocity blazing in his eyes but then they dimmed as the heart slowed and the blood flow stopped. Dante could feel the life leave Vinny—one pull on the switch and all of it gone forever.

The stench of shit came to Dante, and he gripped the handle of the knife and pulled it out. Blood came out of the wound. Dante stood up, drew back his arm, and threw the knife over the gate. He heard the splash it made in the night-covered waters. He took Vinny's gun, considered holding on to it but then hurled it into the harbor as well.

I should call Cal, he thought. *I should call the police and tell them I did it because I had to. They'd see Claudia's face and then they would know. It wasn't murder. It was doing what's right.*

Time skipped ahead, and he found himself hunched over, his hands gripping the corpse under the arms, dragging it to the bushes alongside the path. There was a small clearing inside. The thorns clawed at him again, snagged at his skin. An animal rustled in the darkness beside him and then fled. He gazed down at the body and wondered what to do next.

The only way out was to dig a hole so deep that nobody would ever find him. Make this no-good fuck disappear.

There were lakes and reservoirs where desperate people dumped their cars for insurance money. There were the quarries in Quincy and the Mystic Lakes in Arlington and Medford. His mind fired off possible solutions, but he couldn't come to a decision yet, and he walked back into the night toward the city streets.

35

THE STAGGERED WHITE lines separating the lanes seemed to elongate under the headlights' glare. From the sides and from behind, darkness pressed against the car. Slowly, sensation came back to Dante. He felt as if he'd just risen to the surface and was now opening his eyes to the reality of what had happened earlier. He rolled down the window and tried to air out the car. It smelled of Vinny's feces, the stench of death taking over.

He was driving a stolen car, a Plymouth Plaza, light blue, white interior. He remembered spotting it on a side street off Washington and jimmying the lock with ease. How lucky he was that nobody had seen him.

An exit sign for the Medford Mystics materialized from the night. He eased the car off the main road. The houses on quiet lawns silver with moonlight were as silent as crypts. This was a part of Greater Boston he wasn't that familiar with. Maybe this was a mistake, coming all this way.

Headlights flared on the road up ahead. He prayed that it wasn't a cop. Closer, the headlights beamed through the windshield and lit the interior of the car, and he could hear the voices, the rock-and-roll music blaring shrilly from the speakers of a convertible with its top down. The Pontiac went by in a blur, and Dante glimpsed a teenager's blond hair and a kid with a crew cut in the backseat finishing off a whiskey bottle.

And then came the shattering crash of the bottle, and, in the rearview, the taillights bent and swayed at a turn in the road.

On the dash, the gas gauge showed he had less than a quarter of a tank. That wouldn't be enough to get him back to Boston, but then he'd be walking home anyway.

To kill the silence, he turned on the radio. The owner had left the dial on a station playing a big-band number, all strings and saccharine, and he reached over and turned it up.

He had to squint at his watch: 1:15.

The closer he got to the Mystic Lakes, the bigger and more stately the homes appeared, all of them sitting behind well-manicured hedges on lush, green lawns with weeping willows and Japanese maples.

The car passed under a streetlamp, and the white light slid over the hood and moved through the interior of the car in a liquid motion, illuminating Vinny's body in the passenger seat for a dragging moment, showing all the blood covering his neck and shoulder.

Did he just move?

Was that a twitch?

A smile?

Dante tried to quiet the panic in his head while straining to hear if the man was breathing. He listened for the slightest whistle of air escaping his nostrils, the tremble of phlegm in the throat. Out of the corner of his eye, he saw movement, but when he turned, the body was still. The right front wheel hit a pothole and the body shuddered and leaned closer to the door, head resting against the window.

"Don't fuck with me, Vinny."

Dante lit a cigarette with the car lighter and sucked at it until it flared bright, a lone ember in the dark cavity of the car. He eased his foot off the gas pedal, slowing down to twenty miles an hour, then reached over with the cigarette and ground it into Vinny's cheek. The hiss of it burning and the charred smell of skin immediately hit Dante's senses and turned his stomach. But that was it. Nothing left. Vinny really was dead.

Dante flicked the cigarette out the window, where it bounced and sparked on the tarmac. He passed through a rotary and then on his left came the glitter of moonlight rippling on the lakes and he knew he was close.

Dante found a dirt road that led down to a wooded lot that was wide enough for the Plymouth. First thing he had to do was check to see how deep the water was.

At the lake's edge, Dante undressed down to his boxer shorts. Above him, the sky was full of stars that momentarily captivated him, made him feel dizzy and small, a miserable speck in the universe.

He took a long stick and walked out. Muck curled up between his toes. The water cooled his feverish skin and awakened his senses. The bottom took a quick drop, and he was submerged up to the chest. Another step, and he was up to his neck. *This will have to do,* he thought as he let go of the stick and swam back in.

Onshore, he dressed again. In the dark around him, the cicadas buzzed their nighttime song.

He scrabbled in the dark brush until he found a rock weighing about forty pounds. The underside of the rock was moist. Something slithered across his knuckles, and he assumed it was just a pill bug or some other type of insect. He laid the rock back down on the ground, opened the passenger-side door, leaned in, and dropped the rock on the body's lap. Blood spotted his jacket and spattered his neck. He pushed back out of the car, took off his jacket, and used it to wipe at his skin.

Wearing just his white, bloodstained undershirt, he stood there in the quiet, undisturbed dark. He found a prayer gathering in his head but he turned it away and let it fade into nothing. A man like Vinny could rot in hell for all he cared.

Even with the tank running low, the car started with ease. Dante found another heavy rock, smaller than the one on Vinny's lap, and propped it against the gas pedal. The engine rumbled, the smell of gas rising from the hood, and when he thought it was time, he slammed the door shut, reached through the window, and put the car in drive. He got out of the way just in time.

The dark husk of the car disrupted the placid, moonlit waters, and he couldn't tell if it was floating or if it was grounded in the shallows. Seconds passed, and the air churned, belched, and bubbled from the open window, and then the car went down quickly, thank God, and soon there were just ripples on the surface.

Mosquitoes attacked Dante's face and neck, buzzed hungrily against his ears. He didn't want another cigarette but he fired one up, hoping the smoke would keep them away. He waited and smoked and paced the dark brush, took off his shirt and put the jacket back on. Perhaps Vinny wasn't really dead. Perhaps the door would open and somehow he'd swim to the surface. Dante couldn't think this way. What was done was done, and there was no going back.

The walk home would take him hours unless he hitched or miraculously found a taxi. Thoughts collided in the husk of his head. Soon, his feet were traveling the road. On his right, between the gaps in the trees along the shore, the lake looked even more beautiful, glimmering shards of moon coalescing on the water. The song "Moonlight in Vermont" came to him. He hummed the song loudly, but no matter how loud he hummed, he saw the Plymouth settled into the silt and scum at the bottom of the lake and, above, the moonlight dancing on the surface but unable to penetrate deep enough to illuminate Vinny's grave and its forever-dark silence.

36

THE INTERCONTINENTAL CLUB, DUDLEY SQUARE

MARTIN BUTLER LISTENED to the music playing from the ballroom, but tonight it offered him little peace. He was thinking about the call he'd received from the bank, and now Donal had mentioned seeing the detective at the wake. Donal was standing in the shadows against the far wall, his arms crossed, the light from the sconces highlighting the severe edge of his jawline. The fan thumped steadily above their heads. Donal had just come from evening services, and Butler could smell the incense and beeswax on him; it clung to the fibers of his jacket like a second skin. He imagined a room as smoky as a bar and the low chanting of a hundred mendicants with their arms uplifted to heaven, and heaven oblivious to their pleas. Butler had left God behind a long time ago but out of respect acted as devout as he could around Donal. Still, sometimes he wished the religion would temper the man some.

"Well?" Donal said.

"Well what?"

"Brennan was right about that detective—I doubt it was a coincidence that he was here the night of that dance."

Butler waved him away. "There was no other reason for him to be here and the rest is merely him doing his job. But you're right not to underestimate him, and now that we know that he's connected with this other fellow—"

"O'Brien."

"O'Brien. And you say the priest knows him?"

"Yes, him and his father played their part back in the day."

"Any point in reaching out to the priest, convincing him to talk some sense into this O'Brien?"

"I think we're past that. I thought he'd take my warning, but that didn't work. He's a right hard case, that one, and he's got a death wish. I think that he's in it just for that, for the trouble that he enjoys stirring up—can you believe a man coming into a church and expecting to be shot?"

Donal shook his head, his brow creased and his lips pursed. "I don't trust this at all. The two of them there, together. And now you say the detective's been looking into Mr. de Burgh's finances."

"There's nothing there that would warrant much attention—Mr. de Burgh spreads his money far and wide. He owns much but he gives much."

"Something's going on," Donal said, "and we need to fix it before it gets out of control." He stared at Butler, absently touched the pin on his lapel. "Why haven't the guns been moved yet?" he said. "They're getting impatient."

"The guns are going out within the week. We had to wait for the right passage aboard a boat that no one will suspect, but that doesn't change a thing. You're right, this does need to get fixed. What else do you know about this O'Brien fellow?"

"He served in the war and runs a security business in Scollay Square. They say the mob killed his wife."

"So he has nothing to lose," Butler said.

"Nothing at all."

"How do he and the detective know each other?"

"They're related—cousins, I think."

"If we bring one to heel, the other might follow, perhaps." Butler sat back in his chair and turned so that he could see out the window. From the street, music came up to them, the sound of a woman's voice in laughter, the clanging bell of a trolley. In the other room there was a cessation of sound, a break between sets.

"How are our friends settling in?" Butler asked.

"As I said, sure they're getting antsy. They feel like we're wasting their time."

"Us? We're wasting their time?"

There was the almost imperceptible movement of Donal's shoulders shrugging. His face remained indifferent, cold. The planets revolved around the sun; the sun moved through the cosmos; stars died in distant galaxies and flung their last light toward Earth, and through it all, Donal Phelan remained immutable, unchanging. The glow from the sconce at his back burned a corona around his head and shoulders.

"Not much longer," Butler said.

"They need to know."

"Will they take things into their own hands if we keep them waiting?"

"They will if they feel they have to."

"We need to be the ones in control of what happens here. Tell them they have leave to go ahead."

"You're sure?"

"I am. The guns are going home, Donal, and, in the end, that's all that matters."

"*Is maith Dia.*"

"He is good," Butler said, nodding in agreement. "He is good."

An arc of lightning illuminated the dark rooftops and caught his eye. The shape of a chimney, a water tower, a group of young men on the tarpaper passing a bottle back and forth, and then the scene faded into blackness again. He could feel the floorboards trembling beneath him with the vibration of a hundred dancers. It merged with the vibration of close thunder so that for a moment he could no longer tell the difference between the two. He thought of his brother at home in his wheelchair in the dark, trembling with fear as the night thundered about him, no one there but the old woman asleep in her cot, and him with no voice to call out for help, to tell the world or another of his fear. "For the love of Christ, Donal," he said, "will this heat never break?"

37

IT WAS EARLY Sunday morning, and, in the final days before the aquarium's doors closed forever, the place was mostly deserted. Cal, Dante, and Owen walked the shattered galleries where fish and marine animals had once been, rare species imported from the corners of the globe. This had been a mainstay of all their childhoods, even Owen's, despite the fact that he was younger. For him it had always existed in squalor but it was, nonetheless, something distinctly Southie's, and there was still a sense of pride that it was theirs, even in its neglect by the city.

Cal and Dante had seen it in better times and both felt a certain melancholy as they peered at the empty tanks covered with slime and stained dark by dirty water, at the unwashed glass and cracked plaster and the rusted, incessantly dripping pipes, the sound of which reverberated throughout the cavernous space. The dank, slightly putrid smell reminded Cal of mudflats at low tide. It was Boston's but Boston had also been its ruin. And, to them, it mirrored all beautiful things in the city that had over the years gone to ruin, including many of the old neighborhoods.

They had brought the girls with them—Owen's four-year-old, Fiona, and Dante's Maria—and the children ran ahead, Maria limping slightly from her stitches and with the bandages showing above the top of her saddle shoe. They were eager to look at the displays, excited to be free of adult constraint, and didn't seem to care about the building's decrepitude or its smell; their voices rose, high-pitched and joyful, up through the basilica-like caverns and grottoes. The once-elaborate entrance portal still showed a semblance of its rich past, with its wide ornamental pillars and intricate wood carvings of fish, sea turtles, sharks, dolphins, and mermaids that opened onto the grand space of the cupola in the main viewing room and the seal pool beneath the dome.

Dante called out to Maria, and she stopped and looked back. "Don't run, Maria, your foot is still healing. Go slow."

She nodded, smiling, and dramatically half skipped, half limped to Owen's daughter, who stood, openmouthed, staring at a rusting display embedded in the wall two feet above the floor and from which a green light glowed. The tanks were lit by the skylights above them and by electric light diffused through the water, but the water was so unclean, the whole place seemed to shimmer unpleasantly with an algae-tinged light.

At one time the aquarium had attracted over fifteen thousand people a day but during the Great Depression and through the Second World War it had been neglected, and it had declined quickly. Now, almost half the tanks were empty, and besides a small group of tourists from Canada—Cal could tell from their accents—they were the only ones here.

The Canadians turned away from the fish tanks with looks of disgust on their faces, and he didn't blame them. The place was depressing. It seemed as if the building were collapsing around them from the inside out. Corroded pipes slowly leaked rusty water across sections of the once-remarkable terrazzo, leaving long black runnels. The mayor had refused to appropriate funds for the building's repair and within weeks it would be closing. Cal knew that this would probably be their last time here.

Only one seal of the colony remained, flapping and barking in its open pool beneath the dome, plunging suddenly into the water, surging around its circumference, paddling onto its rocky island, and then doing it all over again. It didn't seem to be aware of any other part of its environment. Maria and Fiona cooed and called to it and then watched for a bit, but when the animal failed to respond to them they moved on to the other exhibits and tanks.

As they walked, Owen caught Dante and Cal up on the case. He told them the names of the murdered on the night of the Fourth and said he was at a roadblock and didn't know what to do next.

"The dead," Dante said. "They were all Irish, like you thought?"

"They were all Irish. And all situated locally. They had different jobs around town."

"The type of jobs where they might have access to the boat, the way Flynn did?"

"Longshoremen, dockworkers, truck drivers, laborers, thieves— what you'd expect. A couple worked on local fishing vessels, so they might have been part of the crew who brought in the guns. We got word from New York that two of their locals with ties to the IRA may have been on the boat, but there's been no sign of them. Between us and New York and the Rhode Island and Connecticut authorities, we might still find more bodies."

"Ready-made production line to move heavy guns and transport them," Cal said.

"Yeah, the Feds think the Irish are planning something big. They've intercepted four boats in the last year smuggling arms and they assume they've missed at least twice that many."

"Were any of the other victims musicians?"

"I checked the list I got from the Intercontinental, and two of them played at regular gigs around town."

"Just like Flynn," Cal said.

"Just like Flynn, but that's not enough to think there's some kind of connection. A quarter of the Irish in town play out at the local halls. For every musician, there's a dozen who know one or two of their fathers' old tunes on the accordion or tin whistle."

"Did you ask the wives if they knew any of the other deceased?"

"They knew them, all right, but only casually, through the dance-hall

240

scene and the Irish social clubs. A few attended classes at the cultural center or were a part of the Gaelic Athletic Association games out in Brighton. There's all manner of connection, and none of it stands out."

"Someone is pulling the strings here, someone's giving the orders," Dante said. "Someone who has the same type of connections."

"That's an awful wide net, and I don't see a way of narrowing it."

"We need the name of your informant," Cal said.

Owen paused to look at a tank and peered, squinting, into the murky water. Something there glided briefly into view; it was translucent and pale, a gelatinous eye on the end of a thinly veined protuberance. He looked up at Cal and shook his head.

"Jesus, Owen, you want our help—"

"I do and I'm glad for it, but that name is staying in the books. Even if Giordano asked for it, I wouldn't give it up. I'd be putting him at too much of a risk, him and who knows how many more people with him who have access to the same info. I don't want another night like the Fourth. There's a reason he trusted me in the first place. I won't jeopardize that."

"Yeah, and there's a reason the guns were gone before you got there and there are now six people dead, maybe more. Whose side is this informant playing on, anyway? How do you know he wasn't playing you all along?"

"I know, trust me. He wasn't. He's fed me stuff before and it's always been straight. So, discussion over. No informant's name."

"What has he fed you?"

"Stuff."

Cal looked at Owen. Dante watched as they stared each other down. Owen was the first to blink. He pursed his lips and his cheeks hollowed.

"Little stuff, all right? A year ago it was a stolen car carrying small arms, the same six months later. Both times we set up a sting with the Staties and nailed them. His word is good."

"You ever wonder why he was doing this?" Dante asked.

"Why he was doing what?"

"Ah, will you stop!" Cal said. "Why he was giving you the shit in the first place."

"That's how you build trust, slowly, over time. You know that. He gave me the stolen cars with the guns and it led to this, a huge arms shipment."

"Yeah, but what's he getting in return? He throws you a couple of bones—no skin off his nose—but now the big one, and they know they've been tipped off?"

"Not by him, they weren't. I won't give him up."

Owen looked from Dante to Cal. Squinting, he rubbed at a spot above his right temple.

"Are we good?" he asked. "Are you two still with me?"

A strange and unpleasant odor passed through the gallery, as if sewage water had suddenly been released into the aquarium's reservoir and tanks. Dante held a handkerchief to his mouth and Cal's face blanched. His eyes watered as he nodded, but it took him a moment to speak.

"Yeah," he said, "we're all good. If we don't have the informant, we'll pretend he doesn't even exist and we'll go at it another way."

"How?"

"I don't know yet."

Fiona and Maria stood quietly before the tank that contained the five giant turtles. They stared through the plate glass as the turtles rose and fell and glided through their murky world. One, the giant green female weighing over four hundred pounds, came close to the glass and held the children's gaze with her own, and held in fascination, they were stilled by it.

The men watched the children and the turtle and they too were momentarily transfixed by the image—the two girls with their hands upon the glass in silent communion with the quiet behemoth that had emerged from the murk. Sunlight from the skylights above cast a flickering illumination down through the water, and for a brief, transitory moment they could forget the decaying state of the building around them, the killings, their conversations of death, and their separate places in all of it.

38

DAY BOULEVARD, SOUTH BOSTON

FITZGERALD SAT IN the car parked at the curb beachside a ways down from the house and smoked a cigarette while he read the paper. Bobby and the two others stood on the beach in their undershirts and trousers with the cuffs rolled up. It was a little after seven o'clock and the sun had just cleared the surface of the blue horizon. It felt good to be in the sun and feel, even this early in the morning, the sand warm beneath his feet. The humidity had broken for now—a series of heavy thunderstorms had passed through during the night, keeping Bobby awake as he stared at the ceiling and watched its crackling light show displayed across the walls, listened to what sounded like distant artillery pounding an enemy's position, and then the rain had come lashing at the window, sending the panes shaking.

Far out, above the outer harbor islands, silver heat shimmered as everything began to build again, but for now the temperature was hot but pleasant. High white cumulus clouds like dandelion clocks, with fat mushroom heads, moved slowly across the sky. Bobby and the other two were attempting to throw a baseball like the Americans did, and they had difficulty not laughing as they tossed the ball back and forth, repeatedly failing to catch it in their fumbling hands. They didn't know the proper mechanics to throw and so instead merely pushed the ball from one to the other, and it kept falling into the sand. For a while, in the absence of Fitzgerald, Bobby could forget why they were there. One thing they had feared was being noticed as outsiders—here in Southie, it seemed everything and anything out of the ordinary was detected, the locals being far more vigilant and safeguarded than any police force; they patrolled their own streets better than the cops. But so far, being on the beach had served the men well. New Irish immigrants were hardly given a second glance, and at this time of the morning, the Avenue was mostly deserted, but four men sitting cramped in a car and smoking cigarettes, one after the other, on a warm July morning would have drawn suspicion.

Here and there, he noted people—someone walking a dog; a runner, shirtless and sweating, pounding the pavement toward Pleasure Bay. Farther down, a couple of men left the bathhouses with small duffel bags, presumably containing their clothing from the gym.

Kinsella stopped throwing the ball, sat down at a park bench, and watched them, shaking his head and offering advice but mostly criticizing. "Jaysus! What a right pair of goms the two of you are. You couldn't hit a sack of potatoes the way you're throwing that yolk."

"You give it a go, then," said Egan.

"I will in me arse. I'll let you two make the fools out of yeselves."

"Shall we get to a baseball game before we head home? Go see the Red Sox?"

"What? And sit there for hours watching a game that we don't know the rules of, like right fucking eejits?"

Fitzgerald came up the pathway to the beach, the newspaper folded under his arm. "He's left," he said. "Same time as before. Do you know the route in and out?"

"I do," Bobby said.

"Show me on the map. I want to know how we're getting out once it's done."

"No maps. Maps are dangerous things to have on you." Bobby tapped his temple. "It's in my head."

"Well, tell us."

"I'll show you on the way out."

Kinsella shifted on the bench and stared out at the sea. "As long as we're not doing it on a Sunday," he said.

Fitzgerald looked at him. "We do it when I say we do it."

"Not on a feckin' Sunday, I won't."

"The same here," said Egan.

Bobby tried to hold his tongue, knowing anything from him was sure to irk Fitzgerald and perhaps put him into a rage. "Every morning, he says farewell to his wife and child at the door," he said now. "I won't be party to killing a man in front of his family. We need to pick another place, another location, anywhere, just not in front of his family."

"What do you think this is? Who do you think we are? The Society of St. Vincent de Fucking Paul? We've put too much time into this for it to be wasted now. This is the most straightforward way and the easiest. We have, as you said, clear points in and out. The streets are mostly deserted in the morning. By the time police get here, we'll be on the highway heading north or south in the other car. We do this the way we planned to on fucking Monday, and that's it. Am I clear?"

"There's no reason to do it before his family."

"Are you walking away from this one? Like you did before? They're giving you one last chance to prove yourself. I already told them they were fools for sending you with us, that you'd find a way to bollix it up. If you're not up to this, you can fuck off now and we'll settle it later. I need to know."

"I'm ready, but I'm telling you it's wrong."

"You never mind what's right or wrong. You leave that to me."

"When all this is done, we're going to have some things to settle between us. Just you and me."

"I'll look forward to it with pleasure."

245

Bobby nodded and Fitzgerald held his gaze, then said between barely parted lips, "If you fuck up, I'll put a bullet in you meself."

The four men walked back to the curb and got into the car, Bobby at the wheel. He drove like a tour guide, mindful of the speed, reminding them to take in their surroundings. They traveled along Day Boulevard before Old Harbor, gulls shrieking over Pleasure Bay, and, to their left, Marine Park and the decrepit cathedral-like aquarium, the cod-shaped weather vane flashing above its peeling cupola, and there was the statue of Admiral Farragut, casting his impressive bronze gaze out to the gray sea. Then they turned west onto the Shore Road and East First Street, toward the Edison plant stacks pumping gray smoke into the blue sky, and with the sea breeze coming through the open windows, ruffling their shirt collars and heavy with the smell of fried food from the few small eateries by the park, and the airplane from Logan arcing slowly above the fort at Castle Island before them, they might have been tourists out for a lazy drive on a summer day in Boston.

39

GREALISH BOXING GYM, DORCHESTER

CAL, IN A T-shirt and boxing trunks, stood before the wall with its faded photos of champions who'd trained at or visited the gym. There was Jack Dempsey and Gene Tunney, who'd come to the ring as part of a marketing campaign promoting their second fight and had posed in boxer's stances for the picture captioned *The Manassa Mauler and the Fighting Marine,* and legendary John L. Sullivan, the Boston Strong Boy from Roxbury, the last heavyweight champion of bareknuckle boxing.

Then there were the boxers who'd become local legends even if they had never made good in the professional ranks. There was even a picture of Cal himself there, as a much younger man, standing with Conn Grealish and his brother Matty, but Cal rarely looked at it even when people new to the gym noticed it and asked if that was really him. Only the older locals had known him before the war and before the damage to his leg. He knew the younger boxers referred to him among themselves as the Gimp—his injury was like a disease, a contagion that, in their fear of mortality, eventual decline and decrepitude, they believed they might catch if they came too close. Hell, some of them wouldn't even spar with him.

His father was in the picture too, smiling and proud, apparently, and handsome too, Cal had to admit. He could almost smell the sweat off him as he had as a teenager, sharp and sweet from whiskey, and combined with concrete dust, a fresh scent that seemed to come through his pores as if he'd just stepped out of a furnace. There was a cruelty that hid beneath the smile and the good looks that made his father all the more foreboding, the strength in those massive hands that could snap finger bones in their grip. God help the man or woman who took that look for anything other than what it was. And, over time, even the trainers—Conn and Matty Grealish and Conn's sons—came to recognize it.

Cal thought of his meeting at St. Anthony's with the Pioneer and the warning to keep out of their business. If the man knew him at all, he would've realized that that was the last thing he should say. Cal went over to the heavy bag and worked it with more anger than he'd had in some time.

He kept at it until he was drenched and the wooden floorboards were stained dark with a pool of his sweat, and then, to cool down, he did twenty minutes of jump-rope work, slowly and off balance because of his bad leg, but the warmth and the exercise helped, and after ten minutes, the muscles and tendons, though they would hurt later, began to loosen. When he was done and still breathing heavy, he toweled off, and with the towel draped about his neck, he walked through the gym and, thinking of his father, searched out one of the Irish boxers that he knew well.

Packie McGuire, whom everyone called the Lip, was climbing out of the ring in the back room, Matty Grealish holding the rope for him. Packie had come over eight or so years before Cal shipped overseas, and everyone knew him because he was with the city's Department of Public Works. Most of the neighbors tipped the sanitation men at Christmastime, and Cal and Lynne had always received a thank-you card back from Packie. Cal waved to him, and Packie, bowlegged and canting to the right, sat heavily on the bench. He removed his mouthpiece and put out his hands for Cal to pull his gloves off. Grunting, Cal got them off and laid them on the wood. Packie was breathing heavily and wincing with each breath, although Cal could see no damage to his face; he looked like he'd just barely broken a sweat.

"What are you panting about? You couldn't have been in there for more than two rounds."

"I wasn't, but sure didn't Matt get me good in the kidneys, the bollix. He kept going low too, and tapping my feckin' balls, the effer." He eyed Matty as he headed to the lockers.

"Drive him into the ropes next time," Cal said, "and put your thigh hard in his crotch and he won't do that again."

Packie nodded and lowered his head, inhaling and exhaling deeply. "Aye," he said after a moment, "I'll certainly do that."

They talked about family and recent fights and upcoming bouts, about the June match between Rocky Marciano and Ezzard Charles and the approaching rematch.

"I tell you, that Ezzard Charles is some fighter," Packie said. "Jesus, Rocky couldn't get him down."

"He took a ton of punishment."

"They both did. Rocky looked as if he would drop from swinging his arms so much. I don't think he could believe that Ezzard was still standing." Packie shook his head and wiped at his mouth absently; it was a smoker's gesture, and Cal could tell that he was dying for a cigarette, but Conn Grealish didn't allow smoking in the gym. The same was true of alcohol.

"Packie," he said. "You've always got an ear to the ground. Has anything come up lately among the Irish to do with the IRA?"

"IRA?" Packie looked at him quizzically.

"To do with all the recent shootings. You've heard about them?"

"Yeah, terrible stuff."

"Well, what are people saying?"

Packie looked about the room and then stood, pressing on the muscles of his thighs. "C'mon," he said, "I'm still winded by that gobshite. Let's see if I can't get me breath back. Lend us a hand at the heavy bag, would you?"

Packie put out his hands again and Cal pulled the gloves up over the tape, made sure they were secure, and tied them, and then they went to the heavy bag and he held it as Packie began with slow, methodical combinations, and focused on his breathing.

"They say," he said, and he punched, left-left-right, left-left-right, "that the bodies of the dead are going back home, with condolences and prayers for the departed."

"What the hell does that mean?" Cal said, his head against the bag, his body dripping with sweat even though he wasn't the one working. Packie looked about him and then paused. There was a group of three men in the corner of the room lifting weights; Cal and Packie heard the resounding clang of metal against metal as the bars banged the braces of the bench. Every now and then, the three looked in Packie and Cal's direction.

Packie mock-blocked and then laid off six combinations in a row. Just watching him made Cal exhausted. "They say," he continued, "it's not just the bodies that are going home to Ireland but also some gifts for the Cause. Lots of the lads are already patting themselves on the backs that they got one over on the cops."

Cal listened intently and considered what Packie was saying. The absence of the sound of metal striking metal drew his attention. The group of men lifting weights had stopped what they were doing and were eye-balling them.

A pulse pounded hard in Cal's neck. The Pioneer's warning came to his mind, and he wondered if he had been followed, if he'd become so complacent he'd let something like that happen. He was filled with an immense anger, but there was fear there as well.

"You know those guys?" Cal motioned with his head toward the corner, and Packie glanced over his shoulder, turned back, and struck the bag twice. "Some Irish lads—I think I've seen them here before but I'm not sure."

"What the fuck are they looking at?" Cal said. "Hey," he called out, "you lot, what the fuck are you looking at?"

"Would you whisht, Cal. Sure they're not doing any harm."

"Then why are they eyeballing us like that?"

Cal stepped away from the bag and limped toward the men. Packie watched him silently.

He stood a few yards from them and shouted again, "What the fuck are you looking at?" The rest of the gym had fallen silent. Cal was aware of the eyes of others on him.

"I can remember every one of your faces, you got that?" He tapped his head. "So now it's up here and I won't forget."

Joe Castiglione, the manager of the gym, and Conn Grealish, the owner, were at his side. Joe touched his shoulder. "Whoa, Cal. What's going on here?"

Cal kept his gaze on the three men. "These—" He glanced briefly at Joe and Conn, and then nodded toward the men. "They fucking won't stop staring at me. If they want to have a go at me, I'll give them a fucking go." Cal was shaking now, trembling with rage, and he spit as he spoke. He felt Joe's hand tighten on his shoulder.

"You guys," Grealish said, "what's your problem?"

"You know who we are, Conn."

"That's right, I know who you are, but I asked you what the fucking problem is. Are you here to work out or what?"

"We're here to work out."

"Yeah, we're here to work out."

The third man nodded.

"See, Cal," Conn said, turning to Cal, trying to placate him, "they're here to work out, that's all."

"Tell them to get out of my shit. Tell them if I see them doing it again, there'll be trouble."

One of the men laughed, and the man to his right slapped a training glove against his side. He continued staring at Cal.

"They've got it, Cal," Joe said. "Don't you, lads? They'll be no trouble here."

"C'mon, Cal," Conn said, and he guided Cal back to Packie. "Let's get you set up at the bag."

Cal allowed himself to be led but waved Conn away. "Nah, Conn, that's all right. I was getting ready to leave anyway." And he turned to look at the men, who had picked up their weights again, and raised his voice so that they could hear. "There's a fucking stink in here that I can't get out of my nose. I'll take a shower and head home."

40

THE MEN TOOK the route they'd taken the three previous times, over the silent roads, the streetlamps still blazing, less bright now as day came on. The gray waters of the harbor on their right stretched out toward the sea, where the sky was beginning to lighten. In their laps they held their balaclavas and their weapons. Fitzgerald had his sawed-off at his side, half hidden in the shadows of the door panel. He'd loaded it with rat shot that could blow the hinges off doors, punch holes in mortar and plaster; Fitzgerald took a perverse pleasure in its pure brutality, in how close he needed to come to the man or woman he was about to kill.

Owen rose a little after dawn, a light mist coming in from the water chilling the still, gray air, but in it the suggestion of the heat that would come once the mist burned off and the sun was full in the sky. Dressed, he sat at the kitchen table with his coffee and the morning edition of the *Globe* as the streetlights went out along the Avenue and Anne came down the stairs with four-year-old Fiona. Anne had her blue terry-cloth robe wrapped tightly about her, and she looked haggard—Fiona had been waking in the night, calling out to Anne and insisting that some of her dolls be moved from where she'd placed them. In the end Anne had removed the dolls and lain down with Fiona. When Owen, groaning, glanced at the clock at two in the morning, he saw he was surrounded by the lot of them, half a dozen bushy-haired dolls with leering faces staring at him. It was no wonder Fiona was frightened; he'd been frightened himself, though eventually he fell into a fitful sleep.

He grinned sheepishly at Anne and made her coffee as she put Fiona in her chair and then sat heavily. "I'm sorry you had such a rotten night," he said. "If I can get home early, I'll take night watch."

Anne shook her head, took a sip of the coffee, then looked wearily at Fiona, who was spooning Cheerios into her mouth and looking at them both with large, wide eyes. "She'll do better tonight, now that the dolls are in our room." She smiled. "How'd you like sleeping with them?"

"Oh, it was a fantastic change of scenery. Another night with them and you might as well send me up to Danvers."

"If this case doesn't send you there first."

Owen shrugged and pushed the newspaper across the table for her. The headlines declared that two more turf shootings had taken place during the night and that in the days ahead Boston was in for a record heat wave and that power consumption should be kept to a minimum.

"All the case takes is time, and with Cal and Dante helping me, we'll get it done. That's what I'm looking forward to, that and the expression on Giordano's face."

"What about me?"

"What about you, girl?"

"When are you looking forward to coming home to your wife?"

"Ah," Owen said, and he got up, crossed the linoleum, held her against him, and squeezed, and she wrapped an arm around his waist. "I look forward to that every day, every single day—you and Fiona, coming home to you two is the only thing that makes the job worthwhile."

❧

He kissed Anne at the front door with Fiona leaning against her mother's hip and looking up at the two of them. "You be good for Mama today, okay?" Owen said, and she nodded, and he bent and kissed her on her pursed, wet lips, held his mouth there until she pulled away, laughing.

He strode down the pathway to the sidewalk, glancing back once and waving. When the three hooded men stepped before him with raised guns, he was so taken by surprise that his first thought, which he realized was ridiculous, was *How on earth can they be wearing balaclavas in this summer heat?*

The man before him held a sawed-off, and Owen registered this right before he heard the close gun blast, and his hand went to his face in self-protection but uselessly, as half his face was already gone. Owen fell forward and another shooter stepped up and pumped three bullets into him. The three stood there for a brief moment, hooded faces looking down at Owen's body, and then they took off at a sprint toward a gray car idling at the curb twenty yards down the Avenue.

Anne rushed from the porch, screaming for help, her robe fluttering madly about her, its belt undone. Fiona stood at the door, wide-eyed in fear, not really understanding what she'd just seen, and she began wailing. Anne knelt on the path and pulled Owen's body toward her so that he was lying with what was left of his bloodied head in her lap, and she tried to rouse him as if he might still be alive and continued to scream for help as the blood pooled around them and finally neighbors came rushing from their doors.

41

BOBBY MYLES SAT on the cot, the whiskey gurgling as he drained the bottle. No matter how much he drank, it didn't help. Eyes closed or open, he could see all of the dead parade before him, like a film reel looped over and over, and he watched with relentless clarity the horror that clutched them in their last moments as living, breathing things. Skin cooked off the bone, faces torn open, limbs sheared off torsos; a young girl holding back her insides as she stumbled into the street. Now joining them was the man they'd killed this morning, a man who had just said good-bye to his family and then, in one loud flash of gunfire, tumbled down onto the walkway with half his head obliterated in a red mist.

Before Myles knew it, the pint bottle was almost empty. Bile burned his throat but he wanted more whiskey. He'd have to go downstairs to the bar and grab another. Maybe it would help knock him out and allow him a moment to hide from his thoughts and cower in a temporary blackness. Maybe it would just make it worse.

He stood from the bed and walked to the dresser to grab a cigarette. He got one in his mouth, and after lighting it, he realized he'd lit the

256

wrong end. This made him laugh, but it was the laugh of a broken man. He dropped it to the ground, stamped on it, brought another to his mouth, and picked up the almost-empty pint.

The heat in the small room doubled, and the walls started to close in on him. His hand went numb and the bottle slid from his fingers and clattered to the floor. Voices came to him and he could hear somebody cursing through the walls, and for a brief moment, it was comforting to know that somebody else was suffering too.

The tobacco burned quickly and he found himself at the window, looking out at the street. It was the same shade of filth that he'd seen in the factory towns of England when he'd lived there with his father, a year in Manchester and two more in Liverpool. *Hell on earth,* he thought. Would he ever get to that place where he could breathe clean air again?

"Bobby."

Myles turned from the window and saw Egan standing at the open door.

"Thought I'd ask if you wanted to go for a drink. But it looks like you're already on your way." Egan gestured to the bottle on the floor.

Myles lowered his head. "Where are the others?"

"They went into town again."

"With who?"

"Some men they met. Locals."

Egan came in and closed the door behind him. "You don't look so good."

Myles ran his fingers through his hair, which was damp with sweat. "I'll be fine once we leave this fucking city."

Egan laughed uncomfortably. "It's not that bad."

"You don't think?" He shook his head. "You know what we did today? Do you know?"

Egan could never pull off a stern, authoritative tone, but he tried anyway. "We don't ask questions, you know that, Bobby."

"It was dirty, I tell you."

"We were told to—"

"Fuck what we were told. What we did, that wasn't for Ireland."

The short man turned away. "I'll go down and get you another bottle. And then you try to relax. We'll be going home soon."

"Home, right." Myles smirked. "I'll get my own bottle. Be off, then."

"Suit yourself."

Bobby shut his eyes and pinched the bridge of his nose. The dead were still there, waiting for him. He knew that no matter how far west he went, they would always follow. He took the bottle off the floor and sucked down the small amount of whiskey that remained.

42

CAL DROVE THEM out of South Boston, leaving the funeral home and following the police down East Broadway. The going was slow but the traffic lights were held by police on motorbikes who somberly waved the procession through. Cal watched it stretching a half a mile ahead of them, squad cars and motorbikes from across the Commonwealth of Massachusetts and the rest of New England—Maine, New Hampshire, Vermont, Rhode Island, Connecticut—and Cal recognized some black-and-whites from New York and Philly, Nevada and California, all with their spinning, flashing blues and reds.

As Cal drove, Dante, beside him, looked out of the window. Another storm had come through during the night—it had been a week of them in quick succession—and the rain was still coming down, pooling in gutters, on the awnings over storefronts, on the chrome of parked cars. Pedestrians lined the funeral route, many in their Sunday best, many curious, some impatient with the length of the cavalcade. Somewhere a driver honked his horn twice, bright and sharp, and he noticed the motorcycle cops looking in that direction. The driver didn't blow his horn a third time. Gulls floated down on unseen thermals and alighted on the buildings. The bells of St. Anne's continued to toll solemnly, as if marking Owen's final passage through Southie.

They passed the West Broadway police station, where uniformed officers stood assembled, saluting the passing hearse, then Amrheins, one of Owen's old haunts, where, standing curbside, four drunks hooted and hollered and held beers aloft as the cars passed by. Over the West Fourth Street Bridge, the Cabot rail yards, and into the South End, to the Cathedral of the Holy Cross on Washington, the mother church of the Roman Catholic Archdiocese of Boston. The inbound El, two stories above, squealed before the church's Gothic façade and its massive stained-glass rose window.

They parked southeast of the church, beneath the Dover Street Station, and climbed out of the car. Men and women, all nursing their own private grievings, raced beneath the overhead rails and before the traffic to escape the rain, newspapers and umbrellas held over their heads. Outside Harry the Greek's, its windows steamed over, a homeless beggar rattled his pail for coins.

Without speaking Cal and Dante walked the three blocks to the cathedral, toward the flashing lights of the halted police procession, merging with other mourners attired in black, the rain slanting at angles through the El's lumbering metalwork above them.

Cal glanced at his reflection in the windows of cars parked along the curb but did not recognize himself—it could have been someone else, a stranger, walking in his shoes. But there was Dante, he could see that, walking on his right, in his dark suit and black tie, head slightly bowed to avoid the rain, his features pinched, either in thought or in consternation. But this other person with Dante—the one reflected back in the rain-stippled glass—he simply could not place. Even when he grinned and showed his teeth to see if the reflection was really him, he could not convince himself that it was he who had made the expression. He told himself that perhaps he had the DTs or some nagging mental fatigue that a shot of whiskey would set right and quick, but he knew it was not that at all.

He felt panicked; a sudden instinctual urge to flee grasped him, an irrational fear telling him that he must run, that they were heading into danger, that their lives were threatened—he eyed the passersby stepping from storefronts and alleys, splashing through puddles beneath the El, convinced that one of them was an assailant, and he worked to keep his nerves in check. He forced himself to continue moving toward the lights. The blurry pinpricks of red and blue coalesced into small halos narrowing and growing smaller, as if they were receding, pulling farther and farther away from them, and the distance continued to widen. He squinted against the sensation, which felt like a migraine pressing at his skull, like an ice pick through his eyes, and he closed them for a moment and focused on his breathing, slow and measured, and his and Dante's footfalls upon the sidewalk.

"You all right?" Dante at his shoulder, but his voice was muffled, as if it were penetrating a fog.

Cal nodded but didn't open his eyes immediately. The concrete smelled of rain, of wet cigarette butts, and there was the sluice rushing from a sewer, the blare of car horns, of voices, the grinding of the subway car's brakes, metal and sparks above them in a darkness he could sense beyond his closed eyelids. When the curb ended, Dante reached for him and Cal opened his eyes. Everything still seemed too bright even though the hulking tresses and supports of the El blocked out most of the light and when he looked up it was still overcast and gray. Neon beer signs shone in bar windows, merging with the lights of the traffic signals before them and the swirling blue and red of the parked procession a half a block ahead. Dante took his hand away. He was looking at him with concern.

"Are you sure you're okay?" he asked.

"Yeah, I'm all right, I'm all right."

They crossed beneath the El at the intersection as the cathedral's bells began their shimmering peal. On the sidewalk they could hear the grand pipe organ from within the cathedral sounding Mozart's Requiem Mass.

❧

After the Mass they followed the hearse and police procession to the grave and another rain shower came on suddenly and Cal was glad for it. There was a numbing effect to watching the rain beading down the glass, hearing the metronome-like thump of the wipers, seeing the bleary train of cars before them, the red and blue police lights fractured and split by the rain so that they shimmered like prisms, and he could dissociate from what they were doing: burying Owen. His heart was a flat thump in his chest that he recognized dully; surely it was failing him, he thought. He had the sense that he and Dante had spoken during the trip to and from the cathedral but he couldn't remember what they'd spoken about.

At Cedar Grove Cemetery they laid Owen in the earth and Father Nolan said the final prayers and now Owen was back with his father and mother and their parents before them.

There had been no traditional laying-out and viewing for Owen, not with half his face gone, and the coffin had remained in state in the front parlor, but Cal knew that Anne had had the funeral home place a crucifix at his breast and rosary beads in his hands, with the beads slipped through his fingers. Cal had stopped in at their house the previous three days and nights and said the rosary with those present, and the prayer and response had been a calming balm of sorts, if not a numbing one.

Fierro came by on the final night to pay his respects, and Giordano also, talking to the men charged with the honor of the casket watch, holding vigil over the coffin. Little Fiona peered around the doorway and Anne took her into the kitchen, where Cal heard the metal hinge on the refrigerator opening, the brief clink of a glass taken from the cupboards, and the sound of a glass of milk being poured. Then their soft footfalls on the carpeted stairs.

As she had for the past nights, shortly after the clock on the mantel in the living room chimed ten o'clock, Anne came back down from Fiona's room, and an old man with a tuft of white hair brushed back with oil on either side of his head—a cousin of Anne's on her mother's side—said the Rosary for the Dead. As Cal prayed, he asked God to bear Owen's soul directly to Heaven and to allow some manner of peace through His love to enter Anne's and Fiona's hearts. He asked that God look after them and keep them in His blessing and in His care.

As the old man spoke, eyes downcast and brow furrowed, focused on his intentions or on those he prayed for, his false teeth moved and slipped in his mouth, creating a soft, wet smacking sound that Cal tried to ignore. "We implore Thee, O Lord," he prayed, "to absolve all their sins from the souls of Thy faithful, so after that having risen again, they may live in the glory of the Resurrection, amid the saints and the elect. Through Christ Our Lord, Amen." And all of them made the sign of the cross, then rose from their kneeling positions. They slowly said their farewells to Anne, who was sitting before the coffin and staring at it as the mourners left, and Fiona cried out from some new horror that had come to her in her sleep.

Father Nolan was done with the final words. He clasped his hands together and they watched as Anne and Fiona came forward. Anne took up the shovel, and Fiona placed her hand over her mother's, and they tilted a blade of dirt and stone down upon the coffin. Owen's captain began the Last Radio Call; he talked of Owen's Irish background, his length of service, his many commendations and medals, his love of family.

"Gone, but not forgotten," the men in blue chorused, their badges shrouded in mourning with black cloth, and Cal echoed it. "Gone, but not forgotten."

The honor guard stepped forward without rifles—Cal had spoken with Anne and then conveyed her wishes to the liaisons: there was to be no gunfire, not again and not with Fiona present. Instead, there would be a twenty-one-bell salute. As the bell was solemnly rung—a sweet, clear resounding chime—the honor guard, one by one, turned to face the grave and, upon each peal, snapped a salute to their fallen comrade, white gloves held to their caps.

The color guard took the flags that had draped the coffin, folded them, one after the other, and handed them to Anne. Two bagpipers, each dressed in traditional kilt, sporran, and feather bonnet, filled the bellows and played "Amazing Grace," then "Loch Lomond," and finally "Danny Boy."

> *But when ye come, and all the flowers are dying,*
> *And I am dead, as dead I well may be,*
> *You'll come and find the place where I am lying,*
> *And kneel and say an Ave there for me.*
> *And I shall hear, though soft you tread above me,*
> *And all my grave will warmer, sweeter be,*
> *For you will bend and tell me that you love me,*
> *And I shall sleep in peace until you come to me.*

During the last refrain, a holder released a dove, and Cal watched the bird climb above the trees, over the Dorchester skyline, and then, in a flickering white blur, it disappeared into the gray. He gazed after it for a long while and then it began to rain again, and the drops fell softly on his face. The umbrellas came up as the mourners filed out of the grave-yard. Anne's brother was at her side, and she and Fiona were flanked by police liaisons who escorted them to the waiting cars. Cal had seen the officers during the wake, standing guard outside the house in black-and-whites and, in dress uniform, performing the casket watch, two of them facing each other and keeping vigil at each end of Owen's fallen body, relieved by another team every thirty minutes, all through the day and night, up until this moment, when their vigil and Owen's journey was finally over.

Fierro was still smoking after all these years, or at least he took every opportunity to smoke when his wife wasn't present. A butt, thick with white ash, dangled from the side of his mouth. His eyebrows were mea-ger things receding into his brow that looked as if they'd been singed by a close flame. He took out the cigarette and tapped the ash to the ground, lifted his hat and ran a hand through his thinning hair. "Cal," he said. "Dante."

They watched the slow skein of family and then the cortege of police from the cemetery grounds, black umbrellas glistening with rain, the color guard lowering their flags and winding them tight against their poles. Cal, Dante, and Fierro stood in a comfortable silence—the *familiáritátés* of mourners at funerals—listening to the bells from the small chapel across the grounds, their usual peal on the quarter hour echoing the twenty-one-bell salute of the honor guard. Cal knew that this must be difficult for Fierro—he and Owen were friends and he'd seen the body and done the autopsy. Cal could only create images in his mind of what that must have been like, how Owen would have looked. He wondered if, using putty, Fierro had tried to reconstruct Owen's face before they put him in the coffin. Before they'd arranged him in the front parlor of the house on Day Boulevard with his rosary. To make him resemble the man he remembered.

43

DAY BOULEVARD, SOUTH BOSTON

LYNNE STANDS ATOP the roof, smiling at him. The wind at this height sets her hair flowing, and she has to push it out of her eyes. She is saying something, calling to him, and she lifts an arm and waves and he laughs because he can't hear her and he tells her to wait, he must come closer, but there is no sound and then she goes to the edge of the roof and steps off, and she falls as she bursts into flame.

Cal opened his eyes. He was sitting in the car, smoke twining lazily upward from a cigarette in his hand, the ash fallen onto the seat and his lap. A soprano was singing the Ave Maria on the radio, so achingly beautiful it left him cold, and he switched it off.

There was a rap on the passenger-side door, and Cal turned his head. Dante was on the sidewalk; he'd struck the door with his knuckles, and now he leaned in the window. "You ready?" he said.

Cal ground what was left of the cigarette into the ashtray, worked his way out of the seat, shirt sticking to the vinyl, and climbed out. He reached into the backseat for his suit coat and put it on while Dante watched. Dante wanted to say that it was too fucking hot for it, that most of the mourners had already disposed of their jackets, but he said nothing and instead took his own coat from the backseat and put it on. For a moment they stood looking at each other and then Dante nodded his head toward the house and Cal stepped onto the curb and they walked the block down Day Boulevard, past the parked cars, to Owen's house. As they went up the steps, a slim, snow-white herring gull—a female, perhaps, or a young male—swooped low across the boulevard, shrieking, scattering the fat, beach-fed seagulls, and Cal paused, watching it climb back into the sky and turn toward the sea, moving toward a distant point he could not see and so quickly that it was soon gone. He hesitated on the steps and then, sensing Dante watching him, walked up onto the porch and opened the screen door.

In a corner of the parlor, Anne sat with a group of family members, her face blanched of color, and Cal worried that the shock of Owen's death and the heat had taken a terrible toll upon her. When he and Dante paid their respects, she looked at them with the eyes of a noctambulist. They went to the drinks table, where bottles of liquor were arranged alongside trays of sandwiches. On the floor, a tin tub filled with melting ice held half-submerged bottles of beer. Cal opened two beers for them and gulped deeply from his. He turned his face, streaming with sweat, toward the fans placed in the wide windows that looked out on the street and the beach. He tugged at his tie. The fans swept the curtains back and pushed the hot air about the crowded room, but otherwise they didn't do a damn thing. Out on the Avenue the sun glinted in the puddles of water left by the rain, and he could see the steam rising off them.

Dante sat at the upright piano with a beer and considered the songs that three years previously he and Owen had sung together after Lynne's funeral. He didn't know what Owen had thought of him or if he'd ever seen him as anything other than a junkie, but in the end, perhaps it didn't matter. Owen had treated him with respect—asking him to stand up and be there for Cal and be more than the junkie he was. He'd expected something of him, something a junkie could never have done and would never have been asked to do. Dante stroked the polished mahogany, lifted the piano top, and laid his fingers gently on the keys. The phonograph was playing in the other room and so no one could hear him. He leaned his head to one side so that he could hear the soft notes. The piano was out of tune—he doubted Owen had played it since Lynne's funeral. Slowly, he closed the lid again. Cal came and sat by him on the bench, handed him another beer, although he'd barely drunk any of the first one. In the other room, the phonograph played a tinny version of "Carrickfergus" and the singer was flat and without emotion, but Dante thought of Owen and listened to it anyway; they had played the same song together three years before.

I'm drunk today and I'm seldom sober, a handsome rover from town to town.
Oh, but I'm sick now. And my days are numbered, so come ye young men and lay me down.

Giordano greeted Cal and Dante as he and the other high-ranking police officers were leaving. Although he'd glimpsed him at the wake and at the funeral, he had aged since the last time Cal had seen him up close. His cheeks sagged and the skin was sallow. The once-lustrous black hair was gray at the temples. He looked as if he'd lost weight. Like a dog with its hackles up, ready to pounce at the slightest sign of aggression, Cal expected to feel something in preparation for the encounter, but he felt nothing, only numbness.

"I'm sorry for your loss," Giordano said, and Cal was surprised when Giordano held out a hand, which Cal shook. He had to admit he was grateful for the condolences, even if they came from Giordano. In a week or even days it might be different, but for now he'd take it.

"Thanks. It's a loss for all of us."

"He was good police."

"The best."

"We're going to get the fuckers who did this." Giordano looked at

Cal as if he expected an argument. Cal didn't know if the commissioner had said it to console him or to warn him.

"Good," Cal said. "Owen deserves that."

Fierro came over, and his presence seemed to make Giordano feel he'd been relieved. He nodded at them and then turned toward the door, and his junior commanders followed.

"What did he want?" Fierro asked; his eyes were red-rimmed and even more tired-looking than usual. The ever-present cigarette butt hung from the right side of his mouth.

"Told me he was sorry for Owen's death. Said Owen was good police."

Fierro nodded, took the butt from his mouth, and tapped the ash into an ashtray on a side table. "I thought he might be trying to recruit you, get you back on the force. Owen always bemoaned the fact that being a cop had changed so much, said they needed more cops like you."

"More cops like me? That's a laugh. Owen might have wanted me to be a cop again, but I can guarantee Giordano wanted no part of it."

"And what about you?"

"What about me?"

"What do you want?"

"If Giordano ever offers to take me back, then he's more of a fool than I ever gave him credit for." Cal shook his head, swallowed the rest of his beer, and put the empty bottle down. He looked toward the door, where Anne was saying farewell to mourners. Suddenly, she broke down, and an older woman held her, trembling, in her arms and then left the room with her. The record that had been playing ended and then the tone arm slipped and there was the hiss and pop as the needle skimmed across the acetate. "No, Fierro," Cal said, "that boat sailed a long time ago."

Fierro was looking at him the way Cal had often seen him look at an eviscerated cadaver, as if he might somehow work secrets from the desiccated flesh, the layers of skin and bone. A secret that might explain the life the victim had lived or what had happened in the moment shortly before his death that had led him to be stretched out on his examining table.

"If you say so," Fierro said.

Owen's daughter, Fiona, wide-eyed and disoriented, came into the room and walked aimlessly among the mourners as if she were looking for her father, as if she expected that at any moment he might step out and surprise her. Cal watched her, then placed his beer on a windowsill and went to her side. She was looking at the throng of people in the room, bewilderment on her face, and when Cal touched her shoulder, she glanced up at him. "Hey there," he said. "How're you doing?"

She stared at him with her large blue eyes and then, after a long while, blinked. "Mommy says Daddy is in heaven now," she said.

Cal remained silent, waiting. He was on his fifth beer and he didn't know what to say. Her hair had been put back with two red barrettes and he could smell that it had recently been washed. A line of perspiration beaded the top of her brow, at the hairline.

"She says that he's with God because he was so good."

He squeezed her shoulder reassuringly.

"God takes all the good people," she said and looked at the room again.

She leaned her head against his side and he put his arm over her and held her there and they stood that way for a long time as Cal heard from upstairs the distant sounds of Anne's wailing and the women with her trying to soothe and comfort her, pleading with her to be quiet, while outside, beyond the glass, in the full glare of the noon sun, Lynne was stepping off a rooftop and falling to her death over and over again.

44

NORTH END

THE LATE-AFTERNOON SUN sucked the color out of everything—the intensity and vastness of the sky was gone, and all the buildings and cars appeared bleached out and blurred in the heat. Dante had been at Uphams Corner since seven that morning, and after hours of being in the humid darkness of the welding pit, his eyes still hadn't adjusted, and the light made him dizzy. He was hungry and realized he had to eat something before he felt even worse. The European Restaurant was close by and he decided to treat himself to an early dinner.

The past week had been good for business at Uphams Corner Auto. The endless heat wave had caused many car radiators to break down; there were multiple blown gaskets and countless tires in ruin from the hot asphalt. Money was coming in steadily, and at any other time, he'd have been grateful, but now his mind was occupied so frequently with Vinny's murder that he couldn't think of much else.

He had already visited the lakes several times this week. What would he accomplish by going there and standing vigil yet again? Yesterday afternoon, he had taken Maria along with him, and while she played at the lake's edge, grabbing twigs and sticks and throwing stones into the water, he sat on a rock and tried to figure out the exact spot where the stolen Plymouth had settled into the muck below. He'd seen the sun rippling against the water, mallard ducks gliding along the surface, the shadow of carp patrolling the shallows, and the occasional outdoorsman paddling a canoe off in the distance, but he had noticed nothing out of the ordinary. Yet the ominous feeling persisted—something was going to go wrong.

It was nearly dusk when Dante returned home, his stomach full of pasta and clams, his head light from a few glasses of wine. In the kitchen, Claudia was packing the fridge with groceries. She had on the same unflattering dress he'd seen her wearing the past few days, her slender frame hidden by its puritanical cut and stiff, boxy waistline. Taking a quick glance at her, one would assume she was wearing too much eye shadow and rouge, but it wasn't makeup; her face was still bruised, although the bruises were slowly healing, each purple-hued and tinged with yellow. Beneath the swelling and the scabs, her old face was reappearing, but it was not the one she had worn when she was with Vinny—it was the one from before, when she'd lived in Scollay Square, desperate and alone. It was the face of a woman afraid of life, afraid of living.

Dante reached into the fridge and grabbed a bottle of beer. He pried off the cap, flipped it into the trash bin, and, after his first haul off the beer, asked, "Why so much food?"

"I'll be away."

"Where's away?"

"I'm going to stay with Daria in Connecticut. They have a room for rent. I'm going to see if I like it there."

Dante was staring at her, and she knew it, but she kept her eyes on the lunch meats wrapped in wax paper that she was placing on the bottom rack next to a jar of applesauce and several tins of sardines.

"Maria is already in bed. Just so you know, she has a temperature." Her voice was monotone and terse.

"Okay."

"And I talked with Mrs. Berardi earlier. She's going away for a couple of days to visit her son. She won't be around to help out."

"Okay," he repeated. He wanted to ask her more questions but he knew what the result would be. "I'll check on Maria in a bit."

She closed the fridge, folded the paper bags, and put them under the sink. "I'll be catching a Greyhound out of Saint James. Tonight." With her eyes downcast, she walked around him.

"Let me drive you."

"No. I can handle it."

"When do you think you'll be back?"

"I'm not too sure. I'll call sometime and let you know."

She padded into the hallway and he heard the bedroom door click shut, quietly, as though she were trying not to wake Maria in the next room.

Dante drained the rest of his beer, opened a second bottle, sat down at the kitchen table, and looked out the window. He watched as people moved about the sidewalks, gathered on stoops and in front of shops and restaurants, all of them seeming no more real than images on a cinema screen. And as the last of the day's greasy light fell through the gaps between the buildings, he smoked and finished the beer.

How long would it take for Claudia to forgive him?

In the end, he knew there was nothing else to do but give it time. And if time couldn't heal that wound, then nothing would.

After taking a cold shower, he dressed quickly and came out to the sitting room to see that Claudia had already left. Traces of a lilac perfume lingered in the air.

He entered Maria's room, sat down on the cot, and put his hand on her forehead. It was damp and warm. From deep in her pale throat came a tremulous murmur—she was dreaming. He wondered if he was there in her dreams with her, and he leaned back against the small headboard, one foot up on the mattress and the other on the floor, and cradled his daughter, hoping it would make her feel protected in some way.

He felt sleep press down on him, his breath drawing shallow and his eyes shutting as if from an immense weight. From within the darkness, an image slowly materialized. Ribbons of silver moonlight frantically danced and glinted like polished steel as a hot breeze rippled the lake. Bodiless, Dante hovered above the surface, and without having to hold his breath, he dived into the water and swam down to the murky bottoms. There he spotted the car, as quiet as a grave, and the dark shapes of sunfish and perch taking up residence in the metal husk alongside the pale bloated body in the front seat. The car door slowly opened without sound, and a current pulled at the passenger and made the arms move, the head slowly turn. Before Dante awoke, he saw a cadaverous hand reaching for him, and he knew that if it grabbed him, it would never let go.

45

IN THE DIN of the bar, Dante heard two men arguing toward the back of the room. He walked through the smoky haze and in an end booth found Cal drunk at a table. He was yelling and had his finger pointed at some guy's face. He was also smiling in a cocky manner, his face dark with stubble and his cheeks flushed with drink. Dante hadn't seen Cal look so thin since he came off the ship from the French field hospital in '45. Around the table, there were a few older Irishmen with pinched faces and a young man sitting with his back to Dante.

The man Cal was arguing with stood about six foot four and had wide, sloping shoulders; he was a barrel-chested laborer who weighed about two hundred and forty pounds, all of it solid as stone. His hair was orange and thick and curly with bushy sideburns that covered his cheeks and jaw and went down his neck. His eyes were a dark blue in his sunburned face.

"We'll take on this narrowback to get my boy in shape for his fight in two weeks," he said, "but my boy don't fight for nothing." At this, the men around them became excited and began hollering odds.

Dante realized it wasn't the older man that Cal wanted to fight, but the kid. The mountain of a man was his father. He could see that the kid was thin and wiry, a neck corded tightly with lean muscle—it was a neck built to take a punch. The hair was ginger like his father's and cut so close to the scalp that knotted scars on his head were visible and gleamed palely under the lamplight. And the kid already had a reputation—he had a match with a ranked fighter at Florian Hall in two weeks. Dante could hear the animated talk about the kid's left, which had already KO'd a dozen men.

Another man came over to the table and gave Cal and the boy each a shot, which Cal downed immediately. The other shot sat untouched next to the kid's full beer. More words were exchanged, and men came from their bar stools and gathered around the table, digging out crumpled ones and fives and giving them to a man who'd taken it upon himself to act as bookie. The winner of the match, he announced, would get a share of the overall pot. Dante lit a cigarette and moved closer to the table.

The kid was no more than nineteen and had a mouth missing half its teeth and a nose that had been broken and improperly set. He was wearing heavy wool slacks and a shirt far too large for his slight build. Somebody from the bar hollered, "Take it outside," and the father and kid stood and were followed by nearly a dozen men. The kid's father, towering over everyone else, led the way to the back door, his arms swinging loose at his sides.

Dante stepped in and grabbed Cal's shoulder. It appeared to take Cal a few moments for his eyes to focus. A look of bewilderment passed across his face.

"Dante! What you say?"

"Don't waste your time with it, Cal."

"They're saying he's one of the best out of the west of Ireland," Cal slurred. His breath was sour and hot with whiskey. "He's been training the last four months in the Catskills. Going to fight Scarpelli at Florian Hall. I want a piece of him."

He grabbed the cigarette from Dante's fingers, brought it to his mouth, and took a few hauls off it before staggering slightly and following the dozen men down the hallway to the back door. Dante had no choice but to go after him.

The lot behind the bar was a wide slab of cracked and crumbling concrete. A chain-link fence bordered one side. Four garbage cans sat brimming with fetid trash. A light above the doorway and an alley streetlight were the only illumination. The dozen men moved into a circle of sorts. One of them, the bookie, pulled aside a wooden crate and sat down heavily on it.

The kid took off his shirt, tossed it to the ground, and raised his fists, showing large, scarred knuckles.

Some of the crowd were shouting at the kid in Irish, urging him on, while others called out bets and Cal listened as the odds grew against him—"Five on the kid," "Another two on the Paddy," "He's gonna fuck that gimp up," "All in for the Mick"—and then he shut it out and focused on his breathing and his feet, always breathing and always moving, and feeling the strength in his bad leg from all his days working the bag for hours, from his limping runs in the morning along the docks and the Fort Point Channel, and now the sharp snap and pop in his wrists and fists as he jabbed and struck the kid two stinging punches to the face and was surprised that the kid took it, had even seemed to nod at him before dancing back.

When the kid came close again, Cal surprised him by quickly moving to his side and using an uppercut to open him up for a roundhouse to the kidneys. He felt the kid's abdomen contract under the blow and he knew he'd hurt him, and when he came in again he knew he had him. But this time when he swung the kid moved faster and popped his head back with two straight left jabs before he could cover up, and then the kid came in fast on him again, evading, jabbing, and then pulling back, and then again a third and fourth time, sticking and shifting, sticking and shifting. Within a minute Cal knew he was in over his head, and he tried to focus his thoughts on defensive jabs and lunges just to set the kid back on his heels so that he might get some time to breathe and set himself properly.

Repeatedly, the kid landed his shots, and none of them glancing blows. As fast as Cal tried to counter, he wasn't fast enough to evade the kid's punches and the kid easily outmaneuvered him.

His bad leg did him little service now; he had almost nothing to push off when he jabbed. It caused him to be flatfooted in the moment before he punched, costing him speed and power. And this slight hesitation was a clear sign to the kid that Cal was setting up the jab, which he now had to deliver with a lurching lunge. Cal knew this, and what made it worse was the kid's range—he had arms on him like long tree limbs. His jabs continuously sent Cal's head snapping back on his neck.

Quickly, Cal grew tired and he leaned against the kid, held him until the boy forced him away with an uppercut or a straight arm to the solar plexus. Cal, breathing heavy, tried to slow things down by moving and blocking, countering the kid before he had a chance to set up for the combinations Cal quickly learned he favored.

The kid was as good with his right as he was with his left and whenever Cal forgot the left, the kid made him pay. Whenever he could avoid getting hit, Cal repeatedly struck the kid's left biceps and the kid would jackrabbit backward and come in a bit slower the next time, more cautious, but after six savage blows to his left arm, the kid could barely lift it and then only in a defensive manner. As a weapon, it seemed next to useless but in one moment, as Cal was moving back, the kid's left seemed to come from nowhere and it momentarily stunned him and turned him blind. He stumbled, shaking his head, and knew that if he couldn't cover up or gain some time to recover, it would be over.

Cal lowered his hands, made himself even more defenseless, as the lights of the alley and the sounds of the shouting men bounced in the cave of his skull—he fought to hold on to something concrete and squinted to focus his eyes as the kid took the bait and came in for the kill. At the last moment Cal dived forward low and hard like a wrestler and threw his arms about the kid, held on as the kid tried to shake him off. But this time he didn't have the strength to force Cal's arms off. Cal lowered his head into the kid's chest and pounded his ribs and kid-

neys with punches, and the kid fought to get away, and Cal fell almost
eagerly into the blindness that enveloped him. In this place, the alley
and the clamoring men were gone; even the kid was gone. There was no
pain, barely any sensation of the physical world at all, although he was
aware of his body still continuing to function—to do what it did—like
a machine.

Ash fell lazily in the sky. There was a moon somewhere up there but
he couldn't see it. The heat he felt was the heat of flames. The tarmac was
oozing thick and soft beneath his feet, holding him, making movement
slow. Lynne was screaming, her hair and head ablaze as she ran through
their apartment. He saw her launch herself out into space, hands grasping at air, and then he saw her plummeting and there was nothing that
he could do but watch, watch as the firemen doused her body with water, and then there was only the black and twisted carcass steaming in
the center of the street.

In darkness the ash covered him, muffled all sound, although he was
barely aware of his flesh being struck and of him striking flesh, the heft
and resistance of it against his fist, of hipbone and solar plexus, the hard
grind of heads against each other, skulls cracking, of the kid's breath
loud and rushing in his ear. He couldn't save her, had been the one
responsible for her death. And now Owen, his body lowered into the
earth in the same place where Lynne lay.

Pressing his head against the kid's chest, he could feel the boy's heart
through the thick muscle—it was tripping like a double bass drum—
and Cal sensed his desperation. Cal brought his head up under the kid's
chin, catching him hard, and he tried to pull away again, but Cal stayed
with him, throwing hooks, glancing blows that nonetheless stung and
had the kid backpedaling but too slow and Cal wrapped him up again,
butted him above the eye with his head as bettors howled and shouted,
and he battered his body as if it were a punching bag.

The kid was trying to move away, push Cal's hands off him and get
some space to counter, but Cal wouldn't let go. He bulled and held and
struck and butted and then he had forced the kid all the way to the

chain-link and he laid against him there, breathing heavily, feeling that if he stopped, he might just puke up his heart. He lowered his shoulders and planted his legs and leaned into the kid as if he were pushing a car along an incline and pounded his ribs with left and right hooks.

"Get the fuck off him and start boxing, you bum," someone hollered, and Cal raised his face wearily but he couldn't see through his swollen eyes, and he grinned, showing bloodstained teeth. He pressed the struggling kid against the chain-link again, drove his fist followed by his forearm and elbow again and again into the kid's face until he was no longer moving. He heard Owen's young daughter, Fiona, crying at the casket for the father who was never coming back. He saw Owen in the ground and the grubs already tunneling through the open half of his face and into his skull. *All this, Cal,* Owen said, and Cal stared into the darkness where Owen's face had once been, a darkness that made up the absence of skin and bone and flesh, and he saw maggots squirming there. *All this, for what? And if you're not to blame, then who is?*

And then he and the kid were both falling, one beside the other. On the tarmac, small shards of glass piercing his palms, Cal crawled on all fours and then shakily rose to his feet. The crowd was staring at him in shock. The Irish had moved forward, closing off the circle, their bodies tense with rage. He saw the kid's father, his face red and trembling with passion, the big sideburns bristling.

"You cunt, you!" the man bellowed and he stepped forward, drove a fist as hard and big as a sledgehammer into Cal's cheekbone. The blow took him to the ground and his head bounced hard against the tarmac and then the father came for him again but three men blocked his way.

Blearily he saw the movement of feet as the crowd scuffled, and a donnybrook broke out—a blur of kicks and knees and fists and snarling mouths. It was the Irish against everyone else and the Irish driving everyone else out, fighting and pressing them into the street. Men cursed and threw bottles; he heard smashing glass and boots grinding the shards into the stone. Through the legs and feet he saw the young kid laid out on the ground, his face bloodied and his eyelids fluttering. Cal thought the kid looked at him, but he showed no sign of recognition. The kid stared at him dully and then he closed his eyes once more. There would be no fight at Florian Hall. The kid wouldn't be fighting in two weeks or even in two months and Cal wondered if he'd ever fight again.

"Get up!" Dante hollered, grabbing at him, trying to lift him amid the press of men. "Get the fuck up!"

He hauled Cal to his feet, and Cal, holding his head, bending low against flailing fists, followed Dante and they pushed their way through the crowd and back into the barroom, empty now but for two bartenders and an old man sitting at the far end of the bar, out of harm's way.

"I've called the cops," the bigger of the two bartenders said. "You have to stay until they come."

"The fuck we do," said Dante, and they kept moving.

"They'll want to have a fucking word with you," the other said and he came from behind the bar to block their way.

"I am a fucking cop," Cal said, and he spit blood on the floor. "Get in our fucking way and you'll regret it." That made the man pause but Cal could see by the look in his eye that it might not be enough. Then the old man spoke up. "Will ye look at the state of them. Sure they haven't had enough for one night? You should be more worried about the mob in the fucking alley."

The bartender stared at Cal until they were at the door. "You're barred from these premises," he called, "and if I see you in here again I'll take great pleasure in giving you the thrashin' of your life meself."

They walked two blocks before either of them said a word. Cal waited until he had his legs back and his breathing had evened out. His leg burned; his ribs ached; sharp pains shot through his lower back when he breathed. He didn't want to look at his face but he could feel how swollen it was. He touched his mouth and cheeks tenderly. One eye had stuck shut but he didn't want to think about that. At the street corner he squeezed the bridge of his nose and, wincing, blew bloody snot onto the sidewalk.

Dante was watching him. "Did you get it out of your system?"

"Get what out of my system?"

"Whatever the fuck is eating at you."

Cal stared at the traffic moving along the Avenue. Sparks from the wires above a passing streetcar arced blue in the night. Men and women talked and laughed as they walked the sidewalk; there was the smell of fried food and the lit neon of stores and bars. The sound of the Red Sox game coming from a second-story window. His skin was caked with blood, and he thought of Owen's description of the tarred-and-feathered murder victim. In his mind he heard the reverberating boom of the shotgun that had taken off half of Owen's face. The beers from earlier had soured in his stomach but the pain in his gut was from something else.

"He kicked your ass, you know," Dante said, to bring him back.

"Yeah, I know. He was a hell of a fighter."

"I thought you'd never get up again."

"But I did, didn't I?" Cal looked at him through his one good eye and grinned. His teeth were black with blood, and with the damaged eye swollen shut he looked as if he were winking.

Cal stood before the sink in his room, wincing as he eased his hands into the water. Once they were submerged, he moved the fingers slowly, opening up the cuts so that fresh blood flowed. Gradually, the pain ebbed, and he moved his hands slowly, one over the other—an ablution of sorts. He didn't look up at the mirror; he didn't want to see his face or his shame. If he looked up he would surely hear Lynne's voice in recrimination or, worse, disappointment. He didn't need to be reminded that once again he'd failed her.

After he'd washed his hands, he cleaned his face, wiping away the hardened blood. He rinsed his mouth with water from the tap and spit repeatedly into the sink until the water ran clear. Then he drank, swirling whiskey in his mouth, burning the cuts and gashes there, and the whiskey spilled from his swollen gums onto his split lips. He drank the whiskey down and clutched the sink, wincing in pain.

He lit a cigarette and lowered his head, puffed on the cigarette tenderly as he clutched the basin and straightened his arms, feeling the bruised muscles across his back and shoulders go taut and rigid with spasms.

He put the last of the whiskey in his mouth and swirled it about, wincing again as it set the inside of his mouth and his inflamed gums on fire, and swallowed. He ripped off some tissue from a roll and bundled it up into small pellets and packed his nostrils. As swollen as his nose was, he couldn't breathe through it anyway.

The blood vessels in his eyes had burst and a bloody film lay across the whites. He could feel it there, pressing against the undersides of his eyelids when he closed his eyes. When he opened his eyes and finally looked in the mirror, he saw bloodshot slits peering through swollen flesh already beginning to discolor and darken. He looked at the whiskey tumbler in his hand, turned it slowly beneath the light so that the beveled glass sparkled, then lifted it up and threw it down, shattering it in the basin.

46

SOUTH END

THEY WERE COMING along Harrison Street toward Chinatown, the windows down and the night air heavy with humidity, the stars above the buildings lost in a haze illuminated from below by the city lights. Cal was searching the street for a bar where they might stop for a drink when Dante slowed the car and Cal looked up and saw the flashing blues and reds of a dozen or more patrol cars up ahead, blocking the road.

"They're detouring us to Franklin and Chandler," Dante said.

"Yeah, something big's going on. Pull over where you can."

Dante glanced in the rearview and eased the car into a spot halfway down the block, and they climbed out. Where the cops had diverted traffic was a notorious stretch of the South End known for its drug dens, prostitution, and loansharking. There were the bars that most people knew better than to step into and the diner that served only eggs and coffee and the corner store with an inch of dust on its boxes of sanitary pads and shaving supplies, all fronts out of which small-timers ran their meager businesses, but the area attracted only the true down-and-outs and there was a limited mob scene here. Violence usually involved beatings or brawls that escalated to stabbings. Cal had been called down here many times when he'd been a cop and there was such a chaotic and arbitrary nature to the crimes that were committed—all mostly acts related to drug use or despair. He remembered the john who'd fallen so obsessively in love with the prostitute he visited every weekend that out of jealousy he'd attacked one of her other clients and hacked off his penis with a broken bottle, and when the screaming woman rejected his advances, he'd done the same to himself.

Twenty or more people stood at the roadblocks looking at the scene unfolding; on the street beyond, the police lights caused flickering shadows to shudder and shake across the building fronts. A fire hydrant that had been opened by a resident earlier in the day due to the heat continued to gush, and the sinuous bands of water streamed across the street. The police were wearing padded riot gear and, in two teams, one from either end of the street, were systematically breaking down doors with battering rams and charging the interiors of homes and businesses. Cal and Dante watched as they led out the inhabitants of each building, men and women with bowed heads and hands cuffed behind their backs. A few struggled or yelled something at the cops, earning a billy club to the gut or the side of the head. Some at the roadblock began hollering and hooting, urging the police on, and when Cal looked at the officers at the barricade, he saw an excitement there also, a type of restrained fervor in their eyes and postures, as if at any moment, if given the signal, they might take off running toward the other police and join them in smashing property and banging heads.

Cal recognized one of the young cops and called out to him, and the kid came over.

"What's going on?" he asked.

The kid was beaming, sweat trickling down his narrow face, and Cal realized he was even younger than he'd thought. He still carried the gangliness and the energy of a late teen. "They're getting the bastards that did Owen," he said.

"This lot?"

"Oh yeah, the chief has us planned to do a bust-up like this every night this week. See if we don't get those fuckers." His eyes gleamed in his pale face and sweat beaded at the tip of his nose. There was the sound of splintering wood and breaking glass and the young cop looked behind him.

"Is Giordano here?" Cal asked, and the kid slowly turned back, the lights of the patrol cars swirling in his eyes.

"He's been here all night," the kid said. Distracted, he looked away again, searched the street, and then pointed. "Over there, by the pharmacy."

The kid's sergeant called for him and he said, "I've got to go," and Cal watched him sprint toward the older man.

They'd smashed in another door, raided the building, and were pulling more inhabitants out—Dante nudged Cal, and Cal leaned in to hear him. "I know some of them," he said. "They're just regular down-and-outs. What the fuck is Giordano doing?"

Cal nodded. A lot of them were down-and-outs, and the others were mostly low-level hoods and small-time drug dealers—and the cops were bending them over cars without discrimination and clubbing any who protested. They beat one guy particularly bad—Cal could hear his screams over the sounds of the crowd—and when they were done, they threw him to the ground, where he lay, unmoving.

Around the cops, the crowd was becoming more excited and agitated; Cal knew the heat had a lot to do with it, building up as with a pending thunderstorm. The crowd pressed against the blockade so hard that the sawhorses slid forward a few inches on the wet concrete; they cheered every time another door was smashed off its hinges or bowed inward beneath the police battering rams and when men were pulled, struggling, from a building and kicked relentlessly to the concrete.

At the far end of the street, Giordano, beneath the weak blue glow of the neon sign that read *Pharmacy*, stood with his commanders and captains, watching grimly as his men raided the flophouses, bars, and homes along Chandler and Essex, the flashing blue and red police lights reflected in the water winding into the gutter at his feet.

47

WITH THE DEMOLITION of Scollay Square, Charlie had moved his newspaper stand to the back of the Old South Meeting House on the corner of Milk and Washington, by the subway. It was here that the colonists had gathered to organize the Boston Tea Party, and knowing it was a breeding ground for revolutionaries, the British had gutted the building, using it as a stable and letting horses shit all over the place. They destroyed much of the interior and stole anything of value. Now it was a museum.

Charlie sat on his stool in the shade of an awning, chewing on a fat unlit cigar and dabbing at his forehead with a cloth napkin. Dante paid for the *Herald*, looked at the cover, and whistled under his breath. The police raids were front page, a black-and-white picture showing a street scene similar to what he and Cal had witnessed the night before, the streets ablaze with lights and the suggestion of flame and looking more like a war zone than the site of a tactical police maneuver.

"This town's goin' to shit," Charlie remarked, looking up at him.

"Hasn't it always been?"

"Worse shit than before. We've got more murders than New York."

"The police say they're taking care of it."

"End of the fucking line, Dante. It's all gonna sink back into the sea."

"Think it's worth it to play the sweepstakes before we go?"

"Only bums and chumps play the sweepstakes. It's a loser's racket. All that money goes directly to the government. You ever know someone who's won?"

"Didn't Isaac Kennedy win it all a few years ago?"

"Isaac Kennedy?" Charlie grimaced and spit. "They found him dead in his apartment down in the garment district last summer—he'd been dead for three weeks and no one knew. He didn't have a penny to his name or a pot to piss in but he had a hundred goddamn cats. Little fuckers waited a week before they started eating him."

Dante bought two Italian subs with peppers and onions from a vendor working the grill of a food cart outside the Old State House. A few tourists were staring at a spot on the ground that a guide, done up like John Adams, was pointing to. It was the site of the Boston Massacre, where the first martyrs of the American Revolution—Crispus Attucks and four others—had been shot down. Trying to cash in on the meager trade, a bum with a tin whistle was attempting a sad, discordant version of "Yankee Doodle." The tourists moved on quickly, and Dante watched John Adams, impressive in his period garb despite the heat, stalk up to the bum and tell him to fuck off.

Dante crossed State toward Brattle and into Scollay, momentarily surprised by the glare of the sun in the space where buildings had once been and the dark spans of metalwork at the far end of Hanover. Pilgrim Security was one of the few remaining businesses left and it showed the signs of struggle. The bottom-floor windows were splintered and cracked; a layer of dirt coated the building from the heavy construction traffic and from the earthen upheavals that seemed to press a constant stone ash into the air. The stairwell held the heat like an oven, and Dante climbed up slowly, measuring his steps on the rippled and cracked linoleum. The third floor was quiet; the secretarial services had moved out the year before and Scollay Realty had simply closed its doors. Scollay Square would be gone soon. There'd be no realty left.

Cal brooded at his desk. They'd lost the Chinese Merchants' Association Building contract in Chinatown and he'd spent the morning writing up half a dozen bids on various jobs around the city, including the Boston Garden and the John Hancock, all the more important now. Both potential accounts were extremely particular—he knew that—and he only hoped that his reputation for hiring ex-cons wouldn't derail him. He was bonded and insured but, in the end, that might not matter. He glared through the glass at the Pole and the Greek sitting on the visitor chairs in the outer office, drinking his coffee. They were still in their Pilgrim Security uniforms with their caps slanted rakishly on their heads. He felt like going out there and beating the shit-eating grins off their faces.

The ceiling fan above ratcheted out its revolutions, a dull grinding followed by a soft thunk as the fan caught, shuddering, and then turned again. The papers under his forearms were damp from his sweat; he peeled them off his skin and pushed them aside.

Dante tapped on the door frame and stepped into the office as Cal looked up. He dropped the paper on Cal's desk, gestured with his head toward the outer office. "What's wrong with those two?"

Cal shook his head. "The question should be, what's right with them? They come here between shifts like they've got no homes to go to and they drink all my coffee. I wouldn't be surprised if I came in one of these days to find them napping on the cot in the back room."

He looked down at the newspaper. "What's this?"

"Check out the front page."

Cal stared at the headlines and then read aloud: " 'Boston Police Sweep Through Gambling Dens and Bars of South End. After a wave of unprecedented violence in the city since the beginning of the summer and the shooting death of one of their own, Boston Police have stepped up their tactics in the fight against crime. Police commissioner Anthony

Giordano says that police operations will continue in neighborhoods until those responsible for the shooting have been apprehended and the streets are safe again.'"

Dante pulled a chair up to the desk, pushed one of the subs over to Cal. Cal looked at it and then back at Dante.

"You never pack a lunch," Dante said. "I know you're not eating well."

"I'm eating just fine." Cal sighed and picked up the sub. His jaw still pained him, and, carefully, he began eating without much joy.

Dante watched him. "One of these nights I'm bringing you into the North End for a real meal."

"I can't believe that I thought Giordano might actually get something done," Cal said after a few minutes, and he put the half-eaten sub on his desktop. "I thought that he'd get a bead on Owen's killers and nail them to the wall."

He rose from the desk and went to the watercooler, filled two cups with water, and handed one to Dante. He was silent as he drank, then he threw the paper into the wastebasket, stood at the window, and looked out at the Central Artery bisecting the view of the waterfront.

"He never bought into the IRA story," Dante said.

"No, he never did."

Cal thought of what Father Nolan had told him: *Don't forget that to them, they're not in America. They're three thousand miles away but they're still home.* A fat dump gull swooped down onto the rooftop of the building opposite, almost immediately sensed Cal staring from the window, and eyed him beadily. Cal was the first to break eye contact. He hated gulls, especially the big ones. He had since he was a child, when he'd witnessed a group of bigger gulls tear a smaller gull apart on Tenean Beach. They'd pulled its thin legs from its body and ripped its wings straight off the muscle and tendon. In the end, his mother had pulled him away from what remained of it, a small sack of bloody yet still feebly flailing plumage.

"Owen asked us what we were going to do," Cal said, and paused.

"They won't be in the usual places where Irish Americans gather," he said, and he turned to Dante. "They won't show up at the dance halls, but we have to go where they are. We have to get in their faces, push their buttons, and see what happens."

"Where do you want to start?"

"I want to start with the tall guy, de Burgh's right-hand man. What's his name...Donal. He's the key. For all the control he shows, I think he's a powder keg with a short fuse. We push enough and he'll go off."

He strode to the door. "Albert!" he called out. "Jimmy!"

The two men in the outer office put down their coffee cups and came to the door. The taller one looked in over the shoulder of the ruddy-faced blond. He was clutching *Bettor's Weekly* in his hand. They were big hands, the size of baseball mitts.

"You two, get in touch with everyone and tell them that whoever isn't working a shift tomorrow has a free night of drinking on the boss. It's been a while but I'm taking you all out on the town."

Jimmy slapped the *Bettor's Weekly* against his thigh. He was grinning again. "This is a joke, yeah? April Fools', right?"

"No joke. Tell them to meet here at six sharp."

"You got it, boss."

As they were turning to go, Cal stopped them. "And don't forget to let Willie, Chow, Rolls, and Fitzy know."

The thin one's eyes shot up with the names and he gave a knowing nod. "This is gonna be a blast," he said.

"Sure it will," Cal said and forced a smile, and the two left, rough-housing at the front door like a couple of schoolboys before they stumbled into the hallway.

Dante was looking at him. "Willie, Chow, Rolls, and Fitzy?"

"You'll see," Cal said, and he bit into his sub with what seemed like a little more enthusiasm. He chewed and swallowed. "Just wait. You'll see."

48

BRIGHTON

NIGHTTIME, AND CITY lights sliding down the windshield of the van as it banged and rattled over the rail crossing on Commonwealth and along Washington into Brighton, the headlights of an oncoming trolley car momentarily illuminating the interior as the operator blew his horn. The eight men in the back of the van bounced on the bench seats and were thrown against one another, but they didn't mind because they were drunk. And Cal had been drinking as well and he was behind the wheel. Dante, in the passenger seat, shouted over the noise of the men singing in the back and told Cal to take it slow, but Dante was smiling as he said it and there was a glassy sheen to his eyes.

"I'm good," Cal said, taking one hand off the wheel and raising it in mock surrender as he stared at Dante to convince him, and the van swerved into the gutter and banged against the curb. "I'm all good!" He reached into the well between the seats and lifted a fifth of Powers whiskey, unscrewed the cap, and tipped it back while keeping his eyes on the road.

Dante found out why Cal had called for Willie, Chow, Rolls, and Fitzy—together they looked like they could have made up the defensive line for any National Football League team, weighing in at over three hundred pounds apiece. Even the Pilgrim Security van, a beaten-up, decades-old Plymouth, complained of the additional ton in its rear, the shocks and springs squealing and groaning and the chassis lurching when the large men exited and then climbed back into the van. Throughout the night, every time Cal began a song from the driver's seat, the others could sing along, a discordant and raucous hollering. As the men wound their way through Boston from one bar to another, the van filled with their energy, growing more and more rowdy as they grew more and more inebriated, as if the energy were looking for some manner of release, a safety valve or vent, and Dante had the feeling that Cal was allowing it, pushing it to build toward some type of detonation. At one point, as a song reached a wailing crescendo from the back of the van, Dante looked at Cal and saw that his shoulders were hunched and he was wincing from the reverberating sound in the tin hollow of the vehicle. When Cal saw Dante watching, he winked and turned his attention back to the road, his shoulders still hunched and shaking, and Dante realized that he was laughing and that he was miraculously sober.

Their last stop was just outside Oak Square in Brighton and when Cal parked, the men piled out of the back of the van. Most of the slum houses along the street were frame and clapboard and this one was no different. It had black-painted windows, and if it weren't for the fact that it had the faded name *Cronin's* etched in filigree into the dark wood above the door and music spilling out from within, you might have mistaken the place for a residence. The inside was a long shotgun-style barroom with old, warped wood and a long lacquered bar where men sat on stools. The floor was covered in sawdust and smelled of years of beer spills.

They walked to the end of the bar and claimed the space for their own. There was a music session going on around a table on the opposite side of the room—three men, playing fiddle, tin whistle, and bodhran—and some of the locals were stamping their feet to the rhythm; others were turned away at the bar, leaning in to each other, shoulder to shoulder, talking softly. Cal's men banged the bar jovially and Cal got them singing again, discordant and harsh, and the other patrons in the bar looked at them. Chow put an arm around a stranger sitting next to him as if they were old friends and began to sing along to the melody.

The bartender took his time getting to them, regarded them coldly. "You'll have to quiet down that lot if you want me to serve you," he said to Cal.

"Ah, there's no harm in them," Cal said. "It's a bachelor party. You can't begrudge a man that, and I'm not going to be the one to tell them you won't serve them a beer."

"Which one's getting married?"

"The big fella, Rolls. With the scully cap. The black guy."

The bartender looked at the man, then at Cal and the others. They were jostling for room at the bar, pushing one another playfully. Chow, having given up on his new friend, was attempting a jig of some sort, oblivious to the stares of the regulars, and the floorboards were creaking under his boots. Fitzy was crooning something that was almost in tune with what the musicians were playing. Cal grinned when the bartender looked at him. "See, they're having a blast."

"They're right gas, so," said the bartender. "I'll serve yis as long as you keep them in check."

Cal ordered them a round of whiskeys with stout, and when the men had put back the whiskeys, he ordered another. After a while the tension in the room shifted but did not dissipate—Cal was aware of the looks and the stiffened shoulders of the regulars, the way they shoved off the stools to head to the restroom, the way they glared at the interlopers. Some began speaking in Irish to hide their conversations. Others openly commented on the group of men, but some of the regulars closest to Cal and Dante's group were pulled either willingly or unwillingly into their jubilant disregard for appropriateness.

Cal took out bills from his pocket and bought one round after the other. Dante was having a deep discussion with the man to his left, who was talking loudly over the music and din of the men singing. Chow was still dancing but had sequestered a thin, older man wearing a cap to show him how it was properly done, and Rolls had his arms over the shoulders of two burly farmer types, and they were laughing as they talked about their exploits with women.

Cal cheered and shouted but kept his watch on the doorways at the front and back. To the right at the end of the bar was a hallway that led to the restroom and an exit. At the back was a doorway closed off with heavy red drapes. Every so often they parted and Cal could see men within, seated around a long table covered with bottles of stout and beer and ashtrays overflowing with cigarettes. The curtains had parted exactly three times since they'd gotten here—twice for the bartender to bring drinks and once for a man who took a left down the hall and didn't come back again.

"This is your last round," the bartender said flatly as he placed the glasses on the bar top.

"I don't think so," said Cal. "Pour us another right now."

The bartender stood his ground. He was a hard case, Cal could tell. There was a purple weal of an old scar across his forehead, maybe the result of a blow from a crowbar, and when he frowned, it grew darker. His eyes were unflinching, bright but tired-looking at the edges, as if he'd spent the better part of his life squinting into the sun. A fisherman at one time, Cal thought. Or perhaps a crewman on a boat, the type that carried cargo back and forth across the Atlantic.

"I said that was your last round."

Cal continued to smile. "There's more of you than us," Cal said, "but do you really want this group to start? Look at them"—he gestured to Rolls, Fitzy, and Chow—"those three alone will make sure you don't have a bar to open in the morning. They'll smash up the place so bad it'll take you weeks to clean it up. Never mind that when the cops come, you'll have your liquor license revoked and then the doors will stay shut for good."

Cal put back his shot and turned the glass over upon the bar. "Another round," he said, "or I tell them you're cutting us off."

The Pioneer came in promptly at nine thirty just as Jimmy, who'd trailed him for the better part of a week, had said he would. The Pioneer didn't see them right away, his gaze first catching the session musicians in the corner and then the bartender and then, finally, the rowdy Americans at the corner of the bar to his right. He glanced at Cal's smiling face and stopped. He frowned and his brow furrowed. He didn't seem to know whether he should continue toward the back or go to the bar. He looked at the bartender, and the bartender shook his head. Finally, the Pioneer approached.

"I knew you'd eventually show up here," he said.

"You did?"

"Of course I did. Sure you've had your man on me the last week. Do you think I'm stupid?"

Cal didn't answer. Instead, he lifted his glass.

Rolls thumped the bar with his big fist. He was bent double, laughing at something one of the farmers had said, and the Pioneer glanced in his direction. He looked at Cal and Dante and then took in their entire company. Cal could tell he was doing the math in his head.

"You'd best be going about your business," Cal said. "They need you in the back."

"When we come for you, these men won't help you."

"I'm sitting here in front of you. We can take care of this right now. Me and you."

The Pioneer didn't blink or smile. He nodded to the barman and strode to the room at the back of the bar. The barman quickly followed. They stepped through the curtains.

"You're not half as clever as you think you are," the man beside Cal said drunkenly. His mouth was slanted to one side and thick with spit. It seemed he had difficulty keeping his eyes open and bringing Cal into focus. With the greatest of efforts, he steadied his head.

"Why's that?"

"You know who that man is, the one you just spoke to?"

"I know who he is."

"Ah, if you did, you wouldn't be talking to him like that."

"But I did, didn't I?"

"Oh, you did, you most certainly did." The drunk nodded and cackled. "Sure you're a right mad one altogether. Right mad. Whoever follows you will be having communion with the angels, by God they will."

The bartender parted the curtains and stepped through, and two men followed. He went behind the bar, spoke to the other bartender, and both reached under the counter.

Cal leaned toward Dante. "It's on," he said. "Be ready for a brawl. And they've got guns." Dante watched the men striding the length of the bar toward them. He turned to Rolls and grabbed his shoulder, and the big man looked at him. Cal watched the barmen coming down the line. He said, "Fitzy, Chow," loud enough for his other men to hear and they looked up, sobering quickly at the sound and measure of his voice. The music from the trio of musicians seemed to swell and rise. The bodhran player was beating the skin so loud and fast Cal could feel the blood rushing through him in a frenzy.

The bartender came up to them, mimicking the smile that Cal had used all night. He waited and when the two other men had positioned themselves at the door he brought the sawed-off up above the bar. "Now, you fuckers—" he began but Cal was waiting and grabbed the barrel at its side, pulled it and the bartender toward him, and struck the bartender in the nose twice with the butt of his gun. The man fell backward, releasing his hold on the shotgun and banging hard into a shelf, knocking bottles of liquor to the floor.

Rolls and Chow went for the men at the door, grappled with them as they pulled out their guns. Rolls grabbed the hand holding a gun and squeezed; the sound of bone splintering resounded loudly in the room and the man screamed. Chow held his man by the throat, thrust him up against the door so hard that the glass shattered. He raised him to the transom, his feet dangling off the ground, and the gun dropped to the floor with a clatter. The drapes parted again and four more men came into the room slowly, young men in dark trousers and jackets, ties loosened and shirt collars open at the neck. Each one had a gun in his hand, held at his side. Fitzy stood between them and all the regulars, who'd risen from their stools, Dante and the others flanking him. The music had stopped and everyone was standing, warily watching the men.

Cal held the sawed-off on the bartender with the purple scar, who was leaning back into the wreckage of wood with a hand to his mashed, bleeding nose. The other bartender had a .38 pointed at Cal's head. "Dante," Cal said, "take this gun, would you?" Dante came to his side and took the shotgun, kept it sighted on the bartender with the blood streaming down his face, and Cal turned so that his automatic, glistening with blood, was leveled at the bartender with the Smith and Wesson.

"I'm going to blow ye fucking head off, mister," the bartender said, his mouth twisting with anger.

"Not with that, you won't," Cal said. "You might try, though, and then I'll shoot you, my friend here will shoot this other fool, and those two big lads over there? They'll tear the others apart with their bare hands."

"You're forgetting the rest of us."

"I don't give a shit about the rest of you."

At the end of the room, the drapes parted and the Pioneer stepped out. He pulled the drapes all the way open so that the wooden hooks rattled on the rail. He looked down the length of the bar at Cal and Dante, the shattered shelves, the splintered door, and his men in a standoff, one with a smashed nose, another in the grip of Rolls, his head bowed in pain, and a third held aloft by his neck, his face swollen and purple. He kept his eyes on Cal and Dante for a moment and then slowly strode down the hallway to the rear exit, and the other men from the back room and the four that had come forward with their guns drawn—a dozen in all—followed. Everyone in the bar listened to the men's footsteps as they walked down the hall and then out the back door. Cal had the sense that he could hear the others breathing heavily about him.

The bartender took a step forward. "Whether it's tonight or not," he said, "you're a fucking dead man."

"It's not tonight, asshole," Cal said, straightening his arm, sighting the man down the barrel of the gun. "You good, Dante? You've still got him?"

"I'm good, Cal."

"Chow, let him down," Cal said. Chow released his grip and the man crashed to the floor, gasping for air.

"All right, boys, we're leaving."

Cal stepped back from the bar and the rest of his men did the same; Dante held the sawed-off aimed at the broken-nosed bartender. Cal kept his gun leveled at the other. When all the men had filed out, Cal and Dante stood before the door.

Dante tilted the sawed-off upward but otherwise kept it trained on the bar. "I'll be taking this," he said, and stepped through the door. Cal followed, eyeing the bartender with the gun, his .45 aimed directly at his head, and backed out of the door. Willie pulled up with the van, brakes squealing, and Cal and Dante waited curbside while the others climbed in. Willie leaned out the window, and Cal said, "Drive a block and we'll meet you. We'll make sure no one's coming out."

A little after eleven thirty Cal finally climbed the stairs to Pilgrim Security. He unlocked the door and deposited the van keys in his desk. Then, as he did most evenings when he'd been out of the office, Cal checked the answering service, just in case one of his men had called in sick or there was an emergency at a client's building. Tonight there was only one message, from a man named Martin Butler, and he'd left a Chelsea phone number.

It was late but he called the operator anyway. He waited for her to connect him. There was the warped ringing, and then someone lifted the receiver and the operator gave Cal's name and number. Then a voice, Irish in cadence and soft-spoken, said, "This is Martin Butler."

Cal let the voice hang there, and the silence lengthened. On the other end of the phone he heard a radio playing a waltz.

"Detective Mackey may have spoken about me," the voice continued.

The man must have known that Cal had been aiding Owen, and he seemed to think that Owen had told him more than he had. "Yes," Cal said finally. "That's right. It's late to be calling, but I got your message."

The man laughed softly. "I'm not one for much sleep. Besides, I think it's time we talked."

"I agree."

"Will you come to Chelsea? It's where I live."

"I can do that," Cal said.

"And is tomorrow good for you? Perhaps in the afternoon?" Butler asked in that soft, mannered way, like a schoolteacher or a librarian, Cal thought, and he wondered how Butler would respond if he said no. In the background the waltz continued but he thought he heard a wailing from a distant room and then a door slamming shut.

"I'll be there around two," Cal said, and listened as the man gave his address, his accent stronger now as he emphasized the number and then the street and asked Cal if he knew it, and Cal said he did and then he put down the phone. In the office it was strangely quiet—sound reduced to singular sensations that briefly enveloped everything else. When he rose from the chair, the squeal of it seemed incredibly loud, as was the rustle of his pants as he moved to the watercooler, a static rubbing in his ears, the overhead fan turning erratically in its ratchets like metal washers tossed and rattling in a tin can. He poured himself water and gulped one cup down and then another, waiting for some manner of relief. In the end, he turned off the overheads, locked the door, limped down the stairs, and walked the dark waterfront, inhaling the putrid sea air and trying to clear his head. It took miles before he felt right again.

49

BENEATH THE WIDE trusses and vast shadows of the Mystic River Bridge, the small two-story house with gray asphalt cladding sat, separated from the other buildings along the terrace by empty plots on either side where houses had once been, their foundations still visible through tufts of withered grass. The man, slight and unassuming, opened the door. Cal had expected to recognize him—he'd been trying to place the name Martin Butler on his drive through the city, although nothing besides the talk in the back rooms of bars came to him—but his face elicited nothing new; Cal had never met him before.

The man led him down a narrow hall to a kitchen. Cracked linoleum peeled at the edges where it met the baseboards; stained prewar wallpaper bubbled in places on the walls. The room smelled of old milk and boiled foods, antiseptic cleaning solution, cigarette smoke, of strong tea brewing in a pot on the stove, and of the stale sweat of the old woman who passed in and out of the kitchen, the sharp snap of her thick wooden heels clattering on the floor as she attended to the young man in a catatonic state down the hall. Cal had seen him when he'd first come in, strapped into a wheelchair so that he wouldn't fall, head lolled to one side and rheum caked about his nostrils and at the side of his mouth.

"You'll have some tea?" the man asked.

"Sure," Cal said, and the man turned back to the sink. Cal watched him and slowly it came to him. He'd been there the night of Owen's birthday at the Intercontinental, the accordion player leading the band onstage, directing everything from the edges. The man in the shadows. How could no one have mentioned his name until that night in the pub, and why would Donal not have spoken of him?

Cal watched him pour the tea into mugs, place the pot back on the sputtering flame on the stove, and sit opposite him.

"I'll let you take care of your own milk and sugar," Butler said, looking at him and slowly turning the spoon in his mug. From outside came the deep, heady thrum of traffic passing on the metal girders two hundred feet above their heads. The sound of the boy hacking reverberated down the hall followed by the muttering Irish of the old woman.

"Donal says he's been seeing a lot of you and the other one, your friend there."

Cal smiled but not with malice; he felt strangely comfortable talking to the man, although he knew he probably shouldn't. "And he'll be seeing a lot more of us."

"Donal's not one to let slights go."

"Neither am I."

"You know that sooner or later this will have to come to a head. There's no other way."

"That's what I'm counting on."

"You were close with Detective Mackey."

"He was my cousin."

"Family is important."

"That's what they tell me."

Martin Butler held his mug to his lips, tilted his head slightly, quizzically. "You're not a family man?"

"I was. Not so much anymore."

"Is it on account of your father?"

Cal wondered if Butler was trying to bait him, and he frowned. It had been a simple question, a direct one, and he realized there was no hidden intent. "On account of a lot of things," he said, "but yeah, my father didn't set the best example."

Butler nodded and didn't push it further. Cal wondered what Donal had told him about his father, and though Butler seemed inclined to let the subject drop, Cal asked, "Did you know him?"

"No." Butler sipped his tea and placed it back on the saucer. "I didn't know the man, but I've heard about him."

"From Donal?"

"From Donal, and others. They say he was good at what he did."

"Like Donal."

"Yes. Like Donal."

From down the hall came a long, tremulous wail, like a dog trying to pull its paw from a metal trap. It raised goose bumps on Cal's skin and he felt a sudden chill, although he was sweating.

"The boy," Cal said. "What—"

"My brother," Butler said. "It happened when he was young. Thirty years ago now, but to look at him you would never think so.

"My father, Gerard, went to fight in the Great War, served in the Irish Guards—have you heard of them?"

"No."

"They're an Irish regiment in the British army. Earned their regimental colors in the Boer War from Queen Victoria. *Quis separabit* is their motto. It means 'Who shall separate us?'

"He fought because he believed it was the right thing to do, he fought as an Irishman, but when he came back after the war, he came back to the War of Independence, and his countrymen treated him as a traitor."

"Why would they do that?"

"We were at war also, with the English." He sipped his tea and then smiled grimly. "Before the British executed some of the Irish leaders of the uprising in 1916, you'd barely find a man or woman who didn't denounce the rebels. During the War of Independence and after, our country was divided. And we became a smaller people, I think. More guarded, more vicious, less kind to one another. When men like my father came back from the Great War, men who'd actually done something heroic—and so many didn't come back, lost at Marne, Ypres, and the Somme—I think it ate at the hearts of those small-minded, shameful people. Suddenly we had a new scapegoat for our woes and our struggle."

"Your father didn't do well after the war, then."

"He tried. Dear God he tried, but they wouldn't let him. No one would give him any work. He faced their abuse every day and took it because he knew his family depended on him, the cowards who had never braved anything in their lives, who only knew how to gossip and speak ill and condemn men with their tongues. So many little men who'd shoot you in the back from the shadows of an alley rather than show their faces. My father finally found a job, cleaning pigsties for a farmer out on the Muckross road, six miles out in the morning and six miles back in the evening on his pushbike. And they paid him half nothing and yet he never complained—we always heard his whistling as he came up the lane, and I think that he began to whistle only once he was within earshot and that there had been no whistling in his day at all before that. He never told us about the type of abuse he faced from his own, but we guessed. We were frightened for him every day and then the day came.

"One night after Mammy had just bathed Colie and was preparing to put him to bed and Daddy was sitting by the fire in the front room, a knock came at the door, and Daddy put down the paper and rose to answer it. At the last moment Colie rushed to his side and took his hand, tried to pull him away from the door for some reason, as if he knew what was going to happen, as if he could sense it, but Daddy just laughed and opened the door, and four men came in wearing balaclavas and shot him dead in front of Colie. We heard Colie scream and when he was done screaming, that was it. We never heard him say another word.

"They don't really know what happened to his mind, but the shock of seeing our father killed—the terror and brutality of it—they say it caused a seizure, and the seizure left him like this. I like to think, and I often pray, that with the advances they have in medicine, one day they'll be able to help him recover. That's what my life is about now.

"I spent decades looking for my father's murderers. One by one, I tracked them down. First in England and then in Europe. I even went to Australia. I found the last one here in America many years ago."

"And you killed him?" Cal said.

Butler sipped slowly from his tea and nodded. He put the mug gently on the table. "I did," he said.

"I've worked for Mr. de Burgh for a long time now and he's been good to me, just as he has to many Irish in this city, and I've done what he's asked of me."

He paused, and in the shadowed, stifling room, he seemed to be listening to the sonic thrum of the traffic upon the bridge—it entered the air like the electricity that hummed through the condensers and cables stretched along the street. A tanker passing beneath the bridge on its slow trawl along the Mystic blared its horn in the distance once, twice, and, after a moment, it was echoed by another boat farther out in the channel.

"A great man," he said, "a great man for"—and he slowed and pronounced the words bitterly—"the Cause."

"Why are you telling me this?"

"Because," Butler began, and he stared at Cal, his pale blue eyes unblinking, "I want to convince you of my intent. This is my truth and I want you to understand it. I want you to know me, to trust me, to let you know that what I say is what I mean."

He rose from the table, chair squeaking on the linoleum. "Come, I'd like to introduce you to my brother Coleman."

❧

The boy wasn't really a boy at all but a man who looked like a boy be-cause his face was devoid of emotion or response. In the years since the incident, Cal doubted a line of worry had ever creased his features or a laugh had ever shaped the skin about his mouth and eyes. Up close he could see the fair stubble on his jaw and chin. He smelled slightly of urine and sour milk.

Butler stroked his head as he spoke to him. "Colie," he said, "I have a man here I'd like you to meet. His name is Cal O'Brien. He's been looking into the shootings I told you about."

Cal was surprised to see something flicker in the man's eyes, and his head shifted slightly on his neck, but it might have been merely a muscle spasm. Cal came close to the young man and looked at Butler, who nodded for him to proceed. He laid his hand over Coleman's and told him that he was glad to meet him, and he watched for a moment as the eyes—the same pale blue as Butler's, with large, dark pupils—regarded him, saw his own face in miniature in those irises staring back, and when the man blinked, Cal knew that he could see him.

Cal stepped back and Butler swiveled the wheelchair so that it was facing the bay window, where sunlight had forced its way through the towering shadow of the bridge and shone on the terrace houses on the far side of the street. In silence they watched two municipal trucks rumbling toward the warehouses down along the docks while Butler ab-sently stroked his brother's hair.

"Why did you stay here, in America?" Cal said. "Once you were done, once you'd found your man, why didn't you simply return home?"

"Home," Butler repeated, letting the word fill the silence, consider-ing it. "Coleman is my home. We were here and I thought we might have a shot at something, a grand life together where I might provide for him the way I'd always wanted and where I could get him the care and help he needed. I didn't see that happening back in Ireland. I wanted an end to the vendettas and the violence."

306

"Well, you certainly don't have an end to it here. Your boy Phelan there, he's not stepping quietly into the New World. He's brought a ton of trouble with him."

"He's not my boy, and trouble isn't something you always go looking for."

"But sometimes it is. And it seems as if you've gone looking for plenty of your share."

"Sometimes," Butler said, and sighed. "Ah, Boston, sure it always seemed like a good place to start."

"Start?"

"Start a beginning, start over, when it was all done."

"But isn't it all done? The last man to be a part of your father's death is dead himself. You're finished. There's nothing more for you to do."

"I still hear that sound at nights sometimes," he said and he nodded toward his brother, sunlight glancing and bending through the shadows and brightening the side of the young man's face, setting sparks alight in his hair; Cal wondered if Coleman could hear them and if he was listening. "And I suppose that's what he still hears, stuck in his skull the way he is, the memories of it as sharp and bright as they were then, all those years ago."

The old woman's shoes sounded in the hallway and she came into the room carrying a tray with a cloth napkin, a bowl of broth, steaming vegetables she'd cut up, and some buttered bread. She laid the tray on a side table beside the wheelchair and turned on a lamp, suddenly brightening the room. As he'd listened to Butler, Cal had been unaware of the lengthening shadows across the street as clouds had moved in. The air seemed to be charged, as if the skies were about to open in a storm. Cal could smell it distinctly but knew that it would merely swirl above them, pushed by the coastal winds, and then move on without providing any relief.

The woman looked at Cal, said something in Irish to Butler, and he nodded. "Dymphna says it's time for Coleman's dinner," he said, but Cal suspected that wasn't what Dymphna had said at all. She continued to stare at him and he didn't see any kindness in her face, but he'd seen good people who'd suffered so much hardness and grief that the kindness had been wiped from their features even when it still remained in their hearts. She reminded him of some of his father's sisters, the ones that had never gotten along in America and had remained outcast, isolated, and alone the rest of their lives, the estranged caste of the immigrant. "I'll show you to the door," Butler said; he held an open palm toward the hallway, indicating that their meeting was done.

"That's all right. I can see myself out."

"As you wish," Butler said and he turned away, reached for a stool, and pulled it up alongside his brother's wheelchair. He draped the cloth napkin over his forearm and began to spoon the broth into his brother's mouth, blowing on it briefly before pressing it between the man's lips.

Outside a sputtering rain fell; it seemed filled with the ashen traffic exhaust it had come through and was warm and greasy on Cal's skin. Thunderheads moved above the rooftops and kept going like promises of something better intended for other people and other places. Cal looked toward the bay window of the house, the rain lightly stippling the glass where Martin Butler sat feeding his younger brother, wiping at the food that dribbled out of his slack mouth and down his cheek. Somewhere in there was the old Irish maid also, standing beyond the glare of the side lamp and, he felt, staring back at him. He didn't believe that Martin Butler was done, not by a long shot. But he had no sense of what was coming next.

50

THE CAR WAS raised on the hydraulic lift and beneath it Dante worked to remove the exhaust, cursing as he broke off a piece of the tailpipe with his gloved hands, the section so rusted it crumbled and flaked down onto his face. He had to weld the axle and the struts, but he needed to remove the exhaust first. He'd already cut through four sections that were rusted to their hanging brackets, and still he couldn't get the thing down. Rust and oil streaked his face. He was sweating like a pig, his overalls were stuck to him, and the bastards he worked with had changed the station on the transistor radio from jazz to the Sox game, like anyone gave a shit. He could hear the other two mechanics, Joe Garibaldi and a new part-timer, Hernandez, jabbering at the other lift instead of working. Four empty sixteen-ounce Schlitz cans lay on the workbench and they were still drinking; he was going to go over there in a minute and pull one from the icebox whether they invited him to or not.

"Built like fucking tanks. Jake couldn't believe it. He tried to persuade him not to spend the money, that it was a waste." Bits of their conversation came to Dante through his grunting and the rattling of the

309

metal as he hauled the remains of the pipe from the mountings and let it fall with a clatter to the concrete.

"You could drive a wagon of Clydesdales to the cemetery in this now, he says. You'll never have that type of weight, but O'Flaherty wasn't hearing any of it. He said he was paying him well to do what he wanted and if he didn't want the business, he'd go elsewhere. So what he'd do? What do you think he did? He welded the fucking chassis."

Dante kicked the piping aside, wiped at his brow, and came out from beneath the car, squinting at the two men, black shadows that turned at the sound of him. His eyes were used to the glare of the hanging work lamps beneath the lift and it took a moment for them to adjust. "You mean O'Flaherty the funeral-home director?"

"Yeah, that's him."

"He had tanks built?"

"No, no," one of the men said, shaking his head. "Not tanks, funeral cars, hearses...Coen's on Columbus Avenue got the order to refit the whole fleet of O'Flaherty hearses."

Dante walked to them so that he could see better, and hot as it was in the garage, he felt a certain relief at being out from beneath the car. A warm breeze came in from the garage doors and Garibaldi and Hernandez were lounging against the bench, sipping beer. He could tell by their eyes that they were well on the way to getting smashed; they looked at him blearily and smiled. Hernandez reached beneath the bench, opened the icebox, took out a can, and tossed it to Dante. Dante cracked it open, brought it to his lips, drank deeply, and let the cold beer settle in his gut. Hernandez was talking again.

"I was just telling Lou how crazy it was, and Coen, the lucky son of a bitch, gets the contract—you know how many cars that is? How much a job like that costs?"

"So he refitted all the original hearses?"

"Yep." Garibaldi swigged from his can and licked his lips. "Six heavy-duty chassis bulked up and point-welded to shit so they could transport ten times the weight they'll ever have to carry. Jake said he thinks

O'Flaherty's going crazy, paranoid that the government is after him for back taxes, but there was no way he was going to turn down a payday like that."

"When did he get the contract?"

"Two months back. He had to deliver them by June fifteenth or the contract would be null and void."

"Jesus, that's a crazy demand—how the hell could he bang them out that fast?"

"For the type of money he told me O'Flaherty paid, he fucking did it."

Dante shook his head. "You think O'Flaherty would at least have let others bid on the job."

"Fucking straight you'd think he would, the mick bastard."

Hernandez and Garibaldi took wooden-backed chairs from along the wall and dragged them to the bay of the garage and sat, half in and half out, in shadow and in light. Dante did the same. The passing traffic created a sense of movement, of stirring air, that fooled the mind and the eye into believing it was cooler than it was. Down the avenue there were other men sitting in the shade of their porches or on their front stoops. At McGuire Park, water spouted and pulsed from a fountain at the center of the kiddie pool but it was too hot for any kids to be about and in the moments of quiet, after traffic had passed, they could hear it spattering onto the aquamarine-colored concrete. The sun blazed down and cast everything in stark relief, the elongated shadows so dark they appeared solid and so sharp it seemed they could cut and draw blood.

"That lucky Jew bastard," Garibaldi said after a while.

"Why's he lucky?"

"To get a contract like that? That's not luck?"

"Maybe O'Flaherty knows he'll get the job done. You think you two could turn around six hearses done out like that in six weeks? No fucking way. They know Jake will do what needs to be done."

The beer had soured in Dante's stomach. He stood, put the empty can on the ground.

"Where you going?" Hernandez asked.

"I'm going on my break."

"What about the car you're working on?"

"What about it? We're still waiting on the differential, which won't be in until the end of the week. Whether I finish today or tomorrow doesn't fucking matter. Not to you two, anyway."

Coen's Auto Wreckage and Salvage was on the Dorchester-Roxbury border, on Columbus Avenue south of Blue Hill Avenue, a DMZ of sorts where the once-regal Victorians and brownstones owned by the Jewish families who had migrated from the North and West Ends a hundred years before had fallen into disrepair and dishevelment, and now many of those same families were leaving for suburbs like Brookline and Sharon. Coen's had been on the same corner for decades and no one knew if the original owner had been Irish or Jewish; both communities had given business to Coen's over the years based on the assumption that it belonged to one of their own, but for as long as anyone who lived around there now could remember, it had belonged to Jacob Anielewicz.

His family had come to Boston from Eastern Europe and had been part of forming the Blue Hill Avenue Shul. Jacob was mild-mannered and hardworking and tried to stay away from alcohol because he was a bad drunk. Dante had seen that once when they were younger, when another Jewish kid had been condescending to him. That kid came from a German family and was studying at the Boston Conservatory and he'd made fun of Jacob's family and their roots in a logging town outside of Krotoszyn, Poland. Jacob, who'd been drinking, had struck him, knocked him to the ground, and then stomped on his hand with his work boots until the bones in his fingers shattered. The kid's family had wanted Jacob to go away for that, but the local rabbis had persuaded them to deal with it out of the Boston courts and within the Jewish community. In the end the kid's relatives had sued Jacob's family, taking almost everything they had and reducing them to living at the fringe of the neighborhood, an area that most of the Jewish families had left and where no one in the black community there trusted them enough to do business with them. Yet his family had persevered and so had Jacob, and gradually he'd won people over. Dante knew that his getting the O'Flaherty's Funeral Homes contract was a big deal.

Jacob was sitting on a metal pail outside eating his lunch, two slices of bread and roast beef and mustard, which Dante knew his wife had made for him. On the ground next to him was a thermos that smelled of thick, heady coffee with some manner of spice. From the bays of the building came the sound of pneumatic tools, the *thunk-thunk* of ratchet winches lifting engines. In a fenced-in lot behind the garage, there were a couple hundred cars, some crushed, some piled atop one another, as well as fenders, metal panels, grilles, and windshields.

"Dante!" Jacob said through a mouthful of food, and he raised his cup in greeting. "Sit, sit!" he said, and drew up another pail for Dante. "Are you hungry?"

"No, no, I ate an hour ago."

"What brings you around? I haven't seen you in a long time. Do you need work?"

"No, I don't need work. Was passing by and thought I'd say hello."

"You can always come to me if you need work—if I have it to spare, I promise I'll give it to you. You're a good welder and a hard worker—always, until that stuff got in the way—" Jacob looked at him apologetically, pursed his lips, and said again, "Always a hard worker."

Dante smiled and gestured with his head toward the sound coming from the garage bays. "You're doing all right?"

"I'm doing very good. I just finished a big contract—it's unbelievable. Look, I never think of it before I see you, but why don't you come work for me?"

"I'm down at Uphams Corner."

"With Sheehy, Gus?"

Dante grinned and shook his head resignedly. "With Sheehy and Gus," he said.

"Oh, that's no good. Listen, they are good guys but they are lazy and that is why no one goes to them. People know the work won't get done. God is good. If you work hard, He provides. Look at me, a minor miracle, some might say. I'm still here. After everything, I am still here, and look, a contract that pays my men and keeps me in work. One of the biggest contracts we've ever gotten. I might even be able to take Lily and the kids on a vacation this year. Perhaps we go back to Europe to visit old family. The kids have never been."

"Well, barely anybody I know is making it above the red. Everybody's struggling still."

"Wait." Jacob put up his hand. "You don't believe. I'll show you, then you'll believe."

Jacob rose from his pail and proudly strode toward the building. He stepped into one of the dark bays and Dante squinted up at the towers of crushed cars, sunlight glancing sharply off their mangled metal and chrome. A rust-colored dog hobbled through the yard, half dragging its hindquarters. It stopped at a bowl by a stack of pallets and for a long while lapped up water.

Jacob was coming back across the dirt yard, grinning and waving something. It was the work order with a check stapled to it. He dropped the paper in Dante's lap and picked up the rest of his sandwich. Between mouthfuls he said: "Look at that amount. It usually takes more than a year for me to make that much. I haven't even cashed it yet. I want to be sure they're happy with the work, then I'll cash it and put some in the bank."

Dante looked at the document. The order was for work to be done on six hearses for O'Flaherty's Funeral Homes, with the address of a particular funeral home on Dot Avenue, but the name and signature on the check wasn't O'Flaherty's, it was de Burgh's. He handed it back to Jacob, who took it and waved it once more, emphatically.

"See, Dante. I'm not bullshitting you. If you need work, come to me. I think things might be changing; good things are coming. You come here and I'll make sure you have the work to do. Never mind that garage. They're good guys—I've already said this—but blech!" He pretended to spit something bad-tasting out of his mouth, and Dante laughed.

Dante looked at Jacob, at his sweaty, earnest, kind face, and then at the dog swaying drunkenly out of the yard, and he knew suddenly that Jacob had left the bowl of water there, that he refilled it three times a day during this summer heat, and that in the morning and evening he also left food for the dog. Dante knew that Jacob's kindness to him was more than he deserved and that he shouldn't take advantage of it no matter what Jacob said. He squinted up at the glare of the sun, and bright orange and red orbs bloomed and burst before him. He had to close his eyes for a moment.

"Thank you, Jacob," he said, and he reached out to shake Jacob's hand. "I'll remember that."

51

DORCHESTER AVENUE, DORCHESTER

NEAR DUSK ON Hallet Street, Cal drove past Florian Hall, pulled the car over, and sat with the engine running. Outside they still had the posters announcing the Liam McDonagh / Joseph Scarpelli bout, their edges lifting slightly in a humid breeze. Cal looked at the picture of the two men standing in typical boxing stances, gloves held at the ready before them. *Liam McDonagh.* So now the kid had a name, and Cal would never forget it. In the poster he looked even younger than Cal remembered, with close-cropped ginger hair and a long, boyish face. He appeared determined, casting a steely gaze at the viewer, but the expression seemed affected, put on and unnatural. Cal saw him instead farming his father's fields, perhaps a tract of bog land, sinew and lean muscle developed by hard work that was never considered hard but essential and necessary. Cal had seen that in Liam's body type, muscles created not in a gym but, like many of the other immigrant fighters he'd met, by all manner of hard labor. In the boy lay the hopes of his entire family; in him lay their pride and their faith and their culture.

If Cal hadn't done what he'd done—if he hadn't gotten drunk and badgered the boy's father, or if he'd boxed instead of brawled—the kid would have been on the card fighting a ten-round ranked bout. Cal suspected that within the rules of the ring and with accredited judges, the boy would have taken it and taken it easily and then he'd be moving up, with a chance at the real big time. Cal had taken plenty of punches in his life but he had felt the kid's full left only once, and that had been enough. A second shot would have done him in.

The red-pink neon lights spelling out *Florian Hall* glowed brighter for a moment during a sudden surge and then, like the rest of the area darkening around him, went black. From the surrounding streets he heard car horns and then a fire engine coming from the Ashmont firehouse blaring down the Avenue. His body tensed and he stopped sweating; he could feel the sickness of adrenaline coiling in his belly. He held his hand aloft and found it was shaking. He closed his eyes and waited for the sensation to pass, then lit a cigarette to relieve the gummy taste in his mouth. He ran his tongue across his teeth and spit out the car window. *Time, Lynne,* he said silently, *it all takes time. And I thought we had all the time in the world.* He nodded and exhaled. *But that's all right,* he told himself, *it's all right now.*

He watched kids running screaming through the gushing water from an illegally opened street hydrant; dozens of them had been opened in the neighborhood, and through the mist of spray Cal could see miniature rainbows cast by refracted sunlight—thousands of gallons of water a minute arcing into the air and thundering onto the tarmac. When he and Dante had been kids they'd done the same thing. Lynne too; he saw her in the face of one young girl, in blue and white swimming togs, laughing as she held her hands over the spout and redirected the spray onto a boy who fled, running for cover behind other kids. He listened to their shouts and their laughter and their bare feet slapping the wet road.

If the water continued to flow from all the opened hydrants throughout the city, there wouldn't be a damn thing left for when a fire broke out; there wouldn't be enough pressure for the firemen to get water through the hoses, and then they could all just watch it burn.

52

O'FLAHERTY'S FUNERAL HOME, DORCHESTER

"HOW MANY HEARSES does it takes to move five tons of guns and explosives?" Cal asked. He and Dante sat low in their seats, not out of an attempt to remain unseen, but because they were tired. It was dark and they were parked outside the address from Jacob Anielewicz's work order, the same funeral home where Cal had, a week before, sat watching the living grieving for the dead. They were waiting for the funeral home to close and sharing a six-pack. Cal was feeling punch-drunk from the heat, and the beer didn't help.

"I don't know," Dante said, going along with the joke. "How many?"

"All of them."

Looking down the Avenue, they saw the neon of bars and taprooms and the lights of the Fields Corner Theater, at the intersection of Adams and Dorchester, which was showing a stage production featuring Howdy Doody and Clarabell the Clown and Chief Thunderthud, head of the Ooragnak tribe of American Indians. Farther down the road was Charlie's Ice Cream Parlor, where young men and women mingled, and the sounds of their talk, animated and loud, came to them on the night air.

Earlier that day they'd circled the block and spotted two of the gleaming hearses in the back lot. There was a wake taking place, and Cal had entered, written his condolences in the funeral home's guest book, and then paid his respects to the dead stranger, the way that his father had taught him, while Dante crawled under the hearses and confirmed the work Jacob had done on their chassis.

Cal sipped his beer and then sat up straighter and put most of the whole can back when, across the street, the front doors opened and the funeral attendants left, followed by the director, O'Flaherty, and the mortician. They watched as O'Flaherty locked the front doors, and then he and the other man stood talking at the edge of light cast by the street-lamps for several minutes before heading south along the Avenue.

Cal and Dante climbed from the car. Cal emptied what was left of his beer into the gutter. They crossed the street and went along the out-side of the building in the dark. At a side entrance Dante watched as Cal tried the door. Cal turned the knob, his hand working something at the latch, and then he was grinning and the door swung open. He held up a business card with the O'Flaherty's Funeral Homes logo on it. "Took this earlier," he said, "and placed it over the latch hole. I was hoping it would hold."

The interior of the building was still lit, lights turned down low in wall sconces, creating shadows in the corners, but gradually their eyes adjusted. They passed through the lobby and the viewing rooms smelling of fresh-cut flowers and the extinguished beeswax candles and incense. There were coffins in two of the rooms, chairs arranged with funeral cards on them, the first row with a placard that read *Family*.

They walked the carpeted floors quickly and quietly, along a vestibule to the office, through a room for casket and urn selections, past the chapel, and to the rear of the building, where an anteroom led to stairs going down to the loading room, the prep room, and the cre-matorium.

In the prep room, smelling of formaldehyde and methanol, the naked body of an old man, embalmed and prepared for the next day's service and disposition, lay on the mortuary table, a modesty cloth placed over his genitals. He looked jaundiced from the embalming fluid and they had yet to apply makeup. Cal glanced at the face and quickly blessed himself; the man looked extremely tired, extinguished after a life of struggle that had also included the minor and remarkable successes that are part of a life. Cal knew that in the morning, the mortician's heavy makeup would, sadly, wipe all of that from his features.

The loading room smelled of diesel and oil, and four coffins sat gleaming beneath the diffuse light. Cal looked to Dante and gestured for him to turn on the lights. They waited as the fluorescent bars above them hummed into life and the room was bathed in their stark, white glare. Taped to the top of the first coffin was a transfer-of-remains cer-tificate and a shipping bill of lading. Dante looked at the paperwork. "It says Michael Cleland," he said. "Boston to Galway aboard the Cunard vessel MV *Georgic* via New York and Liverpool."

"And the others?"

Dante walked the row of coffins, glancing at their bills of lading. "They're the names that Owen gave us of the shooting victims, all bound for Galway."

"What are they waiting for? Why haven't the bodies already shipped? The funerals were more than a week ago."

Dante shrugged. "Someone's holding them up."

"Someone or something." Cal tried to lift the coffin lid but it was locked. He nodded toward the supplies rack. "Give us that church key."

He took the key from Dante and with a couple of cranks there was a hiss of air as the vacuum seal of the coffin was broken. They slowly pried the lid back, and they were staring at Michael Cleland, done up in a charcoal-gray three-piece suit. Heavy wax filler had been used for the part of his face that was missing, and on top of the wax was a trowel's worth of makeup and powder, but it looked as if at some point the mortician had simply given up. The dust of the powder clouded the air. Only his hair seemed real, combed and gleaming with pomade. They stood before the coffin and stared at the man. "They weren't going to show him after a bullet to the head anyway," Dante said.

"No, I suppose not." Cal waited for the smell of the perfume and powder to dissipate. He frowned and then looked at Dante. Dante went to the corner of the room for the rolling examining table. He pulled it alongside the casket, its casters squealing across the tile, and then went to the bottom of the coffin and took the man's feet.

"Ready?" Cal said, and he grasped the shoulders of the suit tightly. "One, two, three," he called and they grunted and swung the body up and out of the casket and onto the metal table. They looked at each other. Cal exhaled deeply. "Jesus," he said. Sweat had broken out on his brow. Dante ran his forearm across his face. "That fucker is heavy," he said.

"Yeah," Cal said and he moved to the coffin, tried lifting one end of it. "But this coffin is heavier."

He reached into the interior and tapped on its bottom, which echoed hollowly, then he tore through the lace cloth, grasped the wood, and pulled it up.

"Bingo!" he said and they looked down into the deep belly of the coffin where four recently oiled German StG 44s, four Russian Kalashnikovs, and two Bren guns arranged in two parallel rows gleamed up at them. Beneath the smuggled assault rifles they could make out ammunition, bullets sparkling dully, small arms, land mines, grenades.

"All that's missing is a bazooka," Dante said. "And I'll guarantee that there are other O'Flaherty's Funeral Homes in Southie and Dorchester with similar coffins going back to Ireland on the same ship later this month. Five tons of the stuff."

Cal grinned. "De Burgh," he said. "You are a sneaky bastard."

He stared at Dante and then asked, "Who do we know who could move something like this?" even though he already knew the answer. There was only one person in Boston who could move stuff like this, one man who, even with all the heat that was coming down on local mobs, would get a kick out of it, and that was Shea Mack.

53

THE SISTERS OF Mercy home was a squat, miserable block of a building, its brick sapped of its crimson and its windows appearing impenetrable to light, as though they were shielded from the sun by black paint. Over the phone, Father Nolan had told Dante it was a "quaint, peaceful place," but here before Dante now, it looked like an asylum or a school for delinquents. What exactly had it been, he wondered, before it became an orphanage for girls?

"You don't have to do this, you know?" Cal framed it as a question, although to Dante it sounded more like a command.

"There may be no other way," he said, still looking through the windshield to the building atop the hill.

"Claudia...she'll come back, won't she?"

"I can't say," Dante answered. "I hope she does."

He could tell that Cal's curiosity was in high gear; he was still waiting for a clear answer as to what had happened and why they were sitting before an orphanage.

"Cousins in Rhode Island, eh?"

Dante corrected him. "Cousins in Connecticut. Greenwich."

"That guy must have really broken her heart. Just getting up and leaving her like that."

"Yeah, I never liked him. Could tell he was up to no good. She'll be better off, though. She just doesn't know it yet."

Cal's voice was congested, as if he were in the grip of a bad head cold. "She seemed so happy last time I saw her. Like a new person."

"Well, that didn't last long."

Cal sneezed, blocking his nose with his forearm. Dante appreciated the distraction and lit up another cigarette.

"Fucking allergies up here. It's like we're in the deep woods of New Hampshire or something."

Dante leaned back in the passenger seat, his hat on his knee, his right elbow resting atop the door with the window rolled down. "It does feel different here, doesn't it? And it's only Everett. So close to Boston."

Cal sneezed again, took out a handkerchief and blew his nose. He crumpled up the linen and, with his knuckles, wiped at the persistent itch that burned his eyes. He looked over at Dante with a bloodshot gaze. "I can go in there with you."

"No, you've done enough. Asking Father Nolan to help me out, and the ride here…that's enough."

Dante took his jacket and hat and stepped out of the car. The gray jacket was severely wrinkled, and Cal wondered if Dante had ever used an iron in his life. The poor guy looked a mess. Even though he had shaved, a rash of razor bumps scattered along his neck. Dante tucked in his white shirt and then put on his jacket. He checked to make sure his zipper was up—miraculously, it was.

"You don't mind waiting?" Dante asked again.

"No, I don't mind."

He leaned in the open window, seemed like he was going to say something but then paused. Cal could tell he was stalling.

"If I don't come out soon, call the cavalry. You know those nuns and me never got along so well."

Cal laughed. "Like oil and water. They didn't like me much either.

Just don't curse, and remember, you're here to find out about the place, see if it's what's right. You don't have to make a decision today."

"I know," he said.

Cal watched Dante walk away. He avoided the set of crumbling stone steps and labored up the grassy hill. Cal thought about how Dante never did anything easy, always took the route that pained him the most—perhaps the suffering reminded him that at least he was still alive.

In the lobby between two sets of double doors, Dante stood and waited. Despite the damp air, it felt far cooler here than it did outside. He took off his hat and fingered its brim. Glancing back through the door's windows to the outside world, he noticed Cal's white car reflecting the sun and blazing as if it were heaven-sent. He could turn around and get in the car and get back to his life—he didn't have to do this.

Two teenage girls came through the doors, each wearing a wool dress that looked to be secondhand, most likely donations from a church.

"Excuse me, sir," one of them said with what seemed to be feigned politeness.

The other one had a narrow face and a hawkish nose and was cursed with bad acne; her skin had an oily sheen to it. Dante and she exchanged glances. "Do you need help, mister?" she asked. Dante could tell she wasn't from Boston, was perhaps from the South.

"I'm looking for the headmistress."

"She's on the second floor, on the other side of the building."

"Thank you."

Before she and the other girl went out, he asked, "Strange question, perhaps, but do you like it here? I mean, is it a good, safe place to be?"

He knew it must have been an odd question because she grinned and then looked at her friend in an inquisitive way. "I guess it is what it is. It could be better, it could be worse."

The other girl laughed. "If you're here to fix things, mister, you should start with the food."

The two of them left, and Dante could hear their laughter fade away as he walked deeper into the building.

There was a churchlike silence to the place. The corridor floors were as dark as obsidian, and the tiles gleamed from a wax polish. A peculiar array of scents came to him, of pencil shavings, mildewed books, candle wax, the subtle sourness of children in need of a bath. He remembered some of Margo's stories about her many stays at different orphanages when she was a child. In their first year of marriage, he had asked her what it was like to never have a home; how could people remain hopeful when they knew that the place they were living was only temporary? Margo had grinned in that crooked way and said she'd gotten used to it because she had no choice.

She had no choice.

"May I help you, sir?"

Startled, Dante looked up and saw a nun standing beside him, hands clasped at her waist, a smile on her rounded, cherubic face.

"Oh yes, I'm here to speak with Mother Counihan."

Even in the shadows, the woman's eyes shone a bright emerald. Dante noticed that her upper lip was dewed with sweat, her cheeks flushed from the heat. He had no idea how old she was—the outfit made her age ambiguous, anywhere from twenty-five to forty-five. But she looked kind, gentle, not like the sisters he remembered from his own childhood.

"Please follow me, then. She's up on the second floor."

There were classrooms on his right. He peered into one and saw two children cleaning a chalkboard with wet rags. Holding a mop far taller than she was, another girl wiped at the floor with great, sweeping arcs. Dante could smell the ammonia, felt it sting at his nostrils.

"Do the children take classes here?"

"Yes, the younger ones do. After age twelve, they are bused to schools in Malden, Chelsea, Charlestown. It's good for them to be around other children."

"So this was a school before?"

"Yes, a private one for girls. The building was vacant for a long time before the church came in and made it Sisters of Mercy. There's not too many places like this left, Mr...."

"Cooper."

"Mr. Cooper. We take great pride in the alms of Our Father. For the children. As long as we can take care of them, this place will remain a haven for the lost wanderers of a burdened youth."

They walked up a staircase to the second floor, where there were bedrooms, their doors left open. Looking into one of them, Dante saw four small beds, each of them with a wool blanket tightly tucked in beneath the mattress and a pillow squared at the top. The walls were painted a pale institutional green, and there was only one window, which was curtained with a heavy material and allowed in meager light.

"Some of the rooms are empty now," she said, watching him. "Please, follow me."

She led him to a wooden door, the carvings intricate and shadowed by the dark amber of the finish. "Mother Counihan is in her office expecting you. Good day, Mr. Cooper."

"God bless," Dante said, watching her walk back the way they had come.

Suddenly alone, Dante felt that heavy weight return to his chest, and in his gut, his stomach tremored and threatened to heave bile. There was a morbid feeling surrounding him, the sensation of a hushed collective, as though unseen but very close by, a group of children hid and waited, holding their breath as they peered out and watched him.

Cal was right. He didn't have to do this. But these women knew how to care for a child. How could he raise a child on his own? A man who just the other night had killed another in cold blood and dumped his body where hopefully nobody would ever find it? A man who hadn't asked for a child, although he'd taken on the task as best as he could?

The doorknob in his hand felt warm, clammy. He thought of things he wanted to say but nothing seemed right. Inside, there was a pleasant musky odor, and he imagined a masculine presence inhabited the office until a large-boned woman got up from her desk and approached him, her hand reaching out to shake his. "Mr. Cooper, it's a pleasure to meet you today."

54

SHEA MACK OWNED the block on Shawmut and Lenox, and the biggest of the apartment buildings, a grim five-story, was the one he called home. Even though it looked like a derelict tenement, it was the place he ran most of his business. It didn't surprise Dante that these buildings had remained unscathed in the police raids last week—Shea Mack knew a good number of the city's powerful and had fed their guilty pleasures with a discreet professionalism that belied his reputation as a trouble-maker.

Dante hadn't been inside this place in years, though occasionally he found himself walking by it with a certain longing for the good old days. There were plenty of glorious times then, and plenty of rotten ones too. At any given moment, there were pimps, dealers, thieves, whores, runaways, gamblers, and crooked cops inhabiting the rooms. And their host, Shea Mack, sadistic as he was, could carry himself with a sense of class and charm, which contributed to his reputation as the royal pa-tron of the gutter. He was an enigma of the underworld; one day you'd see him reciting Yeats and Shakespeare with the dramatic flourish of a well-seasoned thespian as if he were Boston's own Laurence Olivier, but then he'd do something that would turn your stomach, like string up a bad client as if he were a side of beef and carve him up with a sociopath's delight. Shea didn't give two shits about the blood that covered his hands—he knew he could always wash it off. And he never wallowed in the past. The future was his and always would be. Ahead of the curve, he'd say. *If there's money to be made, I'll be the first in line.*

Dante had to take a deep breath and focus. The hour he had spent at the orphanage earlier today kept replaying in his head. He stood there in the rank heat of the alleyway, the garbage festering in overstuffed bins, and tried to think about how he was going to make the proposition to Shea.

There was sudden movement from above, and he looked up to the neighboring building. There was a complex latticework of steel ladders and rusted platforms and steps going nowhere. It looked more like an Escher drawing than a fire escape. A man was standing outside at the third-floor level. Dante heard the trickle of water splash on the ground before him, and then realized the guy was taking a piss. He waited until the man zipped up and went back inside, and then he walked farther in until he came to a gated door twined with ivy and weeds. Inside the back lot, there was a small garden, and tomatoes shone in the dusk's light, dark-hued and ripe for picking.

At the back door, he knocked three times. Nobody answered.

He found a crate and propped it under a window, which was covered with a heavy curtain. From behind it came a bright white light that shone through the sides. Dante wondered what the hell was going on that Shea needed a 200-watt light.

When he stepped off the crate, he saw a man standing at the steps with the door half open. "And who the fuck are you?"

The man was thick, with a bodybuilder's girth, ice-blue eyes, and a gold tooth that gleamed when he opened his mouth. "White boy, I asked you, who the fuck are you?"

Dante noticed there was a gun in his hand, but it was by his side.

"I'm Dante. Shea is expecting me."

"You mean Mr. Mack?"

"I've known Mr. Mack a long time," Dante said. "I call him Shea."

"Yeah?"

"I ain't here to start trouble. I've known him so long I remember when he first arrived in Boston and used his real name, the one his mother gave him."

"And what was that?"

"Oscar."

The man laughed in a high pitch that contrasted sharply with his imposing bulk. "Bullshit. Oscar?"

"Don't tell him I told you."

The black man eyed Dante. "Mr. Mack is finishing up something, but come on in."

They went through a bare hall and another door and entered a large kitchen decked out with modern appliances, each shining brand-new as if it had just left the showroom. The room smelled of jasmine incense and strong reefer. Wearing nothing but silk panties, a woman stood at the stove cooking. At a kitchen table so big it could seat twelve, plates were filled with cheeses and aged meats, and there were glass pitchers of tomato, orange, and grapefruit juice and, beside them, bottles of vodka, gin, and beer. A woman sat at one end, a man's oxford shirt open half-way and exposing the swell of her breasts, the nipples dark and pressing at the fabric. Her ginger hair was done up in rollers, and her face was thick with makeup. A man who looked to be half Asian sat beside her, scribbling notes on a pad of paper, a stick of reefer in one hand and a pen in the other.

The black man still held on to the gun, and with it, he gestured to the hallway off the kitchen.

"Cecil B. DeMille is down the hall." The black guy grinned, showing that twenty-four-karat flash of gold. "And don't make too much noise. I think they still in action."

Dante moved down the hallway. A flood of that same bright white light he'd noticed outside poured into the hallway. A high-pitched electrical buzzing came from the room as well.

He shielded his eyes and saw a circular light propped up on a large tripod. Beside it a shirtless man hunched behind a camera, its engine buzzing loudly. It took a few moments for Dante's eyes to adjust so he could see what was being filmed.

The room was empty of furniture besides a couch and a bed. On the bed, a woman was on all fours, wearing a blond Doris Day wig and nothing else. Other than the wig, no part of her bore any resemblance to Doris Day; her eyebrows were thick and black, and she had a long nose and almond-shaped eyes. Her ass was turned up to a naked man pumping behind her. This man wore a black eye mask like Zorro's and his hair was slicked back with grease; a thin mustache was penciled in sharply above his lip. But it was the man on the other side of the bed who got under Dante's skin. His body was so thickly covered with hair, it could have been a coat, and hiding his face was a plastic monkey mask just like the ones worn in *The Wizard of Oz*.

"Now suck it again! Don't just kiss it like it's your first time," Shea commanded just off camera, crouched on one knee, his sharp profile outlined by the high-wattage light. The man really did think he was Cecil B. DeMille—he was wearing a French beret and smoking a ciga-rette in an ivory holder.

The actress in the wig went at the man and took him in her mouth.

"That's it," Shea cheered her on. "Now you got it."

Dante stepped farther into the room. He knew that Shea Mack could never be underestimated when it came to new ventures—the stag film, and a hard-core one at that, had now entered his business reper-toire.

The monkey man soon worked himself up to a full frenzy and then came, much to the delight of the director. Shea stood up and barked out, "Absolutely stunning!"

All three actors perspired in the bright light, and an assistant to Shea took a towel and helped clean up the actress, wiping at her face and smearing her makeup, which in the heat of the lamp looked as soft as putty. The cameraman stopped filming and the engine in the camera stammered and then cut off. He reached over and flicked a switch and the stage light's bulb dimmed, its thick coils glowing amber.

Shea caressed the actress's back, then handed her a cigarette and, doing the gentlemanly thing, lit it for her. No longer blinded by the lights, Shea turned around and saw Dante standing there.

"Take twenty, you lovely people. Go eat something. Have a drink. We got one more scene, and then we can gussy up and take to the night."

Everybody walked out of the room back to the kitchen. Dante lit a cigarette, exhaled smoke through his nose to clear out the stink of sweat and cum.

"Dante, you look like the type that has a big cock. I need a big cock, and this guy I know said he'd do it, but he's on a bender and I'd be surprised if he could get it up halfway with all the powder he's been dosing twenty-four seven."

Dante smiled. "Shea, it's good to see you too."

"I'm being serious. The actress is a fine Oriental girl from Shanghai. Gorgeous, I tell you."

"Not my thing to be in front of the camera, but thanks anyway."

Shea raised his chin, cocked his head slightly to the right. "Well, I'm bringing Hollywood to little old Boston. It's your loss." He grinned. His teeth glistened as if he were salivating. "Did you like what you saw?"

"A masterpiece. And with Doris Day, no less. How'd you convince her?"

Shea laughed in that hyena-like way that Dante had never gotten used to. "I know she ain't a dead ringer, but she can suck the green out of an emerald, I tell you."

"What are you going to call it?"

"Fuck, I don't know. We'll make a hundred copies, probably give it a name like *Three's a Crowd*, print out another hundred and call it something profane like *Her Monkey Lover*. Smut palaces from Fort Lauderdale to Seattle will eat it up. They'll buy both, thinking they're different, and nobody will notice but me and my accountant."

Shea had lost weight, and his hair was longer, curling at the nape of his neck. Maybe by letting it grow he was trying to compensate for the hairline creeping back from his prominent forehead. "Take a seat and get comfortable."

Dante sat on the sofa, an old Louis XVI–style piece that had been refurbished with purple velvet. It looked comfortable but once he sat, he felt the springs grind up through the seat.

"Business or pleasure?" Shea asked.

"Business."

"As I figured. Go on then."

"Have you heard anything about a shitload of stolen guns?"

Shea laughed again, but this time it was less natural. "What would I do with stolen guns?"

"I guess that's up to you."

Shea shook his head slowly from side to side. "Don't waste my precious time. I have things of utmost importance to attend to. Playing cowboys and Indians is not one of them."

"I'm not talking about a few pop guns. Somebody who wants to start a war would gladly pay our big-time."

"Are you saying I took them?"

"No, I'm not saying you took them. I'm asking you if you want them."

Shea's jaw tightened as he clamped down on the cigarette holder. "Well, how about that. What's the price? There's always a price."

"Well, that's for you to set. We just need your help."

"Who is *we*?"

"Me and my friend Cal."

"The war hero?"

Dante nodded.

"Well, I guess you and your friend are in over your heads again." Shea's eyes glimmered, and apparently, in a split second, he completely abandoned his dream of becoming a smut king. "What kind of help do you need, Mr. Dante Cooper?"

❧

At the Pacific Club, Dante fed a nickel into the pay phone. He dialed Cal's office at Pilgrim Security but all he got was a buzzing silence. Not even the operator from the answering service picked up. He reinserted the nickel and called home—maybe Claudia had returned to the apartment. He let the phone ring a dozen times, and then he hung up, took the nickel, and placed it back in his pocket.

He went to the bar, which, on a weekday night, was quiet. Men along the bar kept their voices low, as though concealing their conversations from curious ears. Moody manned the bar and seemed out of sorts. Even the most optimistic types, like Moody, seemed to be souring in the heat. He poured Dante a beer and a Jameson on the rocks, asked if Dante could pay up right away because he was getting ready to head out. The new bartender was on the way and would arrive in a few minutes.

There was no band playing on the stage, just an old piano man, Louie Bierce, working solo.

Dante leaned against the bar, elbows on the curved edge, and listened to Louie hit all the somber notes of "I'll Remember April," plinking out the ballad as if he were playing the song for his own funeral. At the other end of the bar sat Roland, a dealer who seemed eager to unload his stash. He nodded to Dante, and Dante nodded back.

"Another drink, mister?"

It was a woman's voice. Dante looked up. Moody's cousin Isabelle.

The breath rushed out of him and he managed to say "Yes" and "Please." She glided over to the rows of bottles, plucked the right one, and poured it into his glass, the muscles of her arms taut as rope.

"I don't know how you drink this stuff," she said.

"It's an acquired taste, I guess."

"It must be."

Dante pulled out a cigarette. His hand was shaking, and the flame bowed and swayed as he tried to light it.

334

She was looking at him straight on.

"Wanna smoke?" he asked.

"I don't smoke. Never did."

He searched for something to say. "I heard you're Moody's cousin."

"That I am."

Dante's pulse raced like he was a schoolboy at his first social, his palms sweaty and hot. "You tend bar here often?"

She smiled with the radiance of a model hawking toothpaste. Except he'd never seen a colored woman in *Cosmopolitan* or *Redbook* advertising Colgate. "C'mon, you can do better than that."

"I wasn't trying. Just asking if this is your thing. What you do."

"It's not what I do but it helps pay the rent."

"What is it you do?"

She glanced down the bar at the other patrons. Maybe the question was too personal and she was looking for a way out.

"I clean apartments, the homes of people who make more money in a week than I do in a year. And I go to school."

Dante drained his whiskey. "School for what?"

Again, she looked right at him, seeing him for a fool who asked too many questions. "To be a teacher."

One of the patrons barked for a refill. She grabbed a clean glass and put it under the tap. Foam hissed but she worked the nozzle just right. Dante noticed she was comfortable behind a bar.

"Then you must like kids," he said.

"You could say that. I'm much more at ease with the young and innocent than with the old and tarnished that come in here."

She brought down the beer and joined in a conversation with two men as if she'd been part of it from the beginning. With how attractive she was, it wasn't surprising that the men entertained her with wide eyes and flattering words. Five minutes turned into ten, and Dante stood up from the stool and put down a five-dollar bill.

She came back to him. "Leaving so early?"

"Yeah."

"I was just going to offer you one on the house."

"I couldn't do that. By the looks of the crowd, you'll be lucky to scrape two dimes together for tips."

She grabbed a rag and started wiping down the bar top. "Moody told me about you. He likes you, you know. And he's a good judge of character, so sit back down and let me buy you that drink."

"Only if you'll let me buy *you* a drink. Not here, somewhere a bit more respectable."

She took his glass and refilled it. "I'm not sure that's too wise. On your end or mine. I guess we'll just have to wait and see."

And with that, a group of four men, three black and one white, came to the bar and pulled Isabelle's attention away from Dante, who sat and finished his drink, hearing her charm the men and them charm her back. He wondered if it was all an act or if she'd really meant what she had said.

On the stage, Louie Bierce fumbled at the keys and started over on a song he seemed unfamiliar with. At the bar, one of the men bought everybody a shot of vodka, even Isabelle, who downed hers with ease. Dante dropped another dollar on the bar top and left the club.

55

A FADED RUST-COLORED bloodstain still marked the concrete pathway leading up from the sidewalk, and Cal and Dante paused briefly before it and then proceeded up the porch steps to the front door. Cal had been dreading this and he glanced at Dante as he rang the doorbell and it chimed somewhere deep in the house. A large dump gull, fat as they always were from the greasy french fries beachgoers threw to them, the type that sat on the roof of Sullivan's food stand at Castle Island, landed on the sun-bleached lawn, nosed about for a bit, and then stared at them. Footsteps padded down the hall, the curtain parted for a moment, and then the door opened. Anne looked worse than she had the day of the funeral, and she hadn't yet dressed. She was still in her robe, a green thing with gold shamrocks or flowers—Cal couldn't tell—filigreed across the collar and on the sleeve cuffs. It looked like something that had been given to her as a present and that she might only have worn once.

"Cal, Dante," she said and stared at them. Cal noticed the unfocused quality of her eyes, the slow contraction of the pupils, and assumed she was either still in shock or heavily medicated. "Come in, please come in." They went to move forward but Anne stood in the doorway, gazing out, and it took her a moment to realize she was in their way, and she shook her head and laughed awkwardly and stepped back into the hall. "Sorry, sorry, please come in."

Anne closed the door after them and they stood in the hall, the light through the side window casting a pool of amber on the wood floor and creating the effect of a puddle shimmering about their feet. A clock ticked on a side table. Along the wall hung various family pictures, one of Owen in uniform directly out of the police academy. Cal had been at that ceremony. Anne didn't speak, merely hugged the robe tightly about her and looked at them.

"How are you?" Dante said.

Anne nodded as she considered the question. "I'm holding up, I think." She tried to smile but it seemed manic and stretched on her thin, pale face. Cal reached out for her hands and held them. "Could we look through his belongings, Anne? We think there might be something he left that could help us find his killers."

He thought she might shy away but her grip tightened as if with a reflex of fear, uncertainty. There was a blur of movement, a small figure rushing through the rectangle of light at the end of the dark hall, and Fiona sped from the kitchen into the living room, out of sight. She called out to her mother then, plaintive and questioning, but it took a moment for Anne to respond.

"It's all right, Fiona, it's just Uncle Cal and his friend. I'll be there in a minute."

Anne sighed and let go of Cal's hands. "The detectives have already gone through all of his stuff," she said, "but if you think it would help."

Upstairs, Cal and Dante searched through his drawers without luck. Mechanically they slid open closet doors, parted his suits, pants, and shirts upon the rack, felt for anything that might have been left within them, ran their hands along the wall edges of the closet tops and bottoms. Cal felt an immense sadness as they went through Owen's clothes, as he touched the fabric, trying not to think of the man who would never wear them again. It reminded him of when he'd packed away Lynne's clothes and given them to the Salvation Army. The smell of the living was still here, in all of these things, and he imagined that Owen might come walking into the room at any moment and ask them what the hell they thought they were doing.

In Owen's small office, a personal safe sat by his desk with its iron-plated door left open. The police had rifled through it, and Cal noted that they'd had the decency to neatly stack the items they hadn't taken. Anne watched them from the door. A strange, resigned smile touched her lips but her eyes were far away—perhaps lost in a memory of standing in this same spot and watching Owen work at his desk.

"Owen always used the same combination," she said. "Fiona's birthday."

Inside there were citations, one medal, a rolled-up award, a Boston City Hospital card showing the imprint of their daughter's infant feet and her weight and length, all of their baptismal records, the deed and title for the house, envelopes filled with canceled paychecks and tax forms, and a bundle of small notebooks, the kind that Owen kept in the pocket on the inside of his suit, bound in elastic. Cal pulled them out and glanced at them—a list of contacts, cases opened and closed, suspects, names of innocents and the wrongs done to them, names of villains and their criminal pasts and prison records, dates of various events, leads, questions—the dialectic of the cop searching for some manner of illumination. Pedantic, measured, patient, methodical, dating back to his first year as a detective.

"They went through those," Anne said. "Took a bunch but said they weren't hopeful that they'd help any."

Cal nodded. "Yeah, they pretty much took everything that was necessary."

"They took some of his clothes too."

"When they're done with them, do you want me to ask for them back?"

"No." She shook her head. "That's all right. He has other clothes too—" Anne waved distractedly, as if thinking were causing her pain or distress. She winced. "Downstairs," she said. "I have so much laundry to do, Cal...I just haven't gotten around to it."

"What?"

"Downstairs, in the cellar. He has clothes I never washed. I can't...I can't touch them...not yet. And Fiona's clothes too. She's been wearing the same thing for almost a week..."

"Did you tell the police?"

"I didn't, I didn't think—" She put a hand to her face and began to cry softly, and Cal and Dante looked at each other. Finally Cal went to her and held her shoulder, and with her eyes closed she placed her hand over his and they stood there for a while longer as she cried. She opened her eyes, red-rimmed and bleary, and stared at him. "I didn't think it mattered," she said. "Why would it? For Christ's sake, it's only his dirty clothes. What kind of woman am I that I can't wash my husband's or my daughter's clothes?"

At the top of the stairs, they pulled on the chain for the bulb and then descended into the dirt cellar. The furnace heaved and sighed in the middle of the room, the flames through its grate showing in the dim light. A single bulb hung suspended over a washer and dryer lifted on four wooden pallets arranged side by side. The rest of the basement was dark. To the left of the washer were two laundry baskets full of soiled clothes and a gray slate soapstone sink in which a dirty rheum of waste-water sparkled. It smelled like laundry detergent, old sweat, the ash and oil belches from the furnace grate, and all of it cocooned in the damp heat. Cal began to lift the clothes from the first basket—dresses, skirts, tights, underthings—carefully placing them on the dryer. Beneath their clothing lay Owen's shirt and blazer, pressed down in the basket, where Owen had put them perhaps the day or night before he'd been shot.

Cal lifted out the crinkled shirt and creased jacket and spread them atop the washing machine. From upstairs came the sound of the child crying. He ran his hand along the top of the jacket and felt the bulge. He looked at Dante, his eyes wide, then reached into the inside pocket.

It was another of the small notebooks, bound in elastic to keep the pages intact. Cal stripped off the elastic, opened the book, and leaned into the light of the bare bulb.

On the first page in Owen's tight, small script were his notes on the victims of the recent shootings and their possible connections to the first murdered man, the tarred-and-feathered victim, all leading back to the arrival of the boat, *Midir*, in Boston Harbor. Cal turned the page and scanned its contents: the arrival date of the boat, when Owen had first expected it to arrive, and its contents, the cargo of arms and ammunition, the letters *IRA* underlined twice.

"Here it is," said Cal; he looked at it, squinting for a moment, and then abruptly thrust the notepad toward Dante. Dante looked at him. Cal's jaw was working, the muscles flexing as he ground his teeth. Dante leaned over the washing machine, held the open book toward the bulb, scanned the sheet, and stared at the bottom. Next to the informant's telephone number were initials in bold capitals: *M.B.* Cal said, "And I know the number, because I've already called it."

It took a moment for his words to make sense to Dante. "Jesus," he said. "The informant, it's Martin Butler."

56

STRIPPED DOWN TO his undershirt, Cal leaned over the sink and splashed water onto his face. He emerged from the bathroom wiping at his cheeks. For a moment he held the towel there so that only his eyes, bright and blue, were visible. Dante was at the window staring at the dark thunderheads that had turned the skies above Boston black. The air was still and charged. Even the breeze had died. A colony of gulls reared up over the rooftops and, shrieking madly, swooped toward the northwest. Then there was silence again.

When the phone rang it startled both of them. Cal draped the towel around his neck and picked up the receiver.

"They're coming," the voice said, lilting and formal. "There's nine of them."

"Butler—" Cal began but the line was already dead. "Bastard."

"What is it?"

"It was Butler; he said they're coming and there's nine of them."

"What's his game?"

"He's playing us off one another, using us to take them out. They think they have the drop on us and he wants them to keep thinking that."

"How long have we got?"

"I don't know, twenty minutes? You should call Shea Mack now."

"He may not get here in time."

"Then we'll do the best we can. We can't run. They'll just track us down."

Dante nodded and went to the phone. Through the window, beyond the pile drivers and wrecking-ball cranes, Cal could see the first arcs of lightning breaking like spiderwebs upon the bay. The thunder, when it came, was still so distant it seemed almost playful. This was going to be a big one and it was going to last. The table lamps flickered and ebbed, then grew bright again.

On the other end of the receiver, static crackled and popped and Dante had a difficult time hearing the operator. He almost had to shout the phone number to her. The storm was descending on the city and in a short time the skies would let loose—everything was about to break apart.

He had just gotten off the phone with Shea Mack when the lights flickered again and dimmed. This time they went out and stayed out, and Cal and Dante looked at each other in the dimness. Outside, the darkness pressed at the corners of the streets and alleyways. They could smell the charged air, the sense of it crackling like fire racing along a fine line of ethanol. Dante shrugged and put the dead phone in its cradle.

"Well, he knows," he said.

"And?"

"I didn't ask him what his plan was. We have to hope he keeps his word."

Cal lay the green duffel bag on the table and dumped its contents out. Two land mines with trip wires, two StG 44 machine guns, a pump-action shotgun, and four automatic pistols. Four boxes of bullets, a half a dozen 9 mm clips, and as many machine-gun magazines. He looked at the German S-mines, tapped their steel casings.

"We have to be in position when they come. We'll take watch at the front and back windows in the hallway; that way we'll have an eye on both stairs. We'll use the fire escape in the office as a retreat point if we need it. Once we're in the alleyway, we can use the dumpster for cover and return fire."

He picked up the land mines and considered them. "And these," he said. "These we'll use to slow them down at the door."

"And we'll hope Shea Mack comes through," Dante said, and paused. "You don't look scared."

"Not scared? Jesus, I'm shitting myself right now. I was just hoping you wouldn't notice."

Dante smiled but in the dim light his face was pale.

They took their time loading the guns, taping extra magazines to the machine-gun stocks, and then Cal set the mines by the door to the front office. When he was done, he stood and looked about the room. A strange sense of fondness for its dirty walls and cracked plaster, the windows with their taped glass, came over him.

The black sky had opened up and rain came down in a loud torrent, quickly flooding the streets. White lightning burst over the city, striking the highest points, and very soon they could hear the distant wail of fire engines. They looked to the north and watched as the lights of the city went out block by block, and then they were in darkness, listening to the rain and the thunder. Multiple lightning strikes came again—Cal counted ten strikes within seconds of one another—and as the room shuddered with thunder, they heard in the distance a distinctive electric popping followed by a succession of booming explosions.

"A bunch of transformers have blown," said Dante. "Looks like we're stuck in the dark."

"That might be a good thing."

They stepped out into the hall, Cal taking the top of the front stairwell and Dante taking the back. They stood in the dim hallway sixty feet apart and looked out the windows onto the rain-washed street.

"What time is it?" Dante asked.

Cal didn't want to look at his watch; some superstition about bad luck nagged at him. The time was no longer important—that was for people who expected to be living in the next hour, and although he was trying to keep up a good front, he didn't know if that would end up being true, and he didn't want to dwell on it.

"Does it matter?"

"No. I suppose not."

Dante lit a cigarette and smoked for a bit. Cal rested the StG 44 against the wall. The windows were open to their screens and rain splashed in off the windowsill and peppered him with water, but it felt good and kept his senses sharp. Every time lightning ripped across the sky the hair stood up on his neck and arms, created a brief buzzing at the back of his mouth. Three cars moved slowly down the street with their headlights on and then pulled up to the curb opposite the building. Dante put out his cigarette, leaned the pump-action shotgun against the wall, out of sight, and took up the StG. The men exited their cars wearing rain slickers and walked quickly across the street. Cal counted nine, just as Butler had said. They split into three groups, one group at each door of the building and one in the side alley toward the rear.

"You ready?" Cal said.

He stepped away from the stairwell and pressed himself against the wall. In the gloom Cal had the sense that Dante nodded. "Right, then," he said and, hoisting the machine gun, he nodded too.

"Wait until they're on the stairs," Cal said.

The front door and back-hall door banged open and they heard the men's voices and then their footsteps on the stairs, quick and methodical. Cal stepped from behind the wall and Dante did the same. Together they emptied the magazines down their separate stairwells.

Cal's bullets tore up the plaster walls and wooden banister and shattered the glass of the front doors after going through the two men. Their bodies, riddled with bullets, thumped heavily down the stairs and then lay together in the vestibule, still and unmoving.

In the back-hall entrance the rear man had died first and fallen forward, trapping the lead shooter, and now he slumped against the wall, six ragged bullet holes in his shirt spouting blood and an empty gory space where his left eye had been. Dante stared down at him, at the young, pale face still gleaming from the rain, and felt the gun in his hand hot and its barrel steaming slightly, then he grabbed the pump-action and broke into a run toward the office doors.

Cal, breathing hard through his nose, met him there, slammed the door behind them, and quickly set the trip wires.

From the back office they climbed out the window and onto the fire escape and were immediately soaked. Directly below was an industrial trash dumpster into which hordes of rats were streaming, slick and black from the rain. Cal and Dante faced the brick rear of buildings and a crooked rectangle of three alleyways. To their left was an open shot to the North End, or they could take the alley back to Hanover. The right took them to Cambridge Street. Across from the fire escape was the alley that eventually came out on Brattle.

The rain was beating down so hard they could barely hear anything above the downpour. Only the thunder, when it came, was louder, and the ground seemed to shake beneath it. The rain pounded the walls and the railings, blinding them as they descended to the alley.

They were halfway down the fire escape when they felt the concussive blast of the explosion and the windows blew out above them. They lowered their heads as shards of glass razored down and the railings shook. Dante dropped his gun and slipped as he reached for it and then they were descending again as fast as they could on the slick metal. Bullets ricocheted off the railing close to Cal's hand. They made it the last ten feet down the fire escape to the dumpster, where they crouched, listening as more bullets pockmarked the metal and pinged, scattering into the corners.

"I can't see," said Cal. "Where are they?"

Dante squinted through the rain and then leaned back. "Two of them, both on this side of the alley, just down from the street."

Cal nodded. "I'll have to get across to the other side of the alley to get a position on them." He looked at Dante, his hair flattened and rainwater dripping down his face into his mouth. "Ready?" Dante nodded. "On the count of three. One. Two. *Three!*" Dante rose from behind the dumpster and opened up the StG 44, spraying the top of the alley with bullets, and Cal lunged across to the other side, running the twenty yards as best he could on his bad leg.

He stepped into the protection of the wall, and before Dante had finished firing he began his own volley, seeing the dark figures of de Burgh's men positioned in the far alley across from him. He heard one of them scream out a slew of curses, and then the brick and mortar before Cal's head exploded, sending shards into his cheek and across his face. He stepped back, pressed himself against the alley wall, and breathed deeply. He could feel the blood seeping down his left cheek and jaw, and his left eye seemed to be filling with it. He turned his head up into the rain and let it wash the blood away, then stared out across the alley again.

Dante was pinned down for a moment behind the dumpster, but Cal could tell by the rate of gunfire that, for now, he was facing a single shooter. He'd shot one of them, he was sure, and he ran the numbers through his head again. Two in the front stairwell, two in the back. At least one dead at the door to the office from the land mine, and now one more, wounded at least. And the other one accounted for with Dante. That left maybe two more men.

He put another cartridge in the assault rifle, watched as Dante rose and fired, and then leaned out and sprayed the corner again. One man was down—he could see his legs sticking out, flat on the ground, and the other shooter was forced to slip back into cover as Cal and Dante kept up their fire. Cal paused, waiting a moment, and then the shooter came into view again. It was Donal, the Pioneer. Cal was about to let another volley go when he felt the gun at the back of his head. He hadn't heard the man come down the alley behind him.

He turned his head slightly, glimpsed the face, but couldn't place it. Blondish hair plastered against the scalp, and bloodshot eyes, rain dripping from his brow. "Easy now," the man said.

"What are you waiting for?" Cal asked. Rain banged and clattered off the tops of trash cans in the alley. It gushed from overflowing roof gutters and spilled down on them. The gunfire and the thunder seemed to have no effect on the rat population—their only concern was drowning, and they moved about the men's feet, sniffed for a moment, and then kept going.

"You knew we were coming," the man said. "Someone tipped you off."

Cal could hear the thump of his heart, at first quick as a trip wire, and now slowing. He sighed, waiting for the bullet. There was nothing more to say, and he only hoped Dante could get out of this, that Shea Mack might arrive in time, that he hadn't deceived them both.

Another man from the far alleyway was shouting, screaming at the shooter to kill Cal; sharp and distinct, Cal saw the sawed-off at the other man's side, slipped through his belt loop, the weapon that had killed Owen. The large, bald man was waving his other gun—an automatic—madly.

"I'm not going to kill you," the man behind him said. "I'm done with it, done with all of it." He stepped back farther into the alley. "There was only one other person knew we were coming here. It was Butler, yeah? All along, Butler, and now he's sold us out, just like he sold out the others." He didn't wait for a response. His gun was still raised on Cal as he moved quickly backward.

Through the rain and before a peal of thunder silenced him, Cal heard the man across the alley shouting: "Myles, you're a fucking dead man. We'll be coming after you, ye bastard! We'll be coming for your head, you fucking tout!"

When Cal looked again, the man was gone. It was as if he'd parted the rain like a curtain, stepped through, and closed it after him. Cal flattened himself against the wall. The man with the sawed-off was still shouting about how they were going to come after the other man and kill him.

Cal lifted the gun. He spit rainwater from his mouth and waited for

348

Dante to emerge from the dumpster and start shooting. His heart began to speed up again and the sickness of adrenaline swirled in his stomach. He tried hard to focus on the shooters that remained, fought to maintain his hold on the gun and resist the shakes that he felt throughout his body. He exhaled deeply and briefly closed his eyes. "It's all right," he said to himself. "You're still alive. We're still alive. It's all right, Lynne, Jesus, Lynne."

A series of lightning bolts shredded the sky, so close he could feel the air ripple with their charge, striking the high rooftops, and Dante began firing again. And then Cal took a deep breath, stepped out from cover, and ran toward the shooters, the StG 44 shuddering with bullets pumping from the magazine and ejected in a stream of smoke from the chamber.

The man with the sawed-off in his belt emptied his 9 mm and reached for the shotgun. Cal's bullets seemed to strike everything but the man—they spattered and skittered through the puddles about the man's feet, tore divots out of the brick at his back—but he continued shooting, and then, from Dante's angle, multiple machine-gun bursts punched holes in the man's side, his arm, and his shoulder. A chunk of his neck erupted in gore, and he fell to the ground soundlessly.

Donal sprinted for the top of the alley and Cal continued running forward. The rain was so dense it was blinding, played tricks with his vision, and Donal was merely a gray shape in the wavering darkness, firing absently as he fled. Dante had left the shelter of the dumpster and was coming up behind him. "I'm here!" he shouted so that Cal wouldn't turn and shoot. "I'm here."

The man on the ground was still alive, but barely. His blood turned the rainwater black. Lightning arced and brightened the sky, making everything sharp and distinct, bleached of color. The acrid smell of its discharge filled the air. The man was reaching, hand flailing, for the double-barreled sawed-off, and then his hand dropped and he was still. Cal continued after Donal. The alleyway was rushing with water and the only brightness came at the end of the street where it opened out onto Hanover, and he could see Donal racing toward the parked cars.

Donal turned to return fire and Cal emptied the cartridge into him. Donal was thrust backward by the bullets and fell in the street, writhing and clutching at his gut. As they watched, sirens sounded from other parts of the city. A dozen lightning strikes, milliseconds apart, struck the John Hancock Tower from different points, and Dante and Cal looked down at Donal in the sudden brightness. His face was pulled taut in pain, his eyes rolling back in his head. Blood smeared the side of his mouth. He was gasping, trying to breathe through the pain. His intestines were pouring out of a wide rupture in his gut, and his hands, slick with blood, were having a difficult time keeping them in.

He looked up at Cal, his eyes momentarily gaining focus, and gritted his teeth. The rain ran down his shorn skull. The sky went black again and then white and then black. They stood and watched him struggling, knowing he would be dead soon, and listened to the rain pounding the concrete, pinging off the cars. He began to gasp and Cal knelt on the ground by his head.

"We need the guns," Donal said. "We've got to get the guns to Ireland. Just tell Butler where they are, and this will stop. Without the guns this will never end." He hacked and thick, black blood came out.

"You're a fool for trusting Martin Butler, Donal," Cal said. "He was your informer. He told them the boat was coming in, he even told us you were on your way."

Donal blinked and his head lolled, his eyes opened and closed, and then he forced them wide again. There was still understanding and clarity there, and comprehension as he took in everything Cal was telling him—the last part of him burning with intensity. Cal had seen the look before, in men about to die who'd had some brief, transitory understanding of what was happening to them. He'd always thought—even in his own father's last state—that it was a sudden and final rage at God for the circumstances that had led them there. And it was a conflict and a terror for such a pious man as Donal. He struggled to raise his head and speak.

"You'll find de Burgh at his home in Quincy," he said, sputtering. "Houghs Neck, that's where he is." He nodded, lay back in the street, rain spattering his face. "Martin—" he began. "Martin said—" and then he stopped breathing, and then there was only the sound of the rain and they watched it falling into his open, empty eyes.

There was movement in the shadows on the other side of the cars, and footsteps coming quickly toward them, splashing through puddles. Cal and Dante raised their guns. Shea Mack's voice came to them, drawling like a Southern catcall: "Dante! Cal! You boys can rest easy now. Shea's here to take care of the bad men."

Shea Mack, wearing a dark, full-length slicker, stepped out onto the street with four of his men. He was grinning and the water ran down his face and off his teeth, making him look like a deranged clown, and he seemed to take a crazy pleasure in this. His hair was plastered to his head, and he held a long-barreled M1941 Johnson light machine gun. His men carried heavy arms, Russian-issue machine guns they'd taken from the Irish coffins.

"Hello, war hero," he greeted Cal and then, still grinning, he said to Dante: "I told you I'd hold up my end of the agreement."

"You took your time."

"We was here, just waiting is all—didn't want to rain on your parade." He looked up into the downpour and closed his eyes for a moment as the rain ran over his upturned face, then he sighed deeply and looked at them again.

"How many were there?" Shea asked.

"Eight dead altogether," Cal said. "This one here, two in the alley, and, if my math is right, that makes five in the building."

Shea whistled sharply and looked at them with something like admiration. He nodded, signaling his men to action. One of them moved into the lot and waved. Headlights lit the street, and a truck with canvas sides and top rumbled through the broken chain-link, over the sidewalk, and onto the street. One man lowered the gate of the truck bed and stepped out of the way while the two other men grabbed Donal roughly by the feet and legs and swung him into the back, his distended intestines catching in the gate when they tried to close it.

"Don't you go yanking on that thing there, Curly," Shea called out.

Cursing, one man reopened the gate and pushed the bruised-looking organs back into the dead man's stomach, then shook his hand in disgust.

"Cal, Dante. You two sure had some fun here."

The truck rumbled across the street and into the alley and then the only sign of it was its lights flickering through the dark. After a moment its engine gunned again and it moved toward the far end of the building.

"We'll take care of the dead," Shea said, looking at the two of them. He removed a handkerchief from his pocket and handed it to Cal. Cal stared at it, unmoving. "You're bleeding," Shea said.

Cal felt his face—there was no pain; merely the lack of feeling, a dull numbness, and he wondered if the nerves there had been damaged. He took the handkerchief and held it to his cheek. What he'd taken for rain-water was blood, and within a minute he could feel it seeping through the cloth.

"What are you going to do with the bodies?" he asked.

"I don't know yet." Shea grinned. "But I've got an idea."

57

HOUGHS NECK, QUINCY

IN THE WAKE of the storm, the city and suburbs were coming alive again. Driving along Quincy Shore Drive, Cal and Dante passed the Squantum and then the Wollaston yacht clubs, their docks ablaze with lights and the sound of calypso coming from the open windows and screened-in decks. Cyclists pedaled slowly through the puddles along the promenade, and there were swimmers sitting on the wet seawall and some standing at the water's edge up to their calves, trying to stay cool but also wary of the jellyfish that teemed in the brownish waters, floating now with night coming on, glistening orbs on the surface of the sea. Sheet lightning whitened the sky and the rumble of thunder sounded from far out beyond the harbor islands and at the edges of the bay. McGettrick's Bar, the ice cream parlor, and the clam shack were doing great business, dozens of people standing in line and in throngs around the outdoor tables.

Cal had the car above the speed limit just to generate some airflow, and the damp air tugging at them through the open windows was just enough to make the heat bearable. Past the beach the shoreline changed to mudflats and rock, and sea grass, tall spears in the darkness. They pulled into the gravel driveway of the de Burgh estate on Houghs Neck and sat for a moment watching the house in the car's headlights, and then Cal killed the engine and they stepped out.

They entered the house through the two-door garage, an old oil smear on the concrete where the car had been the only stain in an otherwise pristine space. The house was also empty. The four-poster beds in the six bedrooms were made up, decorative pillows arranged fashionably on the quilts, and the countertops in the kitchen shone as if recently scrubbed, but there was a staleness to the air and a stillness that made them both pause in the large parlor and listen. They looked at the portrait of de Burgh that hung directly above the mantel of a wide granite fireplace and stared down at them. In the brass grate three ash-wood logs sat, like something captured in a still life. Cal looked at the painting of the swans and the boats with their red sails slicing through the white, high-topped waves, then turned to the billiards table, its balls set in the triangle rack on the green felt top.

"No one's lived here for a while," said Dante.

"No, but someone's worked hard to make it look like they have."

Cal noticed another smell beneath the staleness; it was sharp and cloying and barely there, but the more he focused on it, the stronger it became.

They walked down the hall, opened the door to the basement, turned on the light, and stood at the stair top. "Can you smell that?" Cal asked.

Dante lifted his head, sniffed at the air like a dog. "No. I don't smell anything."

Their footfalls on the stairs stirred dust, and motes spiraled upward and trembled in the air. At the center of the finished floor multiple cracks and veins showed darker than the rest, where damage had been filled in with fresh concrete, perhaps for plumbing to the ancient pipes that ran underground to the septic tank. Out here Cal doubted they were connected to the city's sewer. He could smell the sea as if it had seeped through the bedrock and into the foundation, and there was another smell as well. Dante turned toward it and frowned.

"It's lye," Cal said, "that smell. It's what they use in concrete, and in getting rid of bodies. We used it when we were burying our dead in the war."

He nodded toward the floor. "That look like a professional job to you?"

"No, someone was in a hurry."

Cal limped to the workbench against the far wall where tools gleamed dully, looking as though they'd never been used. He took off his shirt, folded it neatly on the tabletop, and hefted a pickax off the wall.

His first swing was wild and the pick skittered off the concrete but when he swung again, grunting, the pick head broke through the thin layer of concrete. Within minutes he'd shattered the concrete into rubble and Dante grabbed a shovel and began digging out the hole. For a while there was only the sound of their labors and the scraping of metal against stone and then Cal stopped.

"Whoa," he said. "Whoa."

He threw the pick aside and knelt by the hole, pulled the fragments of concrete and dirt free with his hands. The smell of lye, of the sea and raw sewage, grew stronger. His hands touched upon canvas, chalky with crushed stone and concrete dust and turned a whitish green.

"Grab an end, would you?" Cal said, and together he and Dante lifted the canvas bag out onto the stone. A mixture of rancid gases—the odors of fecal matter and the mudflats from the shores of Quincy Bay and Rock Island Cove—came up to them, and they turned their faces from it, gagging. Cal grasped an edge of the canvas and pulled it back. Inside were the skeletal remains of a body, all of the soft tissue reduced to a sludge that stained the bones and clothes a black-brown. The skull was held to the neck by thin strands of worsted, yellowed flesh. They stared at the ruined pin-striped suit, mostly eaten away by the chemical process. In its tattered lapel, glinting dully, were two pins—a Pioneer's pin with an image of the Sacred Heart and a gold Fáinne, the kind they'd seen Donal Phelan wearing. Cal knew that the two of them were extremely close; they had to have been. Donal had been de Burgh's right-hand man for decades, and, before things had gone terribly wrong, they'd shared a faith and an intense love of their country. Cal could see Donal all those years ago being inspired by the man who was changing the futures of Irishmen and -women here and at home and then, somehow betrayed, turning against him, and Butler behind all of it.

Cal worked at something in the remains of the skeleton's right hand; as he pried the fingers open, the bones broke off and the gauze-like skin crumbled like chalk. It was a beret pin of the Irish Guards, engraved with the motto *Quis separabit.* Who shall separate us? Martin Butler must have placed it in the hand at the end, after either he or Donal killed him. Cal considered this for a moment and knew that it would have been Martin Butler who had killed him, but with Donal's assent. There would have been no other way, not after all the years spent tracking him down. The last man left alive responsible for his father's death and his brother's vegetative state.

"Mr. de Burgh," Dante said.

Cal sat back on his haunches and breathed out. He wished there were more air in the room. The smell of lye and sewage clung to his skin. "You sad bastard, you," he said, staring at the corpse. The king of Galway murdered and entombed in a trench three feet deep in his cellar, buried with the sewer pipes beneath Quincy Bay. Cal imagined the lye breaking down de Burgh's soft tissue and organs so that they turned into liquid, the remains of the man seeping like a poison through the stone and pipe and into the local water table.

He wiped his hands violently on the knees of his pants as if the stains and the smell might never come out.

Dante held his forearm to his nose.

"They buried him in the same place where the sewer pipes run. The smell is probably the backwash from the septic tank, that and the sea. It's not the body—it's too far gone and nothing's been in these pipes for years."

"That's why Butler was feeding that small crap to Owen, the stolen cars with the pistols, small arms crossing state lines, all to convince

Donal that de Burgh had turned his back on the Cause, that he was the one informing on them, that he'd become a liability. And after he killed de Burgh, he kept the deception going. The boat was the big one. That probably set Donal off. It was all Butler needed. After that they had to clean house with all of de Burgh's old men."

"Madness," Dante said. Wearily he lowered himself to the floor and pulled out a pack of cigarettes. "He created madness—no one knew who was who or who to trust."

"Including us, including Owen."

"And Butler," Dante said. "Where do you think he is?"

They looked at each other; they both knew the answer.

"Long gone," Cal said. "A new name and a new life in some other city, and with him all of de Burgh's assets. He's been planning this for some time and always focusing the attention elsewhere, away from himself. Hell, he might as well have been invisible, and who's going to go after him now? All of his enemies are gone, he saw to that."

"All hail the new king," Dante said.

"The new king," Cal echoed.

Dante shook his head and exhaled cigarette smoke to the ceiling.

Cal rose slowly to his feet, wincing and reaching for his lower back. His undershirt was drenched with sweat. It had begun to rain outside and it tapped softly on the basement windows.

58

MARTIN BUTLER SAT at a booth in a roadside diner with his brother, spooning oatmeal patiently into his mouth and then wiping it off his face. His brother gagged slightly and pushed the food back out so that it ran down his chin. Butler wiped at it and then dabbed his lips. "You're not hungry today? That's all right. I had enough for both of us. I'll get us home, shall I?"

He rose from the booth and went to the register to pay the bill and tip the waitress. He smiled at the locals sitting at the counter and thanked one of them when they held the door for him, and he wheeled his brother out to the parking lot. It was a beautiful evening—the sky was turning purple and red on the horizon; the heat of the day had dulled and a light wind swept in off the desert plain. They had perhaps another hour of daylight and he felt he had a few more hours of driving left in him. He had a hotel reservation already booked for them in the next city and he was eager to get there. Lost in thought and with the sound of gravel crunching beneath the wheelchair's tires, he didn't hear the footsteps coming up behind him at first. A car sailed by on the desert highway and when it passed, the footsteps were still there. He didn't turn. "You came a long way," he said, and paused.

"A long way," Bobby Myles agreed and came up beside him, three or so feet away, an automatic pistol in his right hand. Butler looked at him.

"How did you find me?"

"The recuperative powers of the hot springs, the mineral water, the dry desert air. You had the brochures on your desk. To help your brother, you said. I knew you'd bring him here."

"You knew I'd leave because you'd do the same thing."

"Perhaps, but not in the way you did it."

"No, but I had my reasons."

"To betray them, you mean. And all the men to do with the boat and the guns."

Butler ignored him and looked out at the sun turning the tops of the buttes the color of burning tinder. He stroked his brother's head.

"It's a grand country, isn't it?"

"It is."

"A country where you can make a new start of things."

Butler looked at the gun in Bobby's hand.

"What do you propose to do?" Butler said.

"There's only one thing I can do."

Butler nodded, squeezed the rubber grips on the handles of the wheelchair tightly. His brother moaned, and Butler realized that he was looking at the man holding the gun and he was distressed. "It's all right, Coleman," he soothed. "It's all right." He reached forward and Bobby raised the gun slightly, watched as Butler softly stroked his brother's shoulder.

"There's no other way, then?" Butler said although he was no longer looking at Bobby; he seemed to be staring vacantly at the back of his brother's head, at the whorl of soft hair there.

"No, there's no other way."

"Will you look after him? Will you make sure he's cared for? We have money, de Burgh's money, lots of it. You can put him some place where he'll be taken care of and keep the rest for yourself."

"No," Bobby said.

Butler bowed his head even as he kept his hand on his brother's shoulder and kneaded deeply. He leaned forward and smelled the top of his head. For a moment he leaned his face there, gently kissed the soft, thin hair, and then straightened.

He looked at Bobby, then glanced toward the diner, its neon bright against the encroaching darkness seeping down from the sky at its back. If only someone were to come out of the diner now, if a car were to pull into the lot. This day had come sooner than he'd ever thought possible and he hadn't prepared for it.

He looked back at Bobby. He had to buy some time. The longer he could keep him here talking, the more of a chance he'd find a way out of this. "Will you at least not do it in front of him?" he said. "He saw our daddy shot down when he was—"

The gunshots—three in succession—reverberated out into the vast expanse of the desert, the sound blooming and then only slowly fading. The bullets pierced Butler's lungs and heart and exited out his back; the third punched through a kidney and lodged in his spine. He fell onto his side, away from the wheelchair, and Bobby strode quickly back to his car.

He had parked at the rear of the diner so even as people came out of the entrance, he was already at the side of the building and out of sight. Once in the car, he rounded the back of the diner and then pulled out of the lot and onto the highway with a squeal of tires and in a cloud of sand. Looking in his rearview he could see other diners milling around the wheelchair and de Burgh's Lincoln, and he quickly got the car up to seventy miles an hour.

The desert stretched out on all sides, red sandstone buttes rising from the vast, flat plains, and then night was coming down, and the desert horizon was lit in pink and purple hues, and he turned on the headlights and tuned the radio to a country and western station and for a while hummed aimlessly to a song he knew neither the name of nor the words to but that was distinctly American.

59

It was still early morning and Cal sat on the edge of his bed in his undershirt unwrapping the gauze from his hands. He stared at the damage from his fight with the kid: bright pink flesh, healing in the places where it had turned a dark purple, and inflamed red streaks spiderwebbing outward from the wound that he hoped weren't signs of infection. He flexed his fingers and winced, ran a hand through his hair. He looked up and about the room. The yellow-stained shades were down; a gray, diffuse light slanted through at the edges of the window. He'd had the windows closed against the storm and now the room smelled mildewed, as if a wet animal had curled up beneath the bed or behind the furniture. From above came the sounds of a couple fighting—a prostitute and her john, judging by the woman's swearing and demands for money—and from down the hall the gurgling of pipes and flushing toilets.

He stood slowly, rolling his shoulders, went to the windows and opened them. The air was cooler than it had been but still hot. The heat pressed back the sheer curtains. He looked out over Fort Point, a place without a fort and no longer a point. From his window he could see people passing over the Northern Avenue Bridge on their way to work. A tug pushed a barge and crane down the channel toward the open harbor. He remained there for a while, staring at the rooftops where puddles of rainwater glistened and large gulls floated, waiting for the sun to rise fully into the sky.

He watched it all without really seeing anything. He was listening for some sound of Lynne within him, but there was nothing this morning—only the weariness of being alive and not even the thought of what he would do next. After a moment he went and put on the coffee. While it was percolating he made his bed, tucking in the corners and pulling the edges tight, then he showered, bandaged his hands again, and ironed his shirt and pants. He dressed slowly, doing his tie and then undoing it and starting over. When he was finished he sat at the small Formica table by the window and lit a cigarette and stayed there for a long time.

Dante had a dream. He was on Tenean Beach. The sky was an unspoiled cerulean blue and the sand pulsated a downy white. The breeze was warm and scented with pine, and the ocean stretched out before him, as clear and still as a Tahitian lagoon. Along the shoreline there were no buildings and no factories polluting the air. Clusters of pine trees dotted the periphery, and above, gulls soared against the blue like kites. From behind him came a great pressing silence. Turning around, he saw an incline of beach rising to a rippling series of dunes that were tufted at the crest with beach grass. There were no sounds of highways or traffic. Perhaps there wasn't even a city there anymore, perhaps it was now just one giant space, a crater, a wide expanse of nothing that once was Boston. The only sound came from the black transistor radio beside him, which sat crookedly in the sand and played a ballad, the piano and saxophone sounding with a ghostly dissonance. He could tell by the melody that it was a song he had written—if only he could remember what he had named it.

This is where Sheila died, he thought, but there she was with all the others who suddenly appeared around him.

362

Sitting cross-legged on a large patchwork blanket, Sheila played cards with their daughter. Maria had grown up, was nine or ten. Her face had lost its youthful pudginess, her cheeks narrowed delicately, her body was lean and athletic, and her skin was a deep bronze. She turned and, squinting against the sunlight, smiled at him. So did Sheila, her smile both coy and mocking. Typical of her to look at him that way after all he'd gone through finding her killer. He watched as she flipped the cards face up and noticed how they were all kings and queens and aces.

Off to his left, Claudia sat with their mother. Claudia's hair had turned white at the temples, but it gave her an almost regal, authoritative appearance, and his mother sat in that all-too-tight bathing suit that she'd worn for years and years, leaning back in the chair, a line of sweat dampening her upper lip as she soaked in the sun. Claudia reached out and put her hand on Dante's forearm. She said something but no sound came out. Whatever it was, he could tell that she had forgiven him.

Lynne was walking up from the water and toweling herself dry. She looked beautiful, vibrantly alive in a bright blue bathing suit, her cheeks flushed from her swim in the ocean. Cal came up beside her, no limp staggering his step, and stole the towel from her. His eyes shone with mischief—the same mischief that the war had taken from him. Lynne swung at Cal playfully, and he dodged her blow as if he were sparring. The laughter between them was swallowed up in the great silence.

The radio played another song, and it was the only sound in the world.

With the towel draped over his shoulders, Cal waved to get Dante's attention, and when he got it, Cal pointed to the shoreline.

She was there by the water. Margo. Waiting for him.

Moving across the sand felt like walking up an escalator that was going down. A flash of panic stole his breath—*Why am I walking so slow?* He began to jog and then launched into a sprint. As he got closer, Margo turned toward him. When she spoke, her voice came to him clearly. "There you are. I thought you were going to leave me here waiting forever."

He reached out and grasped her hand. Even with the sun glaring down on her, it was cold to the touch. He looked her over. There were no marks on her arms, the skin supple and pink. She was wearing a broad white hat and a one-piece bathing suit that showed him she was eating well again. The extra weight looked good on her. "It's a gorgeous day," she said. "I'm so glad everybody could make it."

Two children ran behind them, their breaths huffing and their heels kicking up sprays of white sand. Dante turned and watched a younger version of himself, ten years old again, chasing Cal in a game of tag. Cal with his jet-black crew cut, sunburned but feeling no pain, sprinted ahead and doubled his lead. He was always a faster runner but the younger Dante moved up to an arm's length away. From where he was standing, the beach seemed to have no end, and he watched the two children running until they simply evaporated into the white horizon.

"Look at you two," she said. "Always running from something. And you always one step behind."

Dante stood with his wife for a long time, mesmerized at how the sunlight danced and shimmered against the water and the way the tide rhythmically rocked back and forth, as if it were a living, breathing thing.

Margo's hand clutched his tighter. She was looking off into the distance, and even though her eyes were shaded from the sun, she squinted as if to focus.

On the horizon, he saw a dark blemish against the blue. Perhaps a ship passing along the line where the sky and the water met. But it grew bigger and he could tell it was just a cloud. When he blinked, as though trying to rid his eyes of sand, he noticed there were now three dark clouds and they were growing. A breeze rippled the ocean and then it went still and quiet again. He felt a chill and he stepped back from the incoming tide.

"Dante, love. Just when things seem good in life, they take a turn for the worse. Out of everybody I know, you should know that best." Her teeth were an unstained white, but when she leaned into him, he smelled something rotten.

"What are you talking about?"

"Things are going to get a whole lot worse. You don't even know."

He turned back toward the beach. Everybody had left. Margo clutched his hand tighter and when she spoke, no sound came out. Again, the world had turned mute and he couldn't make out what she was trying to say.

The dark clouds in the sky converged and blossomed like a bruise, blotting out the sun. The ocean darkened, and in the distance, it began to churn as if some great behemoth had stirred and was making its ascent to the surface. Margo let go of his hand, and he couldn't tell if she was laughing or crying.

Dante kicked out his legs and threw off the bedsheet as if it were on fire and burning into his flesh. With his heart hammering wildly in his chest, he sat up in the bed and felt vertigo like he'd never felt before, the light from the window bending and the bed below seeming to topple over on a great rush of water. He coughed into his hand and soon his vision steadied and he could tell it was just a dream. He was back in his bed and it was Boston once again. His brow was covered in sweat and he used the bedsheet and wiped at his face. He stood up and realized he was naked. For a moment, he felt vulnerable, ashamed. On the floor was a pair of boxer shorts. He slipped them on, almost falling and seeing spots dance wildly in his vision. From his dresser, he grabbed the syringe, a foil packet, and a spoon tarnished black by flame. All that time away from the junk, and he still could set up a dose with ease. The flame caressed the spoon and the junk sizzled and wept. Before he knew it, the syringe was half full, and tapping the vein he had used last night, he pressed the tip under his skin and brought it all down.

Not even a minute had passed before Dante's stomach turned. He rushed into the bathroom. As he dry-heaved above the sink, he tried his best not to glimpse the reflection in the mirror. The junk was cut poorly, but it was all he had.

Back in the hallway, he stood before the small bedroom of Maria's. He opened the door and stepped in quietly. The bed was empty. Of course he knew it would be empty, but then why did he expect her to be there, waiting for him to drag her out of bed and bring her to the kitchen for breakfast?

One stuffed animal lay upon the pillow looking sideways at him, and the bedsheets were neatly tucked in, not even one wrinkle. Dante's breath ran ragged again. He sat on the bed, lowered his head into his hands, and sobbed, cried until there was nothing left but snot filling his nostrils and a pathetic wheezing rattling in his throat. He twisted around and lay down on the bed, suddenly shivering, feeling the cold pulse through him. He closed his eyes and tried to go back to Tenean. *That's where they all were; that's where I should be too.*

His eyes grew heavy, the light of the room dimmed, and in the distance, he thought he could hear the lull of the ocean. Sleep returned without dreams. This time, there was only blackness, a great seething nothing. When he woke, it was dark again, and the feeling hung heavy that the world would keep on moving without him. He remembered what Margo had said, *You don't even know,* and tried to look into the future that she'd spoken of but could only make it as far as the syringe, the tarnished spoon, and the last hit of junk that waited for him in his bedroom.

You don't even know.

Epilogue

FROM THE GALWAY docks—where so many doomed coffin ships, their lower bellies stuffed with starving, cholera-sick Irish, had sailed for Boston and New York, St. John's and New Brunswick, a hundred years before—the hearses traveled west, past the Spanish Arch and Nimmo's Pier, and along the shore road.

Beneath gray, churning skies and sudden squalls of wind-whipped rain, they passed through Spiddal and into Connemara. At Rossaveal they turned inland toward the distant Maamturks and the wide, empty plains of bog.

In Bealadangan, the General, Sean Mullen, signaled the driver to take a right onto a bitumen-gravel boreen, rutted tire tracks on either side of a high, grass-covered slope, and the two cars wound their way upward through Muckinagh, black and dun bogs covered with pale, rain-engorged gorse and heather falling away on either side.

They passed a barrow-shaped hill upon which a narrow cross angled skyward crookedly and a lone farmhouse, peat smoke twining upward from its chimney. At the sound of the motor, a head poked from the open half-door, looked at them for a moment, a halo of smoke from a pipe cursed out into the rain, and then retreated. They were in Connemara now and the Galway men had little time for the locals, just as the locals had little time for them.

They rounded a bend, the hearse's springs squealing in distress, and the house slowly disappeared from view. Now they were surrounded on all sides by bog and rock and mist-shrouded mountains.

"Here," the passenger said, pointing at a gate, and the driver pulled in, leaving room for the second hearse behind, and the front-seat passenger stepped out. He opened the gate and the two cars entered an overgrown cart path that led to a courtyard attached to a crumbling cow byre and a long-abandoned laborer's cottage, its whitewash faded and moss growing upon the slate roof where one of the corner eaves had collapsed in on itself.

Their boots sinking in cow shit and bog water, the four men hefted the coffins out of one hearse and then the other, laid them on the mossy droim that fell away to the bog. Three bullocks stared balefully at them from over a stone wall and lowed their discontent at the intrusion. The big fellow with the black watch cap glared back at them. "Shut the fuck up," he muttered angrily, the cold mist already turning his mouth stiff.

It began to rain, as it had off and on during their journey west. From the Atlantic, winds pushed black-gray squalls across empty fields; the wind whipped at their clothes and the rain lashed the coffins, banged on the metal roofs of the hearses. Using the casket key, one man slowly cranked and opened each casket until the top was free from the seal and then they pried all the tops back. For a moment they stared unblinking through the rain at the bodies lying in three of the four coffins, and then as the smell struck them they stepped back. They looked at the men they'd sent to Boston four weeks before, rain spattering their blue-black faces—rigor had long ago left them and after almost two weeks at sea, decay had bloated the bodies and filled the coffins with putrefying gases.

"The fuckers," one of them muttered.

"Check for the guns," the General said.

The men wrapped their mouths in kerchiefs and reached into the coffins. Gagging, they pulled and pushed the weighted bodies aside, the soft flesh sinking and seeming to melt under their touch. "Ah, Jesus," one said, "his bleedin' arm is coming off." They burrowed beneath the cadavers, faces pressed close to their rotting comrades, and then yanked their hands free. The big fellow tore the kerchief off his face and shook his head in disgust.

"Fucking Boston," the General said, and stepped forward, grasped an edge of one coffin, and, grunting, overturned it. The men watched as it crashed down the rocks, shattered, and spilled into the bog. Slowly it began to sink. The bog took the coffin, and the upper torso of the dead soldier, Fitzgerald, rolled out, and then both slipped beneath the surface. The General looked until the coffin and the body were gone. Rain slid down his face and he blinked as it ran into his eyes. "Do the same with the rest of the coffins," he said.

"What about the bodies?"

"Fuck the bodies," he said. "Let the bogs have them. And when you're done with that, make sure and wire Boston."

A curlew cried out somewhere over the bogs, lonesome and melancholy. Cows moved slow and brooding at the edge of the sphagnum. The smell of the rotting bodies still hung in the air. He turned to them, squinting through the rain, and said, "Tell them the Irish are coming."

ACKNOWLEDGMENTS

With gratitude and love to my wife, Jennifer Purdy, and to my daughter, Colette Gráinne, two of the most precious blessings in my life.

—*Thomas*

To Marlynn, my rock and my muse. I don't know where I'd be without your kind, generous soul.

—*Douglas*

We'd both like to thank the team over at Mulholland Books / Little, Brown—Joshua Kendall and Garrett McGrath—as well as our agent, Richard Abate.

And to the city of Boston, which always continues to inspire our imaginations.

ABOUT THE AUTHORS

Thomas O'Malley is the author of the novels *In the Province of Saints* and *This Magnificent Desolation*. A graduate of the University of Massachusetts, Boston, and the Iowa Writers' Workshop, he is currently the Director of Creative Writing at Dartmouth College. He lives in the Boston area.

Douglas Graham Purdy is a graduate of the University of Massachusetts, Boston, and currently lives in Brooklyn. This is his second novel.

Also by Thomas O'Malley and Douglas Graham Purdy

Serpents in the Cold

Post-war Boston is desperate to reinvent itself. But in 1951, during the worst winter on record, a brighter future seems far away.

In the midst of the depression, the murder of a string of women hardly registers; the police and the public have both turned their backs. But the latest victim was loved . . .

Old friends Cal and Dante are struggling for meaning in a world leaving them behind. The hunt for the killer of Dante's sister in law gives them new purpose, and makes them powerful enemies. But they will see this thing through – whatever the cost.

MULHOLLAND
BOOKS

HODDER